The snow came down harder as the day broke, driven down by angry winds. White flakes kissed men and horse alike, briefly gracing them with an almost holy appearance before melting away. Melgit watched his breath form heavy plumes of mist. The morn was sharp and cold. A good day for killing, he decided. Winter never held an attraction for him, though he'd lived through his share of them in the field and on campaign. For now, necessity and revenge kept him warm, as it did with most of the men he'd brought back from Gren Mot. This was what they'd been waiting for. Melgit rubbed his frost laden beard as Roffort returned with news.

"Everyone is in place, Commander."

Melgit nodded his approval. They'd spent hours moving everything where it needed to be for the coming assault. It was arduous and painstaking work, for too much noise would alert the enemy and have an entire army breathing down their necks. Melgit was mildly pleased they were still being unnoticed. He looked up at the cloud filled sky and wondered how much longer before he saw the signal. For now, he had nothing to do but wait, and the waiting was worse than the fighting. Melgit tried counting the falling snowflakes to pass the time.

And then he saw it. A brilliant ball of flame shot from one of the catapult batteries. He grinned savagely. It was time for revenge. Melgit drew his sword and began the advance on the Goblin army.

ARMIES OF
THE SILVER MAGE

A History of Malweir Book One

CHRISTIAN WARREN FREED

Copyright © 2020 by Christian Warren Freed

Excerpt from *Beyond the Edge of Dawn* 2021 Christian Warren Freed
Cover design by Melissa Andres
Cover copyright 2021 by Warfighter Books
Author Photograph by Anicie Freed

Warfighter Books
Holly Springs, North Carolina 27540
https://www.christianfreed

Second Edition: January 2021

Library of Congress Cataloging-in-Publication Data
Name: Freed, Christian Warren, 1973- author.
Title: Armies of the Silver Mage/ Christian Warren Freed
Description: Second Edition | Holly Springs, NC: Warfighter Books, 2021.
Identifiers: LCCN 2021930841 | ISBN 9781734907520 (trade paperback)
ISBN: 9781735700076 (ebook)
Subjects: Epic fantasy | Military fantasy

Printed in the United States of America

10 9 8 7 6 5 4 3 2 1

HAMMERS IN THE WIND:
BOOK I OF THE NORTHERN CRUSADE

"I love this book. This book hooked my attention on the first page and it was hard to put down. There is darkness in this book, you know something is going to happen so you keep reading to find out what. The author writes it so good, it's like you are there experiencing what the characters are. And I love it."

"I purchased this book to read to see if it would be suitable for my daughter to read. She is advanced in reading, but some books for kids older than her can be a little to much content wise. I think this one will work out great for her and she would enjoy it as much as I did. I'm glad I came across this book and can't wait to read the rest of the series."

WHERE HAVE ALL THE ELVES GONE?

"This story is fresh and a little tongue-in-cheek, a nice fantasy change of pace with twists here and there that make you have to keep on turning the pages."

"Christian Warren Freed is a very gifted, well-spoken author and his story took me in from page 1. His descriptions of situations, momentary happenings and his vivid characters of the world within the story made my fantasy run wild. As a reader, I felt like being part of the carefully woven net of this book."

THE DRAGON HUNTERS

"Excellently written. The author is able to really capture the stress, fear, and panic of life and death situations such as combat. Greatly looking forward to the next installment in the series!"

"Mr. Freed weaves the parts of this tale together smoothly, keeping the story moving at a good pace. He uses his own military background to paint powerful battle images and then he moves on. With only a little background, he makes the reader care about the members of the band - to worry about them and want them to do the 'right thing'. He adds depth to the characters through their actions and his dialogue is very realistic."

ARMIES OF THE SILVER MAGE

"Armies of the Silver Mage was a great read...any fan of Lord of the Rings or Game of Thrones will love this book. I'm looking forward to next book."

"The book is almost an homage to the great classics like Sword of Shanara and the Lord of the Rings. The author has cleverly used his past military and combat experience to make the battle scenes more realistic."

Acknowledgements

There are many things in life that just aren't possible doing alone. This book is one of them. I would like to thank the men and women of Combined Joint Task Force 180 (Bagram Afghanistan 2002-2003) for their suggestions and help, especially David Hopkins of the New Zealand Special Forces whose bold tales helped inspire some of the action and Aimee Jaskot who helped me get through the toughest plot twists.

Enough cannot be said for my wife and children or my parents who have stood behind and beside me for many years as I struggled to establish a beachhead in the publishing world. My voice may be what comes out in the words you read, but without all of you there wouldn't be anything at all.

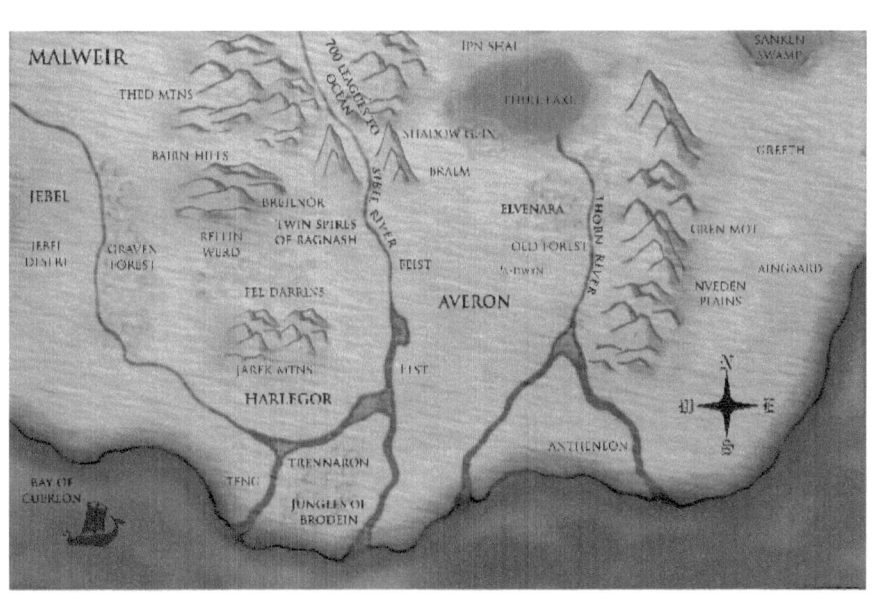

ONE
An Ordinary Life

The day began much the same as every other day for the people of Fel Darrins. Dew coated the blades of long, green grass. Birds flew from tree to tree. Forest animals moved about in search of their next meal. The townsfolk gradually awoke and went about their daily business as if there was no greater world surrounding them. Butchers busied preparing meats for the day. Chandlers dusted off the last of their goods before opening their doors. Herders and farmers were up and in the fields before the first light broke the horizon. Bakers already had the town smelling of freshly baked honey-glazed bread and pastries. All in all, life wasn't bad.

A half a day's walk south of the great forest of Relin Werd, Fel Darrins was a haven of tranquility. The sleepy village was largely forgotten by the outside world, a relic of simpler times. Officially part of the kingdom of Averon, very few travelers made their way this far south. It had been years since the last war had ravaged the land, so long in fact that none but the eldest remembered those dark times.

Yet all was not well. Troubled times were falling on the world of Malweir. Goblins and other foul creatures crept from dark places, roaming the world west of the Gren Mountains. The occasional dragon flew in to steal hard wrought treasures. Ghosts and spirits haunted old battlefields. Elves and Dwarves moved here and there, and it was said a great evil was rumored to be arising in the east.

Sunlight spread across the morning sky by the time Delin Kerny and Fennic Attleford started moving through the woods. Best friends since birth, Delin and Fennic were hardly ever separated, playing and laughing their way through childhood. They shared sweat and the occasional broken bones pretending to be great warriors from legend. They hid from their parents when they didn't want to go inside for the night. Many found their bond enviable, though troublesome. The boys constantly got into mischief, sometimes being punished but most of the time not. It was a life without worry.

They were born just a few months apart and were quickly approaching their eighteenth birthdays, much to the admonishment and denial of their mothers. It was no easy thing for a mother to accept that her son was now a man and not the innocent child she once held in her arms. It was a long-standing tradition for the newly considered men to embark upon a quest to find their path in life. Few ever went farther than the depths of the great forest and that was considered enough.

The natural impatience of youth demanded time speed up. Both were tired of waiting. They wanted to be counted amongst the rest of the men, with voices and opinions of their own that others would finally listen to. The very thought of finally being accepted made it difficult for them to focus. Countless hours were spent dreaming of undertaking a long quest, ranging halfway around the world rescuing princesses and finding long forgotten treasures. The dreams of youth were ever tempered by the restrictions of reality however and the boys remained content with dreams. For the moment.

Fennic worked hard to learn the ways of a miller. His father escorted him down to the mill at a young age and put him to work. Fennic came to appreciate the amount of labor needed. It was no easy task to grind enough flour for an entire village, repeatedly. He often came home covered in fine, white powder. His muscles ached from overuse. When he was old enough, Fennic was allowed to drive the delivery cart. It felt good to escape the confines of the mill but hauling the heavy sacks of flour and grains was backbreaking work.

Oppositely, Delin apprenticed to Ferd the chandler at a young age. Delin learned his numbers quickly. He had no choice. Trader caravans came and went in a steady influx. One small mistake cost money; money neither he nor Ferd had in abundance. Fortunately, Delin had always had a good head for reading and writing. He took his job seriously, earning the praise of several local factors and merchants.

Delin and Fennic suffered from the need for more. Their work kept them busy, but a growing desire lurked deep in their hearts. Fel Darrins was home, but they wanted to see the world. To tread the paths of old heroes and adventurers. To see the great wonders and other races for themselves before old age took hold and mired them to their duties at home.

As with most adolescent boys, Delin and Fennic suffered from the decided inability to focus. Much of their thoughts centered on where they'd go on their adventure, what they'd do. Work drudged on under the dire warnings of the town elders that change led to strife and worse. The boys were convinced such a life was the path to madness but wisely held their tongues.

Having no desire for the drudgery of work, the boys snuck away and went fishing, much as they often did. Big Tom needed to be caught and they both aimed to do it before their birthdays. Everyone in town knew about Big

Tom. He was the biggest fish ever seen in this part of the world and no one had been able to catch him. That was going to change this morning.

"We're going to get our hides tanned when our fathers find out," Delin cautioned as they headed towards Ellif Pond, long fishing poles on their shoulders.

Fennic shrugged. "We can't work all of the time. I don't know how our fathers do it. Besides, summer is nearly over and we've been cooped up at work the whole time. We need a break!"

The argument was good enough to calm Delin's nerves. Besides, coming home with Big Tom on a hook would make them both local legends. Excitement quickly replaced any doubt of misgiving.

"We're going to catch him today, Fennic," Delin finally laughed, as they got closer to the pond. "He doesn't stand a chance this time!"

Fennic joined his friend in a deep laugh. "I couldn't have said it better. Just hope Old Man Wiffe doesn't find out. He might not take kindly to it."

They both suppressed a shudder. Old Man Wiffe owned half of the lands between the town proper and Relin Werd. No one really knew much about him. Rumors said he stood with King Baeleon during the Dwarf Wars, nigh on forty years ago. People spoke of a terrible battle where the king fell and Wiffe lost his arm. Few had seen him since he returned home. Mostly, they caught glimpses of a passing shadow in the forests. He was more legend than man these days; a legend neither Delin nor Fennic cared to know more about.

"Now, why'd you bring him up?" Delin scowled. His voice was barely a whisper.

Both youths stood motionless, watching the surrounding trees. Birds chirped and whistled. Animals scuttled down trails. There was no sign of Old Man Wiffe.

"Do you want to head back?" Fennic asked.

Delin shook his head; the thought of confronting the old man chilled his blood. "We're already going to get it for skipping work, might as well enjoy the day and catch Big Tom."

The boys continued, surrounded now by towering trees and light undergrowth.

Delin suddenly grabbed Fennic's arm and asked, "Did you see that?"

"See what?"

He pointed towards the nearest trees. "Over there. I thought I saw something move."

"You're imagining things. We're the only ones out here," Fennic reassured him.

He wanted to portray the solidity his best friend lacked. It was clear from early on that Fennic was the risk taker, the leader. Delin was more reserved, relying on knowledge and his ability to read and write to get them out of a bind. All their friends knew he'd be a scholar one day, perhaps even in the marbled halls of Paedwyn, court of the king of Averon. At the moment, he wasn't sure he'd make it that far, nor did he care.

"There it goes again," Delin pointed.

A gnawing suspicion crept into Fennic's mind despite understanding the foolishness of it. The very real possibility that Old Man Wiffe was stalking them was too much. A sudden groan of wind knocked branches together with an ominous screech. Suddenly alarmed, Fennic decided it was time to go. The prospect of being caught in the middle of nowhere by the old hermit frightened him greatly. "Come on. I don't like this. Big Tom can wait."

They turned back towards Fel Darrins when a great rustling erupted behind them. Both boys spared a glance at Ellif Pond and ran for their lives. The harder they ran, the closer and louder the noise grew. Leaves burst from several bushes. A crow cawed once before leaping into the sky. The sound of thunder pounding into the earth roared in their ears. Delin looked back over his shoulder, eyes wide with sudden shock. He grabbed Fennic by the shoulder and pulled him out of the way moments before a herd of large deer raced past.

Danger passed, neither willing to admit their foolishness. Both were out of breath and exhausted, as much from the emotional shock as exertion. Fennic stumbled and dropped to his knees. For the first time since deciding to abandon his responsibilities today he doubted his decision. They were both too jittery for their own good. Still, he couldn't help but laugh softly.

"What's so funny?" Delin asked, wiping his mouth.

"Us!"

"What do you mean?"

Fennic stopped laughing long enough to explain. "We were running away from a bunch of deer like two little kids."

Delin was about to reply when he noticed a small cottage on the far side of a clearing.

"Look over there," he said. "I didn't know anyone lived out here."

"Do you think it's…?"

Delin shrugged. "It has to be. Maybe we should turn back."

Fennic shook his head. He'd just been embarrassed by a herd of deer. There was no way he was going to go back to Fel Darrins without something to show for it. Stubborn pride overrode his apprehensions.

The sun was out now, drying the dew and warming the forest. The clearing was a good hundred meters away, but the light green grass and ferns bathed in golden sunlight led them to believe that they were far from civilization. White flowers highlighted in red clung to vines snaking up tree trunks. There was a fresh smell, as if nothing unnatural had ever been here. A nagging sensation crept down Delin's spine.

"I don't think this is such a good idea," he urged. The desire to go home and accept his punishment for skipping out on his chores far outweighed his need to discover if this was indeed Old Man Wiffe's cottage.

"Scared?" Fennic chided with newfound confidence. Truth be told, he was just as scared of running into Wiffe, but he was determined not to let it show.

Delin nodded, "you should be too."

Fennic pressed forward. Now was not the time to show any hesitation. He knew that if he did, he'd never come back out here again. Most of those who knew him considered him a stubborn boy, hardheaded and overconfident. Yet, he was far from dumb. He knew how far to take things and when to quit. This morning happened to be one of those occasions when good judgment abandoned him.

"What happens if he's in there?"

Fennic shrugged again. "We're about to find out!"

The clearing was enormous. Old oak trees lined the way, dotted with a host of saplings and underbrush. A rabbit bounded off at the sound of their approach. Somewhere in the forest a crow cawed. The subtle gurgling of running water led them to a small stream cutting the clearing in two. The only thing missing was a small pond.

The cottage was humble as far as homes went. Faded blue shutters framed the windows. The chimney was still and unused. There were no lights from within. Moss grew in great clumps along the aged stone walls. The thatch roof was barely serviceable. Judging from the size of the cottage, it couldn't have contained more than two rooms. Fennic was almost disappointed when he noticed the front door was slightly ajar.

Curiosity seized him.

"What are you doing?" Delin whispered.

Fennic ignored him and kept walking towards the door. As tranquil as the setting was, he found his mind troubled. He had no desire to get caught breaking into someone's home, especially Old Man Wiffe's.

"Just a quick look and we can leave," Fennic smiled.

A chill settled over the clearing, making Delin ill at ease. "I'm not going in there."

"Suit yourself," Fennic casually replied. "I'm going to see what's inside."

In a moment, Delin was alone. The slightest sound amplified tenfold. The clearing grew cold. He couldn't shake the feeling that he was being watched, certain that a hundred pairs of eyes marked his very breath. The forest was alive and waiting for the chance to strike him down. The deep hoot of a hidden owl was more than enough to send him running inside. A gust of wind slammed the door behind him, and he was alone in the darkness of the cottage. He could scarcely make out his own hands.

"Fennic, where are you?" he whispered.

"You can stop whispering," came the reply. "Letting the door slam was a fool's mistake. I could be dead by now if anyone was home."

"You shouldn't have left me out there like that!"

Fennic laughed. "You shouldn't have stayed."

Delin gradually overcame his fear as his eyes grew used to the dark and started to explore. The main room was sparsely decorated, even for a hermit. A rickety old rocking chair sat next to the empty fireplace, and a small round table by the window. The shelf on the wall held a few colored vases and a handful of books. A brilliant silver sword was mounted on the mantle behind it, drawing Fennic's full attention. Delin grew bolder, knowing that if Wiffe was home he'd have come out by now. He decided to look through the rest of the cottage.

Fennic didn't move. He knew he should be afraid, but the sword whispered to him, calming his nerves and opening his mind to an infinite number of possibilities. Great tales and high adventure lay within the steel, and Fennic Attleford found himself wondering what it would be like to live that life.

"I finished checking the other room," Delin announced. He came to stand beside Fennic and looked up at the sword, not seeing what held Fennic's attention. It was just an old piece of steel.

"All right," Fennic answered blankly.

"He doesn't have much, just a plain cot with a half-filled wardrobe. There are lots of herbs and spices and stuff over there where the kitchen area is. The pantry is stocked with jars of food and dried meat." He paused, noticing Fennic's empty stare. "Are you listening?"

Fennic wasn't. Instead, he was reaching for the shining sword. It called to him, begged him to take it from the mantle and carry out their destiny together. What deeds they could accomplish! Folks would tell of the unstoppable Fennic and his silver sword for generations.

"You shouldn't mess with that," Delin warned.

Nonsense. "Who's going to know?"

Fennic opened his mouth to reply when the baying of an old hound dog echoed around the clearing. Old Man Wiffe was coming home. Delin ran to the door in time to see the recluse entering the clearing. They were trapped. He turned and was astonished to see Fennic brandishing the sword like a professional armsman.

"Put that back! We need to get out of here now."

Fennic marveled at the way the sword cut through the air, whistling with superiority. What a wondrous thing this silver sword was. Delin snatched him by the wrist, breaking the spell. Wild eyes stared back at him.

"Didn't you hear me? Wiffe is back!"

Panic struck Fennic. He hurried to replace the sword, lest he was caught with it in his hands. What would Wiffe think? That he was stealing the sword? Chances were the old man would kill both of them. He ran to the window and peered out. There was nothing out there. No dog, no sign of the old man.

"I think it's safe. I don't see anyone," Fennic said.

The door groaned open and the old hound snapped at them. A heavy shadow fell on them.

"Well, well. What have I here?" the deep voice rolled like thunder across the mountains.

Panic gripped them. The youth briefly considered running out the back window but the dog snapping and barking at his feet stopped him immediately. Fennic's heart skipped. The sword whispered, begged to be used, but Fennic couldn't move.

"Would be thieves come to rob an old man? I don't think so," said the newcomer with unmistakable menace in his tone.

TWO
Old Man Wiffe

The boys were herded into a pair of high back chairs and told not to move while Wiffe finished deciding what to do with them. They sat across from each other, watching as the old man finished stoking the fire and made his breakfast. His hound sat at their feet with a perpetual scowl. It wasn't until he got the fire going that Delin overcame his fear and noticed the man only had one arm. The scene, frightening as it was, reminded Delin of a cold winter night with hot spiced cider and drifting snow.

Old Man Wiffe was a proud, strong man. His right arm was missing from the elbow down though it certainly didn't diminish his overwhelming stature. His demeanor drew men to him in times of crisis and his skill with the blade surpassed that of most. He had a light beard and moustache accompanying the lines on his weathered face. There was nothing about him which suggested weakness. Nigh on eighty years old, Wiffe had seen better days. There was a certain wariness in his eye, a hint of potential danger. Decades of sword play and a hard life had left him with a heavily muscled body. He turned his attention on the boys.

"How long do you think it will be before anyone comes looking for you?" he asked with a tight smile.

"They're al...ready on the way," Delin answered.

Wiffe laughed. "You're no good at bluffing, young Delin Kerny. I know better. These are my woods." He laughed again after watching their eyes widen. "Oh yes, I know you, both of you in fact. And I'm willing to bet neither of you told anyone about your little adventure to my forest. Two fools blind to the world and her ways."

He left them thinking long enough to shift the embers around and add another log. The smell of coffee filled the quaint home.

"Are you going to tell me why you broke into my home, or shall I guess? Hmm?"

"We got lost in the forest," Fennic lied.

"Did you? Here's what I think. I think you stole away from your work just to go fishing. Probably after Big Tom. But something turned you around, forced you in this direction. You found my home all by itself. It wasn't long before curiosity set in and you invaded my life. Just to see if the rumors are true." He paused. Fear poured from them, dominating the atmosphere in the room. Wiffe sat down across from them and stared with hard eyes. They fidgeted on the floor, wanting nothing more than to get away from this place.

"How close am I to the truth? Speak quickly. My patience is almost gone these days."

Delin broke down and babbled the entire tale. Tears trickled down his cheeks, much to Wiffe's silent amusement. He was sure Old Man Wiffe was going to kill them. No one would ever know what happened.

"That's the best you can do? I might need to send you home missing a few fingers. Perhaps that will keep you from breaking into people's homes," he snapped.

Delin finally broke down. "Please, sir. We meant nothing by it."

Wiffe snorted derisively. "You break into my home and I find you holding MY sword. That sounds like you meant to rob me, or am I mistaken?"

Fennic blinked rapidly. "The sword wanted me to take it."

Delin's mouth dropped. He looked over to his friend in wonder but Wiffe merely settled back into his chair and nodded slowly.

Rubbing the gray stubble on his chin, Wiffe exhaled slowly. "I had wondered when this day would come. I'm surprised it is you, Fennic. Relax. I'm not going to hurt either of you."

"You…you're not going to kill us?" Delin asked.

"Kill you! Darkness no. It's been a very long time since I was last forced to kill anyone. No, you'll be returned home for your fathers to deal with, unharmed. Besides, do you have any idea how long it's been since I last had a visitor out here?"

The boys exchanged a cautious glance.

"Granted, the forest is peaceful and calming, but folks don't venture out here like they used to. Most folks I know are long dead. The rest are getting on and passing to the next life. Most others, like you two strapping lads, fear hokey myths and tales, and for good reason. The roads aren't as safe as they used to be. Not with the Silver Mage rising in the east."

Neither was totally sure who this Silver Mage was, but the number of peddlers and travelers moving through Fel Darrins was dwindling and there was talk of gods, both light and dark, returning to claim the thrones of Malweir. Prices were rising due to the lack of buyers, making times hard for the common townsfolk.

"I bet you want to know how I know who you are and why you're here," Wiffe said.

"Yes, sir," Fennic replied.

Wiffe grunted. "Why else do you think I've been wasting good air explaining things to you?" He paused until their confused looks faded. "A long time ago, when I was still young and vigorous, the world opened up for me. Life was good until the Silver Mage rose to power and began the great

Mage Wars. Hundreds of us answered King Baeleon's call to arms and joined the war. We knew that if Paedwyn fell, so too would the rest of Averon."

"You went to war with our grandfathers?" Delin asked.

Wiffe smiled warmly. Old memories embraced him suddenly. "That's when I first met your grandfathers, Gisle Attleford and Sharn Kerny." The boys looked up in shock. Neither could remember their parents admitting they knew Wiffe. They looked back at Wiffe in genuine surprise and many questions. He held up a hand to quiet them. "I know what you want to say. That your families have lived here for generations and never been involved in any war. Those are half-truths at best. They told you what they wanted you to know. Your grandparents were afraid that one day the urge to see the world might grow too strong and you'd wander blindly into war."

The hound growled and stretched before laying its head back down.

"I can't say I blame them. Your grandfathers were good men with clean souls. They came away from the war relatively intact and ran off to a far secluded part of the world to spend the rest of their days. I stayed in Paedwyn and in the army, only coming back home when I could no longer serve the king.

"Maybe I should have left with them, but I was never that smart. Then again, war seemed about the only thing I was ever good at. King Baeleon died in the same battle I lost this," he wiggled his right arm at them, an amused smile creasing his face. "But we won the battle. The Silver Mage disappeared after his defeat at the mountain fortress of Gren Mot. I stayed long enough to see the king buried and made my way here.

"It's been a long while since I told that tale. Doubt if I'll be around to tell it again. I've known you were going to come here. It was written on the winds."

Before either of them could start asking questions, Wiffe got up and strode to the fireplace. His gaze lingered on the sword, now back in its proper place.

"What did the sword say to you, Fennic?" he asked in a plain and forceful tone.

"I don't know how to explain it. It called to me, whispering that I was destined to hold it," Fennic quietly admitted.

Old Man Wiffe turned on them, a grave look etched into his features. "Come forward, young man."

Fennic slowly complied. He was unsure what his punishment was going to be. His father always frowned on his natural curiosity.

"This blade sang to you, did it not?" Wiffe asked. He had the sword in hand, golden fire light dancing on the immaculate silver.

Fennic's eyes locked on the mystical weapon, mesmerized by the simple perfection of it. "Yes. It was like a golden song in my head."

Wiffe was faintly impressed. "This is no normal sword, young Fennic. It has peculiar abilities. Very few have held it. Even fewer have come to understand the power locked within."

Fennic almost drifted off again, lost in the lullaby spun by the sword. The urge to reach out and seize the magnificent weapon was too much to resist. Fennic failed to understand why he was so drawn to it. It was just a sword after all. *Where is this supernatural desire coming from?* All he knew was that the sword seemed to call his name. It wasn't until Wiffe slapped his hand away that he realized what was happening.

"Careful lad. This sword has seen the best and worst of men." He eased it back into the sheath. "Enchanted it is. The Elves made it long ago out of friendship with man. It's said that only one in every generation may use it, and the sword always chooses who that person is."

"Does it have a name?" Fennic asked, his voice slightly dazed.

"All items of power have names and legends surrounding them. This one's name is Phaelor. It means Heaven's Eyes in Elvish and it's made of pure star silver. Phaelor has been around for a thousand years. I've had it for almost fifty of them. At last I can give it to another. My time has come to an end."

Delin rose suddenly, conscious of the fact he was the only one still sitting and not included in the conversation. He blurted out, "What do you mean?"

"Young Fennic has been chosen to bear the sword," Wiffe announced.

"Your father is going to kill you when he hears about this!"

Fennic wasn't listening. Every slumbering desire throughout his short life was culminating in the folded grain of this weapon. Scholars argued it belonged in a museum for the world to see, magicians laid claim to its inherent powers. Regardless of what the more civilized folk believed, Phaelor was a tool of war and had a role in the shaping of the future of Malweir. Whether he wanted to or not, Fennic was now part of that legacy.

If he looked close enough, he could make out the pure crystal gemstones for which it was named. They grabbed the light and radiated a confidence and power seldom seen in this quiet part of the world. He could see the wrath laid out by the blade. The blood and horror. He saw brave men die, begging for their lives, and kingdoms topple while the sword remained cold. The images made him shudder.

The sword had claimed him, bonding them until another came along, and that frightened Fennic. He'd always had dreams about what the world was like but had never had the inclination to find out for himself. Phaelor wasn't going to give him the choice. Wide eyed, torn between the quiet home life and high adventure, Fennic suddenly became aware of whispered urgings.

"You have been accepted by Phaelor, and I pass it to you freely," Wiffe said in a voice mixed with relief and sadness. "Though I warn you, do not let the sword consume you as it has others before. It can neither show you the right path nor solve your problems with a sharp swing. I looked long and hard for someone, anyone, capable of unlocking its secrets, and every time I came away empty handed. Ware the future, my young friend, for Phaelor is destined for greatness and ruin, as are all who dare hold it."

Wiffe handed the weapon over; a king knighting a squire. The youth gasped as the cool steel and leather straps met his flesh. Electricity danced through him, prickling his body and fluttering his eyes. He felt stronger, more confident. The world opened up and he could see clearly. Wiffe stepped back, a strange combination of sorrow and pride waging war in his face.

"Go now," he said. "My part is ended."

Fennic remained quiet almost the entire way home. Every time he touched the naked steel, a host of memories assailed him. He watched men go mad with power and be consumed by fire. It was one of the trappings of the magic, Wiffe had explained. The sword was neither good nor evil, it simply was. Man was responsible for determining greatness or despair.

"What do we tell our parents?" Delin asked at the edge of the village.

Fennic looked at his lifelong friend. "I don't think we should. They never mentioned going to war. Think of how they'd react if they knew we went to see that crazy old man. Or if they saw this sword! We need to keep quiet about this until we can come up with a plan."

Delin wasn't so convinced. He'd been raised not to lie and this most certainly was a lie. He started to rethink the idea of going on an adventure. Staying at home seemed perfectly acceptable considering how visiting Wiffe changed them. Whispered promises of war or worse clung to the sword. They never should have taken it.

"What are you thinking, Delin?"

Confused, he just shook his head.

Fennic put his hand on his best friend's shoulder. "Go home and get some sleep. We don't need to rush into anything."

Delin left him to face his father's wrath. Through the long lecture all he could think about was the sword. Delin and Fennic both went to sleep that night wondering what life might be like if they weren't in Fel Darrins.

THREE
Troubles

Weeks passed. Leaves turned the hillsides into paintings rich with fall's colors. Crops were harvested and stored for the coming snows, and life in Fel Darrins continued as it always had. That was how the townsfolk wanted it. Many of the old had already seen other parts of the world and the turmoil that came with them. Locked away in this forgotten town, they had a chance to live peacefully. Soon it would be time for the harvest ritual, a grand festival rival to those rumored in the king's court at Paedwyn. The mood was bright and cheerful in anticipation of the coming festival. The streets would soon be crowded with merchants and peddlers. Smells of fresh breads and roasted meat would fill the air. Troupes of travelling performers would erect small stages and perform the latest in popular theater.

Fennic, however, was of a different mindset; a sense of foreboding troubled him for reasons he couldn't explain. He didn't know what or when, but events were well beyond his control now. Phaelor whispered secrets to him late at night when only shadows roamed the lands. He found himself wanting to see the legendary smiths of the Dwarves. The great mountain fortress of Gren Mot where his grandfather had lived and waged war. Most of all, he wanted to see the sparkling whiteness of the royal palace of Averon under a moonlit winter night.

The desire became almost torturous. He was the one who had never wanted to go any further than Relin Werd. One morning and a chance meeting with a crazed old man and his life was changing forever. Work kept his days filled, but they felt empty. He hardly saw Delin as the time of the festival approached. He began to find it difficult to speak clearly to Delin. How could he explain the sword wanted him to take it far away from Fel Darrins? Every day Fennic felt the pull. The desire to pack a light bag and head north.

Fennic stepped into the early autumn morning and regretted not wearing a heavier shirt. He clutched his jacket tightly and walked to work as fast as he could. A heavy frost covered everything, and his breath came out in thick vapors. The bitter cold this early in the year meant winter was going to be severe. Unfortunately for Fennic, the mill was all the way across town. Tightening his jacket around his neck, he set out.

He spent the day in relative misery. Phaelor seemed bound to hundreds of mystical thoughts and mysterious dreams. Wiffe had tried to warn him about the possessive powers of the sword but had not mentioned how to combat them. The sword demanded his attention. It beckoned with horrors and riches. Fear and elation blended convincingly enough for Fennic to feed his desire. He wanted to ride into battle with Phaelor held high and an army at his heels. He wanted to do a great many things but didn't know how to tell anyone.

Fennic hadn't been able to tell his own father about Phaelor or his encounter with Old Man Wiffe. There was a stigma about the hermit that left people with worried looks. He was a reminder of a more violent time when the people of Fel Darrins sacrificed almost too much. Fennic found it hard to ignore Phaelor's call. Fennic knew he would be leaving Fel Darrins soon.

He spent hours coming up with a rough plan. When he decided it was sufficiently worked out, he met Delin for dinner at the Tavern. It was the first time they saw each other since his self-imposed isolation. The success of his plan lay in whether he could convince his best friend to come along. Still, the hope far outweighed the gloom. Fennic entered the common room and looked around for his friend. He spied Delin sitting at a corner table close to one of the fireplaces, talking to Tarren Brickton. They'd been flirting for seven years though neither of them had realized it until recently. The only question was when the wedding would take place. Tarren offered him a flashing smile so simple it melted his heart and for an instant he was jealous of his best friend. She danced off to make her rounds of the tables, leaving them to their business.

Fennic was immediately glad for the fire.

"What are you so glib about?" asked Delin.

He shrugged. "Maybe it's the weather."

Delin shrugged back. He struggled with trying to understand Fennic. Understand why his best friend had been ignoring him since they returned from Old Man Wiffe's. None of it made sense. He looked into Fennic's eyes but didn't recognize him. There was a distance coming between them. A distance he could only attribute to the sword.

"I can't see what about snow would make you this cheery. All this means is that your little sword is warping your mind."

"Much like your pretty girlfriend, no doubt," Fennic replied with a rueful smile. He was doing his best to remain calm, to project a sense of levity. He regretted the comment the moment it left his mouth.

"Leave her out of this!" Delin scowled. "She doesn't have anything to do with your queer behavior." His defensiveness was ridiculous. Everyone knew he and Tarren were in love. It showed in their eyes when they looked at each other. The way they couldn't stand being apart for too long. How they tried, and failed, to keep the knowledge from their parents. It was the worst kept secret in the village. Oddly, neither had come out and said those three magical words yet.

"No, I don't suppose she has. I'm sorry."

Delin smiled. "Forget about it."

"I've been thinking. All this stress about Old Man Wiffe and the sword and then our parents …maybe we need a change of scenery for a while?"

His voice was quiet, and he sounded tired. He'd languished for hours trying to think of how to best put the idea before Delin. The onset of an early winter dealt him a severe setback but did not discourage him. They'd grown up with snow but had never traveled more than a few leagues before going home again. If things worked out right, they wouldn't be going home for some time. This storm was going to be their toughest obstacle.

"What are you saying?"

"The same things you have for years. Everything about you has been looking for a different place in a different time. I'm starting to share that dream. I'm tired of being the miller's apprentice. There's a better world out there. One in which we can make a name for ourselves."

Delin's eyebrows peaked. "We? Or you and that sword? What's happening to you? You were always the voice of reason. Even the elders would condemn this as insane. Think about it! Why now? Why after that crazy old man filled your head with impossible stories?"

"Why anything?" Fennic protested. "I don't know why or how, but I need to leave Fel Darrins. This is our chance, Delin. Our chance to travel the world and see those places we've only learned about in our lessons. I can feel Phaelor in my bones. It's giving me confidence. I feel like I can do anything! Come with me Delin. Do you want to look back on your life and wonder what if?"

"What are you two being all secretive about?" asked a sweet voice.

They looked up to see Tarren Brickton standing beside them. She was the same age as them, and had grown up next to them since her parents had moved to the village twelve years ago.

Delin blushed, much to his friend's amusement. Fennic laughed and said, "Nothing Tarren. We were just talking about work and the like."

"I'll bet," she replied. The twinkle in her eyes suggested otherwise. "More like two young boys plotting mischief."

"Miss Brickton, I'm shocked you'd even suggest such a thing!" Fennic announced in mock surprise.

Tarren giggled and joined them. "Well don't let a silly girl stop you. I'm off duty now and don't plan on leaving until I get to the bottom of this scandal."

The boys exchanged wary looks. It was going to be a long night.

Tarren began drumming her fingers on the table. "I can wait just as long as you."

"We weren't talking about anything," Delin insisted.

She knew better. The game went on for a while; the boys doing everything they could to avoid her questions. Truth be known, Delin was still too unsure of what he wanted to do. He'd always been the one to want to see the world, but he had lacked the initiative. Winter promised to arrive early, making this a bad time to try and live out ridiculous dreams of fancy. His defense for the sudden weakness was the solace of Tarren's beauty. Her eyes were brilliant amber. She had high cheekbones, lending her an air or regality. The way her hair framed her smooth, tan face melted his heart. She wore a green dress that, while simple and modest, betrayed a willowy, strong body. She had rich, dark hair that flowed well past her shoulders and she was by far the smartest girl Delin knew.

Delin quickly became enthralled with her. Everything about her enchanted him. Her smile, the way her golden eyes warmed him. What he enjoyed most was the way she made him feel. There was completeness whenever they were together. He didn't know how to explain it, but every part of him wanted to be with her. She complimented him, often making up for areas he lacked. The way she smiled made him forget his worries and left him feeling warm, satisfied.

Her parents lived on the outskirts of town, but owned and ran the tavern, making them some of the most popular people in Fel Darrins. They had been able to afford a private tutor all the way from Paedwyn to ensure their children had the very best education possible. Tarren was the youngest of three daughters and the only one to show a genuine interest in the earnings and day to day business of the tavern. She already had designs to add a small wing for weary travelers to rest. The only problem with this plan was the lack of travelers in Fel Darrins.

Tarren brushed a shining locket of hair from her face and Delin felt his heart flutter. Words jumbled in his mind, suddenly incapable of coherent thought. He couldn't help but stare. More than anything he wanted to come out and tell her he loved her. To kiss her and not care who saw it.

"Like what you see?" she giggled.

He gulped in embarrassment.

Fennic burst out with laughter. "I'd say that was a yes."

Delin answered by punching Fennic in the shoulder.

Tarren saw her opening. "If you like it that much perhaps you can tell me what you were talking about?"

Delin had finally reached his breaking point. He started to open his mouth to tell her everything when three hunters burst into the common room. The door slammed with a crash in their wake. Each bore a haggard look. The common room fell silent in anticipation of what they had to tell. They wore the usual leathers and furs marking their trade, but something about them was different. Their beards, normally blond and brown, were coated in a black substance, as were their clothes. Gilley Brickton came out of the kitchen wiping his hands on a towel.

"Can I help you lads?" he asked with his deep, rumbling voice.

Gilley was a strong and proud man with little fear. He was gentle and generally considered one of the easiest going people in Fel Darrins, despite his burly features and menacing appearance. Folk often complimented him on his willingness to hear them out when times were rough. He knew the hunters, as did most of the townsfolk. He also knew how unusual it was for them to come into town so spooked.

The lead hunter dropped his coins on the bar and said, "Ale. Three of the strongest."

Gilley nodded. "Rough day?"

"Aye," the hunter answered. "We were out hunting near Ellif Pond."

"Out by Old Man Wiffe's?" Gilley asked.

"Not anymore," the man on the far end said in a hushed voice.

A dozen heads turned towards them.

"How do you mean?"

"We'd come out on the far side of the pond just past noon. Was on the trail of a herd of black deer. Hadn't seen anything but tracks so we kept moving. Nith here was the first to smell the smoke. By the time we made it to the clearing, we could see the ruins of a cottage. There wasn't nothing left but half a chimney and some scorched stones. A couple of skeletons lay out front. One was a dog and the other a man with one arm."

"Old Man Wiffe," Gilley announced with a stunned voice.

Rumors were already spreading. Wiffe was considered unfriendly and eccentric by some but was generally known to be a harmless old man by most of the older villagers. Making the situation worse, Wiffe had been seen in town not more than a week ago. To think someone could kill the old man so malevolently was bound to change life in Fel Darrins.

"We're thinking he was robbed first. That's about the only reason I can think to kill him," the hunter explained with a casual coldness. "Aside from that, I'd say whoever done it was looking for something."

"But he weren't nothing but bones already!" the middle hunter practically shouted. His eyes flickered back and forth in a nervous jitter.

Fennic looked at Delin with horror filled eyes. The boys had heard every word and sat mortified. They'd been to Wiffe's only scant weeks ago and now he was dead. Neither had much concern until the hunter mentioned the prospect of the killer looking for something. It was all Fennic could do to keep from panicking. Phaelor! The killers were after the star silver sword. There was no doubt about it. And if they'd gone out of their way to Wiffe's to look for it, he was sure he and Delin weren't safe here in Fel Darrins. All the dreams of adventure suddenly seemed like a sick fantasy. He had to get away. He had to leave before Wiffe's fate befell his family.

FOUR
Rising Darkness

The world transformed into a dangerous place for the people of Fel Darrins in just three short weeks. The village council sent a party out to the ruins of Old Man Wiffe's in the hopes of learning what had happened. The only thing they could decide on was that the hermit was indeed murdered. No one knew what the killers had been looking for, or even if there was a reason for the crime. A handful of the town elders gathered under the anonymity of nightfall to bury Wiffe and his beloved dog in the peaceful clearing he loved the most. Those few were the only ones who remembered Wiffe for what he once was, not the hermit he'd become. A quick prayer was mumbled over the small cairn and the elders of Fel Darrins went home to ponder this sudden turn of events.

Delin Kerny stood looking out across the now barren corn fields. The crops had been brought in, leaving broken stalks jutting up at odd angles. Crows drifted in, picking at the leftover corn cobs. He felt like the fields: a shell of the young man he had once been. News of Old Man Wiffe's death felt surreal. Unspeakable pressure suddenly dropped on his shoulders.

Fennic's arguments didn't help much either. Delin couldn't deny the logic behind them. Whoever killed Wiffe had to have been looking for the sword. The chances of a trail leading back to Fel Darrins and Delin and Fennic were too great to leave to chance. That meant everyone he cared about and loved was in jeopardy. That meant Tarren. He knew what he needed to do but he was afraid to commit. He'd never been far from home before. The prospect of leaving now, at the onset of winter and in the wake of a murder didn't make it any easier. He knew the time had come to give Fennic his answer.

For Fennic, life was growing increasingly more miserable. The death of Old Man Wiffe hit him hard, sparking apprehension and latent fears. He spent long nights awake wondering if the killers had been looking for the sword, and if they were now coming after him. Day by day he grew more convinced it was time to leave Fel Darrins.

Perhaps the worst part came from not being able to tell anyone his concerns. A magical sword. Who would believe such an outlandish story? He knew he wouldn't if he hadn't been there himself. Fennic knew in his heart that Phaelor lay at the heart of this mess. He secretly began packing to leave before the same murderers found his family. He had no idea where to go, or how long it was going to take to get there, but he couldn't let harm come to everyone he knew. Even if Delin decided not to come, Fennic was leaving home. His thoughts drifted back to the night they learned of Old Man Wiffe's death.

"You two know something," Tarren accused quietly one night as the trio sat at a quiet table in the corner of the tavern's common room.

Fennic shook his head in a vain attempt at silencing his best friend.

Delin burst open. The pressure of holding too many secrets finally getting the best of him. "We were there, Tarren."

She gasped. "You went to Old Man Wiffe's cottage? Was he dead?"

"Tarren, keep your voice down please," Fennic begged.

Delin passed a nervous glance to Fennic. "No, he wasn't dead. All he did was scare us a little. Then we left."

Tarren pursed her lips. She could tell when Delin was hiding something. She also knew when not to push. She let them keep their secrets, for now. Her mind was already racing through the different scenarios that might greet her in the days to come. Little could she guess what the friends were planning on doing.

Fennic sighed whenever he thought of Delin and Tarren. He saw the pained look on her face every time she spied them talking quietly. As much as he wanted Delin to go with him, he wasn't willing to steal his best friend away from his life and love. Then again, Delin had been to the old man's house as well and that made him just as much of a target as Fennic was.

His other concern was the sword itself. Wiffe never explained anything about it. He merely said the sword picked who was going to bear it. Fennic knew nothing about swords. Maybe someone in Alloenis could help, or an Elf. They were the ones who created it after all. If not Alloenis, then perhaps one of the king's vaunted advisors would know in Paedwyn, the grand capital of Averon.

Another day came and went with awkward tensions rising throughout Fel Darrins. Messengers were riding through much more than ever before, stopping just long enough to tend their mounts and spread the word to the cautious. War was coming to Averon! The Silver Mage was raising great armies in the east and King Maelor was hard pressed to gather levies from all territories. The Elves were keeping silent, unwilling to commit to another of man's wars. No word had yet returned from the Dwarves. All signs pointed towards Averon standing alone.

Tipper's Tavern was abuzz with rumors. A small group of men were assembling to march to the main army encampment on the plains surrounding Paedwyn. Their deeds would make the high and mighty of the world remember the name Fel Darrins again. Most were single, slightly older than Delin and Fennic. A few married men were involved, but the majority weren't willing to leave their families unprotected for an extended period, especially after what had happened to Old Man Wiffe. The council ordered the formation of a local militia to further protect the village.

Tarren greeted Fennic with her usual charm and grace. He responded in kind and followed her to a table away from everyone else. He couldn't help but think how lucky a man Delin was. The evening crowds hadn't begun arriving yet, and that suited him just fine. What he had to say was only for her ears. A messenger dressed in green and gold, the royal colors of the court at Paedwyn, sat off to himself, finishing an early supper so he could be on the road again before dusk.

"Isn't it pretty?" Tarren asked.

Fennic was confused and made no effort to conceal it.

Seeing the look on his face, she quickly added, "His uniform I mean. So formal and important. I think Delin would be splendid dressed so."

"He probably would," Fennic absently answered.

"What's wrong? You haven't been the same since Wiffe was found dead."

He shrugged, not wanting to go into detail but the weight of his secrets was becoming unbearable. "Have you ever felt that events are moving too fast? Like you don't have any control over what's going to happen from one day to the next?"

She slipped a comforting arm around his shoulder. "Lately I have, but I know you Fennic Attleford. There's more to your troubles than current events. Who can you tell if not me? I'm one of your closest friends and you know I'm not going to tell anyone else. Besides, I know when Delin is hiding something important from me."

Fennic smirked. "When are you two going to come out and tell each other I love you?"

"I might need to after all of this," she said flashing a warm smile. "Now are you finally going to tell me what's got the two of you acting so strangely?"

He let loose a deep sigh and went on to tell her the important parts of his story, leaving out a few details here and there. It felt good to be able to throw the weight off. He'd felt like he was drowning for so long to be able to breathe freely again felt so good. She sat quietly and listened to everything, not quite believing some of it. But these doubts she kept to herself, for Delin would tell her what really happened. He never lied to her. Talk of the sword aroused a desire in her, and for the briefest of moments she wanted to see this magical item. She'd been daydreaming of the sword when Fennic told her his plans to leave.

Her mind reeled from the shock of the simple statement. Leaving? Fennic and Delin? No. Delin wouldn't leave her. He couldn't. There were so many things they had yet to do together. Her mind leapt to the worst possible conclusions. She hadn't even told him she loved him yet and here he was planning on sneaking away in the middle of the night!

"I don't want him to come with me. I really don't. I see the way you two look at each other. The happiness it gives him when you smile. The last thing I want to do is take him away from you," he told her with genuine concern.

Her heart jumped to her throat. "But?"

Tarren felt her stomach twist into knots as he told her his fears about something evil happening to their families. Bloody visions went by so fast she felt she was going to vomit. Unseen assassins running wild through Fel Darrins in search of a mystical sword and uncaring how they gained it was enough to keep her dreams tormented. Nothing bad had happened in this village since her parents and she moved here decades before. Tarren suddenly found herself wanting to sneak away and hide.

He saw the look in her eyes and felt his pain deepen. "It's not going to be safe for us here anymore."

"Safe?" she asked. "What makes you think anyone here is going to be safe once you leave? Whoever stays is in just as much danger as you are if what you're saying is true. They'll stop at nothing to find that sword, if that's what they are after. That puts every one us at risk, Fennic."

Her emphasis on the word *they* sent shivers down his spine.

"The militia guards the streets at night and I doubt anyone looking for the sword will bother tangling with a bunch of angry family men. Besides, we'll be long gone before they even come looking for us."

That, she doubted. "How do you know they aren't already here waiting?"

He was about to answer when the king's messenger got up and left. Their eyes met for a moment and Fennic found a new hope. The king's man offered a nod and was gone. Tarren knew her arguments were finished.

"When are you planning on leaving?" she conceded.

"Tomorrow night," Fennic admitted.

"Is Delin going with you?" Tarren asked quietly.

A single nod.

Their conversation ended, nothing else needing to be said. Her mind was racing ahead with future events and possibilities. Delin was leaving her and there was the very real possibility that he wouldn't be coming home. There was much she needed to do before tomorrow night arrived.

The moon had barely risen, leaving most of the kingdom of Averon lost in the darkness. The people of Fel Darrins were nestled away in their beds, save those few sturdy hands finishing their ale and talking of the days to come. A handful of villagers armed with pitchforks and the occasional sword marched up and down the main road of the village. They were far from being called soldiers, but times were growing more desperate and necessity urged protection. So the husbands and fathers of the village offered their nights in exchange for keeping their loved ones safe.

Three two-man teams constantly circled the village streets, all the while hoping they didn't come across anything out of the ordinary. Fel Darrins wasn't big as villages go, with a population of less than a thousand, but the people were proud and determined. The dangers awakened by the hands of the Silver Mage and his armies of Trolls, Goblins and other foul creatures known only to legend and myth were hundreds of leagues away. Still, no one was willing to take the risk of being caught defenseless. If times were so dark as to bring King Maelor's emissaries all the way to Fel Darrins, the village needed strong men to watch the night. All knew that wars and battles were often fought and won far from the main cities. So long as Averon was at war, the men of Fel Darrins were going to do their part. No matter how far away, they were still a part of the kingdom.

Jeck Trile and Agen Reins were moving down Business Alley, named so for the handful of shops and tinker's huts lining the way. They talked quietly as they walked, trying to alleviate some of their growing boredom. This was just their third night on the job and it had already grown monotonous. Working all day and a few hours during the middle of the night was beginning to take a toll.

Jeck and Agen talked and carried on with their route, paying little attention to the sleepy town and her secrets. Thus, they failed to notice the trio of cumbersome figures shuffling through the shadows. Quiet and unimposing, they went at a measured pace in soundless, precise movements. None of them spoke, instead hissing subtle signs. The lead shadow sniffed the wind, catching the scent of the guards and held his comrades up. Burrowing deeper into the darkness, the creatures watched the men pass.

No one knew how long they'd been stalking the quiet village, but their mission was unmistakable. The old, one arm man was just the first step. They'd been told he possessed a mighty sword and had been ordered to retrieve it. His death was as much of a pleasure as necessity. The two guards had passed without detecting them, the trio continued their quest.

Delin Kerny pulled his hat down over his naturally curly, brown hair with a frown, still unsure if they were doing the right thing. The part of him that always wanted to see what was beyond the sunset and the mighty forest of Relin Werd suddenly found himself loathe to do so. His whole life had been spent wondering, wishing what if. He always saw himself as a soldier in the service of the king, or a high priced mercenary gallivanting around Averon and the surrounding kingdoms to save helpless victims from doom and despair. Recent events shattered those fantasies, throwing everything once dear into broken misconceptions.

The world, once bright and carefree, grew dark and foreboding. He still didn't want to leave the relative security of Fel Darrins, but times were far from being safe. People whispered of strange creatures stalking the night. Some of the guards had caught sight of them from time to time. But always when they gave chase the creatures disappeared back to shadow. Then it happened. A lone man stumbled from the tavern, drunk beyond measure, and was never seen again.

The disappearance compounded Delin's growing fears of his family being next. The last thing he wanted was to see his mother or father torn to pieces at the hands of some ruthless killer in the dark hours of the night. Delin regretted their chance encounter with the old man of the Werd. So much had changed since. He cursed his luck and at that moment made up his mind. He and Fennic had to get as far away as possible to ensure the safety of all that they knew and loved. Not even his blossoming love for Tarren was enough to keep him here.

Dawn crested the southern mountains in shades of purple and blue. Still far from breaking the clouds, the sun was already stealing the chill from Delin's bones as he waited for Fennic. A songbird lazily chirped from atop a nearby brush, as if encouraging the lad to keep his head up. Delin watched the red and white bird and sighed. If only, he wished. Footsteps behind interrupted his somber mood.

"Don't you stand there with your mouth open, Delin Kerny," Tarren scolded in a soft voice. "I didn't get up this early in the morning to see you make a fool of yourself."

She rushed into his arms before he could say a single word, holding him as tight as she could out of fear of letting him go. He closed his eyes to fight back the tears before giving Fennic the same look.

"Don't look at me like that either," Fennic said in his defense. "She didn't leave me with much of a choice. I found her waiting outside my door when I snuck out."

He still wasn't sure how she found out about their change of plans from leaving at night to the morning. Common sense, he supposed. No one wanted to chance the night with those things out there. The look in her eye warned Fennic from saying too much. He wasn't very wise when it came to women and their beguiling ways, but he knew enough to keep his mouth shut.

Tarren, on the other hand, struggled to fight back her tears. She didn't want Delin's last memory of her to be one of sadness. The road ahead was going to be long and arduous she was sure, and she wanted Delin to be strong. Still, the dreams of a long and happy life seemed to rip from her heart the longer she held him. Tarren forced a laugh.

"Tarren, I…," Delin began before she silenced him with a soft finger to his lips.

"I know," she said. "But I wasn't about to let you sneak off without saying goodbye. Besides, I know you, and in knowing that I'm betting you didn't pack half of the things you're going to need on this adventure."

"I asked my mother to pack my extra set of long johns," he said in a weak attempt at humor.

Tarren laughed despite herself. They both knew that neither boy could risk telling their parents. If the killers were indeed looking for the sword any admission to friends or family put them all at risk.

Cheeks turning a dark red, Delin accepted the pack with mumbled thanks. His thoughts were anywhere but on the contents of the pack. He desperately wanted to profess his love for her but didn't want to break the spell. It took great courage for her to step to him the way she had. Delin wasn't about to undermine her inner strength with a moment of his own weakness.

Tarren leaned forward and kissed his cheek. "You'd best be getting on. It looks like it's going to be a good day. Well enough for the two of you to get as far as you can without trouble." Her voice waivered. "I don't like what you're doing and don't really know why, but I say this too. Bring yourself home to me, Delin Kerny. Bring yourself home to the one who loves you."

That was the first time the barrier was breached. He tried to respond but found himself softly kissing her tender lips instead. Euphoria swelled his chest and he felt ready to take on the world. The look in her eyes strengthened his resolve. He knew that his heart was forever hers and was going to do everything in his power to come home again. Satisfied, Tarren ended her kiss and walked away before her strength failed her. She didn't want him to see her crying. Fennic placed a comforting hand on Delin's shoulder and nodded. It was time. Hefting their packs, the two boys said their farewells to Fel Darrins and began the journey of their lives.

FIVE
Relin Werd

Fennic and Delin walked until their feet burned and their muscles grew too sore to carry on. There wasn't any urgency to their actions, for they didn't have a specific destination. Packs filled with travel rations and trinkets to remind them of home, they managed to snare a rabbit or two and even caught a few trout from the stream running parallel to the road. The weather was as good as it could be for traveling on foot, and they prayed it remained that way, at least until they reached Alloenis and a cozy inn to wash away the grime of the road. Soon enough the smell of roasting meat clung to their little campsite. Fennic set Phaelor down beside the fire and stretched.

He was more excited by far. He enjoyed working in the mill, but there was an indescribable freedom from being alone on the path into the unknown. For the first time in his young life he held the power to make his own choices, regardless of the circumstances in which they were delivered. Maybe it was Phaelor whispering in his mind at night, or the Gods themselves that opened this new window to his soul. Whatever started it, Fennic knew it was a long road to wander before the journey was over. They'd left Fel Darrins three days ago and his body still hadn't accepted the task imposed upon it.

"I don't know what I was thinking all those years I wasted in trying to convince you to do this," Delin admitted as he lazily stretched out next to the fire. "All of this walking is doing murder to my feet!"

Fennic's laugh lacked the innocence it once held. "I never thought you'd be the one to want to go home. This is supposed to be your adventure."

"Oh no! This is all you, my friend. You and that fancy sword of yours. You know why I'm here," Delin protested. The hours spent daydreaming of a time like this turned out to be far from what reality had in store.

Fennic shrugged it off. "How far do you suppose it is to Relin Werd?" He chewed casually on a mint leaf. Fennic had a whole pouch of them and it was his grandmother's fault. She'd gotten him hooked on them at a young age and now he found himself chewing on them after almost every meal. These were a gift from Tarren.

Delin shook his head. "It can't be more than a day the way we've been marching."

"I've set an easy pace and given you every opportunity to speed up or slow down," he replied. "Besides, the exercise is good for us."

"I got enough exercise working in the chandlery, thank you very much. You just figure out where we're going after we get to Alloenis, providing we make it there in one piece."

They'd grown up on stories of life in the bigger cities. Alloenis was far from the grandeur of Paedwyn but still much larger than Fel Darrins and her surrounding farmsteads combined. The increased population meant heavier trade and entertainment, more profit, and doubtlessly, a horde of thieves and pick pockets. The best thing going for the boys lay in not having anything of value to steal, nothing except the silver and diamond sword.

"We still need to figure out what to do with your sword," Delin idly continued.

A sudden whisper among the trees stole Fennic's attention. The movement was slight enough that he normally wouldn't have seen it on his best days, especially over the glare and cackling of the fire, but holding the sword heightened his senses, making him more aware. Moving as slow as he could, he reached for Phaelor. Touching the steel opened a new world. He felt it speaking to him, soothing him in a voice as old as time. It told him there was no danger in the forest, no threat from the enemy. Fennic's heart slowed and he released the sword. He looked over to Delin, who was already asleep.

It was dawn again and reasonably cool. The boys were coated with dew, for the fire had gone out sometime during the night. Delin awoke with a slight shiver. He was starting to hate this life. Fennic on the other hand, rose refreshed and ready to take on the world again. Delin scowled at his friend. Darkening skies didn't do much for his spirits either. Today was going to be decidedly miserable.

"Looks like rain," Delin said. "Perfect."

Fennic agreed. "We might be able to make the forest edge without getting caught. Come on, let's hurry and finish breaking camp."

A strong gust of cold wind announced the fringes of the storm. They might make it a few more leagues, but nowhere near Relin Werd. Delin cursed himself again for not thinking enough to bring a map of the kingdom. If it weren't for the occasional traveler, they wouldn't even be sure if this was the right road to Alloenis. They'd barely been on the road for an hour before the first sprinkling of rain came.

The rest of the day was spent ducking from tree to tree on the edges of the road and cowering under a heavy bough when the storm grew angry. High winds pelted hail down on them, littering the boys with welts and bruises. It was already mid-afternoon and they barely managed a handful of miles. Delin spied a huge, bored out oak not far ahead and felt his spirits rise.

Together they dashed forward to safety. The shelter was large and mossy, and more importantly, vacant. It had just enough room for the two of them, which was no problem seeing as how all the natural fuel for a fire was soaked. They huddled together for warmth and road out the storm.

"What are you thinking?" Fennic asked to break the boredom.

Delin blew into his wrinkled hands. "About going home before this nonsense gets worse. You'd do well to think the same. We should have told our parents about the sword the moment we came home. Nothing good will come of this. Mark my words."

Maybe it was the weather and the miserable conditions he was in, or maybe he was simply tired of being treated like an incompetent. Whatever it was, Fennic wasn't taking any more.

"The only reason I have this sword is from listening to your bright ideas. You wanted to go fishing. And you filled my head with fancy tales and daydreams of faraway lands. The last thing I need is your attitude about my responsibilities in keeping our family's safe and seeing to Phaelor doing what it needs to."

Delin was left speechless. He didn't like being the one with the negative energy, but someone had to be thinking with their head now. His guilt over the situation was as much as Fennic's, probably more so. He owed his friend for putting up with his own antics for so long, and he owed himself the gift of dream.

"What's gotten into you?" he asked quietly. "I didn't mean anything by it. We're in this together." He shook his head. Drops of rain fell from the brim of his hat. "Things will get better once we get out of this rain and into a soft bed in Alloenis with a hot meal in us."

Fennic stayed quiet. He knew Delin wasn't trying to be mean. Maybe it was the stress of leaving home and not really knowing what he was doing? They'd been best friends almost from birth, and in more arguments than any other people they knew. He put an arm around Delin and squeezed.

"Don't worry about me. My whole world changed the moment I touched the sword. I've seen visions of a history no one could possibly imagine, even you Delin. It's like Phaelor is alive. It has a will of its own. Old Man Wiffe was right. I don't know what's going to happen in the coming days and weeks, and that scares me. Fel Darrins may have been boring, but it was home and comfortable. But now. I don't know."

Neither of them spoke for a long while. Both had expunged their childish behaviors and insecurities and that was the end of the matter. They were at a critical junction in the adventure and needed to be whole if they were going to survive. Soon, before either of them knew, they were fast asleep.

Delin awoke just before dusk. The rains were gone, though the sky was plagued with grey clouds. It was depressing, but not so much as a few hours earlier. Birdsong told him the rains wouldn't be coming back soon. Delin rubbed his hands over his waterlogged clothes, surprise at how dry they'd gotten from their combined body heat. Fennic was still asleep, and Delin wanted him to stay that way. He liked being alone from time to time and felt he needed the extra space right now. Satisfied for the moment, Delin got out of the tree and stretched before going off to look for flammable materials. If they didn't get dry from a fire they'd both catch pneumonia.

The fire, when he finally found enough fuel that was dry enough to light, was warm, though decidedly small due to uncontrollable circumstances.

Fennic awoke a short while later and they ate a meager meal of dried fruits and nuts before agreeing to move on a few more hours. The trip, short as it was, proved to be relatively safe and uneventful. They even managed to collect enough wood and kindling to start a healthy fire strong enough to dry their clothes and cook a hot meal. Fennic instinctively checked Phaelor for sign of the enemy before going to sleep.

Finishing off a roasted grouse for breakfast, they were packed and moving again not long after the sun rose. They joked and sang songs, carrying on like children without worry. Lunch came and went. The sun was high and beaming. They were dry and marching on full stomachs. Nothing seemed like it could go wrong.

"What do you suppose wants to become our dinner tonight?" Delin asked with a chuckle.

They'd been fortunate thus far, but even the best hunters knew better than to rely on luck keeping the satisfied.

"Rabbit sounds nice," Fennic answered. "I've still got a few potatoes and carrots. Even an onion, I think. We could make a good stew with that."

They couldn't snare a rabbit, though Delin managed to kill two squirrels with his slingshot. Meat was meat after all. Fennic's stew proved to be every bit as tasty with the squirrel meat. They had at last reached the borders of the great Relin Werd. The trees were enormous and every shade of green he could imagine. Giant ferns scattered the ground in vast fields. Pockets of light and shadow played with their vision in beautiful patterns. In short, Relin Werd was everything they were told it was, and more.

It was also much further than they anticipated. The skies darkened, forcing them to stop for the night. A strange man in grey robes burst into the campsite and collapsed just shy of the fire. Fennic jumped back and drew Phaelor. Delin loaded and aimed his slingshot. They inched closer, ready for a trap. Phaelor warned caution in subtle undertones. Fennic slowly leaned down to try and turn the man over so they could see his face. The wild man's arm shot up in a silent plea for help before letting it fall again. Both boys stood wide eyed. What were they going to do about this?

SIX
Dakeb

"What should we do with him?" Fennic asked.

Delin, unwilling to loosen his aim, said, "You had the right of it with that fancy sword. Finish him quick. He's probably the one who killed Old Man Wiffe."

Fennic shook his head. Phaelor would have told him if he were. "I don't think so. He seems harmless enough at any rate. Besides, Phaelor's not warning me."

"Harmless! He could have killed us both if he wanted to," Delin argued.

"Precisely my point. You do a good job of proving yourself wrong. My point is that if this man wanted to kill us, he would have."

"It could be a trap. He might be working for the enemy," Delin cautioned. "I say we tie him up and get some answers before he does something."

"How does that make us better than the enemy?" Fennic asked. He knew Phaelor was making himself unstable, but Delin's newfound obsession with the *enemy* was growing dangerous. The entire situation was spiraling out of control. The wild man groaned and tried to roll over. The boys jumped back; weapons raised. His hand dropped back down and Fennic laid a reassuring hand on Delin's wrist. Having had enough, Fennic knelt to get a good look at him.

Age and experience etched deep lines in his face and hands. He had a peppered beard and moustache, more scruff than beard really. His high forehead was scarred and creased. All he wore were simple grey robes and appeared without purse or wallet. All in all, he seemed a simple man. Exactly the reason Delin felt defensive.

"I have a bad feeling," Delin continued.

He was back far enough to cover Fennic, providing his best friend leapt clear of his shot in time. The old man groaned again and reached a shaky hand up to massage his temples. Fennic felt his heart leap. Could Phaelor be wrong, he wondered. There wasn't time to worry about it, because the man was soon sitting up and staring back at them with pale green eyes.

"Well," he finally said in a groggy voice. "I seem to have taken a terrible stumble. Don't suppose either of you boys could tell me where I am? I've never been good with navigating. At least I'm not a pilot on one of the great ships of the oceans. We'd be lost for years!"

"Ah, I don't mean to sound rude, but we have no idea who you are, or why you are here," Fennic stated.

The old man offered a quizzical look. "You don't catch on very quick, do you lad? I already said I don't know where I am and you asking me isn't going to make me magically recall. Or perhaps your ears don't work quite right? I knew a man back in, oh bother, what was the name of that place? Seems I bumped my head harder than I thought."

Delin eased forward. "That's all well and fine, but we still want to know who you are."

"By my reckoning that puts us on even ground, wouldn't you agree?"

Neither boy moved.

"Fine, fine. Allow me to introduce myself. I am called Dakeb by some. Worse by others of course, and I am more than pleased to make your acquaintances," he smiled. "It's been a frightful spell since I last entertained guests so I may not be very good at it. Forgive me if I lose you from time to time."

"Guests?" Delin asked. "Old man, you came crashing into our campsite. How do you figure we're your guests?"

Dakeb gave them a confused look. "Ah, yes. I see your point. Am I interrupting then?"

"Nothing special if that's what you mean, Master Dakeb," Fennic said.

"Master? I rather like the sound of that. Makes me out to be nobility of a sort. Speaking of rudeness though, I've gone through great pains to let you know who I am and you two haven't said a peep about yourselves. Your parents must have raised you better than that," Dakeb scolded.

Fennic blushed, forgetting they were supposed to be in charge. Delin, on the other hand, had no misconceptions about what was developing. Dakeb had come upon them, whether by mere chance or not, and quickly stole their initial superiority. He'd effortlessly turned the table and it could only get worse.

"I'm Fennic Attleford and this is my best friend Delin Kerny. We're from Fel Darrins," he said before Delin could stop him.

Dakeb tilted his head. "Fel Darrins. It's been a long time since I was last there. Nice little town as I recall. Quiet and out of the way. Not very important in the grand scheme of things."

"You know more than you lead on," Delin accused.

Flames reflected in his green eyes. Dakeb had seen his share of the world and knew more than either of them could begin to imagine. Dangerous times were gripping Averon and Delin and Fennic were too far from

32

understanding how deep the repercussions were going to stretch. The old man chose his words carefully.

"Well met indeed," Dakeb said with a smile. He looked down at the dwindling fire. "It might stand to add a few more logs and twigs. My blood doesn't flow as well as it did. I must be getting old. Hmm. Imagine that. If this keeps up I shan't be around much longer. Don't suppose you've got an extra spot to eat? Traveling is hungry business, as I'm sure you know by now." He paused. "Exactly how far is to your little town of Fel Darrins?"

"A few days," Fennic answered. "Probably a lot closer than where we're heading."

Dakeb's eyebrow raised. "You make it sound as if you're running from something."

The old man shifted his gaze to the darkening forest. An owl's call brought a thin smile to his weathered face. "Soothing isn't it? Owls are among the brighter species but have a nasty tendency towards aggression. Wouldn't want to get nipped by that sharp beak. You know, I just remembered you still haven't mentioned what forest we are in. My memory isn't what is used to be."

Delin returned with an armload of small branches and firewood. "This is Relin Werd, old man. You should at least know which great wood you've stumbled into."

"Old man? Well, I suppose youth sees experience through veiled eyes. I seem to recall the forest being much smaller, but that was years ago. Still, I almost feel at home here."

Delin shook his head and fed the fire.

Dakeb slapped his thigh and laughed. "So, what's for supper? It's got to be heading towards the mid of night and I haven't eaten since the sun went down."

They ate in relative silence, a simple luxury Delin had never been so thankful for. He found the old man intrusive and overbearing. Definitely not one to be trusted he decided the moment Dakeb came awake. He refused to believe that the old man accidentally bumped into them. The sheer convenience of it all was alarming. Fennic, on the other hand, seemed enamored with the grump. That put them both in a bad situation.

"What was it exactly you were looking for in Fel Darrins? You've mentioned it twice already and not said how you knew our little out of the way home," Delin said.

There was a twinkle in Dakeb's eye. "I was going to visit an old friend if you must know. A very good man."

"Anyone we know?" Fennic asked. The slow rising tension between the other two was setting him on edge. Yet whenever he touched Phaelor the sword radiated calm. A nasty cough from the old man eased Fennic's mind, if only slightly.

"Ahh, a tricky question at best. You can live in a village your whole life and not really know the man next door. There's always someone you haven't met. So, the answer to your question is both yes and no. We are old friends and let us leave it at that for now," the old man said.

He yawned. "The hour is growing late and I'm not as young as I once was. I hope you lads don't mind if I retire until the morn?"

Without waiting for a response, Dakeb scooped together a small pile of leaves then pulled his hood over his head and lay down. He looked asleep the moment his head hit the soft leaves. Delin and Fennic stayed up and watched him for a time. Neither tried to go to sleep until he began to snore.

Delin eased closer to Fennic and whispered. "I'm still not sure about him. He may be a decoy for the enemy. He makes the hairs on the back of my neck stand. This is too dangerous, Fennic. I think we should leave before he wakes up."

"I don't know. Phaelor hasn't alerted me at all. I think Dakeb is just a harmless old man looking for a friend before the end. My father used to say the old get like this before they pass on."

Delin scowled. "Say what you will, but that man is dangerous."

Fennic stifled a laugh. "Him? He's older than your grandmother. Look at him. He can't weigh more than a five stones. We should be safe enough."

Tired as he was, Fennic followed Dakeb's example and was soon fast asleep. Delin managed to stay awake a while longer, before succumbing to sleep. A sudden rustling in the dead leaves brought him wide awake and fumbling for his weapon. His fears were being realized. The old man had gotten up after they were asleep and led the enemy right to them! Delin resigned himself to death, hoping to take some of them to the grave with him. By the time his eyes focused all he saw were a pair of forest hares rummaging for a meal. Delin exhaled a long, shaky breath. Only then did he realize he was trembling.

Regaining his composure, Delin checked on Fennic and the old man. Both hadn't even stirred. The fears from earlier in the night were gone and dawn was beginning to crack the night. He found himself oddly satisfied that Fennic kept him from acting out his fears. Smiling, the youth gathered his sling and a pouch of stones and tramped off into the forest to find some food for breakfast. He returned an hour later carrying a dressed pheasant over his shoulder and whistling a song. The look on Fennic's face stole that good mood.

"He's dead," Fennic said.

Delin dropped the bird and rushed over to feel for a pulse. "Must have passed in his sleep," he said.

Fennic shook his head. This was the second time a person they'd come in contact with had died. Ill fortune was following them. How much longer before it struck them down?

Together they gathered enough stones to cover Dakeb's body, seeing as how they lacked the tools to dig a proper grave. Grabbing his legs, Fennic let Delin take the upper body and they lay him in the shallow pit between a pair of tree roots. Something small and dark purple slipped from the old man's robes. Delin reached down and picked it up, staring at the perfection of it. It was no bigger than the palm of his hand and remarkably light. Angles refracted the firelight in a hypnotic way. He didn't know why, but the purple stone was important.

"What is that?" Fennic asked curiously.

"It looks like a crystal," Delin answered. "It's unlike anything I've ever seen." It was that moment Fennic knew things could not get more bizarre.

SEVEN
Gren Mot

Half a continent from the sleeping forests of Relin Werd stood the Gren Mountains, the treacherous boundary between Averon and the wicked land of Gren. Here the war was very much a reality, not just mere speculation over a mug of ale and a leg of venison. Soldiers of Averon met the enemy in engagements that no one ever heard. Skeletons littered the rocky pass between kingdoms. Whatever fragile peace the capital of Paedwyn pretended to enjoy was lost in this largely forgotten part of the world.

Strong winds ravaged the rocky terrain, funneling through the mountain passes and picking up speed and intensity before unleashing across the open slopes of the Gren Mountains. Dark skies kept the air damp and dour enough for the intruders to quickly lose hope and return the way they had come except for the three mounted soldiers, who silently rode through the lower foothills of the eastern range. Black and purple skies laden with thunderstorms kept the sun perpetually hidden here. Lightning raked the slopes around them, warning them to beware. A thunderclap trembled the ground.

"We should turn back!" one of the soldiers shouted.

Sergeant Hallis, the scout leader, ignored him, noting how quickly the young and inexperienced trooper was ready to give up. The land of Gren had been besieged by nature since the Silver Mage first took power, over two hundred years ago. It was rumored that Gren was once a gilded land of a different name, but history was forgotten in response to the great evil threatening the world. Hallis himself had joined the army of Averon out of necessity. A flux swept through the kingdom, claiming hundreds, including his parents. Having nothing to keep him at home, Hallis left to join the army.

He reached the rank of sergeant and was nearing the end of his third decade of service. Most of his duty had been spent on the wrong side of the Gren Mountains, scouting and spying on enemy movements. It was a learned skill that was almost second nature to him. He barely noticed the weather anymore. Normally he wouldn't have taken such a green trooper, but there was little choice. Despite years of waiting, the army of Averon wasn't prepared for the war everyone knew was coming. There just wasn't enough time to get ready.

Hallis didn't have the luxury to worry about what was happening back at Paedwyn. Assigned to the garrison at the mountain fortress of Gren Mot, his job was to scout out the enemy and report any actionable intelligence.

"Keep quiet and watch me, Troop," Hallis barked at the lad. He wanted to say more but knew it was useless. This was the boy's first mission and no amount of class work or indoctrination was enough to prepare him for the horrors surrounding them.

Flames pockmarked the landscape as far as the eye could see. Scrub brushes void of greenery were the last remnants of a pristine empire. All the Fair races fled west after a brutal campaign to oust the Silver Mage failed. Nothing now grew upon the soiled plains. Nothing lived in the fetid waters. The mountains were filled with hordes of Trolls and worse. Goblins and other foul beings lived in the low country, dwelling in vast underground caverns. Hallis knew his patrol was being watched even now.

Most patrols were fielded with the instructions of monitoring only. King Maelor had been concerned with enemy movements and troop buildups for years now and was eager to learn the disposition of his foe. For Hallis, this patrol was unlike any other. Three separate patrols had been sent out the week prior and none returned. Concern was rising that the enemy was at last ready to move. He'd accepted the task because it was a soldier's duty to follow orders, whether he liked them or not. What he didn't accept were the men assigned to him. His complaints fell on deaf ears and three short days later they were inside the realm of the enemy. The third scout reined in close to Hallis and said in a low voice, "Do you think he may be right?"

Hallis finished a hasty drink from his canteen. "I've been thinking that since we left Gren Mot, Jinse."

Older than Hallis, Jinse offered a weak laugh. "So have I. We shouldn't be on the same patrol, at any rate. What good would it do for both of us to get killed at the same time?"

"Orders are orders," Hallis answered.

His friend picked up on the meaning even as the words left his mouth. They both knew the garrison commander at the mountain fortress was an intolerable man who expected his subordinates to obey his every command without question. Jinse also knew that Hallis had been around long enough to put the lives of his men first. The rest of Averon may still be safe behind the illusion of peace, but combat was very real here on the border.

"We should have seen signs by now," Hallis scowled after they rode another hour. "I don't like this at all."

Lightning and thunder emphasized his point.

"The winds are picking up," Jinse remarked. "This is getting dangerous."

Hallis smiled. "It'll make the ale that much better when we get back."

He was going to say more when they rounded a corner and came face to face with a vast plain, normally empty. His eyes widened in horror at what he now saw. Thousands of campfires and campaign tents stretched as far as they could see and into the darkness beyond. Squat, grey bodies in leather armor blanketed every inch of the land. Hallis just barely made out enormous creatures pulling siege machines closer. He'd seen and fought Trolls and Goblins before but had never imagined an army so large. The people of Averon long believed the impending war was inevitable. Not even the king's top advisors could predict when though. Hallis stared at the answer and the fear that came with it.

"This isn't good," Jinse said, his throat suddenly dry.

Hallis sat still and watched. He'd already given up trying to count. The rookie didn't fare so well. Barely past his teen years, the trooper was on the verge of snapping. Never in his days did he expect to go to all out war. Yet here he sat, locked on the brink of a fate inescapable. Doom was returned to the world of men. The veterans noticed his wild look and moved to keep him from doing something brash.

A lightning bolt blasted a nearby rock into a shower of sparks and pebbles, spooking all their horses. The rookie was thrown into a boulder before his horse ran off in the direction of the Goblin camp. Jinse was the first to recover and desperately dashed after the horse before it was too late. Hallis immediately went to his fallen trooper. He was halfway there when Fate intervened.

Black arrows rained down on the fallen trooper, killing him instantly a dozen times over. Hallis snatched his shield in a useless effort, for the enemy was on both sides. The assault ended with a horrible roar from the rocks above. A Mountain Troll burst from cover, mighty war hammer in hand and squads of Goblins at his heels. Hallis was cut off. Jinse wheeled about and drew his sword. The odds were against them and they knew it. Then Jinse did something Hallis didn't expect. The grizzled old veteran roared back at the Troll and charged into their ranks.

"Go!" he bellowed to Hallis.

The last thing Hallis saw was his friend plowing into the enemy. One of them had to live to warn Averon. Jinse chose Hallis. Both men spurred their horses hard; one into certain death and the other back into the mountain passes. Jinse offered the ultimate sacrifice and Hallis would be damned if he let it go to waste. The garrison at Gren Mot had to be warned. The fate of the entire kingdom depended on it.

EIGHT
Tolis Scarn

Heavy rains kept the townsfolk indoors over the last few days. One of the fields south of Fel Darrins was flooded, drawing a fair portion of the able-bodied men to try and stem the tide of the rampaging creek. The recovery took most of the day and they were able to prevent the waters from reaching the village. For most, it was a trip to the warm fire in the Tavern and a pint or two. The storm raged on unabated.

So it was the lone rider came into town unnoticed. He wore clothes of the darkest black and had a menacing scowl. He was half a head taller than most of the townsfolk and heavily muscled. His body was lean and hard from years of constant warfare and hardships. He ignored the houses and closed shops. The rider stopped long enough to watch the men valiantly trying to save their town from the flow of water. While it piqued his curiosity, he didn't find who he was looking for so he rode on towards the Tavern. His horse, the purest color of darkness, snorted displeasure. The rain was slightly tolerable but night was falling and with it the temperature. Winter was but a suggestion away. Hopefully he would find his quarry and be done with the affair before the first snow fell. Otherwise....

The tavern door opened and closed with a bedraggled moan. Heads turned as the stranger in black strode through. The intent in his shadowed eyes made many turn back to their ale. He took in each of the men. Disappointment flashed across his face for a moment only. The man he wanted wasn't here. *Damnation.* The rider abandoned his search and moved closer to the fire. Gilley Brickton laid a restraining hand on his daughter's arm and went to greet the stranger himself.

"What can I get for you, friend?" he asked in a pleasant voice.

Both men stared hard at one another, silently conveying their intent. The rider finally smiled and stripped off his soaked gloves and hat. Gilley almost balked at the sight. The man had a clean-shaven head and deep set, almost hollow eyes. Gilley stiffened.

"Ale, and make it strong," the rider said. "That storm's enough to make a man thirsty for days. Don't you agree?"

"Well enough," Gilley agreed and went off to the bar.

"This is a quiet part of the country," the rider said as he paid for the ale when Gilley returned. "Probably don't get many visitors, I wager."

Gilley eyed him suspiciously. "We get a few here and there. Not as many as in one of the bigger cities closer to Paedwyn, but enough to recognize a familiar face when one passes through."

"Good, then I don't need to tell you I've never been here." Lightning flashed through the windows, heavy thunder following. "Name's Tolis Scarn. I'm an independent trader out of Keesis in the south."

Gilley had never heard of Keesis but he knew enough to spot a trader when he saw one, and whoever this man was, he most definitely wasn't a trader. This man was dangerous.

"There's not much call for a trader around here, friend. We kind of like to stick to ourselves. Makes for a nice quiet place," Gilley said.

Scarn laughed, deep and resounding. "The story's the same much the world over. I've been through just about every kingdom in Malweir, but I never stay in one place for more than a season or so. A year at the most. I make enough to fill my pockets and move on. Most towns profit from my business and I don't stay longer than I'm welcomed."

"It takes a wise man to know his limitations," Gilley agreed. "Enjoy your ale, friend, and don't be shy to ask for another. My name's Gilley Brickton."

Scarn nodded, offering a pleasant, if entirely false, smile.

Gilley stalked back into the kitchens, a dark look troubling his eyes. A lifetime of running inns and taverns taught him how to recognize danger, and Scarn's poise screamed danger. Gilley took a hand towel from the counter and wiped the corners of his mouth.

"What's wrong, Papa?" Tarren asked once Gilley had returned.

He dried off his hands and sighed. "That stranger in the common room. He says he's a trader. I don't believe him for a second."

She watched the odd man. "Maybe he just has a few secrets. Lots of folk do these days."

"Aye. The wrong sort more often than not," Gilley snorted. "Best we tell folk to keep clear of him. A watchful eye in the least. It wouldn't do well to find a friend dead in the middle of the night."

She leaned over and kissed her father on the cheek. "Yes Papa, I promise to be careful around him."

Despite the sweetness and confidence in her voice, Gilley had his doubts.

Tolis Scarn remained in Fel Darrins long enough for the storm to blow out. He spent the time gathering as much information as he could glean. Several of the lesser liked townsfolk took to him the instant his smile graced the Tavern. Most of his days were spent wandering the darker side of life. He killed when it was necessary, and often when it wasn't, and had no morals. The money in his purse came from generous benefactors for services well-tended. His specialty was acquisitions, and he had yet to fail a task. Fel Darrins was but another stop in an endless cycle. Sundown found him again by the fire, warming himself while pretending to care about the petty problems and issues the villagers faced. He responded with tales and grand adventures of his own. Most of his talk was deemed unbelievable, as nothing exciting ever happened in Fel Darrins. Such a recipe often led to long months of doldrums.

"Much out of the ordinary ever happens in this part of the world?" Scarn asked during his third night of visiting the tavern. "Surely there has to be some form of entertainment here."

"Not around here."

"I don't think most folks even know we're a part of the kingdom."

Scarn smiled. "That can come in handy during tax time."

"I've seen strange things, friend," a shaky handed man came forward to say. "Been lots of odd goings on of late. Strange creatures shuffling through the night, making terrible sounds. This place isn't what it used to be. Folks here are scared to go out after dusk."

Sensing opportunity, Scarn bought the man another frothing ale. He'd been waiting three days for a break like this. "You don't say. Well, I don't put much faith in monsters and ghoulies, but I do keep a good blade close by. You never know what you may come across on a dark country road. What's your name friend?"

"Jeck, and I'm with you on that. These things sure weren't friendly or much human even. I know what I saw, and never want to see it again."

Scarn found his fears most interesting. He knew that the Silver Mage had unleashed platoons of Gnaals to scour the world, but he didn't know one was here in this part of Averon. The people here were harmless at best, but the Mage never made a move without being sure of the result. Perhaps there was more to Fel Darrins than met the eye. Scarn decided to press further.

"That would explain the patrols during the night."

They all nodded.

"Then I'm guessing that with so much going on you probably wouldn't have noticed a fragile old man in simple robes passing through?" he asked timidly to leave the impression he didn't want to broach the subject.

"I seen him," Jeck said after downing the last swallow of ale. "Passed through close to a week ago now."

"Me too," said another. Scarn felt his luck shift. Finally.

"Tell me, friend, did this old man say where he was headed?"

"Left right as the storm was brewing. Gilley tried to convince him to stay but he'd have none of it. Said there was important matters needed doing that couldn't wait. I think he was heading for Relin Werd."

Scarn had heard enough. He bought them all another round and quickly changed the subject. He ensured they drank more than he and avoided all talk about his dark past. Scarn wanted to smile but knew better. Relin Werd was too far to make in a day, even on horseback. The hunt was on!

The lurking question of why the Silver Mage had sent a Gnaal here troubled him. Was the Mage looking to be rid of him already? The Silver Mage was a terror from the old times, before the devastation of the Mage Wars, a decayed relic of a once honorable order. Scarn finished his ale and left his companions with their heads on the table.

Keeping far enough away to stay hidden, Tarren followed the dark stranger as he dropped a heavy coin on the table and started down the hall. She didn't like him or what he was doing there. He'd attracted the worst people in town and they all took a shining to him. Her every instinct told him he was dangerous. Tarren couldn't put her finger on it, but Scarn had a foul air about him. He was evil. All her senses screamed it. The longer he stayed here the more danger the people of Fel Darrins were in. Tarren stayed in the shadows until she saw Scarn unlock his door and slip inside. She held her breath until she caught the candlelight flicker under his door. She eased forward to peak through the keyhole.

Scarn stood in the center of the room, his back to the door. A large assortment of knives, swords, and daggers lay on the table, confirming her father's suspicions. She'd been taught not to judge people, but Gilley was right. No honest trader carried so many different weapons. She covered her mouth when he removed his shirt, showing her a body covered by scars, both old and new. Tarren decided she'd seen enough and snuck back to the common room to clean up for the night. She didn't notice the door ease open and Scarn stick his head into the hall. Tolis Scarn smiled and closed the door.

A dozen thoughts crammed into Tarren's head, none of them good. She was convinced Delin and Fennic were in peril and needed to be warned. Trembling, she packed her bag. Tarren knew the stranger would be leaving before the dawn to hunt down her friends. She'd decided to follow him until he got close enough and rush in to give them warning before it was too late. She loathed the thought of leaving home like a thief in the night. Her parents wouldn't understand. They'd been upset when Delin and Fennic left. This would set them over the top. Tarren silently prayed her father didn't do something brash like follow her. He was the last man she wanted to see hurt.

But the task had to be done. Her friends, her love, were in danger and she was the only one not blinded by Scarn's charm to realize it. No monster of an ill-favored man was enough to keep her from the man she loved. She would rescue Delin. Finished, Tarren went and saddled the pony her father bought her a few years back. She waited for Scarn on the outskirts of town. She didn't have to wait long. The lanky man eased into the stables and left a few minutes later. Dawn was still far enough off to give him at least a league before anyone noticed him missing.

Scarn was near impossible to see in the perfect darkness. She barely saw him when he rode by. Tarren clicked her pony forward. It was all she could do to keep him in her line of sight. She'd never followed anyone before and the prospect of losing him frightened her. Sleep wormed through her. She already wanted to go back to bed. But her loyalties went too deep. She loved Delin almost as much as her father and was willing to sacrifice everything for his safety. She drew a heavy sigh, took a backward glance at her town she'd grown up in, and followed Tolis Scarn off into the night and whatever adventures lay beyond. She prayed they didn't last long.

NINE
Alloenis

The town of Alloenis stretched for row upon row of wooden houses. There were markets and shops and an overabundance of people crowding the streets. Neither Delin nor Fennic had ever seen the like. It was like stepping into another world. Swindlers and conmen worked the crowds while countless pick pockets bumped into the innocent not savvy enough to know better. Alloenis was the major trade center for western Averon. On a normal day one could see Dwarves bartering with Men, Gnomes, and the occasional Elf. Today, however, they found dozens of soldiers in the livery of the king.

That wasn't surprising. Convoys of supply wagons and mounted companies heading east were a constant sight on the main roads. Since leaving Relin Werd, the boys watched countless columns of cavalry and infantry marching to Paedwyn from the western lands, all dressed in the green and gold of Averon. Oddly enough, there were smaller columns of peasants heading the same way with but one soldier marching alongside them. Fennic believed them recruits for the coming fight. Some whispered the skies over Gren had already grown dark. With the Silver Mage stirring again no one was safe. Mounted patrols roved the surrounding countryside from the great Relin Werd to the fringes of Alloenis. The war was coming much sooner than they thought.

The boys entered Alloenis with mouths agape.

The sheer size of the town was overwhelming. Until now they doubted there were so many people in the world. Two and three story buildings lined their view for as far as they could see. The Bairn Hills lay far to the west and mighty Paedwyn was to the east. Gren wasn't far beyond. Fennic's hope of understanding the sword and why it chose him lay in finding a scholar or a smithy. The unnatural desire to use it in battle strengthened daily, pushing him to the brink of rash decisions. He needed help if he stood any chance of remaining himself.

"Dragon scale shields! Only a silver apiece. Made from genuine dragons!"

"Magic potions and powders!"

Delin wanted to laugh. "Can you believe this place?"

"Come see the remarkable two headed man from exotic Antheneon. See what people say can't exist!"

"This is incredible," Fennic conceded. "Now I know why father never spoke well of the world. Fel Darrins could never be like this."

"I agree. We need to be careful here. Someone's responsible for killing Old Man Wiffe. They might have beaten us here. I don't fancy the thought of catching a knife in the back," Delin said with a shudder. His nerves had been on edge since finding the strange purple stone in Dakeb's robes. A gem so fine was bound to draw the wrong type of attention.

They'd spent the hours of travel agonizing over the hundreds of possibilities. The stone was by far the most exquisite possession he'd ever come across, certainly rivaling Phaelor in many ways. The biggest problem was not knowing what it was or what to do with it. Fennic offered to sell it when they got rid of the sword, but his comment was met with stiff defiance. No, Delin was going to keep it. Nothing was said on the matter since.

"We need to find a place to sleep and grab a bite to eat. I'm tired of eating travel rations and it'll be dark soon," Fennic said. "And I don't think we want to be caught out in the open after dark. Even with the city patrols I don't feel quite safe."

It took an hour to worm through the crowds and find the right inn. Most of the ones on the main street were already crowded and growing more so the closer it got to sunset. They were just about to give up when they came across an innocent, if not slightly run down, blue inn with a giant golden insect on the sign. Less than a handful of horses were tethered to the hitch out front, and judging from the sudden quiet, there were few patrons.

"I don't know what a scarab is, but there doesn't seem to be too many folks who want to come this way for a night's sleep. Looks like as good a place as we can find," Delin said. He scratched his scalp and studied the sign.

Fennic nodded. They didn't have the money for much else anyway. "Let's hope it's safe."

"Quit worrying. This is your adventure after all."

The door opened and in they went. The boys were instantly met with the scrutinizing stares of those few assembled.

"Welcome. Welcome my friends. You won't find a better meal than here at the Golden Scarab," said the rotund innkeeper. His eyes lit up as he finished drying his pudgy hands. He smelled money.

Delin shook his hand. "Thank you, I suppose."

"We don't get much business since the Trader's Guild added the new road and all those terrible tariffs."

"I can see that. Hopefully this doesn't make you too eager to take all our coin," Delin stated with a stern gaze.

Fennic balked at his friend's straight forwardness.

The innkeeper let out a shaky laugh, patting Delin on the shoulder. "Nonsense. There are plenty of thieves out there to keep a decent man in business. I run a respectable establishment. Besides, King Maelor's men don't take kindly to being taken, if you get my meaning."

His eyes quickly shifted to the table with three men in gold and green.

"But where are my manners? I'm Will Apper. Anything I can do for you, you just let me know."

"Thank you, Mr. Apper. We appreciate that," Fennic smiled. He felt like he found a friend, though he couldn't say why.

Will ambled off, leaving them to find a table on their own. They decided to stay away from the other patrons. The crowd was thin and spaced, affording the boys plenty of room without looking conspicuous. Judging from the neighborhood the Scarab was in, that seemed the wisest course. Aside from the soldiers, there were four men playing a game of bones and a lone Dwarf off by himself in the far corner. None of them were so much as looking at them now.

Fennic's jitters towards civilization ebbed slightly. He'd been convinced they were going to be robbed from the moment they stepped foot into the busy city. They ate a meager meal of house stew, filled with chunks of meat they couldn't describe, and a plate of cheese served with a loaf of fresh baked bread and sliced pears for dessert. The taste and heat hit the spot and both boys pushed away from the table with their bellies full. They sat and talked for a spell. The soldiers got up and left for their barracks bunks. A pair of young traders came in and enjoyed a similar dinner and left and still the Dwarf sat and watched.

Delin cut off a yawn when the doors burst open and a pair of huge men in green and gold entered. One stood with arms folded across his chest and a hand never far from the hilt of his sword. His eyes were dark and narrowed, as if expecting trouble. His partner was slightly shorter and had a more pleasant demeanor. He had fair hair and brilliant eyes and was overly handsome to look at.

"King Maelor of Averon presents greetings," he announced with a graceful bow. "At this time his majesty is looking for fit and eager men to join the brotherhood his armies have to offer."

"Recruiters," Will whispered to Delin while collecting their plates. "Trying to take more men off to fight the Mage."

"Do they come around often?" Fennic asked.

The recruiter went on with a well-rehearsed speech given a hundred times already. There was no doubt about his friendly character and alluring charm to the fancies of young men and boys. Fennic wondered how many men he'd already snared into service. At the same time, he wanted no part in a war. Leaving Fel Darrins was bad enough.

Will shrugged. "Often enough I suppose. Don't let me make up your minds though. The army was never for me, but we need them. The Mage would already be sitting on the throne if those men weren't blocking the way."

Two men got up and went to the recruiters. The Dwarf took it in but made no move. A massive, double headed axe leaned against the wall behind him. His beady eyes were locked on the bigger soldier. The scene took mere moments. No sooner had they arrived, the recruiters left, with two volunteers. Two men in a near empty bar wasn't a bad deal at all. The door closed and the Dwarf finally moved from his seat. He was halfway back to his table with a fresh mug of ale when he spied Fennic's sword. Delin and Fennic watched the diminutive warrior carefully as he sat down next to them and returned their stares. Will Apper watched from behind the bar. His hand drifted to the truncheon he kept for emergencies.

"Damned soldiers, always coming around to spoil the taste of a good drink, I say," the Dwarf grumbled in a deep voice. "Fancy you boys didn't get taken in by all the flowery words."

"Maybe we have a different agenda," Delin replied coldly.

"That's a tricky word. Politicians and thieves have agendas and you don't strike me as either. I'm Norgen, by the way." His grip was crushing as he introduced himself properly.

"Seeing how you're ordinary folk, I'd caution you to keep a tighter eye on your surroundings."

Fennic feigned a smile. "We don't know what you mean."

Norgen laughed. "Yes you do, boy. That fancy sword of yours is going to bring you more attention than you ever dreamed."

He held up a hand to stop Fennic's protests. "I've been watching you since you came in here. I don't like what I see. You two are about as back woods as a man can be and. These people will eat you alive if you keep on. The careful man lives longer."

"Well Norgen, we appreciate the advice, but we can handle ourselves," Delin warned.

"I doubt that. You already have too many eyes upon you. These are dangerous times, boys. The enemy has many eyes and ears throughout the west. Even my kinfolk in the Bairn Hills aren't safe any longer." He slammed the table hard enough to spill some of their drinks.

Fennic tried to calm him down. "It's not that we're trying to get rid of you, Norgen, but we are new to Alloenis and we've never seen a Dwarf before, much less spoken with one. This is all still very strange for us."

"Indeed it is. Indeed it is. But if you wish to keep on, you'll listen to those who offer help," Norgen replied.

Delin wasn't convinced. He'd seen plenty of people like Norgen while sitting with Tarren in the Tavern. "You say we need to be careful and pay attention yet here you are offering all those things you've warned against. How do we take that?"

"Smart lad. Let me tell you a little tale to ease your young minds. Last year a rider came to our might hall in Breilnor. He spoke of a coming war between the free races of Malweir and the dark realm of Gren. He didn't want to tell us, but we worked it out that the Elves were going to sit this one out. They are tired of the wars of men and want no part in this new one. My people debated long and hard before deciding on sending a token party to Paedwyn. We were going to see how bad the situation was before committing the strength of our armies.

"We made it halfway to Alloenis when we were beset by a Gnaal." He ignored their confused looks. "Nasty things, Gnaals. One hasn't been seen since the last war against Gren. Now they roam the countryside. The night belongs to them and it takes much to kill one. Magic some say. We fought hard, as only Dwarves can, but in the end I was the only one to walk away. They all died that night. I suffered a broken arm and deep wounds across my back, but the Gnaal left me for dead before stalking off into the darkness.

"I wanted to return home and warn my people, but two things stopped me. The halls of Breilnor are well guarded and deep within the mountain base. The Gnaal was also between me and Breilnor. The second, and more important of the two, is when a Dwarf gives his word he keeps it until the end. We may be reclusive, quarrelsome and generally foul tempered, but we love our freedom. Gren threatens to rob that from us. I cannot return home until the Silver Mage is vanquished."

Fennic found himself sympathizing with him. All three were far from the comforts of home. War threatened the world. This was the time for all allies to band together and move past differences. Despite Delin's initial reservations, the boys soon took a liking to the Dwarf. Norgen went on to explain his decisions and intentions. His task was to deliver the message from his king and survey the battlefield. Averon was alone until then. They talked long into the evening and finally decided to end their meeting. All promised to meet in the common room again on the morn.

They found Norgen awaiting them not long after the sun broke.

"Good morning to you, young sirs," Norgen said.

Fennic yawned. "Good morning to you, Master Dwarf. I trust you slept well?"

"Well enough, considering I had a double handful of beer in my belly! Will has a good rack of leftover mutton by the fire. It's especially good with a hearty hangover."

They spent the rest of the day talking. The conversation gradually turned to Phaelor and what to do. Norgen confessed he knew little of magical weapons or their whims. He offered to help them find one who could help. The recruiters came again that night, snatching one more for the cause. This time they announced that they were departing for the garrison at Paedwyn at the end of the week and would not be returning. His last minute theatrics snared another but no more. The fact of the matter was that most people didn't tend to worry or think of war until it was on their door. Delin noticed the silent soldier's piercing eyes with a faraway look. He would have given anything to know what that man was thinking.

Another day came and went with a deeper exploration of Alloenis. Thus far they hadn't found anyone else trustworthy enough to mention the sword. Hope started to diminish. Norgen brought up the subject of escorting them to Paedwyn. His wounds were fully recovered, and he was ready to get back on the road. The boys finally caved in and agreed. In two days' time they'd begin the trek for the golden halls of Paedwyn. The morning before they left they watched three full companies of recruits marching out under the fluttering banner of the king. The boys were highly impressed though Norgen passed them off as disorganized rabble. Dwarves, he explained, were brilliant tacticians and professional soldiers much envied throughout Malweir.

"You should retire early tonight," Norgen said after pushing away an empty dinner plate. "We're in no hurry to get there, but you can never tell what might happen."

They nodded, but neither believed for a moment that they'd be able to sleep easy again until they returned to Fel Darrins. Gnaals and armies of green and gold filled their dreams.

TEN

Norgen

"What's Paedwyn like?" Fennic asked. He tossed aside the freshly cleaned grouse bone he'd been gnawing on.

Norgen was spinning his own fowl over the small fire. "Much the same as every other man city I should say. Oh, there are some impressive buildings and statues. Done by Dwarves more than likely. Men seldom create things of beauty. Too bent on conquest and destruction they are."

"You sound as if you don't care much for us," Delin commented with a slight scowl.

"That all depends on how you mean. My folk often come to the aid of the kings of Averon. Darkness threatens us all whether the Elves choose to see it or not." His speech left them wondering if he held more contempt for men or Elves. Dwarves appeared to have lower opinions of just about everyone but themselves.

"They've already come out and said they weren't going to fight. Bah! You'll never see a Dwarf run from a good fight. That I can assure you."

"Forgive my ignorance, but we know almost nothing of Dwarves or any of the other races for that matter. Why do the Elves feel that way?" Fennic asked. Phaelor had shown him much over the past few weeks, just enough to keep him wanting more. "I'd have thought it was everyone's responsibility to rid the evil threatening us."

The Dwarf grunted. "Well spoken. It's a complicated matter. Folk say that most of the Elves are thousands of years old and tired of battles and war. Those are the main ones pushing Elfkind into seclusion. A shame the whole world is being made to suffer through the complacency of a few."

Delin was confused. "What makes a Dwarf so different? The people in our village haven't gone to war in decades."

Rage surged across Norgen's face but quickly faded. "Dwarves know their responsibilities and don't run from them! We may not put much faith in any but our own kind, but our strength and fortitude is unmatched throughout the lands. All the great monuments and statues in Averon, and the lands beyond, were painstakingly crafted by Dwarven artists. We've mined the precious stones and ores from the deepest mountains. The finest blades and suits of armor have been crafted by our smiths. Never, never doubt the will of a Dwarf."

He paused to take a deep breath. "My friends, the world is a darker place than you ever imagined. There are no glories to be found. No heroes or quests left. All that remains is petty squabbling between the Free Peoples.

That's how the Silver Mage came to power. No one was watching while he amassed an army and stole a kingdom."

He fell silent, casting his hood over his head before adding another log to the fire. The smell of roasting fowl filled the small clearing. Soon all three sat back with full bellies. Fennic sneezed when Norgen lit his pipe and the smoke drifted into his nostrils.

"You said that Dwarves crafted the great swords?" he asked, a twinkle in his eye.

Norgen nodded. "Aye. That we did. But not the sword you bear."

Disappointment hit Fennic. He was hoping. Still, he drew Phaelor and showed it to the Dwarf for the first time. "I was told the Elves made it long ago. Do you think you could tell me anything about it?"

Norgen reached out with an unsteady hand and grasped the hilt. The world around him erupted into light and song. Amazement filled his eyes. His heart filled with hope and joy. At that one moment in time there was no violence or strife. Life was in perfect harmony.

"This is beyond a wonder!" he exclaimed. "Dwarves are the first to sing praise of our own work, but this exceeds anything we've ever done. How did you come by it?"

Fennic replied, "One of the men in our village. He was murdered not long after."

"Does it have a name? All items of magic have names to mark their greatness. Surely this is magic as I've never seen. Tell me the name."

"Phaelor."

"Heaven's Eyes," Norgen whispered.

Delin balked. "You know Elvish?"

"Boy, this sword is a legend of the world. The blade is wrought of star silver, and a finer weapon there never was. Many have died in search of this."

The clouds parted enough for the moonlight to strike the blade, revealing a long line of deeply carved runes along the center of the steel. Norgen's eyes opened in astonishment.

"Look here," he uttered. "Can you see them? Ancient runes. No one has used them in generations. You have been blessed to receive so fine a weapon. They speak of great, great power. You could well lose your life by wielding it wrong. No smith in Alloenis has the knowledge to end your quest. The craftsmanship goes well beyond the scope of men."

Fennic went into the tale of how they found the sword in Old Man Wiffe's home and their long, strange journey since. Names and places meant nothing to the Dwarf though he clung to every word. He suspected they knew more than they were letting on, but he wasn't going to pry the information from them. A darker part of him hoped the boys had only good intentions. Else the world was lost to the growing night. Having heard enough, Norgen suggested they all get some sleep. It was still a long way to Paedwyn.

They breakfasted on quail eggs and a rasher of salted pork. Norgen made a pot of coffee. Dark clouds were coming in from the west, threatening to overtake them before long. Lighter grey clouds were already filling the sky, stealing away the warmth of the autumn sun. The Dwarf's compact size and build served as natural protection from all but the harshest weather. The boys, on the other hand, were forced to pull out their winter cloaks before they finished eating. A light drizzle was falling by the time they broke camp.

No one spoke until they were well on the way.

"How is it you don't know how to craft metal?" Delin asked. "I was under the impression all Dwarves could smith." He was fingering the strange purple stone. Thus far he'd managed to keep it a secret. His one fear, and a growing one at that, was that the enemy would try and kill him for it once they discovered he had it.

"Not all Dwarves forge steel or even live under the mountains. There are many places throughout Averon that my folk live in thriving hamlets and villages. Never far from the mountains, mind you. We do enjoy the feel and comfort the hard earth offers. You haven't lived until you've had Dwarven hospitality, my friends. Well brewed mead, meat of all kinds, and tales lasting long into the night. Many in my family forge. I have never had the touch for it. No. I've been a warrior all my life, and a trader beyond that. Long have we taken pride in our military prowess, but I fear now it won't be enough to stop the armies of Gren." Sadness filled his voice.

"Perhaps one day you can come to Breilnor and see how a Dwarf treats his friends!"

They smiled and readily agreed.

Conditions worsened throughout the day. Rain turned to snow. Temperatures dropped. Winds picked up, making it nigh unbearable to continue. Delin and Fennic wanted to stop for the night and find shelter but Norgen merely laughed it off. The worst of the storm wasn't even close he told them. Besides, the road was in the open for at least another league, leaving them exposed.

His predictions rang true. They gained an orchard just as the heavy snowfall hit. Huddled together beneath closely grown berry bushes, the three friends did what they could to ignore the growing cold and howling winds. Ice pelted their exposed areas and not even their blankets were enough to keep them warm. The storm gained strength long into the afternoon before easing back.

Norgen combed the ice and snow from his beard with a hearty laugh and said, "That wasn't so bad. I've seen much worse."

The boys exchanged looks, uncertain of their newfound friend. Their confusion made him laugh harder.

"Winter will be bad this year. Not very good conditions for fighting a war. Come, we'd best hurry along. There's a town not far from here. I'd like to make for it before the storm decides to turn back on us."

They couldn't have agreed more.

Threatening skies were closing across southern Averon but were still far enough out to be inconsequential to the moment, especially for what Tolis Scarn had to do. He didn't care for this part of the country. The people were overly friendly and open and the lands offered practically nothing for a man of his nature. He enjoyed a good drink and an unsuspecting victim with a fat purse. The only way he was going to get that was by reaching Alloenis.

The tracks he was following suggested his prey was heading for the western trade town. Probably hoping to get lost in the crowd, Scarn guessed. He wasn't relishing the thought of scouring an entire city to find one man he didn't care about to begin with. His employer was most adamant about finding him, though. Judging from the Hooded Man's tone of voice and menacing glare, Scarn swore to do his best and be rid of the job.

A murder of crows erupting from a nearby oak tree broke his train of thought. His horse snorted displeasure, sidestepping around a hole in the trail. Scarn's senses were screaming in warning. Danger was near. Darkness was closing in and he was barely at the edge of the Great Relin Werd. Many times he'd passed under the majesty and awe the forest offered, and just as many times he hated coming back. Not that the forest was a bad place, but there were Elves in the deep heart, and they disapproved of his kind. The tracks left him little choice this time. He had to go in.

An unnatural pile of stones caught his eye. He wouldn't normally have given it a second thought but there was something odd about it. Scarn slid from the saddle and drew his sword. Further investigation showed some of the stones were disturbed. Probably by forest predators. Scarn peered closer and felt his heart surge. Buried under the rocks, he caught a glimpse of a plain robe. *Could it be?* This could be the end of his troubles. Scarn furiously tore the cairn apart and at last felt desperation.

"Dark gods!" he hissed.

Gone. The body was gone. Rage seethed deep inside. He'd already wasted four months on the trail of the old man and came up empty handed time and time again. Growling and cursing, Scarn flung a rock into a nearby tree and mounted his horse. He started to believe the powers that be were working against him. A wolf bayed in the night as the lone rider took off for Alloenis.

ELEVEN
To War

Darkness swelled and grew for as far as the eye could see. Sunlight hadn't fallen on the ill land of Gren since the Silver Mage returned to proclaim his quest to rule Averon. His armies were growing by the day, so fast that the armies of Paedwyn would be no match from sheer weight of numbers. Tribes of Trolls and Goblins poured down from the mountains to his banner. Scores of Gnaals already scouring the western kingdoms in search of the one item capable of thwarting him. Even a red dragon answered his call. All was slowly coming into fruition.

From his tower high above the keep of ancient Aingaard, deep in the rotten land men knew only as Gren, Sidian the Silver Mage watched his darkness push towards the mountains. Once the ancient fortress of Gren Mot was enshrouded by his will the invasion would begin. He had no intent of joining the battle. It was still early enough to let his captains oversee matters.

Sidian was a tall man, thinly built, and resilient beyond measure. He was over a hundred years old, the last of the first rebellion to steal the world. The others were long dead, leaving him alone to carry on. Long, white hair flowed past his shoulders. He had deep eyes, piercingly hollow and colorless. They made his face appear gaunt and withdrawn. Some said he was more dead than alive, though none living could say. Certain people had a way of disappearing around him.

He waved his hand, changing the scene before him. Clouds were replaced by the vision of Gren Mot. Maelor's men were admirable at best, and constantly improving their battlements and defenses. It was going to be a hard fight, even with the dragon. Sidian spied rows of trenches filled with pitch. Sharpened spikes designed to skewer horses and advancing infantry lay beyond. Battlements capable of holding hundreds of archers sat within range. This alone had the capability to delay the advancing army and inflict massive casualties. Sidian had little doubt that every meter of ground in the pass was already ranged by Maelor's catapults.

Sidian released the image. He wasn't overly concerned with the defenses. Bold as they were, all would prove a useless, pathetic attempt to stave destiny. His armies already outnumbered the western races by five times, with more swelling the ranks daily. His main worry stemmed from the Gnaals lack of progress. He needed to find that man, else all he'd worked for was for naught. Dakeb and his purple stone were the only things capable of stopping his quest.

Less than pleased, Sidian turned from the storm darkened skies and went back to his study with much on his mind. The halls were empty and without decoration. He was never one for flowery paintings or tapestries. Instead, Sidian's heart was dark and volatile, void of pleasantry and kindness. He was the future of Malweir. Robes flowing behind, Sidian entered his receiving room where two Goblins stood waiting with bowed heads.

Their bodies were gnarled and abused. Their skin was a mottled green-black. Hatred seethed from their eyes. They carried black weapons, cruel and serrated. Their armor was thick with leather plates. Each had sparse hair and disfigured teeth, threatening and razor sharp. The larger one stepped forward.

"Master, the first army is assembled," he growled in a deep, hissing voice. "More come daily. Soon we shall have enough to range the world."

Their progress was better than he anticipated.

"Indeed we shall," snarled the Silver Mage. "But all is not in place yet."

"What are your orders, Master?"

Sidian's body tensed. "Go. Open the gates and march on Gren Mot. Clear the mountains so the invasion of Averon can begin."

"We will need the dragon if we're to break the walls. Gren Mot runs deep into the ground. It will take much to conquer."

"You will have the dragon. Now go."

Deep drums echoed thunder throughout Aingaard and the surrounding plains of Gren. Every Troll, Goblin and foul creature heard the rumbling and felt rage grow. The time was finally at hand. Battalions formed ranks. Swords and cudgels, axes and knives, were drawn. The drums beat louder, inspiring the foul masses into frenzy. Slowly they surged towards the gates.

The gates of Aingaard opened with a horrific groan. The front rank of the army marched out. Sidian watched it all from his sacred tower. Companies of horsemen rode through after the infantry in black armor and dark horses. They were the remnants of the once proud race of men from Gren. Torchlight gleamed off their spears until they were but mere specks in the distance. Thousands of campfires lined the valley floor. The day had come when their ilk could spread through the world. Gren would be mighty once again.

Dusk turned to night and the gates of Aingaard still were open. The Silver Mage watched until he lost interest and retired for the evening. It would take almost a week for the armies to get ready for the assault on Gren Mot. Time enough for him to continue his search.

The drums were deep and resounding. The very rock of the earth trembled from their awesome sound. Every living creature for leagues around heard the noise and knew fear. War had come to the free world. Herds of deer and elk fled to the mountain crags. Bears burrowed down in their dens, and even the eagles fled to the south. All that remained were three riders in smoke darkened armor. The leader stared down at the diseased city of Aingaard through a looking glass. His heart despaired. The van of the army was setting forth and their numbers far outweighed the meager hosts of Averon.

They were the last patrol Commander Fynten was going to authorize. With the armies of Gren on the move, it was simply too dangerous for the riders. The leader prayed help was coming. He didn't want to think of what might happen if they were forced to stand alone.

"The enemy is moving. Back to the fortress," he told the others.

Just then a great howl went up, closely followed by a dozen more. They'd been spotted! Soon Goblins and wolves would be swarming over the slopes searching for them.

"Quickly! Back up the trail and ride for Gren Mot," the leader ordered. "Don't stop until you gain the defenses. Ride!"

They fled for dear life, even as the first horn blasted the chill air. Night was falling and it was a long ride back to the fortress. The leader knew it was next to impossible for all three of them to make it back alive. But so long as one man returned to warn Commander Fynten all was not lost. The wind began to howl.

TWELVE
Feist

Norgen stretched with a mighty roar. The boys were just now waking. Cramped in a single cot room, there was neither room to move or stretch out properly. It was, however, warm and dry. Another storm hit shortly after they reached the small town of Feist. Ice and sleet forced them to dash from building to building to escape the fury. Large chunks of hail pounded the wooden walls for much of the night. Norgen wasted no time in finding an inn and purchasing a room for the night. They dined on a fine meal of roast duck and potatoes with fresh dark bread and ale. The Dwarf enjoyed a long smoke from his pipe before they retired for the night. It was the first real night of comfort they'd had since leaving Alloenis, some six days back.

"Up now lads!" Norgen said as he yanked the heavy wool blanket away.

"We've got a full day before us and you two dandies are wasting time."

Delin barely cracked an eye open. "Don't Dwarves ever sleep?"

The deep laugh was the last thing he wanted to hear. "Not when there's work to be done. Come on, breakfast is waiting."

Fennic groaned. "Breakfast? Lunch would be better suited to our needs."

Norgen dunked his head in a bucket of cold water. Droplets splashed across the floor, some striking the walls and cot. He let out a long breath of satisfaction and smiled.

"You snored so loud I don't think I slept more than a few moments at a time,"

Fennic complained to Norgen.

Delin agreed. His eyes were bloodshot and sore.

"Nonsense!" Norgen fumed. "Dwarves don't snore."

"I'd like to disagree with that," Delin laughed. "You were shaking the bed!"

Norgen shot them a scowl and headed out the door for the common room, taunting them that breakfast would be over long before they made it out of bed. Halfway through the meal Fennic pretended to snore, sending the boys into a fit of laughter while Norgen scowled a little deeper.

"What's the name of this town?" Fennic asked between mouthfuls of large, country style hotcakes.

"This is Feist, young sir," answered the serving girl. She set down three steaming cups of coffee. "Be not the biggest town west of Paedwyn, but you'll always find a good show."

Norgen shrugged, leaving them to wonder what her definition of a show was.

"Storm might stick around for a few days," the Dwarf offered at the end of the meal.

"I don't think we should spend more time here than we need to," Fennic hesitantly said. "Something's not right."

"He's been like this since Phaelor came to him," Delin explained upon seeing Norgen's confusion. "It's almost as if the sword's guiding him where it needs to go. I've never seen the like."

The Dwarf grunted. "Powerful is that sword, make no mistake. I fear it leads your friend to a dark place."

Delin leaned closer and whispered, "Do you think there are Gnaals near?"

"Do not speak that name unless you must. Evil things happen when evil thoughts are had. But no, I fear my premonition goes well beyond the dark stalkers. War is fast upon us, my young friends, and it will take all of us to see through to victory."

"I thought you were just here to check things out?" Fennic asked.

Norgen smiled and shook his head. "It's too late to turn back now. I am just as committed as you. This war is mine as well."

They spent the next few days talking of the past and future. Norgen entertained them with tales of days long past. There was no limit to the number of stories he could spin, and he had no hesitation in the telling of them. They were sure he'd exhausted his supply of tales by the time the storm finally passed.

"We need to look into arming you if we're to continue east," he told them the day after the storm. "The last thing you want is to be caught without a good axe. I'm surprised your parents let you leave as such."

They shared a hesitant glance, each still debating whether to trust the Dwarf. He'd given them no reason for doubt and the combination of their need for a true friend made up their minds. Delin slowly explained how they'd snuck away during the night and no one knew where they were. The Dwarf listened intently, grunting through the highlights. His dark eyes questioned their motives, but he remained silent.

"I don't think I'm ready for a battle," Fennic told them. "I can barely manage Phaelor."

"Indeed," Norgen replied. "I suggest daggers and short swords to begin with. Not many of my folk have much knowledge in blade, but there are armsmen a'plenty in Paedwyn. You'll get your turn and probably more."

Delin rubbed the purple stone in his pocket for reassurance.

"Now shall we go and find a smith? Something about the feel of steel gets my blood flowing," the Dwarf laughed.

Feist was unlike any other town they'd been through. Peddlers and trinket makers did their swindling, the norm for civilization. The streets were paved with reddish-brown stones, the same stones used in the making of the great houses on the main boulevard. Awning covered streets announced the start of the market district. The smells of fresh fish and vegetables waxed the air. Fishermen from the Northern Ocean sailed the seven hundred leagues south down the Sibit River, hitting every major town and city along the way. Southerners, especially landlocked countries like Averon, were willing to pay well for the freshest catch.

Norgen told them an arena lay on the far side of town. Gladiator combat was mostly forbidden in the west, but Feist held annual games. Competitors from every kingdom in Malweir gathered once a year to determine the best of the best. Folks paid dearly to watch the event, and the kingdom flourished during that time. The boys asked Norgen when the next games were held and he shrugged.

Halfway through town they were forced to stop as a band of men escorted a small group of giraffes across the street. Not even Norgen had seen such before. All three stood in awe of the long-necked beasts. Strange white horses with black stripes stood in pens on the far side of the road. There were monkeys in cages, and exotic birds chirping and whistling from assorted hanging cages. Women far more exotic moved here and there. Each was heavily tanned with flowing black hair and slender bodies. They walked about in silk clothes that hid most of their bodies. Delin and Fennic quickly found themselves staring at the strange beauty.

"Come lads, these women are more danger than either of you are willing to find," he cautioned before leading them to the first smith.

Personal weapons were tricky to choose. The boys discovered this the hard way and went through three smiths in a half day. They stopped for a quick bite to eat before continuing the search. Norgen warned them about the lack of quality from several more smithies as they browsed. The boys began to lose hope as the sun dipped beneath the distant mountaintops

"Well," Norgen said. "This is the last one in town. I hope he's a man of talent and a degree of honesty."

"I hope so. My feet can't take much more of this," Fennic complained.

The Dwarf said, "Nonsense. There're many leagues left to Paedwyn. You'll have feet like leather by the time we make it."

"Welcome friends," announced the smith. He wiped his blackened hands off on a well-used apron and shook each theirs. "Can't say as that I get too many Dwarves here, but I'm always willing to help where I may. What can I do for you lads?"

"We need two daggers. Short swords if you have them."

The smith nodded. "Ah yes, I can see why. Dangerous times these are. Why, I just heard tell that the Silver Mage's army is moving this way. Finally unleashed to claim us all. Dark times indeed."

"Indeed," Norgen agreed. "Word travels fast these days. When did this happen?"

"Just this morning, but you know everyone has spies and experts in rumors. Who can say what to believe anymore? Wish times were better. Maybe business would pick up."

"Wars have a way of blessing and ruining business when we least have need of it," Norgen said with a curt nod. He found himself liking the smith. The man had an honest atmosphere and that meant a good deal.

They walked back through the shop, past rows of half-finished swords, plows, and hammers. There were barrels filled with nails and tacks. A pile of metal bands for the local cooper sat off in the corner. The shop itself was very clean and orderly. Norgen was impressed.

"Perhaps these will do." The burly smith pulled a covering back to reveal newly forged two foot short swords. Neither was decorated, but even the boys noticed the craftsmanship involved in their making. The smith beamed with pride. "They may not be fancy. That's not what I was going for. See, these here are special. Only three were ever made. I sold the first to King Maelor himself. For his son it was. Your two friends have a familiar look to them, one of royalty. I could part with these for a fair price."

Norgen eyed the man as only a Dwarf could when it comes to haggling.

"Fair for whom? I've no need of untested weapons. They can kill you as easy as clumsiness."

"I can assure you these blades will serve their purpose well. Ask around, my work is as good as gold in times of need."

Norgen hefted the first blade and went through a series of jabs and thrusts. He grunted. The blade danced in his hand. Most of his folk preferred the heavy double headed battle axe, but this was giving him a second thought.

The balance and weight were almost perfect. This truly was a sword made for a king.

"Is it not fine?" asked the smith.

"Fine enough to keep them alive long enough to get back home," Norgen nodded.

The smith smiled. "Shall we discuss a price?"

Norgen set the weapon back down. "A gold apiece."

Disappointment flashed behind his eyes. "I was thinking more along the lines of two. These are finely crafted blades worthy of the greatest lord."

"Good as they are, I have yet to find a replacement for a good battle axe."

"Ah, times are hard all around," the smith tried to say.

The Dwarf agreed. "Tis true. Harder than most care to accept. We do not create the times though. One gold apiece or my friends and I are leaving for another smithy."

They wound up paying a few extra silvers for the daggers and left the smith with an unhappy look. Norgen went over the basics of sword play with the boys later that night, promising to begin their training the next morning. All three went to sleep feeling slightly better about the future.

Night usually made Tarren feel comfortable, seducing her into the never realms of sleep. Tonight was anything but. She figured Alloenis was more than another day away. Distance wasn't the problem. Being watched by everything unseen was. There was no way of knowing how far ahead the stranger in black was or even if he was still there. A man like that could easily have doubled back to stalk her. The thought of him waiting off in the bushes one night made her body tremble and left a sickening thought in her mind.

Traveling through Relin Werd had been a terrible experience. Every sound was a monster. Every pair of eyes an evil coming to claim her. Her fears hadn't been realized and were more than likely absurd if not for the nagging feeling in the pit of her stomach. Doubt was setting in. Tarren wasn't sure how much longer she could go on. Her body wasn't made for endless days of forced travel with minimal rations and an undefined sense of direction. Part of her wanted to go home. The only thing stopping her was her love for Delin.

"What have I gotten myself in to," she whispered to herself.

She was cold, wet, and tired. The storm raged through, catching her in the open. It was all she could do to find some semblance of shelter and ride it out. A crisp hoot from a storm owl answered her. Tarren settled in against a large maple tree and watched the forest. She knew she had to sleep but was determined to stay awake as long as possible. Tolis Scarn hid behind every bush and she wasn't going to be caught unawares. Her eyes drifted close moments later.

She awoke to gentle prodding on her shoulder. Her first instinct was to draw the tiny dagger given to her as birthday present by her father some years ago. Tarren opened her eyes and drew back to attack. She knew she had been caught and meant to inflict as much harm as possible. A gentle whuff made her lower her guard. Her eyes adjusted and a large dark form took shape. It was a pony. Young and golden brown with velvet eyes. And definitely not hers.

Tarren glanced nervously about. She was frighteningly concerned about her surroundings. Her pony was gone without so much as a sign it had ever been here. Scarn! This had to be a trap, but she was alone. The Great Werd looked down upon her in silent judgment. A subtle voice whispered in the deepest corners of her mind. She looked the pony over and noticed it appeared unbroken. Curiously, the pony seemed to be smiling down on her, calming her fears. Tarren smiled back.

"What are you doing out here all by yourself?" she asked in a gentle voice. "I used to know why I was here, but that was before the storm. All I know now is that I'm tired and want to go home. But I can't!"

Tears welled in her eyes. The pony stepped closer and rubbed its muzzle against her.

"My friends are in danger. They need me and I don't know that I'm strong enough to help them," she confided.

She took silent comfort from the animal. It drew away the doubt and suffering she'd been going through and gave her new hope. Tarren knew she had a chance. Her spirits lifted. A new day was upon her and she had much to do to save her love.

THIRTEEN
The Gnaal

Melting snow and ice turned the roads into a muddy slush, slowing travel to a miserable crawl. Temperatures stayed low but just above freezing. Distant mountaintops remained buried in perpetual snow with strong winds swirling the loose powder about. Winter was still weeks away yet the skies were constantly growing darker.

Norgen calmly combed the ice from his beard and watched the boys spar with carved wooden swords. They'd continually improved since leaving Feist a handful of days ago. The Dwarf knew it wouldn't be enough to keep them alive in combat, but it was just enough to give them a chance to run. He prayed they never learned what combat was.

The very night they left Feist Norgen knew his prayers went unanswered. He felt that familiar chill. He knew then that a Gnaal had found them. They were being hunted.

He kept his fears to himself despite their constant nagging. Gnaals were horrible creatures with blood thirsty appetites and never relented. That he survived one already was a miracle. Many good friends lay dead and rotting from one. Axes and swords were useless against their blackened flesh. The Dwarves fought with valor and didn't so much as cut the fell beast.

Having had enough, Delin and Fennic lowered their swords and rejoined the Dwarf in youthful laughter. They were exhausted and drenched in sweat. Norgen had them rinse off at a nearby stream to keep from getting sick. They came back and shared a meager meal of dried meat and traveler's bread. Norgen ignored their protests over not having a fire and bade them eat in silence. The sun was setting and that old chill returning.

Creeping shadows stretched across the world in an open invitation for dark creatures and evil desires. A dead silence settled over their camp and all Norgen could do was watch the night. His knuckles were already white from the grip on his axe. Fennic was the first to notice.

"What's bothering you, Norgen? You haven't been the same since we left Feist," he commented. His own hand dropped to Phaelor.

The Dwarf's eyes were cold and distant. "There is danger near. We would do well to use caution. I like this not."

"What is it?"

"Nothing I care to speak of."

Then came a rustling deep in the woods, followed by a high-pitched scream. Norgen leapt to his feet, axe in hand and ready for battle. His muscles bristled under the tight leather armor. The boys were suddenly aware of how powerful and lethal a Dwarf could be.

"What?" Delin asked before drawing his own short sword.

"I don't know," Fennic whispered, "but I feel it too."

Norgen's deep voice rumbled in the dark. "There is a Gnaal close. We are being hunted. Prepare yourselves."

"A Gnaal!" they exclaimed in unison. "What does it want?"

"Death."

Delin's stomach rose to his throat and he felt sick. He absently fumbled through his pocket. The purple stone offered courage and hope just from a touch. The next scream ended that feeling.

"Death is the only way to satisfy them. Cold and overpowering, they continue their hunt until their prey lay broken at their feet. Whether it comes for me or you, I cannot say," Norgen continued.

"That's not reassuring," Fennic said.

"We must flee. Now!"

Delin hesitated. "Shouldn't we find some place to hide and let it pass?"

"Gnaals do not pass and there is no place to hide. They will hunt us until they die or their master calls them off," Norgen growled. "Quickly. Pack up the camp and let us be away before it finds us."

A horrible, high pitched wail broke through the tree only a few meters away. Fennic strapped his pack on as a huge shape burst into the tiny glade. The odor was overwhelming. It stank of rot and decayed flesh, disease and malice. Worst of all, it stank of death. The beast drew darkness unto it, stealing definition from the writhing limbs and grotesque flesh riddled with boils and lesions. The Gnaal hissed a noxious gas and bellowed.

"Run!"

Norgen shoved them away and took a mighty swing towards the Gnaal's midsection. The axe blade hit the hardened flesh and bounced off. Norgen was slapped to the ground, barely managing to roll away before the Gnaal punched down into the ground. Fennic's shout drew its attention away long enough for Norgen to escape.

The Dwarf dashed forward while Fennic stepped toward the Gnaal with Phaelor in hand. The Gnaal cringed and retreated a step before lashing its tail at the boy. Fennic ducked. The scaled appendage whistled over his head to strike a maple tree.

The tree exploded with a loud crack and sent splinters flying. Norgen scooped up the boy and carried him into the night. Phaelor's golden light somehow wounded the beast. For perhaps the first time, it became aware of its mortality. The Gnaal discovered fear. The creature of darkness clutched the wound and folded back into the night. Norgen wasn't about to trust their luck. He pushed them harder and faster, and easily outran them both.

"Hurry lads," he ordered between deep breaths. "Your sword hurt it, but there's not much time before it'll be back."

Delin dropped to his knees from sheer exhaustion. "We can't run all the way to Paedwyn. Fennic wounded it. We should stand and fight."

"Have you learned nothing this night? Nothing we do can kill them," Norgen spat.

"But you said I hurt it," Fennic said. "And if it can be hurt, it can be killed."

"Not by any of us. Do you have the courage to look into Death's eyes?" He sipped from his canteen before adding, "I do not, not a second time. Both of you are too young to know such horrors. We've run half the night. Let us find a place to rest for a spell. Pray the demon does not return. Once dawn comes we head south for the road to Paedwyn."

"How can you be so sure of where we are?" Delin asked. "I've been lost from the moment we set off this night."

"My people have long looked to the skies to show us the way. Each star has its place in the night sky, as does the moon. See that bright one up to your left? That is named Gru in the Old Tongue, and always points the way north. Once you find her, she will guide your way."

Fennic decided the theory went beyond his working knowledge and let the matter rest but for one question. "What happens when there's no moon to gu…"

A crisp burning sensation ran down his leg. Phaelor's warning came moments before the Gnaal struck. Fire spread across the treetops. Thunder rumbled overhead. The ground began to shake as the Gnaal stepped from the darkness. Fennic vomited uncontrollably. Rotten flesh covered the creature's skull. Two rows of horns ran down the center of the head. Deep set eyes burned the foulest shade of green, whispering pure malevolence. Hugely muscled and standing ten feet tall, the Gnaal had massive wings curved with spikes.

The Gnaal swelled in size, drawing up to almost double the height. The sound of swords being drawn echoed in the glade. Delin couldn't control his shaking for he was sure the end had come. The Gnaal stepped closer. Norgen prayed for his friends, knowing he'd soon be amongst those already slain by the monster. He doubled his grip on the axe haft and prepared to attack.

"Get down Dwarf!"

Flaming arrows sped from the night to strike the Gnaal in the neck, chest and thighs. The monster roared even as the shafts erupted in flame and melted away. Phaelor blocked a swing from the heavy cudgel. The shock struck Fennic in the shoulder and knocked the boy unconscious. Another flight of arrows hit the Gnaal in the face. Then another. And another, giving Delin enough time to dart under and drag Fennic away.

The assault intensified. Arrows were now pouring in from three sides. The Gnaal reeled back under the relentless assault. Four shapes rode out from the night with swords drawn. It wasn't until they stopped to pick up the Dwarf and his companions that Delin saw them for what they were. Their upper bodies were of muscled men while the rest were huge, barrel bodied horses. Centaurs. Each had long hair tied back with jeweled bands. They hefted the three upon their backs and turned to run.

Showing no fear, the fourth Centaur twirled his sword and charged the Gnaal. His thundering hooves were drowned out by the Gnaal's roar as it surged forth to accept the challenge. Delin could only watch in horror as the Gnaal hefted his cudgel and swung. The weapon caught the Centaur in the chest, crushing bone and flesh. A final flight of arrows riddled the Gnaal as the Centaurs retreated. The last thing Delin saw was the monster triumphant over the freshly slain corpse.

Delin wasn't sure how long they rode, only that the sun was up the next time he awoke. Nightmares haunted him. He watched his rescuer die needlessly over and over each time he closed his eyes. He was certain the Gnaal was close on their heels, ready to slaughter them all. Not even the purple stone gave him comfort. Exhaustion overtook him again and he succumbed back to sleep.

There wasn't any bucking when he finally roused. The world wasn't racing by in a green blur anymore. Though it certainly felt like it after enduring the riding motion for so long. The smell of roasting meat on the fire aroused his appetites. More of the Centaurs were milling about. None of them paid him much heed. They seemed intent on learning the fate of their brother. Norgen stood with his arms folded across his burly chest quietly conversing with their leader. The Dwarf smiled upon seeing young Delin awake.

"Well now, I was beginning to wonder if you planned on sleeping through supper. Even young Master Attleford has recovered from that nasty blow. In fact, he hasn't shut up yet," Norgen laughed.

Delin stretched some of the soreness away. "Are we safe?"

"Safe enough for now," a golden haired Centaur said with a smile. He saw the fright still in Delin's eyes and said, "There is no need for fear now.

My men and I were sent to find you. Ah, forgive me, my name is Ris Kaverling and you are safe so long as my band guards you."

"Sent by whom? Not to say that I don't appreciate the help, mind you, but I'm not too sure of many things these days," Delin replied.

Norgen grunted. "The boy is learning."

"Indeed, and inquisitive as well. The help is freely given as a favor to an old friend, though the pain of my loss will haunt me for days to come. Relax your mind. Your friend's sword wounded the Gnaal and I doubt it will follow so close again," Ris said. "Soon enough you will meet the man responsible for saving you. Now come and eat, for we shall be leaving you much sooner than you would like."

The thought of being alone again and in foreign parts displeased him, but Delin knew their troubles were just that, theirs. Ris and his Centaurs came unasked for and were the only reason he was still alive. For that he had no way to offer proper thanks.

"Hoy Delin!" Fennic exclaimed from atop a galloping Centaur. "I'm the one who gets knocked out and you sleep all day."

"A fine friend you are. Going off and almost getting yourself killed like that. What was I supposed to do then?" Delin protested with his hands on his hips in mock consternation.

Fennic laughed. "You're the adventuresome one. I'd expect you to run off and fight Trolls in the Gren Mountains."

"Be careful what you speak of, young ones," Ris cautioned. "The hills have ears and the Mage's spies are everywhere these days. Trolls and Goblins are already on this side of the mountains and in number. Gnaals are merely the beginning of your troubles."

"What news of the Elves?" Norgen asked.

Ris shook his head. "They will not fight this war. We are on our own. My people will offer what help we can, but we were never many."

"There are more of you?" Delin asked.

"Aye. Hundreds. We are a mere rescue party. And now that our jobs are finished, it is time to take our leave. The Gnaal is far behind and there are no enemies between here and the King's road. Travel a league due south and you'll be at the road. Paedwyn is no more than a few days away so long as the path is clear."

"Thank you for all of your help," Fennic told them.

Ris put a gentle hand on his shoulder and said, "Ware those who would be your friends. What you carry holds all our fates. Farewell my friends."

FOURTEEN
Following the Trail

Tolis Scarn had only been to Feist once before and remembered less than he cared to. Much the same as every other city, Feist also had a darker side. Enemies of the king met in secret lodges safe from prying eyes. There they plotted Averon's downfall and a return to the revolutionary times of the Mages. The Silver Mage stretched his influence this far through rumor alone. Scarn didn't really care. The war between Averon and the dead kingdom wasn't his business. His sole focus lay in finding the shard of the Cracked Crystal of Tol Shere that crazy old Dakeb. Political ambitions and empirical desires were well beyond the scope of his future.

Apart from harboring radicals and society's miscreants, Feist was a very good place to stop for ale and go unnoticed for a few hours. Just the place Scarn felt comfortable in. He rode past a hastily assembled gate guard and into town shortly after nightfall three weeks since leaving Fel Darrins. Three long weeks and he was no closer to finding the shard than when he was hired. The Hooded Man hired him over four months ago. Scarn knew time was running out. His instructions were to have the shard before Winter Day and that was a mere four weeks away. He was frustrated at the lack of success and in need of a day off.

Scarn decided to put business to the side for the night and guided his horse through the busy streets to an inn. He had every intention of enjoying a few good drinks before resuming the hunt. Four soldiers marched by without so much as passing a glance. To them he wasn't more than another rider in a city of strangers. Certainly not a threat to the security of Feist. That didn't surprise him much. Most soldiers garrisoned in the smaller cities stopped paying so much attention to the solemn oaths implied in their duties. Talk of the gathering darkness in the ancient land of Gren cluttered the streets. Enemy armies were massing, threatening to spill across the border and condemn Averon under a foul blanket.

Scarn, having found a place suitable enough for his liking, took a chair close to the fire and warmed his hands while he awaited his drink. There were a handful of other patrons spread throughout the common room. Two Dwarves sat by themselves in the opposite corner while a trio of local youths enjoyed the warmth offered by the ale. Scarn received a few suspicious looks that lasted only as long as it took him to return them. No one wanted trouble it seemed.

"Your ale, sir."

He looked up at the serving girl and smiled. Her cheeks blushed as his fingers brushed against hers.

"Thank you, pet."

Giggling as she went off, the plump girl secretly wished he'd order another.

"Not from around here are you, boy?" asked an old voice from behind.

Scarn felt that familiar twinge. "I don't see as how that's any of your concern."

The old man ignored Scarn's sour attitude and took a seat opposite him. "Just like everyone these days. Can't take the time to be friendly. Not like there's harm in it. Folks just aren't polite anymore. Reminds me of the dark times."

"I'm a little young to remember those days," Scarn replied between swallows.

"Aye, as well they were. Many a good man died during those days. But it's our doom that we forget. Thousands died and for what? To establish puppet thrones in case the evil returned. Ha!"

Agitated, Scarn finished his ale and ordered again. "Why don't you go bother someone else before I get angry?"

The old man ignored him and continued to ramble. "That's the problem with youth. Never takes the time to listen. You just may be surprised one of these times. Especially now with all these strange things going on. Very strange indeed."

Now that he found interesting. Against better judgment, Scarn paid for the ale and decided to ask questions. He'd been through this scenario a hundred times already and knew how to play the game. Scarn discovered most people warmed to him after a few drinks but this guy was almost there now. Chances were the old man wouldn't remember the conversation come morning.

Scarn leaned forward and smoothly asked, "What do you mean by strange?"

"Eh? Decided to join the conversation, have we?" He smiled and took another drink. "We've all seen many a strange moment as of late. Dark beings in the streets late at night. I myself have heard terrible wailings coming from the forests outside town. The sounds of demons some say."

"I've heard them myself on the road from Alloenis. They're enough to frighten a simple trader out of business."

"I'll bet."

"Surely there has to be more than that? It doesn't seem like there's any shortage of business here," Scarn pressed.

"Secrets. Too many secrets. Folks been disappearing for no reason and the authorities don't seem concerned. Everyone's more focused on the coming war with Gren. Myself, I don't care. I've already lived too many winters and seen my share of battle. A few more don't matter much." He paused long enough to let out a shallow belch. "A trader you say? What brings you to Feist? We've already got plenty of your profession."

"I'm supposed to meet with an old friend. I wonder if you've seen him." Scarn went on to describe Dakeb, but the old man shook his head. "Maybe he got delayed in the storm or I missed him."

"Could be, friend. Plenty of things like that happen in bad weather," the old man agreed. "Was it business or pleasure?"

"Does it matter? You can't tell the difference once you've been at it for so long. As a matter of fact, he found this rare purple stone and was wondering how much it was worth. Who better to ask than a close friend?"

"Haven't seen this old man of yours. But then again, we all look alike after a while. I do seem to recall two young men with an odd purple stone. Saw them going to Loenx's smithy. They had a Dwarf with them."

A Dwarf? This was news. He just couldn't figure out why two boys had the shard. Dakeb must have gotten spooked and given it to them in Fel Darrins. So what happened to the old man? The grave in Relin Werd was empty and could have been a decoy to throw him off the trail. No one he passed from there to here remembered seeing an old man traveling alone. They did recall a pair of boys heading north. Dakeb must have come upon them in the forest and gave them the stone. He had to have. "Does anyone know where they are now? It's possible my friend couldn't make it and had them come in his place."

The old man offered a doubtful scowl before quickly accepting another tankard of ale at Scarn's expense. Scarn sat in disappointment as the old man downed his drink and mumbled something about going to bed. It was obvious there was nothing more to learn here. Tolis Scarn yawned and walked off.

Dawn was extremely short in coming, much to Scarn's dislike. He was already bordering exhaustion from countless weeks on the road and empty nights trying to gather information. Sometimes he wondered what a normal life would be like. A boring cottage with the same woman and children running under foot didn't seem right to him. He was a free soul, bound eternal to roam the world in search of one more job. Satisfied with his lot, he roamed the world with the self-imposed authority of a god. Scarn strapped on his weapons and went back to the common room for a quick bite to eat before searching for Loenx the smith.

He asked around for directions and was only mildly disappointed it took so long to find someone who knew of the man.

"Loenx? Yeah I know him," said an ex-soldier with one arm. "Down the road on the right. Owns a green smithy. What you want with him is beyond me. There's no talent in his work."

Scarn thanked the old cripple and entered the green smithy. A greasy looking man stepped out to greet him. His smile was false and misleading. Scarn took an instant dislike to the man.

"Greetings friend. Is there anything in particular you're looking for?" Loenx asked. "Perhaps you'd care to see what I have working in the forge?"

"That would be perfect," Scarn replied.

He'd been in far bigger and better smiths over his life, but there most were in the bigger population centers. Still, what Loenx lacked in talent he made up for in cleanliness and layout. Assorted swords in various stages of completion line a row of stone benches. There was a small pile of coal in the far corner with a torn leather bellow next to it. Scrap iron sat in buckets at the foot of the forge. Scarn was almost impressed.

Loenx saw his obvious approval and made the mistake of turning his back to fetch a sword nearing completion. Scarn eased back to lock the forge door and draw his dagger.

"What's the meaning of this?"

Scarn moved closer. "Relax and we'll both walk away from this. Anger me and I promise your blood will stain the floor. Do you understand?"

Loenx nodded.

"Good. I have a few questions I want to ask you. You're going to be very truthful with me, I can feel it. A pair of boys came in here a few days ago, accompanied by a Dwarf."

"Yes, I remember them," Loenx replied.

"Who were they and what did they want?"

Loenx started shaking. "Please sir, take what money I have in my purse and go. I don't want any trouble. I'm just a simple smith trying to make a living."

"Wrong answer."

Scarn pounced on him. He kicked out Loenx's knee and dropped the smith with a sharp cry of pain.

"You're making this very painful," he growled. "Answer my questions and you'll never see me again. I'm not the kind of man you want as an enemy."

Scarn had to stretch once he left the smith. It had been a long time since he tortured a man. Loenx took a bit of work to break, but the man wouldn't shut up once his resistance broke. He'd told much more than Scarn cared to know. In the end it all came down to liability. Any man who willingly talked so much was dangerous. Scarn knew if he could make the smith talk so easily someone else might get the same results. He noticed a small blood stain on his sleeve and frowned. This was a new riding jacket. If Loenx weren't already dead Scarn would have gone back inside.

FIFTEEN
The War Begins

"Fire!"

The catapult battery launched a dozen flaming projectiles into the massing Goblin ranks less than a mile away. Tired men hurriedly reloaded their weapons until they had to be replaced by fresh men from the fortress. A battalion of archers came marching down from the rear of the pass to join the ranks aching for battle. Cavalrymen and infantry were already in place behind a trio of pitch filled ditches.

Hundreds of Goblins were already dead yet still the army pressed forward. Mountain Trolls towered over the Goblins, pulling great siege engines toward the front lines. Tens of thousands more waited on the vast plains of Gren. Once the ancient fortress was conquered the way into Averon would be wide open for invasion. All the vanguard had to do was bring down the walls of Gren Mot and slay her defenders. Commander Fynten watched Goblin engineers with their blackened wooden walkways move closer to the front ranks. They carried more than enough to breach the ditches.

"Archers ready! Third rank. Strike the flames!"

A page ran along the rank of bowmen, setting fire to the small line of pitch. The archer captain walked to Fynten and removed his conical helmet. The commander of Gren Mot nodded to him. Fynten had dark hair with a thick moustache. He was lightly muscled and nearing the end of his third decade. Ahead of his peers in practically every category, the King saw fit to entrust him with the mounting responsibility of defending Averon's eastern approach.

"I was wondering when your boys were going to join us, Wiln," he said with a smile. A cold wind tussled his thick, black hair. "We've been having all the fun thus far."

Another catapult salvo rocketed overhead. A massive cheer rose from the Goblin ranks. Fynten turned to see their engineers rush towards the first obstacle.

Wiln grimaced at their numbers. "I thought it would be a better entrance to arrive just in the nick of time."

"That you have," Fynten agreed. "Are your men ready?"

"We await the order."

The catapults fired again. Fragments of oil and brimstone drifted into stretching trails across the sky. Fynten judged the front Goblin ranks in range. He turned to his friend.

"You have it," he said. "Let's just hope they can strike their marks." Wiln replaced his helm and gallantly strode back to his men with sword raised high. "Ignite!"

Four hundred tiny flames simultaneously sprang to life along the Averonian lines.

"Draw!"

Archers drew back, aiming in on the Goblin foe.

"Loose!"

The burning missiles whistled through the purple-black sky. Some hit only dirt and rock yet the majority struck true. A handful dropped into the trench filled with pitch. A wall of flame erupted on the battlefield. Not even the roar of Fynten's men was enough to drown the screams of the roasting Goblins.

"Ignite and take aim! Second target. Loose!"

The second volley struck the confused mass of Goblins. Hundreds fell while their comrades trampled over the still warm corpses. Fynten watched the display in disgust. He hated war, but fully understood the necessity for it. If he failed here a doom would befall his beloved Averon. Everything he stood for and believed in would meet a violent demise. No, this was the only way.

"Captain Surnish!" he roared. "Move those catapults three hundred meters back and engage."

The Goblins breeched the final ditch halfway through the second night and halted. Fynten summoned his captains to his tent to discuss the coming fight. All were blackened from ash and fire and covered in sweat despite the growing cold of winter. Outside, the catapults continued their brutal assault. Hundreds died with each volley.

Wiln wiped the exhaustion from his brow. "We've killed thousands of them and to what end? Still they press us without regard for casualties. We cannot win this battle."

"Where would you have us retreat to?" asked the disgruntled cavalry captain, Melgit. "My horses are of no use in the keep."

Fynten let them argue for a time. It did good to get the angst off their chests and clear their minds. He knew they merely expressed what everyone of the soldiers was feeling. Sooner or later something had to give. Fynten hoped it was the enemy's will.

"Gentlemen, how many of us have families on the other side of the mountains?" He already knew the answer, but by asking it put their minds in the right place.

"Because none of them will survive should we fail. Make no mistake; this is the beginning of the much dreaded war. Those we killed thus far are insignificant compared to what yet awaits us."

"None doubt you, Commander," Wiln conceded, "but how long can we realistically hold this position? And at what cost? We can only push our men so far before the first wall is taken."

"My scouts have seen more Goblins and other foul creatures than all Averon can hope to withstand. What we accomplish in the pass will be minimal at best," Melgit said. He'd spent most of his adult life fighting one war or the next and had never left the enemy in control of the battlefield."

"We need hold until King Maelor has an army large enough to invade Gren and put the Mage's head on a pike. Don't tell me what we can and can't do, or why. Give me solutions to the problems at hand. What you must realize, is that it is expected we die in the defense of our country should the need arise. My orders, issued by the king's own hand, state that the keep will be held to the last man."

A low murmur spread through the captains.

Fynten held up his hand. "I have no intention of dying in these mountains."

Surnish slammed a gnarled fist into the table. "Nor do I! What do you need of me to break this damned siege?"

"Keep firing as long as the catapults hold. I've already authorized one company at a time to be replaced. This stands for everyone but your archers, Wiln. I need as many shafts in the air as I can get," Fynten explained. The artillery was the least of his concerns. Besides, catapults weren't much good once the Goblins closed on his infantry. "You've been exceptionally quiet so far, Prelin."

The one-eyed infantry captain nodded. "Aside from Melgit, my men have seen the least action. We are rested and ready to fight."

"You'll have your fight much sooner than I'd like. My instincts say they'll hit the wall before sunrise. The pikes and archers will keep them at bay long enough but some are bound to break through," Fynten said. "Melgit, that's where you come in. Swing your cavalry in from the flank. Don't stop until you're clear the far side and back behind the wall again."

"The wounded...," he began.

Fynten suppressed a grimace. "There will be no wounded. You know this as well as I. Archers will provide cover before and after your charge. I want the Goblins confused. Expecting another attack. Captain Jeurle, is all ready for our surprise?"

"All is," Jeurle replied. He was the youngest and most eager of the group. He was also one of the brightest engineers in the royal army. "Hopefully we can take some of those Trolls down as well."

"The battlements in the keep have the Troll killers already in place. They're not my main concern," Fynten turned back to Melgit. "Is there a way to fire their siege machines?"

"The danger to the cavalry will be great."

"And unacceptable, I wager," Fynten agreed.

A single trumpet call rang out across the mountain pass. The Goblins were preparing to attack.

"Gentlemen, to your posts. My guess is they're already too close for your catapults so aim for the siege machines. Every little piece will buy us and Averon time. Good luck," he told them.

One by one they filed from the tent to return to their troops. It was going to be dark for a while longer and the dark gray Goblin skin would be difficult to see. It might also work to Fynten's advantage.

SIXTEEN
Bad Times

The ferocity with which the early winter storm sputtered and raged led Tarren to believe that she wasn't meant to leave Fel Darrins. Hidden in a small cave, she and the strange pony waited out the snows. It was the pony who saved them. Tarren would have been caught in the open when the storm hit. The pony's insistence at following its own desires led them to a shallow valley filled with enormous boulders and broken trees. Finding shelter was the easy part.

She noticed the pony's natural stubbornness the moment she awoke in the clearing some days ago. Initially she didn't want anything to do with the beast. But she was alone and on foot and hunting a man who was going to harm her one true love. What real choice did she have? Besides, there was something about the butterscotch colored pony that soothed here, comforted her enough to trust it. The decision to climb aboard came naturally.

They followed the main trail for another league or so before the pony ambled off through the lightly forested hills. No matter what Tarren tried, she couldn't persuade it to turn back to the road. She felt the mow familiar tremor of fear sprouting. The forests were dark and dangerous and a simple girl from a small village shouldn't have anything to do with them on the best of days. The pony offered her comfort, silently reassuring her that all was well. Strangely enough, Tarren found herself relaxing.

She didn't like being without a choice any more than being alone in a foreign land, but her friends were in peril. Of that she was convinced. It became the one sustaining focus that kept her going through the seemingly endless series of blunders and setbacks. Add a stray pony that seemed to have its own issues and she was left wondering what she was supposed to do. They reached the valley an hour before the first snows fell. Winds were already howling by the time they found the small cave and the skies opened up.

The new dawn was considerably less spectacular than the day prior as was the one before that. Winter was fast closing in. Soon all Malweir would become a colorless land of grey and white. Now more than ever Norgen wished for a quiet mountain tunnel they could secretly travel through. Deep snows only served to leave their tracks easier to find. That meant the Gnaal would find them sooner than later. Norgen narrowed his eyes against the morning glare and watched for signs of ambush.

"He's been in a sour mood all night," Fennic whispered from their position a few meters behind the Dwarf.

Delin grunted. "You would be too if you remembered what happened last night. That Gnaal was nearly the death of us. Now I know why he's so spooked."

"Dwarves are never spooked," Norgen growled over his shoulder. "Though we do have a superb sense of caution."

Delin stifled a laugh. "Fine, oh mighty Dwarf. We won't tell anyone your secrets."

The banter raged back and forth until they stopped for a bite to eat. Norgen's mood gradually lightened until he walked with a constant smile. Both boys looked at him in confusion for it was out of character for the Dwarf to be happy. When asked about his sudden mood swing, the Dwarf gave a mischievous smile and said, "You'll see soon enough."

The intrigue went on until the following morning.

Norgen rushed them through breakfast and hygiene. They were back on the road to Paedwyn in no time. Morning mists took forever to clear, but when they did the boys were met by an awe-inspiring sight. Norgen stood back and beamed with pride. At first all they could see were two massive snow-covered mountain tops high above the world. Ever so slowly did the mountains take shape, changing from indistinctive bulks to majestic formations glowing a purplish-red. These were the tallest peaks in all Malweir. Small foothills clustered around the bases, adding dimension to the bulk and importance. Norgen dropped to his knees with tears streaming down his cheeks.

"What's wrong?" Fennic asked.

As moving as the sight was to behold, Fennic felt their importance lost on him.

Norgen threw his arms open and exclaimed, "Behold! The Twin Spires of Ragnash. The most holy of Dwarven places."

Golden sunlight washed across the frozen peaks, bathing them in the light of the gods.

"What you see are the eldest mountains in the world. Every Dwarf must pay respect when he passes. This is where the first Dwarves came into being. There are gorgeous halls of jewels and gold therein, stretching deep into the living world. All our power, our secrets and origins rest inside. Were time on our side I would take you there."

The world suddenly became a much smaller place for Fennic. His empty feeling lessened somewhat. A peculiar kinship formed between himself and the taciturn Dwarf that he couldn't explain.

"My kings lie entombed inside, all the way back to the beginning," he went on. "No greater honor could ever be bestowed upon a Dwarf than to rest forever in the hallowed halls. I doubt I shall ever see such. My lot is already decided."

"Perhaps not," Fennic consoled.

"Nay, friend. I know my fate and it lies along another path."

He wiped the tears away and attempted changing the subject. "Paedwyn is no more than a handful of days away. We should be there before the week ends if all goes well."

"I don't mean to be the pessimist of the group, but nothing has gone right since we left Alloenis," Delin reminded them.

Norgen laughed. "Perfect! There's nowhere to go but up."

"Now you want to be happy."

The Dwarf scolded a finger at them. "Always take advantage of the situation no matter how you find it. There is still much ground to cover ere we reach the city. Much can happen if we're not careful."

The boys nodded and resumed the quest. Farmer's wagons and frightened villagers heading for the homes of western relatives dotted the roads. A wicked scare came from Gren and people fled just as fast as they could. Others chose to stay behind and defend their homes and still others dismissed the threat as immature. The Silver Mage was dead and rotted, they argued. Soon they would learn the error of their thoughts.

Norgen explained how towns and villages gradually got larger the closer they got to the capital of King Maelor's realm. Compared to the heart of Averon, Fel Darrins might as well be in another world. Delin and Fennic assaulted the Dwarf with questions upon questions until they had to stop to regain their voices. By dusk all were beyond tired.

A foul odor woke Norgen shy of midnight. It was the smell of death. Norgen rolled over and clutched his axe. He knew it was a battle he couldn't win. No Gnaal appeared though and the night carried on. The tiniest sliver of a moon hung in the sky. He barely made out the Twin Spires of Ragnash in the distance. Sniffing the air, Norgen frowned. The decay wasn't of Gren, but of flesh and blood. An evil thing was going on.

Ignoring the urge to wake the boys, Norgen dropped his cloak and went in search of the danger. The grass was wet and fresh, making it easier for him to move unheard. It wasn't long before he came upon a recent campsite. There was half a dozen burnt logs in the fire pit and a stack of kindling and firewood off to the side. A burned out wagon lay on its side with several short, black arrows in it. Norgen immediately recognized the threat. The Dwarf ran to the wagon, using it for cover until he decided it was safe to move in the open.

He eased forward to a partially hidden lump in the mist. A Goblin. The throat had been slashed. Norgen search for any other clue of what happened but didn't need any. A half dozen more bodies lay around the site, none of them Goblins. Axe ready, Norgen moved from body to body. The first was burned beyond recognition. He quickly abandoned the corpse and went to the next. His stomach turned rancid after rolling the body over and seeing the face. It was one of the boys from the common room of the Golden Scarab. Having seen enough, Norgen went back to his own camp.

Dawn found him standing watch over the boys. His eyes were cold and bloodshot from horror inspired nightmares he'd witnessed during the night. Packs of Goblins loose west of the Gren Mountains wasn't unusual, but this close to Paedwyn and openly attacking the king's men meant war was already begun.

Fennic yawned. "Good morning, Norgen. I hope you slept as well as I did."

"Pack your gear. We need to move," he replied in a strained voice. "It's not safe here."

"What did he say?" Delin asked from behind the boulder where he relieved himself.

"Is it the Gnaal?" Fennic asked. He hurriedly pulled on his trousers. Painful memories came back to him.

"Worse," Norgen replied. "There are Goblins about."

"What's this about Goblins?" Delin asked. "I thought we were close to Paedwyn."

"Aye. I came upon an encampment last night. There were bodies all over, one of which was a fat, gray Goblin. They attacked right past dusk from what I can tell. Killed a good number of recruits before they got away."

Fennic flinched. "Recruits?"

"Same ones we saw leaving Alloenis. My guess is we'll run in to the rest of them before long. The enemy is moving at last."

Delin groaned. Gnaals were beyond comprehension, but the thought of murderous bands of Goblins ranging the landscape unchecked was simply terrifying. This was not the adventure he dreamed of as a child. His first thoughts were of Tarren and her safety. Little did he know she was but a few weeks behind them along a different path. The simple security of his life was shattered from a whim. He was beginning to regret ever going to Old Man Wiffe's home.

"I think I want to go home now," he muttered to no one in particular.

If they heard him they didn't reply. The tiny band kept walking. Fennic had no misgivings about the journey. Phaelor urged him onward to untold destinies. He and the sword were one now, to whatever end was in store.

They heard evidence of Goblins just after midday. The angry sounds of sword and spear clashing in battle sang a wicked song. Norgen whipped his axe into position and sprinted into the fray.

SEVENTEEN
Flight

The cool afternoon sun was barely enough to melt the patches of snow and ice still clinging to life across the plains and fields. Crows picked through old corn in the hopes of finding one last meal before winter struck. Songbirds fortified their nests against the bad weather and small forest animals sat quietly in their dens. Aside from the crisp sounds of battle raging, it was a normal autumn day.

Delin and Fennic gained the top of the small rise and jerked to a halt. What they saw horrified them. Soldiers dressed in green and gold surrounded a small group of weaponless civilians. Dozens of bodies already littered the ground. The remaining wagons sent up puffs of smoke while they burned. A few men were still on horseback, but it was apparent the horses and wagons had been the initial targets. Across the field massed a large body of Goblins. Delin and Fennic were so absorbed with witnessing their first battle they failed to see Norgen charging into the rear of the Goblin formation.

Dwarven steel bit deep into the under protected Goblin flesh, felling four before they rest knew what was among them. They drew back and tried to rally but the Dwarf was in a battle rage. Another two fell to the gouging blade of his axe. Then he paused and a Goblin club knocked him off his feet. He rolled once, swinging viciously at a nearby leg. He blocked a blow from a rusted sword with the haft of his axe. Norgen easily turned the thrust aside and punched the dull end of his axe into the Goblin's belly.

He uppercut the blade through his foe's lower jaw and spun to his feet.

Sergeant Hallis was prepared to die, though not entirely willing. He'd been forced to leave his friends at Gren Mot after his last patrol was killed. Commander Fynten told him it was for the best if he spent a few weeks off the line. So they made him a recruiter. He protested at first, for Hallis was a born warrior. A sword was as natural to him as a scythe in the hands of a farmer. Recruiter was a slap in the face, yet still he obeyed.

Any rest Fynten had in mind for him was cut short the first time Goblins came upon them in the dark. It was a quick strike, but got the job started. One wagon was destroyed and a handful of men and horses were slain before Hallis readied a defense and fought back. He killed five by himself in a matter of minutes. The half column of cavalry fought hard, eventually driving the Goblins back into the night. The retreat was planned, of that there was no doubt, but Hallis was glad for the respite. The bedraggled band dressed their casualties during the frantic retreat. Hallis regretted the decision of not burying the dead, but many more would have lost their lives in the process. There simply wasn't a choice.

Goblins harassed them for two more days, casually whittling down the numbers until just over half of their original number remained. His captain was already slain by an arrow. Hallis quickly assumed command. The unarmed men were herded to the center of the circle with instructions to snatch up a sword when it became available. A young recruit dropped his bloodstained sword and yelled in horror upon seeing the dark mass forming a hundred meters away. Hallis grit his teeth and growled for them to buckle down. He reminded them why they volunteered in the first place and made ready to meet his doom.

The squat figure bounding down the slope might well have been another Goblin for all Hallis was concerned. Just one more pound bearing down the total weight. He wasn't expecting to live much longer, not with the current odds. Then the figure attacked the rear of the Goblin formation. The formation broke moments later. Only one race was capable of causing so much mayhem: a Dwarf. A glimmer of hope resurfaced in the veteran.

"Marsh! Keep watch against those archers in the trees," Hallis roared. They had to act now or be swept away. "The rest of you on me!"

The remaining soldiers formed a tight wedge on Hallis and charged into the enemy. Dark blood stained Norgen's leather plate armor and beard. An irrepressible rage welled inside. All the friends slain by the Gnaal; the recruits murdered by Goblins in the night. The Centaur giving his life to save the three of them. All of it boiled down into one massive bloodlust. Revenge!

A dull blade bounced off his shoulder, nicking his left triceps before Norgen grabbed the Goblin's arm and thrust the blade into another's chest. The Dwarf crouched to leap but was tackled from the side. Roughly the same size, the Goblin had more mass, easily putting Norgen on his back. The wind drove from his lungs. The rotted smell of his enemy made Norgen gag. Hot spittle drooled onto his cheek and he saw bits of half chewed flesh dangling between the ruined teeth. Pressing down, the Goblin started to crush his throat.

It took every ounce of strength Norgen possessed to keep the long fingers from wrapping around his throat, but Norgen was up to the task. He used one hand to start punching the Goblin's ribs, crushing bones. Still the enemy pressed. Soon the pressure was too much and Norgen could feel his strength fading. One last move and he drew the Goblin's own dirk and stabbed him in the armpit. The Goblin howled worse than a dying dragon, throwing his head back a second before it was hacked from his shoulders.

Blood splashed onto Norgen's flushed face. He didn't hear the long sword whistling through the air. Nor did he see the handful of soldiers hit the exposed flank and break the Goblin spirit. Having lost the advantage, the Goblins broke and ran.

Delin watched the scene unfold with a sickening feeling in the pit of his stomach. He just knew Norgen was going to die. "What should we do?" he asked.

A sharp metallic ring was Fennic's reply. He drew Phaelor and prepared to join the fight. Delin snatched at his arm, jerking him back to reality.

"What are you doing? You'll be killed if you go down there!"

Fennic struggled in the grip and snapped, "Let me go! I'm supposed to fight. Phaelor says so."

"Phaelor's going to get you killed, you dunce! Listen to yourself. What do you know about fighting a battle or wielding a sword?" Delin fumed. He was as scared as he was furious.

"How am I supposed to learn if you keep holding me back? Ever since the sword chose me you've tried to control what I do. That's it, isn't it? You're jealous of me and Phaelor." The blow caught Fennic off guard. He staggered back a step from the force of it. His face turned red and sore.

Delin's fist stayed clenched. "Fennic, you're the best friend I've ever had, but you need to calm down and listen. If you, if we, go down there we'll only be in the way. We don't know about battles or how to fight. Phaelor may want to go, but it doesn't know you. Look into your soul and see the truth. It's the only way we can make it through this."

Slowly the intensity in Fennic's eyes ebbed and caution returned. He was embarrassed and it took all the courage he could muster to look his friend in the eye.

"I…I'm sorry. I shouldn't have said that," he meekly offered.

Delin's shoulders dropped. "I know, but there's no time for that now. We need to figure something out to help."

The battle changed. More and more Goblin bodies lay across the field. Most of them centered on the berserk Dwarf and his deadly axe. Then Norgen fell. The boys needed to act.

"Look," Fennic pointed.

The surviving soldiers were rushing towards the Goblins, leaving three wounded men looking after twenty frightened boys. Norgen was beyond their help. His fate was out of their hands, but they were in position to help the recruits and wounded.

"In the trees. See there? The archers are sneaking closer. Those guys will be murdered if we don't help."

Delin looked closer at the Goblins. Fennic was right. "What do we do?"

"I say we sneak down behind them and attack. Hopefully we kill one or two before they get spooked enough to run. Then we turn their bows on them. We may not know swords, but each of us grew up hunting."

"This is crazy."

"I'm listening if you have something better in mind," Fennic queried.

Delin shook his head in defeat. "I hate when you do it."

"You only hate it because I'm right. Come on."

"When did you become the leader of this adventure?" he asked before following.

They went as fast as they dared without risking discovery. Neither was sure of how to handle the situation so they just eased into it. Patches of sunlight and shadow dotted the lightly forested slope, making it almost impossible to spot their foe. The Goblins were cunning and well camouflaged. Delin quickly realized the only way to kill a Goblin was to view it as a deer. They moved closer.

Gentle thrumming danced across the slope. Lines of fire sped from the trees into the diminishing ranks of the defenders. Delin saw another recruit topple over with a burning arrow in his chest. The world suddenly became a terrible place, more real than his darkest fantasies. The recruits weren't much older than he and Fennic.

Fennic crept closer to the Goblin archer, Phaelor humming softly in his hands. His blood pounded with the warrior spirit of generations long past. The star silver sword demanded justice for blood spilled. And Fennic delivered. He strode confidently forward, the instrument of the gods. Life and death were insignificant compared to the power he wielded. Fennic attacked.

The Goblin archer spun about suddenly. His bow was knocked and drawn. Fennic charged from the trees at the same moment and the Goblin loosed in terror. The arrow sped past Fennic's head, forcing him to duck right. The Goblin was better trained and quicker. The beast dropped his bow and drew the wicked blade from his waist. He was on Fennic in a heartbeat. Steel clashed, with the village boy fighting for his life. The Goblin was much stronger than he anticipated. A brutal slash knocked Phaelor from his grasp and he knew it was over. The Goblin slowly drew back for the killing blow.

Fennic found he couldn't close his eyes, no matter how hard he tried. He saw his own reflection in the Goblin's soulless eyes. He watched the rust stained blade arc down. But the blow never fell. The Goblin jerked back in mid-swing and pitched forward in a spray of blood and ichors. Fennic looked up to see Delin holding a bloodstained sword.

"You saved my life," Fennic whispered.

"I shouldn't have had to," Delin replied.

He was in shock at having taken his first life.

EIGHTEEN
Their First Battle

"What do we do now?"

Flaming arrows were still dropping into the defenders. Only a span of moments had passed since Fennic and Delin joined the fight. Norgen was still alone in the back of the enemy masses and inflicting great damage. Bodies piled up around him. The situation on the slope was much less dramatic. Phaelor lay partially buried under dead leaves a few meters off, close to the Goblin's bow.

"Grab the bow and follow me," Fennic said with a twinkle in his eyes. "If we can kill enough of their archers the rest will break and run. Come on."

Both knew that Delin was the better archer by far. He'd practically grown up in the woods, hunting and fishing. His father taught him everything needed to survive in the wild. Delin's only problem was he didn't know if he could keep killing. Determined to save the recruits, Delin strung the bow and turned to darker thoughts. He tried to focus. Tried to imagine the enemy as wild deer or bear. It was the only way he decided. Delin drew back and fired.

The first was the toughest kill. He'd had plenty of time to study the dark gray body. The way the loose armor covered the torso and the bulging muscles in his arms and neck. These Goblins were stronger than they appeared. The arrow sliced through the back of the Goblin's neck, ripping out the throat and vocal cords. Delin watched the dying Goblin pitch forward down the hill to the cheers of the men below. It was then Delin knew he was making a real difference.

He killed eight more before running out of arrows. What remained of the Goblin archers broke and ran for safety.

Sergeant Hallis pulled the Dwarf to his feet and they watched what was left of the Goblins retreat. Too many on both sides were dead, with others lying in pain across the field. Further fighting served no purpose. Hallis and Norgen stalked the battlefield for wounded Goblins. There were none when the pair finished.

"You and your company came just in time," Hallis told him in an acidic tone. "I don't think we were going to hold much longer. How many did you bring?"

Norgen wiped some of the blood from the blades of his axe. "Myself and two others."

"You attacked a reinforced company of Goblins by yourselves? I've seen bravery in battles plenty of times, but yours was near suicidal," Hallis said in disbelief. "But the help is much appreciated. Name's Hallis."

"Norgen," the Dwarf scowled back. "Who's in charge here?"

"I am now. Most everyone else was killed in the beginning." Just then recognition flashed in the man's eyes. "I know you, don't I?"

Norgen nodded. "Aye. Back in Alloenis."

"I remember. It was you and that pair of boys we couldn't convince to join us." He looked around at the dead. "Probably better they didn't. This is no job for boys."

Norgen couldn't help but agree. He'd been just a lad when he killed his first Goblin and the memory was forever a part of him.

"What brings you this way?" Hallis asked.

Norgen gave an abbreviated version of the story, to the point where none but the vital points remained. Dwarves were long known for their skill at telling tales and dragging them out for hours on end. For Norgen to speak so plainly and quickly was quite a feat.

"Ills news," Hallis said. He looked over his shoulder at the sound of Delin and Fennic returning. The soldier passed Norgen a queer look. Norgen shrugged.

The boys looked him in the eye and nodded once. He could see the difference in them. They were men now, no longer innocent boys from the countryside. It warmed his heart to see them both alive and unharmed. Norgen said nothing about the pair of bows, with two full quivers, they brought with them.

"Survived your first scrape I see," he told them. "Remember what you learned here. A good soldier learns from mistakes."

"I almost died up there," Fennic said shakily. "Phaelor...."

"That's war, boy," Norgen reminded. "We almost die every time we touch the blade. Are either of you wounded?"

"No," Delin answered. He drew a deep breath for the first time. "Just a few cuts and bruises."

Sudden pain lanced through Fennic's shoulder and he instinctively reached up to clutch the pain. Bright red blood trickled down his bicep, coloring his fingertips when they came away from the wound. Funny, he didn't remember being cut.

"Let me see your arm," Norgen said. "I'm no healer, but I've been hurt enough to know how to treat the simple wounds."

Fennic grimaced as he stripped his tunic off. The pain was so harsh he knew he was going to lose the arm. He just knew.

"Relax. Tis just a scrape," the Dwarf said. "Looks like an arrow grazed you."

Delin tried to stifle a laugh and failed.

"What's so funny?" Fennic fumed.

"You! It's just a scratch and you act like you're dying!"

"I don't remember you being attacked the way I was. Ouch," he cried out when Norgen pinched the wound shut.

Delin laughed harder. "Because I wasn't foolish enough to charge into them. If only your mother could have seen you!"

"Enough," Norgen growled. "A wound is no laughing matter. Goblins oft dip their arrows in poison. You are fortunate to be alive. Otherwise the poison would have worked through your system and killed you already."

The reality of war stung Fennic. He looked at the minor wound and shuddered. What was he doing? He wasn't a soldier. Wasn't a warrior from legends told. He was a simple farm boy from Fel Darrins. No one from the village had anything to do with Averon for decades, though he had a hunch that was soon to change. Like it or not, the people of the sleepy village were about to be embroiled in a war of the grandest scale. No one was going to be safe from the armies of the Silver Mage.

"Gather the bodies and burn them," Hallis ordered his recruits. "Jin!"

A battered soldier with a bloody bandage around his neck limed over. "How's the neck?"

Jin did his best to smile through the pain. "It's nothing a pint of ale won't fix."

"Good. I want you to take the rest of the men and bury our dead. Don't let any of the recruits help. Keep them busy with the Goblins. It wouldn't do to see them bury their friends and family right now. Keep them moving so as there's no time to think about it." he paused in thought, recalling the disaster in the Gren Mountains. "How many horses do we have?"

"Three, but one is unable to ride."

Hallis looked around. "Send out two scouts. We need a better defensive position before night falls."

"I'll see to it," Jin told him and then walked off.

Satisfied for the moment, Hallis drifted back to the Dwarf and his companions.

"What are your plans now? The road is not safe."

Norgen finished cleaning and dressing Fennic's shoulder. "Seems to me the enemy is all over this side of the mountains. It isn't wise to travel alone, if you get my meaning."

"Indeed I do. And we can sorely use the help. It's a pity there's not more of you."

Norgen's eyes misted, secreting the agony in his heart. "There were more. We marched months ago from Breilnor and were attacked by the Gnaal. I alone escaped."

"I am sorry," Hallis offered.

"Tis not your fault. The Silver Mage has sent his creatures out in search of something, but what I do not know. I believe whatever they hunt will be the only thing capable of destroying his filth for all time."

"You bear ill tidings. Gnaals haven't been seen outside of Gren in hundreds of years."

The Dwarf nodded.

"Still, if what you say is true, there is time to win the war. King Maelor is assembling a great host. I have no illusions of it being enough. For I have seen them might of Gren and all the world should tremble. These are ill times," Hallis said with a dark voice.

"There's a stream a few hundred meters east of here. I'd appreciate it if you and a couple of my boys went and filled the canteens. Paedwyn is far afoot," he told the boys.

"We'd be glad to help," Delin told him, grabbing Fennic by the collar and pulling him along.

"I wish I still had that innocence," Hallis admitted while they walked off.

"We are long past that time," Norgen said.

NINETEEN
Speculation

Guards and pickets were established for the night on rotating one hour shifts. Jin posted the pickets a hundred meters out for early warning and brought the guards in much closer to the mouth of the cave. He alone would remain awake for the remainder of the night. They'd been lucky to find a shelter big enough for them all, though it wasn't truly a cave. Time and weather had eroded a large portion of the under bank while several downed oak trees provided natural cover in the front. The enemy had only one avenue of approach. The men slept comfortably that night.

Most of them.

"I can still smell them," Delin whispered.

Fennic watched him with sad eyes. "It's all in your mind. The battle was far from here. We need to sleep. I have a feeling things aren't going to get any easier."

"Even if we went home?"

"Especially then. Do you think anyone will be safe from this war? That battle could easily have taken place in Fel Darrins. No, Delin, the only way to feel safe again is by stopping the Silver Mage. Besides, you heard Norgen. The Mage is afraid of something. He knows he can be beaten."

Delin wasn't so sure. Then an idea struck. "What if it's Phaelor?"

The subject touched an increasingly sore spot. Much of their troubles revolved around the Star Silver sword. Delin viewed it with disdain, forcing them from home in a direction neither wanted. Fennic saw it as a powerful gift commanding its own destiny and choosing hosts as the ages passed. What if the sword was meant to kill the Silver Mage?

"Get some sleep. I have a chill going down my spine," Fennic snapped.

"Fair enough," Delin said knowingly. "What do you suppose your mom and dad are doing right now?

A smile crossed his lips. "I can see her pulling a fresh baked apple pie from the stove, waiting for dad to come home. The whole house smelling of spices and roast meat. She has the last of the wildflowers in a vase on the kitchen table. At least that's how I want to think of them."

"I can see myself sitting under the willow trees along the river watching the otters play. Tarren's there too. She's brought a picnic lunch. The sun is shining, and I've got Big Tom landed." Delin fell asleep smiling.

Night grew colder. Delin was snoring lightly in his cloak. Fennic, however, found sleep elusive. Dark visions taunted him. He pictured himself on the ground waiting to die. Phaelor whispered to him, assuring him of his rightful destiny. And there, alongside a stream in the heart of Averon, Fennic Attleford had his first premonition of the land of Gren. All thanks to a foolish idea and skipping work to go fishing, his life, not two months removed, was finished. Voices drifted to him from across the shelter. Their distraction was a welcome relief.

"What happens once we get to Paedwyn," Norgen asked.

Hallis let out a long sigh. "Well, we need to get you in to see the king. These boys will start their training. I only hope there's enough time before the enemy arrives. The situation is far worse than you think."

Even Jin, consumed in his duties as sergeant of the guard, perked his ears.

"As I said before, I have seen the hosts of Gren and they are mighty."

"I don't like the sound of that," Norgen said.

Hallis replied, "This war is going to take more than the strength of Averon to win. We need your help as much as the Elves."

"Would that the Elves still had their will to fight, but I'm afraid countless years of battle and turmoil have turned them against the affairs of others. I'm thinking me and my boys here are all the help you'll be getting for a spell."

Hallis clasped the Dwarf on the shoulder. "Perhaps, but we don't know what the new day brings until the dawn. We may yet find reason to hope."

They were up and moving well before dawn. Hallis kept his mounted scouts ranging in giant circles while the column moved through the wild. The roads weren't safe and the countryside was wooded lightly enough to provide cover. Most of them, Hallis included, were worn out from days of harassment and battle. They were all armed now, and ready for the next fight. The weak had been trimmed from the ranks, as was the case in every army since time began. The Goblins weren't going to find them so easy a target again.

Hallis walked twice as far as the column. The Goblin force was just a reconnaissance raiding party, and that meant the main force was much, much larger. He ranged the length of the column a dozen times over, offering encouragement and barking orders. Always were his eyes searching the flanks for sign of the enemy. The new recruits soon forgot the disaster from yesterday and found motivation in his actions. The pace quickened. Hallis rejoined Norgen and the others when the column stopped for a quick midday meal.

"What do you think?" he asked between mouthfuls of bread.

Jin laughed. "We've made good time today. Right about now I wish I were a training sergeant."

"How so?"

"How many of them get actual combat veterans to train? Their job is easy with this group." Jin went back to his canteen for another drink.

Hallis sat silent in the knowledge that his friends, his brothers, in Gren Mot had once felt the very same way. Now, who knew whether the fortress still stood?

"If all the lands were so fortunate," Norgen said. "Let us see how well they fight when the weight of Gren moves down onto the plains."

"They'll never get out of the mountains," Jin boasted. He was a good man, Hallis decided, one of the best junior noncommissioned officers in the army, but he still lacked a wisdom for all-out war. "King Maelor has sent ambassadors to all the lands. We won't stand alone."

"Aye, but none have answered," Norgen replied.

Fennic didn't like where the conversation was headed so he decided to change it. "What's Gren like, Sergeant Hallis?"

All but Norgen turned to the boy with mouths slightly agape. It never dawned on them that he might have another reason for knowing.

"It is a dark and evil land," Hallis said with careful thought. "The plains are covered in ash and decay. Nothing lives there. There is darkness and despair. The enemy has armies ranging as far as the eye can see, and not just Goblins and Trolls. He has men among them as well. The last descendants of ancient Gren, before the rise of the Mages."

"Do not think that because they are men they can be turned to our side. No, they have become as evil as the very land." His face turned dark. "They are wild to look at, with long, gnarled beards and dressed in course wool tunics and horned helms. They are fierce warriors. No doubt the Mage will have them in the front when the invasion begins."

Delin stared wide eyed as he listened to the description.

Norgen laughed. "Be easy on them. This is their first war! Keep your heads up lads. The world is ripe with turmoil and nothing men or Dwarves can do will change it. Things are as they will be. Nothing more."

"Don't worry on such things now. Concentrate on your skills with bow and sword," Jin offered. "The time is fast approaching when you will need them."

"The bow is no trouble. It's the sword I'm worried about," Fennic admitted. His head dropped with the thought of his previous failure.

"Yet you both survived against a score of well-trained Goblins," Hallis told them. "Impressive. The people of your village are stronger than I thought."

They both smiled.

"I will teach you to become swordsmen at every chance we get between here and Paedwyn. You need not worry," Hallis said. "Mind you though, you'll only know enough to keep yourselves alive. Not to take on the enemy host single handed."

The sun came out from behind the heavy blanket of clouds choking the skies, and for a moment they were warm. Winter birds whistled to each other across the treetops. A small herd of deer crossed their path without so much as looking their way. Hallis found a small measure of comfort. Birds and animals meant no Goblins. He called another break halfway through the afternoon. The scouts had already returned with nothing to report, but Hallis knew two men could not see everything. The enemy could easily have slipped past them.

Fennic and Delin joined the surviving recruits in basic principles of sword fighting and then a series of exercises designed to build speed and efficiency. Much as they wanted to know how to fight, Hallis would have none of it. They had to learn the basics before moving on. They broke camp an hour later.

Hallis was almost sure they'd made it through another day when Jin came riding back into the column. He had a look of despair that needed no interpretation.

"Goblins, and something else," he said through breaths. "I think it's just a scouting party, but even so, the main body can't be far behind."

"How far?"

"Depends if they halt or not. I'd guess no more than an hour," Jin answered.

Norgen and the boys came stalking up, listening intently to every word.

"What is the something else?" he asked

Jin shook his head. "I don't know. I've never seen the like."

"A Gnaal," Norgen whispered once Jin finished describing it. A foul air settled about him.

"Up until a few months ago I would have thought you mad," Hallis said. "Recent events have convinced me otherwise. If what you say is true and they are nigh unkillable, what chance do we have to stop them?"

Norgen spat. "Fennic wounded it the last time we fought. It knows it can be hurt now and might be less anxious to jump into the fight again. Fennic, I am afraid we are going to have to ask you to come with us."

Phaelor warmed his leg. Despite that reassurance, fear spread through him. His heart bade him go and hide, to escape the monster of Gren before it claimed his soul. Duty and friendship demanded otherwise.

"Bringing the boy is risky," Jin said. "I don't want his death on my hands if this goes wrong."

"I know what I'm getting in to," Fennic replied with a shaky voice. He took another step closer to becoming a man.

Hallis wasn't convinced. "Nay boy. Give me the sword. This is too dangerous."

"The sword only obeys young Attleford," Norgen said.

The old veteran looked deep into the resolve in Fennic's eyes. "So be it. Come, we're wasting time. I don't enjoy the prospect of fighting them at night. Jin, bring one squad. Drop their packs here and follow me."

Norgen growled in delight. "Good. My axe was growing restless for Goblin blood."

TWENTY
Counter Strike

Norgen was the first to inch his way over the small rise and peer down on the Goblin position. He hadn't spotted the Gnaal but knew better than to think it was gone. Taking a quick count and general layout of the glade, he slid back down to where the others waited. The Dwarf removed his dented helm and drank deeply from an offered canteen. "There's over a score down there. All scouts. The defense is weak. No one is watching for us. I think fortune is smiling, for I saw no sign of the Gnaal. Let's hit them now and be done with it."

"Not so hasty," Hallis said. "What of the other side, Blaron?"

The blond soldier poured a little water over his face. He'd returned at about the same time as Norgen. "Aye, I saw that Gnaal. Big and nasty. He's hidden in a depression close to a small grove of elm trees."

He took a stick and began mapping out the glade in the dirt. Blaron and Norgen spent the next few minutes going over what they knew. Neither had a plan for dealing with the Gnaal, but Norgen cautioned it would be dark soon. The time of the Gnaal. The sky was already changing from white-blue to the pink and crimson of twilight. They had to move.

Finally, Hallis began issuing orders. "Blaron, I want you to take eight men back to your last position. I'll bring the rest with me. Watch carefully. I don't want anyone to fire until you see the first body drop. Choose your targets carefully. Once the main body of Goblins is destroyed we retreat to the bivouac. Don't wait for us. Just go. And avoid the Gnaal at all costs. Any questions?"

Fennic felt inspired by Hallis' leadership. The way the orders flowed was incredible. There was no doubt about it, Hallis was born natural.

"Move fast and stay quiet. One wrong move will compromise all of us. And do not try to fight that Gnaal. If a hundred Dwarves couldn't defeat it, we won't either. Good hunting."

The gaunt Blaron took his men and wordlessly trailed off through the gathering dusk. Hallis took an instant liking to the man the moment they met. He'd served under Blaron's father back when he was a recruit. That was back in King Baeleon's reign, long before the Silver Mage made ready his war. Averon was more civilized then. Hallis hoped he wasn't going to have to deliver sad news to Blaron's family when he returned to Paedwyn.

A sudden rustling nearby set them into a hasty defensive position. Bows were strung and swords drawn, much to Delin's surprise as he came walking out of the bushes. Hallis felt his face turn dark red.

"What do you think you're doing?" he whispered harshly.

Delin stood his ground. "I'm not going to let my friend go off on his own, especially with what you're about to face. I don't care who thinks different."

A thin smile cracked the old soldier's grimace. "There's a fire in you, boy. That much is certain. I only hope it doesn't get you killed."

"He's a Dwarf at heart," Norgen said approvingly.

Hallis wasn't convinced. "Both of you stay well behind us. This isn't going to last more than a minute or so. You need to be running when I turn back around. Understand?"

They did.

"Not another sound from here out."

Hallis waved the group forward. The soldiers moved stealthily, fanning out in a long line towards the top of the rise. Each took a concealed firing position and waited. Norgen held the boys back five meters off the line. He knew better than to risk himself for no reason and wasn't about to let Delin or Fennic do so either. Besides, everyone knew Dwarves couldn't use long bows. But give a Dwarf a crossbow and see the damage he could do!

Once in position, they waited for Blaron's men to get set. Heartbeats quickened. Throats went dry and palms began to sweat. Fennic was the most afraid. He'd stood face to face with the Gnaal already and barely survived. Now he wondered where the courage to do so again was going to come from.

Slowly, methodically, Hallis drew back and took aim. The light wood colored shaft rubbed against his cheek. Hallis shifted once and let loose. The arrow whistled as it gathered speed. It struck the nearest Goblin in the throat with a wet thump. Hallis smiled long enough to knock and aim again. Arrows sped in from both sides. The battle was joined.

Half of the Goblins were dead before the rest knew what was happening. They scrambled for cover, spitting a futile volley back in return. Only three Goblins were alive by the time the Gnaal burst from cover. The elm stand exploded in a hail of fire and splinters. A terrible roar shook the ground as the decaying monster stormed into the thick of the battle. Fennic saw death searching him out.

Phaelor screamed to be drawn. To exact revenge and finish the job already begun. Dead bodies were flung recklessly aside and crushed under the Gnaal's advance. Blaron did exactly as he was told. His eight men withdrew as fast as they could before the great beast spotted them. Hallis wasn't so fortunate. The Gnaal's rotting head turned his way and those vile eyes locked on the sergeant. The Gnaal smiled and started towards the ridge.

The recruits broke and ran in fear. Some stood petrified. Hallis wished he could find a place to hide. This went beyond the decadence and horrors on the plains of Gren. This was pure and malevolent hatred. He shakily reached back and drew another arrow.

"Save it," Norgen growled.

The Gnaal was coming closer.

Axe in hand, the Dwarf said, "Take your people and flee. Look after these two for me."

"Where are you going?"

Norgen smiled grimly. "I'm tired of running from this bastard."

He started to march out to meet the monster. Too many times he'd been forced to run, each time believing he was free. The Gnaal kept coming. Each knew the only way to be free was for one of them to die.

Fennic watched in shock. Norgen was committing suicide to buy them time. Phaelor in hand, the youth rushed off to stand with his friend. Delin pulled him back just in time.

"Wait! I've got a better idea," he yelled.

The Gnaal's heavy club missed Norgen's head and smashed through a tree.

Delin took one his Goblin arrows and touched it to Phaelor's glowing blade.

"What are you doing?" Fennic asked.

He still wasn't sure. "Just watch."

Norgen slashed and his axe bounced off the Gnaal's kneecap. They knew he couldn't last long like this. Norgen needed help. Fennic stared at the arrow as it started to glow. Hallis joined the fight then, moving halfway down the slope and firing off the rest of his quiver. They were all dead if Delin's idea didn't work. Delin aimed his arrow carefully and prayed to every god he knew. He didn't want to die.

Then the Gnaal saw them. Saw the one thing it hated more than life itself. The sword! The golden light was an insult to all Gren. It was an aberration to his master. The Gnaal remembered the pain it caused and knew what to do. Roaring, it forgot its attackers and made for the two boys on the hill. The arrow flew towards it.

Seconds slowed so that every action was deliberate and purposeful. Norgen hacked at the back of its leg. Chunks of muscle and flesh flew away. Dark blood splashed around him and the Gnaal roared on. The wielder had to die. Hallis slipped and fell in the ichors. Phaelor glowed bright enough to rival the sun. The enchanted missile struck the Gnaal in the eye with a fleshy smack and plunged deep into its fever maddened mind. Golden light spread like a virus, seeping from every wound and pore. The Gnaal tossed back its head and screamed before crashing to the ground. There it lay; Hallis swore under his breath. The Gnaal lay unmoving, not breathing. Norgen stared wide eyed.

"You did it," Fennic whispered in disbelief.

Delin would have smiled if his heart weren't in his throat threatening to explode. "We....we need to make sure it's dead."

Trembling, they helped each other down to the corpse.

"Stay back," Norgen warned.

He knew full well how the Gnaal liked to play dead. Too many friends died that way and he wasn't willing to let these two follow suit. Fennic stared into the monster's lifeless eyes, expecting to learn the true nature of horror. The feeling of dread was gone.

His thoughts were clear and concise again. The Gnaal was dead.

"It's all right," he reassured them.

Holding Phaelor high, Fennic plunged the blade down through the dark heart of the beast. A quiet hiss escaped the body. Together they watched the body melt away, folding in itself until nothing but a putrid scar remained on the ground. A small piece of evil had left the world.

A sense of peace reentered the glade. The surviving Goblins were gone, fleeing at the first sign the Gnaal was in danger. Norgen and Hallis gathered around Fennic. No one spoke for long moments. There wasn't need to. A young boy, plagued by self-doubt and indecision, from an obscure village in the far reaches of mighty Averon was now responsible for destroying one of the most fearsome creatures Malweir had ever known. They stared in awe.

"You have done what they said could not be done," Hallis forced himself to say. "Have you any idea what this means?"

Norgen planted the head of his axe on the ground and bowed low. "Would you and that sword have been there when we first set foot from Breilnor."

"The light to counter the growing darkness. You boys have given men reason to hope again," Hallis exclaimed.

The light against the darkness. That's the reason why I must go to Gren, Delin finally collapsed. Where he should have been feeling elation and pride, he felt only a gnawing bitterness. The Gnaal was but a prelude of darker dreams to come. He rechecked his pocket for the purple stone and relaxed. He couldn't stop smiling.

Twilight was upon them, spreading shadow and night in a protective blanket. Hallis nervously pushed them away from the battlefield. He wasn't an overly superstitious man but having seen more than the common man he wasn't about to take any chances.

TWENTY-ONE
Meetings in the Night

The nightlife of Feist left much to be desired. A handful of rundown bars and taverns drew the usual crowds of derelicts and aspiring thieves. Good and honest folk went to the old theater on the main road for a live show. Most of the talented performers crowded the towns around Paedwyn and Alloenis. Tolis Scarn didn't care for any of it.

He was more comfortable alone. Scarn found people too petty and intrusive. They all wanted more, always complaining how unfair life was. Most weren't any better than cattle being drawn to the slaughterhouse. People too afraid to go and take theirs. Scarn looked upon them all with disdain, for he never lacked in taking what he wanted. Born to parents who died from the flux when he was quite young, Scarn learned how to find and collect the necessary elements of life the hard way.

He lost count of the times he was caught by angry farmers and merchants. They broke his bones, busted his lips and left him covered in bruises, and still he persisted. Time and experience conspired to make him better. To hone his skills until the beatings stopped.

Until he stopped getting caught. Not long after his second decade he found time to stop and think about what could have been. His parents had been decent and hardworking farmers from Braem, a quaint northern border town. That life never came to be and he turned to crime. His entire basis for being was a contradiction to his parent's beliefs.

Water under the bridge, he told himself and never looked back. Perhaps those were the reasons he was here in Feist, drinking cheap ale in a second-rate inn and hunting a pair of boys halfway across Averon for an employer he didn't know.

"Cheers," he said to no one in particular as he downed the last swallow of ale.

He wasn't much of a drinker, and the poor quality offered by this inn was twisting his stomach horribly. So Scarn passed a few coppers to the bar maid and left the common room for the night. A pillow with a heavy down blanket offered much more than the dreary crowds of Feist. Besides, days and weeks of hard traveling and investigating had taken their toll. A few days rest and relaxation were just what he needed before taking up the road again. He wasn't sure his employer would appreciate the delay, but now he didn't care.

Tolis Scarn was many things: a killer, spy, and thief. He'd even done a bit of assassination in his time. But he was not naïve. His employer had secret motivations, a common factor among those he chose to work for. Only a fool would believe otherwise. No student of history, Scarn was keen enough to understand the significance of the purple stones. He sighed halfway up the stair, cursing himself for thinking about work during his self-imposed break.

Floorboards groaned underfoot, marking his passage down the poorly lit hall. Cobwebs plagued the upper corners and ceiling, and a thin film of dust coated the floor. True, he might have found a classier place, but this suited his purpose. Scarn turned the key in his door and stepped inside. The hairs on his neck raised instantly. Instincts drew the short sword in one hand and his dagger in the other. Still too dark to see the danger, he knew stood stone still and waited. A low, erratic breath came from across the room.

"Show yourself or I'll kill you where you stand," Scarn growled.

A rasping voice replied, "You'll have no need of those weapons with me, Tolis Scarn. I am beyond the limits of your imagination."

The lantern above the small table sprang to life, temporarily blinding him. Bright flashes burned his eyes. Scarn raised his weapons higher and readied for the attack. But the attack did not come.

"What do you want?" he asked, blinking the flashes away.

With a power like that, Scarn knew he was dead.

"Look at me closely and answer your own questions," came the answer.

He did. There was an unsettling familiarity in the voice that worried him. Finally able to focus, Scarn looked upon the hunched over man in a dark robe. His face and hands were completely concealed, leaving no doubts as to his identity. Danger screamed at Scarn.

"How did you find me?"

The Hooded Man let out a hissing laugh. "Did you truly think I wasn't going to follow your every move? Your every action? Perhaps I haven't made myself fully clear?"

Dark fear pulsed forward, sweeping the room. It gripped Scarn and threatened to drive him to his knees.

"A war is coming. One that will shake the foundations of the world. Everything you have ever known will be torn asunder. The darkness is stronger but not undefeatable. There are certain weaknesses exposed."

Scarn shook the demons from his head. He didn't much care about wars or darkness. He didn't care about anything but finishing this job and putting it all behind him.

"Where is the stone?" the Hooded Man pressed.

"Not far. I've been tracking…."

"You've been tracking a whisper. Nothing more." The Hooded Man drew to his full height. "The old man no longer holds the stone."

"I know. I came upon his grave in Relin Werd."

The Hooded Man cocked his head in thought. "Where then did he go? I have not felt him for some time now. Winter Day is soon upon us. I need that stone, Scarn."

"The current keepers can't be more than a few days away. Two young boys have it, and they travel with a Dwarf," Scarn said.

The same two who killed the Gnaal? This is most unexpected. He frowned within the shadows of his hood. "They are more than three days from here."

Scarn didn't ask how he knew. He wanted the man to leave.

The Hooded Man began to pace. "This is becoming more dangerous than I thought. You must leave at dawn, for our enemies will soon be in Paedwyn. Take the King's Road and ride hard. The only way to succeed is to get ahead of them and reach the city first."

"What do I do then?"

"Leave that to me."

The window flew open and a stiff wind blew out the lantern. Tolis Scarn waited until he knew he was alone before closing the window and relighting the room. His mind was filled with questions. The most prominent was what made Winter Day so important? Too disturbed to think, Scarn strapped his weapons back on and headed for the common room.

Sidian, the Silver Mage, slumped back into his throne of dragon bone. Cold sweat poured down his face. His old body felt used and broken beyond the strain of his years. His weathered hand caressed his aching temple. The magic was taking more out of him these days. He felt more alone. More fragile since the war began. His fires weren't enough to keep him warm anymore.

A heavy knock took away the pain and weakness.

Two slender Goblins with mottled skin eased their way to his feet and bowed. Behind them walked a strong man with evil eyes.

"My lord," the man said. "We are making progress against the enemy forces in the mountain pass, but our losses are mounting. We need the dragon."

Sidian's eyes flashed. "I will use the dragon at the time and place of my choosing, not a moment before. Am I clear, Grelnor?"

Grelnor bowed. "Forgiveness. I do not presume to overstep my bounds, but losses are heavy. The enemy is much craftier than we believed."

"The lives of Goblins and Trolls do not concern me. They are easy enough to come by. Have the reinforcements come in from the east yet?"

"I've heard nothing. Only recently did I return from the front lines," Grelnor told him. "Wagon trains full of wounded leave daily and there are few enough healers here in Gren. We could well lose this war with the outcome of the siege."

Sidian didn't ask for a progress report. Daily reports and random visions showed him the carnage of the pass. War was an uncivilized affair and it sickened his stomach. With the two largest kingdoms in Malweir embroiled in conflict, his personal task went unnoticed.

"The eastern clans have yet to march," the taller Goblin rasped. "My runners return with word of cowardice. Their leaders claim to be waiting for the final thrust into Averon."

The speech was slow and broken, for most Goblins had a limited grasp on the common tongue.

"Perhaps they need... persuasion," Grelnor offered.

Recent losses meant little in the terms of manpower to Gren, but the more Goblins killed were going to cause serious problems when the war moved down onto the open plains.

"I will dispatch my Gnaals to hasten their preparations. Commander Grelnor, we will be out of the mountains in less than one week. Do not stop the attack and do not fail me," he told the once proud man. "Redouble your efforts and break their will."

"As you command," Grelnor bowed again and stormed from the chamber, the Goblins fast on his heel.

Sidian resumed rubbing his forehead but the ache only grew stronger.

"Where are you leading me I wonder, pony?" Tarren asked through a light yawn. She was tired of traveling and sore from riding so much. She cursed her decisions for the thousandth time. The pony snorted as if to say, trust me.

Tarren supposed matters could be worse. She shuddered to think what might have been if she were caught by the storm in the open. Winter Day was three and half weeks away and already the weather changed for the worse. Her motivation for finding Delin and Fennic grew sharply with each passing day.

They stopped occasionally so the pony could browse on the last of the fall grasses and Tarren could relieve herself. They had no shortage of water, which was much the opposite of her food stores. Food was a serious issue and seeing how the pony stuck to grass and berries, Tarren wondered how much longer she was going to make it with the pony in the lead before she found herself starving.

"We need to find food soon. I don't want to starve out here," she told the creature while stroking its muzzle. "Oh, I wish you understood me."

The pony swished its tail.

Tarren stretched awake with a mighty yawn. After ducking behind a boulder, she came back to find the fire stoked and a large bundle close by. The pony was nowhere in sight. She knew better to question a helping hand so she went to the sack, hoping her pony was coming back. Inside were dried fruits and meat, venison from the smell, and a large wedge of cheese buried under a loaf of dark bread. All told, there was enough to last her another four days, five if she rationed carefully. Tears of gratitude clouded her shining blue eyes.

The pony returned shortly, tail swishing and walking with the same carefree attitude. It was all Tarren could do to run up and wrap her around the soft neck and cry.

TWENTY-TWO
Celegon

Thunder and lightning pushed out from Gren. The wicked land grew stronger, spreading evil with the passing hour. Dark clouds filled the red and black skies. Lightning wreathed the jagged mountaintops and hidden crags. Howling winds tormented the world down to the foundations. The Gren Mountains were dangerous any time of the year. War and invasion increased that threat. Mountain Trolls worked beneath the surface to bring down the ancient rock and dirt while the armies battled nearby.

High above, lodged in a forgotten pass, stood two slender figures in green cloaks. Each had a full quiver and a bow strapped across his back with long rapiers at the hip. Dangerous as they were intelligent, the Elves watched the battle play out in secrecy.

Catapults barraged the surging ranks of Goblins and men, destroying troops and equipment at an unprecedented pace. Fires burned and raged behind the enemy lines. The Elves keen eyes spied a long line of wagons laden with wounded moving back down the pass. Human losses seemed considerably less though they were far outnumbered. The Elves saw evidence of a tremendous landslide leaving a trail into the invading army. Bodies and siege machines were wiped out in an instant.

"The humans have no chance," the younger Elf remarked dispassionately. "Not even with the weight of our people behind them, Celegon."

His long blond hair flowing in the strong winds, Celegon said nothing. Another major assault was beginning. Human archers slew scores of Goblin foot soldiers. Many tried to break and run and would have succeeded if not for the three battalions of Ogres pushing them forward. Arrows darkened the skies. Return fire struck down many of the defenders. Celegon caught sight of a mass of heavy cavalry waiting off to the side of the main avenue of approach. They looked tired, both horse and rider.

"We shall see, my friend," he finally said. "These humans are most resilient. I see thousands dead, and how many more have already been taken back to Gren? The humans are deserving of our help."

"Alsenal has said the Dwarves are ready to commit. Our people aren't needed here."

Celegon smiled. "I disagree. Man isn't strong enough to handle the fate of the world alone. And the bearded folk were never many. We need to help."

"As we always have," the Elf replied. "Man cannot grow if we continue to hold his hands. They must unite and be held accountable for their actions."

"And must we sit by and watch this evil spread across Malweir until even we are no longer safe? Or have you forgotten the horrors of the Mage War? I have no desire to see my children's children buried before me," he argued back.

"The powers of life and death are beyond our control. As is the destiny of Man. Celegon, surely you must understand the potential danger in our involvement? How many died in the last war? How many friends and brothers did we lose? Man has learned nothing in the time since. Nothing! They continue with their petty wars and idle fantasies while the world disintegrates around them. Our paths must separate before both our peoples are destroyed. Your father sees the truth of this. Why can't you?"

"I've always held a soft spot for humans, Derlith. You know this," Celegon said in a quiet voice.

The Ogres joined the battle. Most of the Goblin lines were shattered and combat ineffective. A healthy majority of the Ogres were riddled with flaming arrows and barbed pikes. The humans were bringing ballistae forward to counter the murderous foe. Giant wooden arrows a foot around and six long were loaded and aimed at the charging Ogres.

"Look at them. Not even Elves would stand against so many Ogres," Celegon said. "Each and every one of them is scared to wit's end and still they stand. If only my father had that same courage for our people's future."

"It would be a future laden in grief," came the answer. "Come, we need to get out of this pass before the storms worsen."

Being a prince of Elves had both advantages and disadvantages. His opinions were generally held in high regard so long as they mirrored the consensus of the Elves. Most policies and legislation remained beyond the scope of his authority. His father often included him in private conversations, and every once in a while, allowed Celegon's reasoning to win through. Alsenal alone was accountable when it came to the welfare of the Highland Elves.

High pitched screams and wails drifted up to them. Ogres were starting to die, badly. A further look showed many already on the ground in growing pools of blood. But it was not enough. The defense was folding. Desperation sent the cavalry charging into the Ogre flanks. It was a suicide charge. They had to know that horsemen were no match for the armor skinned warriors of Gren. Tears filled Celegon's eyes. "When was it last you witnessed such bravery?" he asked.

The Elf prince stood transfixed on the gruesome scene.

"They need our help."

"So that we may suffer the same fate? I am not so ready to die for man."

Celegon knew better than to continue the argument, but the courage of the defenders demanded more.

"Think what they could do with a handful of our companies at their side, Derlith. We'd stem the enemy tide and drive them back into Gren long before the war had the chance to spread," Celegon said.

"Join them if you wish, but I'll have no part in it," Derlith replied. "My orders were to scout the battlefield and return with what I saw. Nothing more."

He leaned closer to his prince and said, "This is not our war."

"And when it becomes so?"

"Come. We need to go home. The outcome of this battle was decided before it even began. Time will come and pass and nothing Men or Elves do will stop it."

TWENTY-THREE
A Journey Ends

A light wind tickled Norgen's beard. He and Hallis stood together, arms folded across their chests and watching the distant riders. Two more days of hard pressed travel brought them almost full circle back to the King's Road. The game of cat and mouse with the Goblins had been a series of hits and misses. There were few casualties and nothing more.

Woodland gave way to rock strewn fields which eventually turned back into lightly forested hills. Hallis stopped the column, instructing Jin to set up a defensive perimeter before he and another rider went down into the valley. They already had one over strength company of Goblins hunting them and he wasn't about to be caught in a trap so close to Paedwyn. Most of the morning was gone before Hallis, Norgen and the boys left the protective circle of sentries and pickets to await Jin's return.

"A good sign," the dour Dwarf said. "Of course, we'd be able to hunt down them Goblins if they had more riders a coming."

Precisely what I'd do if not for the urgency of the times. "Unfortunately matters demand otherwise," Hallis replied. "Averon has greater need for trained soldiers. A company of Goblins is of small concern."

"At least there's one less Gnaal to trouble us," Delin beamed.

It took all their combined efforts to defeat the demon of Gren. They bonded that day, in an irrefutable fellowship of warriors since time began. Hope returned and the boys saw the light of the sun again. Even the recruits found a new life and hungered to reach Paedwyn and gain their revenge for the ones left in that cold, distant forest.

"Indeed. We owe you both a debt of gratitude. Were not for your sword and quick thinking we'd all be dead," Hallis said with a smile. "I like you Delin Kerny. My son was much as you are."

Fennic couldn't help but ask, "Where is he now?"

Hallis closed his eyes and his attitude turned sour. "He joined the army against my wishes and went to one of the Troll hunter companies. The last we heard of him was before his company was dispatched to the Thed Mountains north of Braem to put down a local uprising."

The looks in their eyes suggested naivety so he answered their unasked question.

"That was nigh on six years ago. Less than a score of men returned. None of them were in the same frame of mind as when they left. When my days of service end, I will go and learn what fate befell my son."

He was suddenly thankful for the closeness of the riders. The story was hard to tell and it pained him immeasurably with each telling. Jin reined to a halt a few meters away and dismounted.

"What news, Jin?" Hallis asked.

"Good news, Sergeant! The road ahead is clear all the way to Paedwyn. This is Corporal Storr. He's been sent as a guide to escort us in."

Storr nodded his greeting. His dark eyes widened upon seeing the Dwarf.

"Sergeant, I've been assigned to take you to the outpost at Dill Rock. There is a company of lancers awaiting you. The King has heard of your peril and wishes to speak with you once all is settled," Storr told them.

This was news for Hallis. He'd thought none but his own men knew of their plight from Alloenis. "Very well, young Storr." Hallis motioned for the last rider, an unknown boy from a small hamlet west of Alloenis. "Go back and tell Blaron to marshal the men and break camp. We are going to Paedwyn today."

"Yes sir," replied the boy before riding off.

"Tell me, Storr, what is this Dill Rock outpost? I've heard nothing of the capitol's defenses since returning to the flat lands," Hallis asked.

"High Commander Steleon thought it wise to place a series of outposts in a great circle around Paedwyn. He knows that Gren Mot cannot hold the enemy forever and the host has not assembled yet. The outposts are designed as an early warning device should the enemy flood the plains."

"You make it sound like the war is underway," Hallis replied.

Storr swallowed hard. "The fortress is sorely under siege."

"What? That can't be! Gren was nowhere close to attacking when I left."

"Sergeant, matters changed greatly over the last few weeks. We received a messenger from Gren demanding we surrender the fortress. King Maelor laughed at this and dismissed the messenger without a response. Gren Mot was already under attack."

Hallis thought of his friends and comrades fighting for their lives without him at their side. He was supposed to be there. Supposed to be standing the wall side by side with all of them.

"Fynten is a good man, but even he can't hold long," Jin broke in. Plenty of his friends were trapped in the mountain pass as well.

"What plans for relief does Steleon have?" Hallis asked.

Storr stood stone faced and cold. Like the professional soldier he was, he kept his emotions in check. "He's been instructed to build the host. Gren Mot will see no reinforcements for some time."

"There are over two thousand troops there. Does Steleon expect them to sacrifice so much?" he gasped in shock.

"He asks only what the king commands. When the host is ready we will march on Gren. King Maelor desires an end state with this long conflict."

Jin felt his heart sag. "What news from the front?"

"Messengers arrive daily. The enemy is still far from reaching our walls and a great number have fallen. But our own wounded flow back in an unending stream."

He didn't say what was next. He didn't need to. They all knew it was a hopeless mission. The rustle of men and equipment ended their conversation, which Hallis was most grateful for.

Blaron presented the troops with a wry smile and professional salute. "The column is formed, Sergeant. May we please go home now?"

"By all means," Hallis said with a smile. "By all means."

The younger Blaron turned towards the men and barked, "Forward... march!"

Horsemen and Dwarf at their head, Hallis led them down the long road to Paedwyn.

Roast meat and pheasant assaulted their senses. They'd spent the last few hours cleaning themselves and changing into their new uniforms of green and gold. Hallis and his band of companions commandeered a small building for themselves. They'd been told they were going to spend the night at Dill Rock. The rest of the company was quartered in the troop tents. The tents lacked heat, but everyone had a cot and blankets to themselves. More than the harshness the wild offered.

Cooks and the mess staff were busy chopping onions and carrots and peeling potatoes and turnips to throw into those big cast iron cauldrons for a healthy stew. Bread baked in the field ovens and the meats were near done cooking. Some of the poorer soldiers had never eaten so well.

Delin and Fennic got most of the attention once word of their heroics spread. The soldiers of Averon were trained for battle, but none had ever fought a Gnaal, much less defeated one. For those two young boys to accomplish such was unheard of. They were given the best spots around the fire and were the first in line to eat. Seconds and thirds were piled onto their plates. Fresh ale and beer was brought out by the keg, for a small celebration was underway. They were the first heroes of Averon's war.

Unsure of the newfound popularity he found himself sharing, Norgen acquired a pipe and a pouch of the best leaf in camp for a quiet smoke along the picket wall. Men were strange by Dwarf standards. He found no cause for celebration. There was no reason to drink and cheer. Battles needed to be fought and won. Friends were going to die, and others would return home a fragment of their former selves.

Norgen exhaled a thick plume of bluish smoke and was struck by a thought. Perhaps these men celebrated now because of uncertainty. There were never guarantees in war, this one especially. Such was the way of life. Perhaps they celebrated merely to keep the darkness from icing their hearts. He had to admit the idea was appealing, and there was a warped sense of reasoning about it, but a Dwarf could not partake so prematurely.

"What keeps your mind locked in struggle this fine night, Master Dwarf?" Hallis called from behind.

Norgen eyed him, instantly spying the mugs in his hands. He gratefully accepted one and drank deep.

"Your people have a stronger spine than we believed."

Hallis chuckled. "I'm not so sure that is always a good thing. More often than not it leads us down the wrong paths."

"As with all peoples," agreed the Dwarf. "I must admit that I didn't think Averon was going to be able to weather this storm. Those two boys have given me reason to rethink."

Hallis clapped a hand on the Dwarf's shoulder, which came as a surprise but Norgen said nothing.

"Wait until you gaze upon the glory of Paedwyn, my friend. Oh how your eyes will open," Hallis told him.

"Open spaces and towering buildings aren't to my liking, but I will see this city of yours on condition."

"Which would be?"

Norgen laughed. "That you return with me to Breilnor when this war is over. Kindness must be repaid. Once you look upon the wonders of the Dwarven kingdoms you'll find there is nothing comparable. Jewel lined walls rich in ore and treasure. Halls of majestic grandeur. There is a warmth inside, a warmth to keep your heart content until the end of days. You need come to Breilnor."

"When this is over I shall take you up on the offer," Hallis replied.

Mounted to the last man, Norgen included despite much fussing and protests, Hallis and his men began the last leg of their journey to Paedwyn. Many of the recruits suffered from the lack of sleep and hard days on the hunt. They were all anxious to go. Once Storr galloped to the head of the column, Hallis gave the signal to move out. He was eager to return to Paedwyn, and more importantly, his wife. She was the one person he admired above all else and she certainly deserved more than what he was giving her. Any soldier knew how hard it was balancing military and family life. His was no exception. Hallis was deathly afraid he'd devoted too much of his life to his brothers in arms and not her. He could only hope she understood.

Sunlight broke through the clouds, sending long streams across the land and crowning the distant mountaintops in golden halos. The horses seemed more spirited during their march. Songs were sung as the trials of just a day before were pushed towards the back of their minds.

"How much farther?" Fennic asked. Weeks of walking and now riding again after so long was beginning to take a toll on his rump.

Hallis tried his best to keep his laugh to himself. "Not much longer."

"Hmmph. He's been saying that all morning," Norgen growled. "I'm starting to think this city is all make believe."

Just then a large, blurred darkness came into view. Slowly, that blur found definition and that definition became precise until all could distinguish each majestic building from the next.

"Behold!" Storr called back to them. "The glory of Paedwyn!"

They turned their heads as one to gaze upon the throne of Averon and not a man was left unaffected.

TWENTY-FOUR
Paedwyn

There are moments in every man's life when his heart feels like bursting and his senses strain to comprehend. This was such a moment for Fennic and Delin. Neither had been able to close their mouths since the glory of Paedwyn emerged from the haze. Tall spires of white crowned in gold and silver reached up to the heavens as if to challenge the eternal beauty. Sunlight showered the city, punctuating the color and impressiveness. Fennic used to feel his imagination was limitless, but nothing in his dreams ever came close to this.

"You can close your mouths at any time," Hallis leaned over to them and said.

Delin almost giggled. "I can't help it. We've heard stories about the rest of Averon and how beautiful the king's city is but seeing it now I know no story can capture the true essence of it."

Jin and Storr shared a laugh at their naivety.

"Then you are in for a host of surprises," Jin told them. "There is enough to amaze you for the rest of your days inside those walls."

"Remember why we've come here," Hallis reminded. "Have many companies reported in, Storr?"

"Yours is the last to return from the west. I've no idea how many from the rest of the lands are here," Storr answered. "They say more than half of the host is assembled."

Clarions rang out across the plains and towered walls, announcing their arrival.

"Is that for us?" Fennic asked.

"Aye. Word travels fast among the army," Storr smiled back. "Couriers passed the word days ago. By now all Averon knows the Gnaal slayers have come to Paedwyn."

"Don't let it go to your head," cautioned Norgen. "Men have a tendency to forget great deeds as quickly as they occur."

Hallis nodded slowly. "Indeed we do, as must all races through the course of time."

"Sad but true," the Dwarf agreed. "It is the doom of mortality."

"Keep your heads high," Jin whispered down. "These people are expecting a band of heroes, not gawking country boys and grizzled old soldiers."

Hallis couldn't stop the smile from breaking through. "That's enough out of you, Jin. I don't know about you, but I'm not feeling very old today. Welcome to Paedwyn, friends."

Trumpets sang the moment the first rider entered the massive gates. Hundreds of citizens lined the way, eager to catch a glimpse at their reason for elation. Imperial guards keep the crowds back, while priests and clerics formed two ranks at the end of the main boulevard. Behind them sat the castle proper, separated from the city by a natural stream and long stone bridge. A ranking officer with dozens of decorations on his uniform strode out to greet them.

His raven black hair danced on the wind, covering his stern face from time to time. He wore a thick moustache and kept a beard close cropped. Well-developed muscles from years of hard work lay hidden beneath his armor. He was just past middle age and bore the scars of more than his share of battles. All in all, he was as formidable warrior as Averon had ever fielded.

A thin smiled wrinkled his face.

"Sergeant Hallis. It has been a long time," he said in a rustic voice.

"Longer than I can tell, High Commander," the veteran replied with a crisp salute.

Steleon eyed the cast assembled. "I was told of your deeds, but from the queer look of your companions I think some things were left out."

"Yes sir. The story is long and interesting to say the least."

Steleon laughed. "Then perhaps we need to hear it over a cold tankard of ale. I trust young Storr treated you well at Dill Rock?"

"As well as can be expected, sir," Jin answered.

"Good. I'll have my men escort you to your quarters so you can freshen up before your audience with the king. He is most anxious to meet you all."

Fennic caught himself staring wide eyed at the highest ranking man in the Averonian army. And now he was going to meet an actual king. He wished his family were here to share this moment with him. Sadly, they didn't even know where he was or even that he was still alive. All the victories and hardships suddenly felt empty. Meaningless.

"How fares the siege at Gren Mot?" Hallis asked after summoning up the courage.

A foul look came over Steleon. "I know it was hard for you to leave so abruptly. If you are to place blame then use me. The good of the kingdom is at stake and I feel safer with men like you here training our recruits. You've seen the enemy and can compensate for the lack of experience in other instructors. Most of whom haven't touched a sword in battle in years. I need you here."

Hallis was no fool. He listened to the way Steleon danced around the question until avoiding it altogether. A rash of bad and painful memories came back to him. He remembered standing side by side with a Colonel Steleon then at the battle of Elst, watching helplessly while hundreds of friends were captured and put to death. Steleon had saved him that day, but his life was never the same again. There seemed little doubt in the ancient mountain fortress. Hallis swallowed his fears and spurred his horse forward to the bridge. The heavy pounding of drums echoed through the crowded corridors of Paedwyn. Steleon mounted in one fluid motion and led the procession into the castle. Children tossed dried wildflowers into the streets, smiling and cheering the column as it passed.

Trumpets and horns played Averon's anthem. Hallis and the others returned the smiles in kind and waved until their arms grew tired. Only Norgen remained motionless. Dwarves, he argued for the thousandth time, did not ride horses. The insult was nearly overlooked by the shock of him sitting atop the enormous beast. Compared to the relative smooth ride of the Centaur, the horse was turning his stomach on end.

"How much longer afore I can move about on my own two feet the way the gods intended?" he scowled.

Jin clapped his back lightly so as not to throw him off. "Fear not, Master Dwarf. These people are as shocked to see you riding a horse as you are to be on one. We'll be inside the castle soon enough. Try and enjoy this, for it happens but once in a life."

"I'm glad you find my plight so amusing," Norgen growled.

Delin and Fennic snickered from behind.

The last man rode into the heart of the castle and the crowds dispersed, though they were reluctant to do so. Folks knew there would be rare times for such excitement in the coming months. The company rode through the smaller buildings in the castle grounds until they came unto the enormous compound of the royal army. Steleon turned the company over to the ferriers and stable boys. He left a pair of guides to escort them to their guest chambers before returning to his office on the second floor of the army headquarters.

Companies of recruits sparred with wooden blades under the instructor's watchful eyes on the main training field next to the stable. Would be archers loosed shaft after shaft into bails of hail from a hundred paces. The distant thunder of hooves announced the training of new cavalrymen. Pike men danced with quarter staffs. Fennic found it all alluring, for he desperately wanted to learn how to use Phaelor before going through with his plan to enter Gren. He and Delin had spent hours learning and developing the basic movements and techniques needed to keep them alive, but it wasn't enough. Far more knowledgeable from when they left Fel Darrins, they still had much to learn if they were going to survive the coming storm.

"Patience, young ones," Hallis quietly told them after noticing their looks of longing. "You'll be forced to become warriors soon enough. Let things develop on their own accord."

Fennic pretended to agree. He'd told no one yet of his intentions, not even dear old Delin. Marching into Gren and slaying the Silver Mage was his secret for now. Death was almost a foregone conclusion, and he wasn't willing to let his friends, new or old, share the same fate.

"I for one wouldn't mind a go at one of those pikes," Delin broke in. "Arrows are well and fine, but what happens when the quiver's empty?"

"Are all the folk of your village so stubborn?" Hallis asked.

Delin laughed. "Only the ones old enough to talk."

"Come, I've been looking forward to using the baths for weeks and don't intend on being the last in line," urged Hallis. If there was one thing he couldn't stand it was a bath of cold and dirty water.

Together, with Norgen and Jin, they left the others under the guidance of their soon to be instructors and headed for the baths. The water was a great luxury and unlike anything either boy had ever known. Days of toil and sweat were washed away in what seemed like long hours. After only a half an hour, they dried off, dressed and headed for the mess hall. Evening was closing in on them as Norgen finally arrived.

Just then Delin spied a commotion to the east and a rising cloud of dust. A herald soon followed and summoned all able bodied men to the courtyards. A great wagon train was fast approaching the compound. Palace guards marched out to secure the main boulevard.

"What's going on?" Delin asked.

Hallis sat quiet, painstakingly watching the train wind closer. The sheer size of it could mean but one thing. He felt his heart fall.

"Wounded, and a lot of them. From Gren Mot most likely," Jin replied. He too was quiet and sick to the stomach. "This does not bode well."

"I'm going down to meet them," Hallis announced and left before they could stop him.

One by one they followed. They found Steleon standing at the front of the reception. Glancing their way, he offered a dispassionate look and said nothing. Fennic started to speak but Norgen cut him off.

"Careful lad," he whispered. "Tis an ill omen we see. That many wounded means their commander has given up hope of defending the fortress. It won't be much longer before they are overrun."

"Why can't they leave and fight again?" Delin asked, confused.

Norgen shot him a stern look. "Would you? How many will die if that army comes down from the mountains? They are buying time with their lives."

"Indeed they are, Master Dwarf," Steleon murmured. "And their gift is more precious than a thousand gems. We have much to prepare for, else their bravery be in vain."

The vanguard of escort riders rode up, halting their spent horses and saluting the High Commander. Each bore expressions of defeat. Their armor was scored and stained black from blood and flame. All had some sort of wound. Their beards were wild and unkempt, and their eyes stared in to forever.

"What news from Commander Fynten?" asked Steleon.

The lead rider wiped his parched lips. "Dire news, sir. The enemy has advanced to the walls and will make their move within the week. Fynten believes he has yet some time. Their casualties range in the thousands and still they attack."

Wagons were rolling up.

"We all fought bravely, sir, but they keep coming. It's as if their numbers are endless," he went on.

Steleon watched and waited for each wagon to go by. Wounded were jammed into them, some stacked atop each other. The smell of blood and death turned the air rank.

"How many are in this train?" Steleon asked.

"A hundred by seven and fifty."

Steleon paled. *Seven hundred and fifty men out of over the original two thousand and some will not see the dawn. Fynten is paying a higher toll than I would ask.* Norgen cast his hood over his head out of respect. War had truly come to Averon at last. Fennic and Delin stood aghast. They refused to believe what they were seeing. Averon was the most powerful kingdom in the land and a fifth of its army was in the process of being destroyed. What hope did the world have?

The rider saluted again and pressed, "Sir, my men and I request to return to Gren Mot and stand the watch."

Steleon's smile was sad and proud. "I admire your courage, Captain Crespith, but I cannot afford to sacrifice more of my cavalry. I need you here, son."

Crespith hung his head, fat tears stinging his eyes. "I understand."

The High Commander grasped Crespith's calf. "I know your pain. I've known it from the moment we received word the enemy was moving. But there is much to be done if we are to save Averon. The attack will soon be upon us and I have need of every asset I can get. You've seen them. You know their composition and strength. What you've seen may well help us win and put an end to the evil in Gren forever. Will you help me here?"

Crespith stiffened. He had a newfound purpose in life. The pain of abandoning his comrades would never heal, but at least he had the chance to take revenge."

"It will be an honor, sir," he said with authority.

"Good. Report to my office in the morning so we can begin planning. In the meantime, I suggest you see to your men. No doubt they are alone and confused as well. Good night, Captain." Steleon saluted the man and dismissed him.

"Men like him are the future of this kingdom, mayhap the world," he went on to say. "Would that I had ten thousand more."

Hallis agreed. "Perhaps you do. Look at the recruits I brought in. They were ambushed, forced to watch their friends die and not a one broke ranks and ran home. They've killed and been killed without any formal military training. War is a fickle thing. These two boys from a village unknown to most managed to kill a Gnaal single handedly. I think all of them have the hearts of lions."

"We'll see soon enough, I'm afraid. I need to make my report to the king. Fortunate your dinner was postponed until the morrow," Steleon said while walking away.

They watched the saddened warriors for a while longer until each had had enough. More than a few of the wounded spoke with Hallis along the march. He offered what encouragement he could. Their pain slowly shifted to him. Fortunately, Jin saw what was happening and intervened.

"I think we can all use a good drink. The boys included," he announced, motioning towards Delin and Fennic with a smile. "Anyone who can kill a Gnaal is good enough to share ale with me any day."

"Here, here," Delin said with a sparkle in his eye. "It's been a long time since I enjoyed myself."

Jin put his arms around their shoulders and said, "Then come and let me show you how we enjoy the night here in Paedwyn! First round is on me."

The last brought Norgen from his silence. "Now you're talking. Let me show you how a Dwarf drinks!"

Laughing all the way to the tavern door, they bragged and joked through the packed streets. Once inside the tavern the merriment continued. Their mirth quickly spread through the room until all inside pushed the misery of the day behind and found cause to laugh. Jin and Norgen bragged so much they eagerly joined in a drinking game. Soon a large assortment of empty mugs crowded the table.

"I hope they've enough barrels out back to keep this going," Delin said, a line of foam bubbles on his upper lip.

"Mind your tongue, young one," Norgen slurred. "This lad has far to go afore he can best one of the Dwarven warriors in mere ale."

Jin laughed. "The night is still young."

Norgen snorted. "Just don't be heaving on my boots."

The tavern broke into laughter and the night went on. True enough, Jin soon ran from the room and emptied his stomach on the cobblestone streets. Norgen roared in victory and announced the next round was on him. The tavern cheered.

TWENTY-FIVE
Home

Hallis didn't have the taste for drinking. Sticking to water, the old soldier watched over the others, finally escorting them back to their chambers. Norgen wound up carrying Fennic over his shoulder. He'd drunk himself to sleep after but four mugs. Jin and Delin stumbled on with each other's help. Only the Dwarf displayed none of the effects of drunkenness. Hallis made a mental note to never challenge him to a drinking contest.

After closing the door on the last of his friends, Hallis went to his own room and went to bed. He was up and moving well before the dawn. The thought of so many of his friends coming in with the wounded weighed heavily on his mind. They deserved his visit, if for naught but morale. He wasn't surprised to run in to Steleon heading in the same direction. They exchanged a few words, but it was clear each had his own agenda for the day. Steleon soon was out of sight, leaving Hallis on his way alone.

The hospital was almost more than he was willing to face up to. There was a strong and fetid smell coating the halls and it took his very nerve. Healers and surgeons moved around him, ignoring him as much as possible. His was the one clean uniform in the building. There was a room to the right filled with bodies under white, stained sheets. Hallis wondered how many were once his friends.

"Can I help you, Sergeant?" a surgeon finally asked.

"These used to be my men."

The surgeon paused. "Were you there?"

"No. I was transferred before the fighting began."

"It's a difficult thing, leaving friends behind," he replied. "We normally don't allow healthy soldiers in here, but I'll look the other way so long as you keep things quiet."

"Agreed," Hallis said.

He walked through dozens of wounded, not caring if he knew them or not. They were all soldiers of Averon and he was a noncommissioned officer, a leader. Hallis stopped and tried to offer encouragement to all he spoke with. Some responded in kind, telling him how brave the defense was. Hallis occasionally came across one who knew a friend of his and they talked for long moments. That's when he learned of the deaths of more than a few friends.

He was halfway through the ward when a familiar voice called out his name. Hallis turned and found himself staring back at Flyn Arthen. He smiled and reached out to clasp hands. Then he noticed the dark bandages wrapped around the stump of Flyn's arm. Flyn caught the pause and tried to make the best of it.

"Like it? I lost it three days after you left. Goblin arrows went through during a patrol. Shattered the bone and started to turn a little gangrenous. Docs thought it best to hack it off before it wound up killing me," Flyn said with a wry grin.

"You never did have much sense."

"Bah. The hardest part to get used to is still feeling it from time to time."

Even the normally stern Hallis couldn't keep back a laugh. They walked to a quieter part of the hospital.

"How goes the fight?" Hallis asked.

Flyn sighed and shook his head. "Not good. They reached the last of the outer defenses when Fynten sent the wounded away. It wouldn't have been so bad if we had some time to relax between assaults. But they keep coming. Walking over their dead and wounded without a second thought. We thought it was discipline when our catapults pummeled their ranks and they didn't break. But that discipline was nothing more than pure savagery. We could hear them at night, eating their dead. I pray Fynten can hold out," Flyn finished. "What of Crespith and his lancers? Did they go back to the pass?"

"Steleon wouldn't let them. I think he's going to use them to build the defenses around Paedwyn. Still, we cannot stand without aid."

Flyn snorted. "I may not be able to use a bow no more, but I can still skewer my share of Goblins. We can win, Hallis."

Hallis gently patted his shoulder. "Ah the luxuries of being young and single. I wish I were so fortunate."

"Speaking of which, how is your wife these days?"

Again the flashing smile. "Lonely, I imagine. Years of me being gone and our son missing must be eating her away. I wish these were simpler times so I might learn what a marriage is supposed to be."

"Sadly enough, we cannot choose the times we live in. but I do think we can help ourselves along a bit. You don't need to be here with all this death and a crippled soldier, Hallis. Go to your wife and make up for all those years you've been apart."

The aging veteran was speechless. "There's no way I can thank you."

"For what?" Flyn snorted. "Make someone else happy, Hallis. We'll be fine here."

They embraced as friends and Hallis walked out of the hospital. His step was quick and slightly nervous. Flyn's last word to him opened his eyes to a piece of his life he'd been missing for too long. Chella was the only woman he ever found capable of handling his love and absence without so much as a frown. She never complained to him once in all those times he'd been told to go away on king's business. In that regard, she was a much better person than he ever hoped to be.

Finally, after months in the Gren Mountains and more scouring Averon for fresh recruits, he reached his home. Knocking on the door wasn't necessary, but he felt wrong for not doing it. He was, in effect, a stranger to his own home. Hallis knocked. The door slowly swung open after a time, for it was still early. His heart skipped when her sleep absorbed face first came in to view. She was still the most beautiful woman he had ever seen.

She wore her black and white stripped housecoat. Her golden hair had streaks of grey in it and was tied back in a ponytail. She had almond colored eyes and lightly tanned skin. Changing as her hair was, there wasn't an extra wrinkle on her. Tears welled in her eyes when she looked upon her caller.

"Hallis, my love," she whispered and rushed into his tender embrace.

That was all it took for him to cry too. They stood locked in each other's arms for a long time. Neither spoke, for doing so would have broken the spell. When at last they separated, she looked upon him with tear soaked eyes.

"They told me you went back to the fortress when the wagons came in. I was sure you were with them. I... I didn't want to believe," she choked.

He smiled deeply at her. "I've been safe the whole time, love. They sent me off to do some recruiting in Alloenis. Nothing out of the ordinary happens that way."

He wanted to ask her how she managed not to hear of his most recent exploits but thought the better of it. She probably did know but was too proud to spoil his tale. Chella was always like that. Satisfied he was safe and home for the time being, Chella grabbed his hand and led him back to the bedroom. It was a long while before they fell asleep in each other's arms.

"Chella, I wasn't completely telling the truth about being in Alloenis," he admitted in the early afternoon after both had the chance to bathe and eat a hearty meal.

She stared at him with a mischievous twinkle in her eyes. "I always thought that a relationship was built on trust. Maybe I was wrong all along."

Hallis ignored the jibe and began telling the strange tale of his trek from the west. Even he found parts of it hard to believe, occasionally omitting a minor detail. Chella sat mesmerized through the telling, for though she'd heard bits and pieces from her friends and neighbors already, no one told it quite like Hallis. She loved listening to his voice, always had. It soothed her more than any one thing should. Every word reminded her why she fell in love with him all those years ago.

Chella stood and kissed his forehead when he finally finished. "Ah love, I sometimes wish we had a normal life where you stayed home and served my every whim."

He smiled at her with sad eyes. "I know, and I would change if I could. But I've always been a soldier. I'm afraid I shall be for some time yet to come."

She kissed him again. "Nor will I ever ask you to change who you are. I love you for you, Hallis. Promise me you'll come home to me when this is all said and done."

"I promise," he whispered and closed his eyes.

Chella kissed the top of his head once more and said, "Come, let's go back to bed, my love."

King Maelor sat behind the ancient oak table trying to concentrate on the speakers on the floor and staying awake at the same time. He was hardly middle aged and his hair had already turned white. He had a light build with gaunt features. His eyes were a pale blue and rimmed in red. He wore a soldier's uniform without rank or decoration. The gold sash over his left breast told all who he was. And for the moment, he was tired.

"Sire, there is still time to send reinforcements. Our lancers report the enemy has yet to breach the walls," said a tall, thin man in purple robes.

Another in shining yellow with a long blonde beard stood up next. "As you know, the walls are thrice as tall as a Mountain Troll and just as thick. T'would take a dragon to break them down and no dragons have been seen in this part of the world in decades."

Maelor closed his eyes and pinched the bridge of his nose. "How long would it take to organize a massive relief force and deploy them to the fortress? Gentlemen, do any of you truly believe we have that much time?"

"A least a fortnight, sire," the man in purple resigned.

Two weeks. "Though I have no doubts in Fynten's ability, I cannot foresee arriving in time to help."

Maelor pushed his chair back and stood. A portrait of his father was behind the simple desk and they seemed as twins. Many said he was the striking image of King Baeleon.

"The Silver Mage is as cunning as he is wicked. We know not how large his armies are or what the grand intent of this invasion is. He could easily be sending another army up through Antheneon in the south with the hopes of catching us unawares while we are focused on the mountain pass. Any relief I send will only weaken Averon," he told them. His voice was strong and uplifting.

"I will not leave the people, who make this kingdom, exposed to the horrors of Gren. If there's a battle to be fought in the lowlands, it will be at a place of my choosing. Gren Mot will fall, of that I have no doubts. Fynten and his men are buying time for us and we're going to use it. Prepare the army to move."

"Move to where, sire?" Steleon asked. He'd been silent through the discussion until now. Battle was his arena, not politics and scheming.

"We make our stand on the Thorn River. Let them come across and be slaughtered," the king commanded with a wicked grin.

"And if we fail?" the man in yellow gaped.

Maelor shot him a foul glare. "Then we fail knowing there was nothing more to be done."

Steleon concealed his smile. He'd never cared for the king's advisors. They plotted and fast talked their way through situations for their own gain and often lost sight of the people.

"What news of Harlegor, sire?" Steleon asked. With the riders of Harlegor, his armies might have a chance.

Maelor shook his head. "I have heard nothing since the messengers were dispatched."

They had been sent almost three months ago, Steleon remembered. Long before Gren made their opening move. Though he knew little of Harlegor's monarchy, Steleon had been more than confident that the Steward was an honorable man and would stand the line with them. Surely the Silver Mage wasn't going to stop with Averon. And if he went deeper, the smaller kingdoms wouldn't last long alone.

"I do not like the way this is playing out," Maelor confided. "We lack the power to control our own destiny. The Silver Mage holds all the cards."

"There is hope yet, sire. We have the Gnaal slayers among us now," Steleon said.

Maelor thought on this. "If we had more capable of such I'd rest easier at night. Do we know how two boys, children, managed to slay the dark creature?"

"I've been looking into it. It appears that young Master Attleford's blade glowed a golden hue in the battle."

"There is only one sword I have heard of with that type of power. But I thought it was a myth?"

"Apparently not. If all accounts are correct, Fennic holds the Star Silver Sword." Steleon bowed and left the chamber, along with the pompous advisors. Maelor looked up at the image of his father and prayed for the same strength. Courage he had aplenty, as did his brave warriors, but was courage alone enough to stave the tide of darkness? If the Silver Mage managed victory, Averon would topple and become an extension of Gren. He couldn't let that happen. Couldn't let thousands of innocents suffer the fate of the Mage by failing. Sadly, his people had unending questions of the future, and he had no answers.

TWENTY-SIX
Unlikely Heroes

Seamstresses visited them one by one, carefully measuring each from top to bottom. When asked why, they merely laughed and asked what their favorite color was. Delin gave up and went along with them, surmising that they were going to be subjected to the whims of the court for the duration of their stay in Paedwyn. Norgen sat with folded arms and his natural scowl slightly deeper. Jin watched the taciturn Dwarf from across the room and found it all quite humorous.

"Your scowl is quite becoming. Will you be wearing it when you appear before the king this eve?" he joked.

Norgen halfheartedly threw the last of his apple at the soldier. "I did not travel all this way for pomp and ceremony. My own king I could have seen if I wanted to sign and dance like a puppet."

"I've never seen a Dwarf dance," Fennic laughed.

Norgen growled. "Nor will you tonight."

"Come, come," Jin said. "You are about to be in the presence of royalty. You don't want King Maelor thinking your kind uncouth, do you?"

"Enjoy this while you can," Blaron said upon entering the room. "There will be little enough time for pleasantries as this in the near future. Myself, I'm looking forward to this evening. Just imagine all those ladies in elegant gowns just begging for a handsome man to dance with. My future wife might be there!"

In the company of kings and warriors, Fennic found himself thinking, if only my parents might see me now. Who would ever believe it?

Their nerves were on edge, butterflies knotting their stomachs, by the time the royal page arrived to escort them to the grand dining hall. Jin, Blaron and Hallis were all dressed in their formal uniforms, complete with ornamental sabers at the right hip. Impressive as they were, Norgen and the boys held their own. The Dwarf wore a jeweled vest with black breeks and newly made boots tipped in silver. He had a gemstone band around the middle of his beard. Dark blue was Delin's color, from his silk shirt to his pants with yellow stripes running down the out seam. Fennic was in similar garb, though his was of forest green and lacking the stripes.

Hallis made the comment of them looking like little princes and both blushed. Murmurs spread through the crowds. Some swore they were a stately delegation come to aid in the war. Minor lords and ladies lined the gilded halls of the castle in all forms of finery and pretty. Noble born knights flanked the main doors, swords drawn and raised in tribute to the passing heroes. The boys walked wide eyed in amazement.

Applause greeted them. Hallis waved back at the throngs of onlookers and followed the page to the head table. He hadn't expected to sit so close to the king. All the tables were draped in gold trimmed white clothes. Baskets of fresh bread were placed every two seats. There were crystal glasses filled with fine wines and carefully crafted ceramic plates and Elf made silverware. A roaring fire behind the head table warmed the hall. Huge candlelit chandeliers hung from the ceiling in a great star pattern.

"All this is for us?" Fennic asked the page.

The boy nodded. "In your names, yes. It has been a long time since the king had the cause to celebrate this way. He should be in splendid spirits."

Delin asked, "What do you say to a king?"

"Same as any other man, just say sire a lot," Norgen said.

The arriving crowds cut the conversation short as the hall quickly filled. Men and women took their seats without missing a word. Fennic found most of them rude and obnoxious, unlike folk back home. He guessed they were too accustomed to not having to do anything for themselves. Either way, Fennic decided he wanted nothing to do with any of them.

The truth was he hadn't been comfortable since their stay in Alloenis. He was no judge of civilization or the intricate trappings of society, but he knew what he didn't care for. Men were too willing to cheat and steal from each other. Thieves and con artists were as common as cows and sheep back home. He hoped the king was a better man than the representation of his court. Even the knights were purely for display. They were the remnants of the old ducal system not used in hundreds of years. Not since the Mage War. Fennic didn't know it, but knights had fought or held a position of military power since the rise of Maelor. They could hold their titles out of respect and a family history of service to the land.

"My lords and ladies, please take your seats. His highness will be arriving shortly," an old man in royal livery announced.

"Isn't this exciting?" Fennic asked Norgen.

The Dwarf, already pulling his chair closer to the table, said, "I find it drawn out and unnecessary. Give me the quiet fire in a broken down inn and I'll not complain."

"He has a point," Jin said. "It's been a long time since I had to wear this uniform. The collar is chaffing me!"

Hallis said, "Settle down. Every nobleman in Paedwyn is watching."

"Can we just go back to the barracks and be soldiers again?"

The veteran sergeant rubbed his chin but said nothing. Every chair and table in the hall was filled. The people were a rainbow of colors and jewels. Chatter was quiet to a low roar, much to Norgen's relief. Platters of vegetables and greens were brought out before the main course. Roast elk and boar, pheasants and duck came next, filling the hall with a hearty aroma.

"Sure makes all those cold meals in the rain and snow worth it, doesn't it?" Jin asked.

"Actually it makes me wonder why I wanted to leave home," Delin answered.

Fennic kept his mouth shut.

Again rang the horn and the hall fell silent.

"The sovereign ruler of the lands and peoples of Averon, King Maelor, the First."

The audience rose as one, facing the center of the hall to watch Maelor enter. Royal guardsmen pushed the stained wooden doors open and marched to the head table. Maelor wasted no time in following. He was as hungry as the rest and anxious to meet the band of heroes. The crown of Averon sat atop his head for one of those few times he needed it. He wore dark green trousers and a frost white shirt. His demeanor and presence suggested royalty and natural leadership. His boots echoed across the marble floor as he made his way to his place. A young boy pulled his chair back and Maelor offered him a warm smile.

"Honored guests, nobles, and dear friends, I thank you for gracing this hall. Dark times have fallen upon us and the sun still shines. Sitting with me tonight are the ones responsible for destroying two companies of Goblins and a Gnaal ravaging our lands. Their selfless service and loyalty to the throne have ensured to me that we will not fall under evil's spell. Their duty reflects great credit upon themselves and the name of all we stand for. At this time I wish to award them all with the Order of Turnin."

Those gathered let out a collective gasp. Years had passed since the last time the highest military award in the land was passed out. Named for the first king of Averon, the Order of Turnin signified the ultimate heroism. Hallis felt his mouth drop open.

Decorated all, the feast began. Conversations started and stopped between mouthfuls of food. Maelor left an hour later and again all rose until the doors closed behind him. It didn't take long before Hallis and company decided to follow his lead.

The same page returned and told them, "Gentlemen, King Maelor wishes you join him in his private study once you've finished. I shall await you outside the door." He bowed and stepped away.

"Will wonders never cease," Jin exclaimed.

Blaron rubbed his bloated stomach. "I'd rather join the men if it's all the same to you, Sergeant."

"Go ahead. I think the five of us will be more than enough to keep his majesty occupied," Hallis consented. "Looks like you have to wear your uniform a while longer, Jin."

True to his word, the page bowed again and led them through an impossible maze of hallways and corridors. Getting lost proved a simple task. Statues on marble pedestals lined the walls between doors and paintings. Hallis explained some of the work to them, though history was never his strong suit. He was a simple man from a small farming community, much like Fennic and Delin. Hard times led him to the army and there he remained. Come to think of it, farming was never the life for him.

"His majesty will see you now," the king's chamberlain said once they arrived at a pair of massive marble doors. He guided them into the study where Maelor patiently read from a high back chair close to the fire.

Those pale blue eyes settled on his heroes with a measure of warmth.

"My father built this kingdom off lies and deceit. He stole it from his brother who was a wicked man with a fell heart. It took time to turn Averon into a respected land and now I am her steward. Am I to be the last of my line? Sometimes I wonder if all I've managed to do was get a lot of people killed," he told them.

"Sire, our friends are not dying for no reason," Hallis said in a low voice. "I wish that were true. I fear the Silver Mage is too powerful to be stopped."

"Tonight you praised us for killing one of the demons of legend," Norgen said in a stern voice. "If this was possible, so is defeating the Silver Mage. I am Norgen of Breilnor. My lord wishes to send aid based on my recommendations. I have seen the best and worst of man in the past and wanted no part of your wars. These two boys showed me the error of my thinking. They put their lives on the line without any thought of themselves. They are the reason you will prevail."

Maelor eyed the Dwarf carefully, soaking up every word. Finally he said, "There is a tale here for the telling and I would hear all of it. Leave no detail out."

The story lasted well over two hours and Maelor learned much. He felt hope rising with the telling and even dared to chance a peek at victory.

When the last man fell silent, Maelor went to a well-crafted wooden cabinet and brought out two large bottles of dark red wine. Pouring them each a hearty glass, he toasted them all.

"To the future."

"The future," they echoed.

"I sometimes wish I weren't king," he admitted after a moment of silence. "I know I was born to be king, but I was never asked what I wanted. Life is unfair that way. My father was a great man, yet I never knew him as a father." He turned to look at the boys. "I envy you. You've lived a real childhood and spent years with friends and family, played in the forests of your youth. All this is but a dream to me. Perhaps one day I will find a wife and have children to live my life through.

"When this war is done and Gren lies in defeat, I will journey to this little village of yours. I wish to see how life is meant to be lived. But until then, we must focus on the war. Fennic Attleford, this sword of yours bears great interest. If it's what I'm thinking, you may well be the salvation of the land. Is it truly the Star Silver Sword of legend?"

Fennic swallowed hard. "So I've been told, sire. I was chosen by Phaelor and warned by Old Man Wiffe. It appears Fate has decided my life, much as it has done for you."

"I cannot ask this of you, but I dearly wish that golden sword to march with army and lend hope. I fancy even the Silver Mage may turn away from its power," Maelor quietly admitted. "The sight alone would do much for morale."

"As I said earlier, sire, Phaelor decides when and where it must be. I will join the fight if it wants me too," Fennic said.

Maelor rose, feeling unexplainably rejuvenated. He stood tall and proud. The mid of night was already past and he had much to think on before the sun rose. Bidding them all a good night, Maelor closed the door to his study and stared out the window overlooking his sleeping kingdom. He only wished he knew what was happening at Gren Mot and if Fynten was still fighting.

TWENTY-SEVEN
Surprise

League after league of rolling hills and endless plains stretched on day and night until Tarren hadn't a clue to where she was. They might have been traveling in circles for all she knew. The pony kept a steady pace through the journey, confident in direction and purpose. Sunrise followed sunset. There hadn't been a storm in over a week though the skies darkened on several occasions. By luck or fate, the ill wind passed them by.

Always there was the pony. He never missed a step or stopped swishing his long tail. He'd stop so she could relieve herself and snatch a bite to eat. She found him considerate to her needs and always willing to listen. Odd as it seemed, Tarren took comfort in the pony. The simple things started to relax her. The way his ears flipped every time she laughed. How he made a light gallop across an open field.

Tarren prided herself on her ability to take care of herself and her family. For what it was worth, few of those skills mattered out here in the wild. None of her independence or social skills was of use this deep in the countryside. She knew in her heart that she already would have given up and gone home if not for the pony. More often than not she cried herself to sleep.

"I wish I had an idea where we are," she confided after a light snack of berries and cheese. "Everything looks the same to me. Oh, this would be so much easier if you talked."

Loneliness was setting in despite her best efforts to keep occupied. There was only so much one could do alone before the nerves frazzled. The more she thought about it, the worse her plan to sweep in and rescue her love sounded.

Tarren reached up and scratched behind the pony's ear. "Just once I'd like to hear a voice other than my own."

Those deep brown eyes stared back at her, stirring forgotten emotions. He snorted as if to say that all was going to turn out fine. Trust in me and I'll make sure no harm befalls you, the pony stared back. For reasons she didn't understand, and would spend many long nights pondering over the course of her life, Tarren felt her fears dissipate. The sun was high and shining, warming the world. The pony snorted again and nuzzled against her palm. Tarren smiled and packed the meager camp.

She found she wasn't as sore as she had been. The first week had been so horrible she often had trouble falling asleep and the next morning even worse. Her muscles felt tight and abused every time she opened her eyes. She was sure Gnomes came upon her in her sleep and pounded her with their tiny hammers while she slept. She was finally getting past that and used to the road.

The day went fast, much faster than she liked. Shadows crept back across the world soon enough, turning parts of the landscape into an eerie winter land, unsafe for human wanderings. A sharp cracking noise from the nearby tree line made her turn in fright. Moving shadows played with her vision. They taunted her into believing an army of Goblins were closing. The pony kept on without so much as slowing. Once she thought she saw a bear in the forest. It was huge and a dark shimmering black.

The pony eventually came to a stop just past sundown. Again Tarren felt calmed. If there was anything out there capable of doing them harm, she couldn't tell. The pony stood guard over her until she fell asleep.

Her eyes flew open sometime after midnight. A tiny sliver of light was shining down, adding to the haunting quality she'd grown accustomed to. A quick look around the camp confirmed her fears. She was alone. The pony was nowhere to be seen. That's when she heard soft voices coming from a clearing not far away. Chill winds danced across the plains and sent shivers down her spine. Tarren gathered her cloak about her and crept closer to the noise. She knew she needed to be careful yet something in the back of her mind reminded her she was safe. Still, Tarren was cautious and careful not to reveal herself lest the voices belong to the enemy. She settled behind the bole of a large beech tree and listened.

"The ways are not safe," argued a strong voice. "My people are few but we kill Goblins when we find them. I would not trust to follow the paths and trails with a civilian among us."

"You offer more security than I can and you know the terrain. Take her to Ipn Shal and wait for me."

"Were you not a wizard I'd dismiss this conversation," said the first man. "What you ask is difficult. The war with Gren is spreading. We're finding more and more Goblins and other fell creatures. I fear for us all."

"As do I," said the second. "Which is precisely why I need you to escort her to the ruins. I must go east to aid in Averon's defense. They will soon be hard pressed to hold their ground."

"How deep run the armies of the Mage?"

There was an overlong pause. "More than any has seen before."

A horse balked in fear.

The first man spoke again, a much darker tone lacing his vice. "Can we survive?"

"There are many forces at work now. Good and evil are but two. A seer may show us how this war will end, but I rather enjoy how things naturally happen. Gives me a purpose for being, after all."

Tarren caught a light laugh.

"I don't share your views, wizard, but I can understand where your heart is. Your kind and mine are slowly fading from the world. All the magic from the ancient world is being replaced by newer and more powerful forces. I would like to say that I feel the same, but my heart warns otherwise. If Averon falls the western countries are doomed."

The wizard clapped a hand on his friend's shoulder. "There may yet be hope."

"Not without all the races coming together. It is a fight we cannot win otherwise."

"Head to head, I agree. Our hope lay in a select few already chosen to champion the free world. Throw in a wily old Mage and a few tokens of power and our chances seem quite remarkable."

She heard another laugh, from a third man.

"You have a way with words. I hope to sit and drink with you for many hours when this is finished."

"So you'll take the girl?"

"What are your plans?"

Tarren heard the reluctance in his voice, and almost stepped into the clearing to confront them. She immediately understood they referenced how best to deal with her, like she was some sort of chattel. She didn't like being talked about, especially without being given a voice for her own opinions.

"I'm going to bring the walls of Aingaard down around Sidian's head. Take her to the ruins of Ipn Shal and await my return. Spirits willing, the tide of this foul war will shift to our favor."

"Do your chosen few know who they are yet?"

The wizard shook his head. "No, but they have already come together. They've fought and bled as one. Always a good way to start the bonding process for such an adventure."

"I hope they manage to survive long enough for your purposes, wizard. How well do you think they'll handle traveling into the dark land?"

"Not so well as a Goblin, perhaps, but one has already made up his mind. Free choice is what we fight for and that is a powerful enemy to contend with."

"A journey into Gren is hard regardless. When do you want us to claim the girl?"

"Claim is such a terrible word. Almost fitting of Gren. Come in the morning after breakfast. None of us like to travel on an empty stomach."

The first man laughed. "You do look as though you've lost a few pounds."

"Nuts and berries are hardly enough to sustain a man of my stature. I need a healthy plate of meat and potatoes before I starve away."

"In the morning then. We will be there to escort your young friend to the keep. Farewell wizard."

Hoof beats told Tarren the meeting was over so she scurried back to the campsite. The pony still wasn't back, and she hadn't the slightest idea where he was. She wanted to worry, but there were too many things happening for that. She didn't know who was coming to get her or who was trying to get rid of her. Too many unknowns lurked in the night for her liking. Tarren clutched the small dagger she'd brought from home to her chest and told herself she was going to stay awake through the night.

She was asleep in five minutes.

Winter doves cooed from the treetops, unconcerned with what was playing out on the ground. Six men rode into the campsite, most with their weapons at the ready and scanning for signs of the enemy. Spear tips rose above their heads, gleaming in the early light. Each wore long hair in tight braids, held back by golden braids with different colored gemstones embedded in them.

"She likes to sleep late," one of them smirked.

A crow cawed. Tarren stirred from the sound but didn't wake.

"I don't like the feel of this."

The lead rider eased closer to the sleeping girl.

"Wake her. The Goblins are closer than yesterday and I want to be away before they discover us."

Tarren clutched her dagger tighter and listened to everything they said. Of a sudden she jumped up and aimed her dagger at the heart of the nearest man. Her eyes flew wide at the strange sight looking back at her. Half man and half horse, they stood in a loose semi-circle.

"You have no need of that with us, young lady. We are all friends here," the leader told her.

Tarren recognized his voice from last night. And the dagger stayed where it was.

"Who are you?" she demanded. "I'm not going anywhere until you explain what's going on. Goblins be damned."

"I like her already," the Centaur with the dagger aimed at his chest smiled.

"Enough, Beal. We don't have the time for this. I am Ris Kaverling and my brothers and I have been assigned to protect you for as long as we are able."

As much as she was looking forward to speaking to another person, Tarren wasn't about to drop her guard just because a mythical beast told her he was going to keep her safe. She thought of Delin and Fennic and wondered where they were, or even if they were all on the same paths. If she went the wrong way, she might never find her love again.

"Well, Ris Kaverling, I have no need of your assistance and no desire to go to this Ipn Shal," she said forcefully.

Ris cocked an eyebrow. "How did you know that?"

"I heard you last night. You and that wizard. I don't know who you think you are, but I'll not be carried away from my course."

Ris eased forward. "Your life is precisely the reason we've come. There is great danger coming towards us. We need to be gone before the Goblins arrive. Tarren, please. Listen to me. I have given my word to a friend that no harm shall befall you while I draw breath. Would you have that trust shattered for childish fears?"

"A promise made without my consent. I am my own woman. This wizard friend, whom I never met, holds no sway over me, nor do you and your kin. Go away and let me about my business."

He admired Tarren's independence, but this was no time for stubbornness. His life was at risk right with hers. A change of tactics was required.

"Very well, Tarren Brickton. I shall leave you, though I warn you that your life is in forfeit soon. Goblins have been hunting you for weeks now. They won't stop until they catch you. They'll come on you when you least expect and steal you away to their dark master in the land of Gren. But the choice is yours, as you so kindly remind us. I leave you now."

She suddenly wasn't so sure. The Centaur appeared likable enough, and he did have concerns for her well-being. Still, she and the pony had done well enough on their own. If only he was here now. Come to think of it, Tarren hadn't seen him since she went to sleep the night before.

A dark bearded Centaur came galloping into the campsite, a cloud of dust chasing him. A half empty quiver was strapped over his leather jerkin. Dark blood stained his powerful flank.

"Goblins," he hissed in warning.

Ris walked to his friend. "What happened?"

"They came upon me from the south, though I do not believe they knew I was there. I killed five and fled. They are numbered well over a hundred and heading this way fast. I tried to lose them, but they are driven."

Strong as his band was, Ris knew they were no match for a force so large. He turned to Tarren and asked, "Well, Ms. Brickton, what shall it be? I cannot protect you like this."

A deep horn bellowed through the trees. The Goblins had come.

TWENTY-EIGHT
Hunted

The sound of the horn was enough to strike fear through Tarren's soul. She'd never heard such a vile and demanding sound. And now that she had, never wanted to again. Confused and alone, she wanted her pony back more than anything. Tarren could hear the Goblins now. The clank and rustle of armor and mail running through the trees coming to kill her.

"Decide quickly," Ris demanded. "Time has left us."

His brothers formed a solid line, arrows smoothly knocked. Their sharp eyes watched the trees in anticipation. At least six more Goblins were going to die before this was done. Tarren reached a hand out to her appointed guardian.

"I accept," she politely said with a trace of fear in her words.

Ris effortlessly pulled her on his back. "The company is much appreciated. We ride."

A series of successive thrums told her the first salvo was away. Several grunts followed and then heavy crashes. Tarren knew someone was dying. Six more arrows sped true. Ris whistled and they turned and fled. Goblins broke into the open with axes and cudgels waving menacingly overhead.

Tarren risked a glance back. Her fears were realized at the sight of them. She'd never seen a Goblin before. Their stout, gray bodies stunk of malice and waste. Wicked teeth poked up and down, too large to fit in their mouths. Tarren felt hatred seething from their looks. She buried her face into the Centaur's strong back and didn't look back. The gap quickly widened.

She guessed they ran nonstop for close to an hour. The smell of sweat and energy mingled as one, at once revolting and intoxicating. Ris finally held up his arm and the company slowed to a trot. For Tarren, there was no going back. Her fate was solely in their hands now. Ris let her off so she could catch her breath. Her legs felt wobbly and her heart was pounding. It was the first time she'd been in danger of losing her life. Two of the Centaurs doubled back and disappeared. Tarren knew nothing of warfare or tactics but was smart enough to figure out the pair were searching for signs of pursuit. Her stomach growled. She'd forgotten they hadn't eaten yet, and it was nigh on midday. She blushed when she noticed Ris smiling down at her. He wordlessly handed her a pack with some old bread and the last bit of cheese.

"What now?" she asked between bites.

Ris stretched his arms. "Providing the way is clear, we start the trek to Ipn Shal. Winter isn't far off and I'd as soon get there before the snows come. The way is perilous enough in good weather."

"What is this Ipn Shal place? I've never heard of it before," she admitted.

"It was once the fortress home of the order of Mages. Those born with the talent came from all parts of Malweir to learn and develop their crafts. Life was simpler back then. The Mages worked in concert to better all races," he told her.

She stared at him wide eyed. "You can't be that old? We've heard stories about the Mages and how long ago the world fell into war. That must have been a hundred years ago."

"Almost two hundred," he said. "And no, I was nowhere close to being born. My grandsire lived through those times and passed down what he was forced to endure. I think that will be the only thing to save us. Our understanding of the past."

"It is said the Silver Mage first learned the dark arts and slowly subjugated others to his fell cause deep in the underbelly of the fortress. A great war arose between good and evil, and the world took sides. Many of the Mages were killed in a single night and Ipn Shal came down around them. That was the beginning of the dark times. Today the keep is all but a forgotten ruin in an abandoned part of the land."

"Have you ever been there?"

Tarren had always been fascinated by the lore and lure of magic and the grand age of magery. She often imagined herself in flowing robes and gowns of the finest silks as she danced across marbled floors in grand ballrooms. It was an alien concept, her living in a small town practically no one had heard of. Ris saw the dreamy look in her eyes and it warmed him. There was so much violence and mayhem in the world her brand of innocence was reassuring.

"Once," he replied. "The landscape is inhospitable now. Ruined by magic and warped beyond sustaining life. There are several abandoned towns along the way. They say the people fled during the war. Now nothing is safe. Everything north of Thuil Lake was destroyed by the Mages. The ground is broken and unstable. Much of it is hardened rock, sharp and jagged. There is no vegetation anymore and the very water was turned to sulfur. The last livable town is called Braem. Fair enough as far as men go, but I will not set foot within its boundaries. That will be our last chance for getting supplies and good sleep before we reach the ruins."

He tossed the apple core he was nibbling on away and continued. "The people of Braem seem friendly enough, but our races have never been comfortable with each other."

Tarren didn't know what to think. She was lost. Goblins and Mages. Centaurs and wars of unimaginable devastation. It was almost too much for her. Life was a simple thing, only she was suddenly finding out differently. She finished her meager meal and thanked him politely. It was then she realized there was no turning back. Delin and Fennic were going to have to wait. Destiny had chosen her for a different task.

"How long will it take to reach Braem?" she asked him and thus resigned herself to the present course.

"Four days if I reckon right. I'm not too familiar with this part of Averon but we're far enough north of Alloenis to give me a good idea. Braem will be there regardless of when we arrive. We need to concern ourselves with the Goblins and other foul creatures in league with Gren."

"I'm not so sure I like the sound of that," she confided.

Ris sympathized with her. "Goblins are spread across the continent and beyond. Those behind us have been blooded and will not stop easily. They will kill us or we them. It is the way of things. Fear not, we will keep you safe.'

Part of her felt defeated by the bleak prospects of tomorrow. "Tell me, why does this wizard care so much for me? I've never met him."

"He may well be our strongest hope for success against the dark. As I'm sure you overheard last night," he said with a grin. "He has many names in different lands, but I only know him as Dakeb."

The scouts returned then, storming back into the loose perimeter. Vinz took his time to catch his breath and report.

"They are coming. A league, maybe more away, but they do not stop to rest," he said.

Ris scowled. He'd been hoping for a longer rest. "That gives us less than an hour. We need to get moving. Tell the others we leave in five minutes."

Adrenalin eased through her veins again. She really didn't want to see another Goblin. Fate had other ideas.

"Feel like going for a ride?" Ris halfheartedly asked.

She already knew there was no choice. Staying meant death. Tarren accepted his hand and resumed her place on his back. And the tiny band was away. He tried to belay her suspicions of Goblins tracking them all the way to the ruins. He had a few tricks left to play and Goblins weren't overly bright.

The game of cat and mouse went on for the next three days. Ris and his friends ran hard and managed to put good distance between them and the enemy. It gave them enough time to eat and relax before moving again. He sent two teams of two out each night before dusk to sneak upon the enemy and reduce their numbers. And each night they returned with positive results. Another twenty Goblins fell to their cunning, but the war band was much too strong to face head on. Tarren and Ris became friends during those long rides. Their conversations ranged from the simple smell of the golden dragon flower to the first war against the Silver Mage. She found herself liking the Centaur more and more as the time sped. She finally found someone to talk to and decided to make the most of it.

Another two days went by, with the band of Centaurs zigzagging across the endless plains. More Goblins died and the gap between them steadily widened. Ris assured her he knew where he was and that Braem was near. She had no choice but to accept it. They crossed many tracks along the way. Most were normal forest animals and wildlife yet some were intensely puzzling. Booted feet and heavily weighted. Ris had no explanation. His mood darkened and he insisted they proceeded with extreme caution. Something about the type and frequency of the tracks disturbed him. The Goblins must have noticed as much too, for they pulled back into the shadows of the foothills just east of the Sibit River and remained.

Twilight fell upon them, bringing winter one day closer. Ris halted at the top of a small rise overlooking a quaint town.

"Braem," he announced. "You should enter tomorrow morning. The dark is always dangerous regardless of the where. You'll be safe enough with us in the meantime."

"But still no fire or a hot meal," she teased.

Ris tossed his head back. They'd had no fire since joining company. Goblins had an excellent sense of night vision and smell. Fire and roasting meat were more than enough to draw the attention of even a lone Goblin.

"No. No meat. It looks like another night of berries and dried deer meat. We don't want to take unnecessary chances."

Her stomach growled at the thought of having to eat more of the bland travel rations. Tarren settled down for another cold night.

TWENTY-NINE
Gren Mot Falls

Thunder roared so loud it trembled the ground and blasted the Gren Mountains. Men and beasts felt the awesome power and knew fear. Soldiers scrambled to their positions atop the walls of the beleaguered fortress in alarm. The thunder wasn't natural. Another attack had begun.

Fynten emerged from his chambers, naked from the waist up and sword in hand. His eyes were half closed from sleep. Days of constant battle sapped his strength until he found himself at the edge of his stamina. Last night was the first time he'd managed uninterrupted sleep since the siege began. Thousands of enemy soldiers lay dead and rotting on the fetid battlefield. So many, that the defenders of the mountain pass felt sure Gren would not attack again so soon.

The stench of death was fierce. Soldiers heaved their stomachs over the battered walls from the intensity of the carnage. The army of Gren didn't care. They trampled their dead under foot, crushing them into an expensive highway from the wicked kingdom. Ever so slowly the defenders were pushed back towards their last lines of defense. Time was almost up.

"What's happening?" Fynten demanded from a young soldier rushing past.

"We're… we're under attack, sir."

Fynten regarded the boy with a sour look. He'd already guessed as much, but then again, most of his men had never seen such reckless slaughter. The commander of the fading fortress of Gren Mot ducked back into his meager quarters long enough to don a tunic and armor. Dents and blood stains had ruined the once magnificent shine. It was like so much his world had become. The old veteran headed towards the sound of fighting.

"Commander Fynten! You need to get to the tower at once!" Surnish shouted after running into him in a darkened hall.

Thunder rocked the castle foundations. The roar was deafening.

"What in the world was that?" Fynten asked.

Surnish shrugged. "I don't know. The others are already in the command post waiting."

Grim stares met him when they entered the tower. He knew at once this was the final assault. His mind went over recent events and Fynten was glad he'd made some of the decisions he had. He'd sent Melgit and his surviving cavalry back to Paedwyn days prior. He knew that they were next to useless in this kind of warfare and King Maelor would have need of the chargers in the coming war. Melgit, of course, sputtered and fumed at being dismissed, but in the end the long column of riders left the fort. Jeurle, his eyes bloodshot, merely shook his head in frustration. He was on the verge of tears.

"Report."

Captain Wiln saluted and said, "This has been going on for the past hour. None of the lookouts have seen anything, but that means nothing considering the heavy cloud cover. I suspect another trick from the Mage."

Again the thunder boomed, followed closely by a large shadow sailing overhead.

"Dear gods," Prelin whispered.

Fynten stepped forward to reinforce his command and take their minds from the horror about to be unleashed upon them.

"Archers and infantry to the walls. I want every bow in this fortress ready to use. Surnish, I need those two remaining catapults primed and ready. Jeurle, provide back up. I don't need to tell any of you that this is going to be rough. But always remember that no matter what happens here this day we are the defenders of our country and our people. Go with the Gods, my friends."

The older Surnish was about to answer when a fifty meter section of the inner wall erupted in flame. Burning men fell, screaming. A dark shadow raced overhead again, carrying with it the acrid smell of sulfur and acid. Fynten felt his heart fall. A dragon! A handful of arrows sped into the sky in reply, but the commander knew it was a futile gesture. The shadow wheeled about and bore down on the tower.

"Everyone down!" Fynten screamed.

The heat washed over them first, blistering their flesh inside their armor. Fynten's last sight was a thick wall of flame rushing towards him. If he screamed, no one heard it.

Columns of smoke funneled into the early morn. Gray skies and heavy clouds threatened snow. The smell of burnt flesh filled the mountain pass. Vultures perched atop the jagged crags waiting for the living to depart so the feast could begin. Drumming pounded through the pass, dominating the snarls and curses of the hundred Goblins trying to tear down the gates. Ladders and scaling ropes were already covering the walls, allowing hundreds of Goblins and Men of Gren to enter the fallen keep. Those few survivors from the dragon attack were no match for the bloodthirsty enemy. A great cheer erupted when at last the mighty stone gates came crashing to the ground in a storm of dust and rock. Captains and sergeants reformed their companies to enter Gren Mot. Now nothing stood between them and the richness of Averon.

A lean man with the hungry features of a wolf elbowed through the throngs, pushing his way to the very front ranks. Goblin and Man alike bowed and gave him a wide berth. The man had doom in his eyes. Few knew him by name, though his dark reputation ran rampant through the armies. He was the incarnate of evil itself.

"Lord Hoole, the keep has fallen. We now control the pass," a blood-stained Goblin snarled.

Jervis Hoole's eyes lit up. Born a poor farm boy who decided to join the army the day his parents were killed, his ruthlessness and barbarism were of a special sort that propelled him through the ranks. He was twice decorated by the Silver Mage for his actions in battle. Man, woman, and child alike fell beneath his steel and he held no regrets. Life was suffering, plain and simple.

He wore a wolf skin cloak over a wool jerkin and leather breeks. There was no trace of fat on his body. Long years of war and sacrifice made him lean. Scars and burn marks covered most of his upper body. They served as a constant reminder of his personal weaknesses and overcome ordeals.

"Is it?" he asked in a wicked voice. "Then why do I still hear the sounds of fighting inside?"

The Goblin hesitated to answer.

"I want all survivors brought alive to the main yard. Do not kill another unless I order it." he commanded.

The Goblin stepped back. "But my troops."

"Are expendable," Hoole spat. "Never once believe the life of your kind is half as valuable as a man. I want those prisoners alive."

Hoole stalked across the charred battleground relishing the smell and visual torments before him. The lone attack of the dragon managed more damage than his entire army in over three years of skirmishes and battle with the enemy. He wished he could control such power and greatness once before he died. Hoole stared at ancient Gren Mot and laughed. The walls held a power beyond his comprehension. Built when the mountains were still young, Gren Mot was fashioned from the living stone. A part of the world died today and he was here to see it.

Even in desolation, Gren Mot remained impressive. Ornate stone buttresses arched over a hundred feet in the air. Broken gargoyles and other statues of half-forgotten heroes graced the overhangs and courtyards. Jervis Hoole stared in awe at the still pristine statue of a tall warrior striding forward, sword raised in challenge. The artist captured the life of it. It showed a frosted muscle tone and the anguish of knowing too much war. It wore the helm and body armor of ancient Gren, before the Silver Mage. Hoole felt a stirring deep inside.

"The prisoners have been collected as you ordered," the Goblin returned to report. "What do we do now?"

Hoole ignored the contempt in his voice. "Line them up. Segregate the officers and senior sergeants."

The Silver Mage's orders were clear. It was Hoole's job to ensure they were carried out. Once the fortress was entirely pacified his armies could focus on their own dead. This was more important. He considered clearing his army from the pass and letting the dragon fly by and burn the corpses of his dead. It would be far easier in the long run. But that would clue King Maelor too soon.

The line of battered prisoners was escorted into the rubble strewn yard amidst the howls and cheers of the conquering Trolls and Goblins. Hoole watched the fear in their eyes. Averon was a lazy land, consumed by its own sloth and lack of vision. The Silver Mage was going to take back everything they'd stolen from Gren and it began here.

Hoole held up his hand and silence settled.

"Soldiers of Averon, you have been found guilty of taking up arms against the great nation of Gren, murdering her people and contaminating the world with your heathenism. There can be but one sentence for such crimes. You are hereby sentenced to spend the remainder of your days as slaves for the Silver Mage."

He watched as a near broken captain stepped forward. Wiln was close to death, a goodly portion of his body burned from the dragon's breath. His right arm was broken. Despite all this, he remained defiant.

"Averon will never bow," he said, and spat at his captors.

A thin smile split Hoole's face. Goblins drew their swords and readied to attack. "Indeed," he replied. "Though I fear you won't live to find out."

Hoole nodded and his Goblins swarmed over Wiln, hacking him into pieces. Satisfied, Jervis Hoole walked up to few survivors and snatched the youngest by the collar. He dragged the boy next to Wiln's corpse and shoved his face in the gore.

"Go back to your king, boy. Tell him what you saw and what awaits. Tell him what fate is coming for Averon and then find a place to hide. You will die the next time I see you."

A whip cracked and the frightened boy took off running. Laughter followed. "Put the rest in chains and take them to Aingaard," Hoole ordered.

Having seen enough, Hoole turned towards the lands of his mortal enemies and sneered. *Soon, soon your day will come.*

THIRTY
Gloom and Allies

The night life Paedwyn offered went beyond anything either of the boys imagined. They were used to the lone tavern in a simple town where half the population crowded inside once a week to sing songs and talk. Paedwyn, on the other hand, held over a hundred thousand people, not to mention several army regiments and the headquarters.

The city seemed to stretch forever. Taverns, inns, gambling halls, and all manner of entertainment were available in every direction. Theaters and circuses drew throngs of people daily and there was never a lack of stories waiting to be told. Actors and playwrights came from the world over to study and apprentice with the masters. Music was played with the most basic of instruments to a degree unsurpassed in all Malweir. The streets of Paedwyn were every youth's dream.

Yet along with the lighthearted mirth there came a darker underside most public administrators were reluctant to admit. Pickpockets and murderers, waiting for the unsuspecting drunkard stumbling into a dark alley, hid in the shadows. Civic patrols discovered and removed bodies of the less fortunate. Everyone from the king down knew of the troubles and no measure of control had been effective. It was reasoned that such would always happen in high concentrations of people. Even so, Maelor wanted it to end. Delin and Fennic had been here just over a week and were still enamored with the capitol city. Norgen was often with them in their daily wanderings. Tonight however, they found themselves alone in the inn of the Dragon Tail. Two mugs of hot cider sat before them.

Delin rubbed the beard he'd started growing. He had a rue smile on his face.

"What's so funny?" Fennic asked. "I haven't seen you laugh in a long time."

There was a sparkle in his eye. "What do you suppose they're doing right now?"

"What who are doing?"

"Our families. I've been thinking about them for a bit. This is the time of year my mom starts baking her pumpkin pies. Dad comes home with a fresh killed stag.

Friends and family come over for the feast. I miss them, Fennic."

Fennic Attleford stretched a reassuring hand to his best friend. "I miss them too. Part of me wishes I never took the sword, but Phaelor is pulling me. Forcing me in the direction it needs to go. I know what needs to be done but

148

I'm afraid. All our dreams of seeing the world and having adventures used to sound so good. Now look where we are."

"In the middle of a war," Delin replied. "I haven't seen Hallis in a few days. I wonder what he's up to. With all those Gnaals and Goblins roaming the wilds I shouldn't doubt he's out there somewhere."

Delin paused long enough to finish his cider and order another. They'd run out of the money they brought from Fel Darrins a long time ago but were handsomely rewarded by the treasury of the king for their actions in the name of Averon. They were now also in the employ of Maelor. He'd named them heroes and given them the station according to such. The king treated them as if they were his own sons.

"I can think of another smile I want to see again," Delin admitted with a blush.

It was Fennic's turn to smile. "And does she have a name?"

"Who said anything about a she?" Delin protested. "You know full well who it is."

Fennic grew jealous of his friend. True love was a fickle thing and always eluded him, despite his best efforts. It just didn't seem fair that Delin would fall so hopelessly in love and he was left with nothing but a cold pillow on long winter nights. Still, Fennic knew love would find him in its own due time. At least that's what his father often said. Right now, he wasn't so sure.

He watched the way Delin and Tarren looked at each other and it burned a hole in his heart. Now, with Phaelor in his life, Fennic was beginning to doubt the future. He'd been with a girl only once and neither of them really understood what they were doing. Her father found out about it and forbade him from ever seeing her again. Fennic was hurt, but not as much as by seeing his friends shamelessly holding hands and walking through town.

"Aside from you," Delin said, "Tarren is my only friend."

"I'm sure she's working in the tavern hoping you're all right. You should send her a dispatch," Fennic suggested. He was anxious to change the subject.

Delin snorted. "I would but I don't think anyone here has even heard of Fel Darrins."

"I'm thinking that is a good thing about now," Fennic replied.

The tavern door burst open, followed by the rush of cold winds and a light flurry of snow. The Dwarf had become such a familiar sight few patrons bothered to pay attention. Both boys were glad to see Norgen again. The Dwarf's beady eyes narrowed as he sought out his two friends. He wasn't smiling. Picking his way through the crowd, Norgen finally sat down with them and motioned for a barmaid.

"What's wrong?" Fennic asked. Phaelor burned lightly against his thigh.

"There's a column of several hundred horsemen heading this way. Hallis wants us to join him," the Dwarf said in a hushed growl.

Delin's heart froze. "Are they enemy?"

"No. The Silver Mage doesn't look fondly on cavalry. They ride from the east. Finish your drinks and let's go."

"I think I lost the stomach for it," Fennic said.

Norgen shrugged. "Suit yourself. I want you both to remember one thing during the coming months. Do not neglect yourselves during this war, be it for food or sleep. Your strength is all you have."

Fennic reluctantly finished his cider and followed them out into the chill night. A pair of women in heavy, dirty cloaks stood waiting by the door with inviting looks. One was old and well past her prime while the other was especially young. Norgen forced the group briskly by. No one on the streets was even aware of the coming riders. Norgen feared the worst. He had a good idea where they were coming from but wasn't about to be the one to incite a panic in the city. Times were hard enough with the threat of war and a harsh winter coming on.

They found Hallis waiting on horseback just on the near side of the Geise Bridge. His look told them the worst. Disaster had come to the mountain fortress. Norgen led them to the spare mounts.

"We must hurry," the sergeant said. "Steleon wants all key personnel with him when they reach the city."

"What happened?" Delin asked.

"It is not my place to say."

They rode at a goodly pace, past the eastern gates and out to a makeshift camp halfway to the river. Steleon and a handful of commanders were already pacing and developing battle strategies inside a large green tent trimmed in gold. Sentries and infantrymen patrolled the general area. Fennic half expected to see the entourage of the king.

Hallis dismounted and entered the tent.

Steleon looked up and nodded. "I apologize for the sudden summons, but war often follows its own schedule," he told the boys. "Border scouts reported a large body of riders coming from the direction of the Gren Mountains. All indications are they belong to us, which means the worst for Fynten. We've received no word in some time and the trains of wounded all but stopped coming. Four hundred horsemen can only mean ill."

Fennic swallowed hard. "But wouldn't that mean there's no hope left to defend the mountains? Fynten and all those men...."

"Are as good as dead," Steleon finished grimly. "We must look to the defense of the lowlands now. We are all that is left standing between Paedwyn and the Silver Mage."

"Is there any news from Harlegor?" Hallis asked.

"None."

"Our list of allies grows thinner," Norgen said. He gently tugged on his beard. "This will be a dark winter."

Steleon nodded. "Winter is the one thing we have going for us. The mountains are a formidable place, even in summer. The passes are slick and treacherous in the winter months. Not even the Mage can delay the seasons. He has less than a month before the snows set in. If we can hold him until then we just might have a chance."

Delin and Fennic exchanged doubtful looks. There were too many ifs in the plan. What little they knew of war came from firsthand experience and that was a matter of Fate. Or so Hallis once told them. He said a good general can plan until his hair turns gray and it would do little good. Plans tended to go awry once the first arrow flew. Hopefully the Silver Mage was going to be a product of his own cunning.

"Riders are approaching!"

Steleon spun, his bear skin cloak twirling in the torchlight. "Arms! Prepare for battle!"

"I thought they were friendly?" Delin asked Hallis.

Soldiers marched into battle lines. The clamor of steel on steel echoed on the still night air.

"Be they friend or foe, we can ill afford to be caught with our guard down. A handful could be ours, while the rest might easily be imposters hoping to sneak in and wreak havoc. The enemy is crafty so we must keep our vigil."

Delin was confused. "But Goblins don't look anything like us."

"You forget, Master Kerny," Norgen cautioned, "the Silver Mage has more than Goblins under his spell. Many tribes and lands of men have fallen to his will. They now willingly serve his dark cause."

"I wish I never left home," Fennic whispered. "Life was so much simpler."

"Simple or not, we would still be at war and your precious Fel Darrins would be in even greater danger, for no one would have any knowledge of the coming horror," Hallis tried to reassure them. "You being here is a testament to all the hamlets and villes the people of Paedwyn have never known. You and the Star Silver sword have the chance to shape the outcome of the war and that is no small task. None of us know what will happen tomorrow or the week after. We can merely react to the events of the moment. Hold your heads high for you have rightly been named heroes of the realm."

Fennic felt a stirring in his heart, similar to when he first touched Phaelor. He pushed aside the dread thoughts of war and tried to focus on a better world. The world he was fighting to preserve. He still wasn't sure it was a good idea to tell the others of his intent on going into Gren. They'd do their best to talk him out of it, not seeing what was really happening. Sadly, Phaelor controlled destiny and that of the free world. What choice did Fennic really have?

A cold breeze danced over the half frozen plain. The men shivered and their teeth chattered noisily. Delin immediately found winter to be a horrible time for a war. Then a great commotion in the west arose and stole his dreams of heat and warmth. The riders had arrived.

Steleon and Hallis stood shoulder to shoulder as the first ranks came into sight. The old veterans were surprised to see Melgit at the head of the formation. Steleon had always taken Melgit as a man who never retreated. Seeing him now meant certain doom for the garrison at Gren Mot. Fatigue oozing from every pore, Melgit rode up to his commander and saluted. His shoulders were slumped and there was a new hollowness in his eyes. The siege had taken a heavy toll on him and his men. His armor was blackened and battered, and blood stained his equipment.

"Commander," Melgit bowed in the saddle.

"How many did you bring back?" Steleon asked. He already knew the fate of the others.

"Just over four hundred. I lost ten on the way home and the rest in battle." His voice lacked its usual edge. Delin stood in awe of this grizzled warrior and knew it would not be the last time he would be in such a presence.

"All our tricks worked and we reaped a terrible toll," the cavalryman continued. "The enemy lost many thousands and still they advanced. Fynten ordered us to fall back to defend Paedwyn once the last outer defense line was breeched. Thousands more fell before we were forced back inside the walls."

He let out an involuntary shudder. "They marched over their dead without care. I've never seen the like. They had an army of Trolls bringing great siege machines. The Silver Mage isn't going to stop until the western world lies at his feet. I fear for the kingdom."

It was then he noticed the two boys and their Dwarven ally.

"Have the Dwarves come at last?" he asked in shock and hope.

"Master Norgen is an envoy for his people," Hallis said. "They will come."

Norgen remained silent.

THIRTY-ONE
Forced Plans

There was a tiny sliver of moon out by the time Hallis finished bedding down Melgit's men. All four hundred began caring for their mounts before seeing to their own needs. Though he wasn't much for horses, Hallis admired the cavalrymen's dedication to their partners. Slowly the troopers gathered around the growing fires to shake off the chill and share a bite to eat before heading off to sleep. Melgit and his commanders went into Steleon's command tent.

The tent smelled of pipe smoke and oil. Detailed maps of the Gren Mountains and eastern Averon lay sprawled across the tabletops. Additional tactical maps hung from one of the walls. Steleon was already making this his home. Fresh brewed coffee was brought in, much their appreciation. Outside, the noise was dying down. The camp was going back to sleep.

"I'm glad you made it out of there," Steleon told his friend. *You'll be sorely needed soon enough.*

"It wasn't my decision," Melgit replied with a dour look. "Fynten and I fought for two days over this. His logic finally won. Besides, my forces are better suited to the open plain. We would have been all but worthless cooped up in that fortress. Still, leaving them behind was the hardest thing I have ever done."

No one spoke for long moments.

"I had every intention of going back to their aid. We even took our time moving through the pass. At the base of the mountains we made a hasty camp and began planning. Three days later young Graeme here stumbled into our sentries. My story ends there. Graeme, please tell them what you told me."

Graeme was young in every sense of the word. He sat humbled in the presence of the army's senior commanders and was at a loss for words.

Steleon sensed his hesitation and did his best to ease the youth's nerves. "Forget that I am your superior right now. Think of me as a friend and brother."

The boy took a deep calming breath and began. He stopped more than once to wipe a stream of tears from his eyes as the horrible memories came rushing back. When he finally finished, he had a steeled look to him. Part of him wanted revenge for his friends. Steleon politely excused himself and stumbled outside. He was an emotional wreck. His heart bled for those poor men burned alive and their families. So many friends had been recklessly slaughtered. Dragons were near invincible, but none had been seen in years. That Sidian held one under his sway was an ill omen for Averon. His mind slowly drifted away to past conversations with his friend and peer.

Fynten was being groomed for one of the top positions in the army. He was by far Averon's best and most able field commander. And now he was dead. All Steleon's friends were dead. He couldn't help but feel like he sent them to their deaths. What hope was there now?

Summing up his courage, Steleon went back inside and joined Hallis next to the fire. "How are we going to survive this?" he asked suddenly.

Hallis was staring off into the long reaching darkness. "With men like Graeme. He has fight in him."

"And Fennic and Delin," Steleon added.

"Yes sir."

He clapped his hand on Hallis' shoulder and nodded. "I hope you're right. Now come, we have a war to plan."

Steleon turned to those assembled and said, "Gentlemen, tomorrow I ride back to Paedwyn to inform the king. Melgit, your men stay here for the moment, but I need you to come with me. You and young Master Graeme. The army will deploy to the banks of the Thorn River and make our stand there. Every available man will move in three days. I think the Silver Mage will consolidate his forces before moving on the lowlands.

"Begin the defenses immediately. Fynten was a good friend and I will not let his death be in vain. Whether Harlegor, Antheneon, or the Dwarves come to our aid or not, we will make a war more terrible than Sidian's darkest nightmares. There will be no retreat. The very life of Averon depends on our actions. Our war starts today."

"Sir, I wish to remain here," Hallis announced. "I should have been there with my friends. It's the least I can do to stand the watch now."

There was a gleam in Steleon's eye. "I may have to promote you if you keep this up. Master Graeme, I offer you the chance to go home to your family. After what you've endured, I believe you have done more than your share. Go home and live a good life."

"It would dishonor what they died for, sir," Graeme said with all the courage he could muster. "I'd like to stay until the Mage is defeated."

Steleon took heart from his words. "Very well. You are hereby ordered to spend the next week with you family. I can't see the enemy arriving before then. Report back to Captain Melgit or myself. You're going to serve as my aide for the duration of the war. Now go and get some rest. You have a date with the king tomorrow."

Fighting back a smile, Graeme saluted and left.

"Take care of that one, Melgit. He's a good lad," Steleon said.

"I'll treat him like my own son," the cavalryman proudly said.

Fennic's sudden yawn reminded them all the hour and provided enough motivation for them to wrap up their discussions and head to bed. Emotions were heavy and many a man wept himself to sleep. Nine hundred friends had paid a horrible price for them and there was revenge to be had.

Hard winds whipped through the city streets, howling around every corner. No one strayed outside unless they absolutely had to. Winter crept closer with a heavy hand. Pasty gray clouds filled the skies, threatening heavy snows. The very air was thick and menacing. Winter promised to be especially cruel this year. Atop the tower where his private study was, King Maelor felt a hundred years older than the day prior. Steleon had returned at midday with a small compliment of men and news of their defeat. It wasn't entirely unexpected, though Maelor had hoped they would hold out longer. Averon wasn't ready to fight a full-blown war yet.

"A dragon," he whispered, hardly believing his own words. "What chance have we against a dragon? Gren Mot was ancient, carved from the spine of the world. Paedwyn was hand built over the course of a decade. This dragon of his will send us all to ruin and slavery."

Steleon stood quietly contemplating the future. He'd been over all this information before. "Sire, it isn't inconceivable to kill one of the wyrms."

"I admire your determination, but we must face reality. Averon is finally at war. Send out heralds to every hamlet, city, and village. Have them encourage all single men of fighting age to come and make the stand. I think married men would appreciate being left alone to care for their loved ones before the end."

"Do you truly believe our fate is already sealed?" asked Steleon. Simply accepting defeat was too hard for him to swallow. "Remember young Graeme."

"Our fate," Maelor began, "is under extreme distress. The next month is going to see the future revealed. As much as I'd like to see the heroism of this boy, all I can see is a prisoner set free to deliver a message."

Neither spoke for a long while. The prospect of living under the cruel hand of Gren was all too real. Generations of growth and society threatened to be destroyed under a rain of fire. The Silver Mage was too powerful. Unless... Maelor shook his head. No. His allies were not coming. He wondered why the other kings and stewards couldn't see it. Averon was but the first target. Then would fall Antheneon and Harlegor. The Elves were all but memories and the Dwarves were forgotten in their dark caverns.

Maelor suddenly remembered days when he'd play and pretend to beat back hordes of Goblins in the name of justice and right. Those were innocent times, now long lost. He wondered how his father managed to balance peace and war after the brief civil war in which he assumed power. Now he feared he wouldn't get the chance to find out.

"Tell me your plans," the king finally said.

"Word has already gone out to the army to head for the banks of the Thorn River. Hopefully we can be in position and ready to defend before the armies of the Silver Mage come down from the mountains."

Maelor raised an eyebrow. "How long can we realistically hold them on the eastern bank?"

"Sire, we have fifteen thousand men, with more coming daily. I believe I can hold them at the river for the duration of the winter," Steleon answered confidently.

The king wasn't so sure. He liked his commander but doubted his confidence in this matter. Of course, Steleon hadn't told him everything. He hadn't told him how many able troops Gren was throwing at them. Hadn't told him their barbarous intent and the nature of the man who led her armies.

"Let us hope the river doesn't freeze," Maelor said. "Though I'm sure you have something in place to counter that."

"Naturally," the charismatic warrior said with a sly smile. "They may get a few battalions across, but no Trolls or heavy siege machines. Make no mistake, Sire, this will be a costly war. Tens of thousands will die regardless of the outcome."

Maelor moved to his window and stared out at his kingdom. The world was coming down on him and he was powerless to prevent it. A thousand men must have stood in the same situation during various points of time, there was nothing special about him. The only difference he found was that he knew it. He was just another in a long history of men. No one would remember his name in a thousand years. This was the deciding point in his life. There wasn't much he could do to prevent it or affect the outcome. The thought of his people dead and his great city in ruins ached his heart greatly.

"Very well. Move the army. Take as many as you need," he finally conceded. "I don't want word of the disaster at Gren Mot circulating. Panic is going to hurt us more than the invading army. This is a delicate time. One mishap and our world is lost."

Steleon had no reply.

Outside, the wind howled even harder.

"I fear it may not be soon enough," Melgit replied.

THIRTY-TWO
Waiting for the Shadow

Word of the invasion spread much quicker than Maelor had hoped. Wagons laden with household possessions streamed past Paedwyn day and night. The poorer families walked while the richer ones enjoyed the fruits of their wealth. No one wanted to be anywhere near the capital when the enemy arrived. Emissaries and scouts from Gren were already moving through the lowlands spreading word of the impending doom. The people started to panic.

Merchants and traders stopped in Paedwyn on their trek westward, spreading rumors and creating an overall commotion in the city. Maelor ensured that word of the war was passed down to every street and alley; giving people time to decide their course of action. The fall of Gren Mot and Sidian's dragon were ominously left out.

Army units mobilized and a long cycle of deployments began. Winding columns of cavalry and infantry passed from the garrison to the east. Locals and passersby stopped to watch the brave men march off to their deaths. The soldiers held their heads high and sang battle songs to lift their spirits. A chorus of shouts and cheers of encouragement followed them into the plains. Colors and pennants waved overhead.

"We might stand half a chance if they fight half as well as they parade," Norgen said from the walls one day. He exhaled a thick plume of smoke.

He and the boys had spent the majority of the last week running petty errands and collecting gear and provisions for themselves. Steleon's assurance that they were going to be as far away from the actual fighting wasn't good enough to rest on. Weapons were in short supply and smithies were working overtime to meet demand. More people were being hired as a result. The local economy was beginning to boom, much as it did at the start of every war.

Fennic said, "Averon is a strong land. I may not know much about how to fight a war, but I've seen enough in the last few weeks to know strength."

"Strong or no, it takes more than a desire to win a war. Goblins are poor fighters, but they can crush you in numbers. That's what is going to happen here," the Dwarf replied. "Not even the power of my folk can turn this tide."

"Will they come?" Delin asked.

"Who can say? My king is wise and powerful but has little in the way of trust." He clapped both on the shoulder and laughed. "Who can say what the future may bring? I, for one, can't wait to sink my axe into some Goblin meat."

With that they left the walls in search of their last decent meal before joining the ranks tomorrow. The Thorn River was calling, and with it, war.

The midday sun was hot for the onset of winter. Winter's Day was only two weeks away and Tolis Scarn still hadn't recovered the purple stone or found the thief, Dakeb. He knew the Hooded Man was growing more displeased but there was little to be done. Finding one man in all this madness was nigh on fruitless. The longer the search took the more he wanted to quit the job and move on to something more lucrative. Then again, Scarn had never left a job incomplete. In fact, this mission was slowly becoming personal to him. He had every intention of finding the boys and their Dwarf companion and making them suffer. The thought brought a smile to his leathered face as he rode through Paedwyn's gates.

Crowded as the streets were, it took him surprisingly little time getting to his favorite inn. They even had a room open for him. Scarn flipped the rough haired boy a copper to take care of his horse and bags. He'd normally do it himself, but something about the boy reminded Scarn of himself so long ago. Back before power and greed corrupted him. Smirking, he snatched a hasty meal without ale and stalked to his room. He was tired and needed to rest.

A familiar evil rushed at him upon opening the door, clutching him in its grip and dragging him inside. The door slammed shut. Scarn hung immobilized a foot off the floor. His muscles tenses and spasmed, surging with raw power. Struggling to reach his weapons. Darkness seethed and pulsed in the middle of the room.

"I grow tired of you," the center of the darkness rasped. "Winter Day is almost upon us and you continue to fail me. Perhaps a more lethal demonstration of my power is required?"

"You'll have your stone," Scarn said in a ragged breath. "I just need more time."

"Time is a luxury you do not have."

Scarn's look defied the evil. "Why don't you find it yourself if you're so damned powerful? Or are you afraid of the stone?"

The intensity of the spell faltered briefly.

"That's it, isn't it? You're afraid of what this stone can do to you. Ha! All this time I thought you were in control. Fate appears to have a different course of action, eh? You need me more than you think. Now put me down so we can talk like civilized men."

Scarn knew he held the upper hand and planned on taking full advantage of it. A smug look on his face, Scarn slowly dropped to the floor. He suddenly saw untold treasures coming his way and decided to press his luck.

"Why is this stone so important? If it makes you so afraid what will it do to me if I touch it?" he asked.

Dark vapors swirled around the Hooded Man, once again concealing him from prying eyes. His body heaved with aggression beneath those thick robes. "The stone holds a magic more powerful than your mortal life can comprehend. It is a living being, incapable of destruction."

Scarn's curiosity rose. "Then why should I give it to you? I'm thinking I should keep it for myself and start a brand-new empire. Can you imagine the chaos?"

"You forget your place too quickly. I am not so helpless as you believe," the Hooded Man snarled.

"Then why not collect the stone yourself?"

The mists swirled and flared out, seizing Scarn by the throat and squeezing hard.

"Do not presume for one instant that my reluctance to touch the stone will prolong your life. Men like you are cheap and easy to come by, Tolis Scarn. All I need do is snap my fingers and a dozen others are ready to take your place."

The mists relaxed their grip and dissolved.

"Remember that the next time you decide to feel important."

Scarn fell to his hands and knees, eyes bulging and gasping for air. He wanted nothing more than to lash out at the man and it took a concentrated effort to keep from doing so. The Hooded Man, whoever he was, was more dangerous than Scarn had been led to believe. Salvaging his pride, Scarn forced himself off the floor.

The Hooded Man retreated to the shadows again and continued. "I have discovered the identities of those you seek. Farmer's sons from an obscure village in the western reaches of Averon. They are hardly free from their teens and travel in the company of a Dwarf. My spies tracked them here, to join the campaign more likely. Do not let them succeed. Find them, follow them for as long as necessary and take the stone. No harm must befall them ere you take what I want."

The mists swirled and then he was gone.

"Do not fail me again, Tolis Scarn," a voice echoed softly.

Scarn rubbed his throat. His only chance for survival lay in finding that damned stone and discovering how to use it before the Hooded Man. Even then he wasn't so sure.

Morning arrived to the sound of trumpets and clarions announcing the arrival of the last units from Paedwyn arriving on the battlefield. The army of Averon was fully deployed and taking up positions west of the river. Catapults and ballistae were hastily constructed by the royal engineers. Companies of infantry were sent to find stones and suitable ammunition for a prolonged battle. Great supply trains stretched an entire league towards the camp. Cook fires spread the promise of roasting deer and elk. Aside from the impending invasion, it wasn't so bad a place.

Hallis led his own small column into the encampment with a grim look in his eyes and his head held high. Behind him rode Delin and the others. They had finally returned. Bumped and bruised from the ride, Delin stared down at the expansive plain with eyes wide open. He'd spent most of his youth dreaming of epic struggles against the night. And here he was looking down on an army thousands strong. He stared into the faces of the battle-hardened veterans and scared recruits and realized he never had wanted to be in such a place.

His thoughts turned to Tarren and a great longing filled his heart. Only recently did he discover how important she truly was to him. It pained him every time he woke up and when he went to bed. What a fool he'd been to run away from home and join this adventure. Right now, he would have given anything to see her smile one more time.

Fennic, on the other hand, was quickly becoming enamored with the war and the Star Silver sword. The relative ease with which he slew the Gnaal went to his head and the sword filled his dreams with greatness. Sure, he reluctantly admitted Delin's role in killing the foul beast of Gren, but none of it would have been possible without the sword. Something mysterious lurked in the corners of his dark eyes, troubling his mind to great ends. He kept it to himself, waiting until the moment was right to tell his friends. Until then, Fennic Attleford kept his demons to himself.

"This is just one of three camps we've established along the river," Hallis told them.

Norgen scoffed. "No doubt the enemy will strike here first."

"Don't forget that pesky dragon," Jin laughed.

The Dwarf shot him a scowl but kept his tongue.

They spied the command tent with relative ease and rode for it. Guards armed with sword and shield ringed the enclosure. A burly sergeant with a silver beard casually walked out to greet them. Norgen subconsciously fondled his own beard. All around them the organized confusion of the army camp noisily went about its preparations.

"Hallis, you old goat farmer," laughed the sergeant. "I thought they killed you a long time ago."

Sliding from the saddle, Hallis shook his friend's hand. "I haven't met one yet that can do it proper. Good to see you Roln."

"Steleon told us to expect you and the new heroes of the realm. Word of them has spread to every cook fire for two leagues up and down the damned river. Most of us think we got a pretty good shot at winning this thing. There's even rumors of marching into Gren after to put an end to this once and for all."

Fennic's eyes grew wide at the thought of his plan being discovered.

"A bit premature for my tastes," Hallis replied. "We need to win here first." He paused to take in the added security around the command tent. "This can't be all just for us?"

Roln laughed even harder. "You always did take yourself too seriously. No. Steleon feels the enemy has spies running in the army and didn't want to take a chance. The tribes of ancient Gren march alongside the Goblins and Trolls, they say."

Norgen yawned. He enjoyed the casual banter between warriors as much as the next man, but he was tired and hungry.

"Seeing there's no foe to cleave, I'd like a bite to eat and a mug of ale," he told them. Truth be told, he hated riding horses as much as fighting Gnaals and it showed.

Roln laughed again. "Don't fret, Master Dwarf. We've food and drink aplenty. Let's take care of your mounts and see about filling your stomachs before Steleon discovers you're here."

One hour and a good pipe later, they pushed away from the table and stretched and yawned. Not even midday and the skies were darkening. Passing soldiers saw this as a bad sign and made wards to protect themselves. Steleon, being a warrior all his life, recognized the danger and ordered huge barrels of ale to be opened. Older and wiser men knew the real reason and it did the trick. The camp was saved from demoralization.

"I wonder what it's going to be like," Fennic said to Delin. He had intended to stop eating after his second plate of roast pheasant but couldn't help it. It was too good to pass up and reminded him of home.

Delin just looked at him and shook his head. He was afraid to find out.

"This is very exciting. The battle. The war. I want to know, Delin."

Delin eyed him suspiciously. "You're not the person I knew back in Fel Darrins. I feel like I don't know you anymore."

His words were harsh and not altogether unexpected, but Fennic did his best to take them in stride.

"It's Phaelor, Delin. I can feel it changing me, folding me into something I never wanted to be. What's worse, I think I like it," Fennic told his best friend.

Delin shook his head and silently wept for his friend.

There were few people who saw the lone rider in purple and black with the horns of an elk emblazoned on his banner ride into camp. He'd been riding for nearly a week to deliver an important message to the king. After tonight, he could return with the answer.

THIRTY-THREE
Dark Decisions

Fennic walked along the riverbank watching the sun rise slowly over the jagged peaks of the Gren Mountains. The sky was alive in shades of orange and red, appearing as if the very underworld had opened and unleashed hell. That was exactly how Fennic felt. A fever raged deep within his innermost mind. Too many dark and wonderful thoughts collided to torment him. He'd barely been able to sleep.

The top of the sun poked over the highest crag and he was suddenly reminded that his birthday was just two weeks away. Eighteen years old and already a man. Winter's Day was fast approaching and would normally be time for celebration in Fel Darrins. This year he saw no reason to celebrate. Not even his birthday was cause to ease the trouble in his soul. He raised a hand to shield the sun's glare. Then it came to him. An unspoken whisper in shadows of his mind. Fennic knew what he had to do. It was the only way.

He knew there was simply no way to slip in to Gren alone. He needed friends. Fennic clasped his hands behind his back and walked back to the tent. His mind fumbled over the right words to convince the others of the importance of this quest. In the end it wouldn't matter if they said yes or no. Phaelor would not be denied.

Handfuls of stragglers and volunteers walked or rode into the three main camps throughout the day, steadily building up the numbers. Most had little or no formal military training and were sent to the reserves. Steleon ordered instructors to go over the basics with them. He hoped it was just enough to keep them long enough to matter. They were farmers and shopkeepers, peasants without land claims. They were the very soul of what Averon had come to be over the long course of its history. Many a mother and wife were left behind with tears in their eyes. Others chose to come along to see their husbands and sons sacrifice themselves if need be. They cooked and cleaned for the troops, selflessly giving to the men who defended them. Steleon was careful to keep them away from the regular army. They could ill afford any distractions at this point.

Tolis Scarn was in one of the last groups to arrive. He was hooded and carefully disguised on the off chance someone recognized him. After all, he was unpopular in many lands. More than one ruler had put a price on his head and that made him an inviting target for would be mercenaries and bounty hunters. He was spending more time running for his life than working to fix things these days.

So when the Hooded Man came to him one night after heavy drinking with a sinister proposition it didn't take much convincing. Now here he was. He'd been tracking the stone for almost three months and was almost right back where he started. The closest he'd gotten was in Relin Werd but all he found was the empty cairn. The Hooded Man was increasingly becoming agitated at his results and now he was in the middle of a war. Lady Fortune seemed to have abandoned him completely.

A sergeant came out to the assorted rabble barking orders and asking questions. Those with weapons experience were herded to the right while the rest were sent back to the reserve compound to get what training they could before the enemy arrived. Scarn and a group of experienced men were marched over to one of the newest recruit regiments for integration.

Half of them were already bloodied, having served with Sergeant Hallis on his way back from the western lands. They were almost legendary by now, for no one had ever slain a Gnaal. The meager band suddenly found themselves a focal point for the army. The quiet heroes in shadows remained Delin and Fennic. The common man's friend and role model. Most of the recruits were much older than the boys. A sigh escaped Scarn upon seeing them. He just knew he was going to die here. Yet there was a strange sense of determination in him. Tolis Scarn settled down and eased himself into his new role as a soldier in the armies of Averon.

Melgit watched with minor interest as his cavalry drilled on the vast plain. He was normally enthralled by the sleek tactics and the thunder of hooves, but the precision held no joy for him this day. He was tired of war and seeing friends and subordinates fall. Nightmares of Gren Mot continued to plague him. He did his best to put them in place during the day but he also knew Steleon wouldn't hesitate to relieve him on the field if he showed adequate reason. Melgit was convinced the only way to exorcise the demons was by leading his men back into the fray. His cold, blue eyes were shrouded in pain and determination.

Most of the others were already assembled in the command tent by the time he arrived. His eyes sparked when he noticed the ragged man with a travel beard dressed in purple and black. Graeme stood off by the map pointing and talking excitedly. One of the boys sat off by himself fondling an extravagant sword. Another was with Hallis and the Dwarf. Melgit had heard most of the stories by now and was hardly impressed. Too many of his comrades lay dead for him to care much about a pair of boys from some distant village few had heard of.

Steleon came from one of the smaller side tents dressed in a dull and dented set of training armor. Young Jin was with him. Neither said a word. Everyone watched as the bearded man got up and followed Jin from the tent. Questions raged throughout the tent and only Steleon had the answers.

"Our scouts have reported enemy movement at last," he said in a low grating voice. "The dragon is nowhere in sight, but the threat is too real to ignore. The army of Gren has recovered from the sting at Gren Mot and are moving down through the pass. The Dwarves have not come and no other land has sent troops to our aid. The hour grows dark yet hope still flickers. Come forward, Fennic."

Awkward with addressing a group of people, even with ones he was familiar, Fennic slowly made his way to the middle of the tent. He slowly wrapped his hand around the hilt of Phaelor and drew the ancient and mighty weapon. A gasp went up from those who hadn't seen it before. Even Steleon was impressed.

"This is Phaelor, the Star Silver sword of legend. I will not go into details here of how it came into my possession. It has been my guiding hand for weeks now, pulling me towards whatever destiny the Elves created it for." He cleared his throat. "Only recently has it become clear to me what I need to do. I must take the sword to Gren and destroy the Silver Mage. There is no choice."

Silence dominated the tent. Graeme stood with his mouth agape. Disbelief stung his eyes. Steleon rose slowly. He had a vague notion of why they were there, but this went beyond those assumptions. He didn't expect a task so dire.

"Foolishness!" spat Melgit. "You're but a boy. Barely old enough to join the army. We don't expect to put the fate of Averon in his hands do we? I don't care if he holds the cursed sword or not. No child can do what great armies have failed to."

Steleon held up a staying hand. "You forget, he is the Gnaal slayer. I won't judge him by his age. There are many strange powers in this world. Who are we to decide what is clearly beyond us all?"

"All Averon is at stake!" Melgit argued.

"Calm down, Melgit," Steleon warned. "Let them speak."

Hallis stood and eyed them with a stern gaze. "I am no prophet nor scholar, but I know strength when I see it. These two boys managed to kill the Gnaal where companies of men and Dwarves could not. If his path leads him into the foulness of Gren he shall not go alone."

Fennic and Delin shared a surprised look at the outburst.

Melgit rolled his eyes. "You can't be serious. I'll have no part in this. Trusting our land to a mere boy!"

"No one is asking you to go," Steleon replied. There was a hushed urgency in his voice. Sound traveled far at night and this plan was too important to be heard while still in the fledgling stage. Several spies and infiltrators had already been caught and hung.

"You were summoned here for your knowledge of the dread land, nothing more. All I ask is you remain silent to everyone outside of this council. The fate of all us now rides upon secrecy. As far as Fennic's youth and inexperience, well, anyone capable of slaying a demon of Gren has earned the right to risk his life in the name of us all. I will not hinder the quest." He paused to eye Fennic softly. "What support I can lend, I will. You have my word."

"This is all well and fine, but I'll not let the glory of victory fall solely on men," Norgen growled and moved to stand beside Hallis. His heavy battle axe rested on the ground.

Delin let out a long, controlled breath. He was as afraid of uttering his next few words as he was with the troubles in his heart. "We've been friends for a long time, and a real friend will stick by your side through the good and bad. Besides, you'll need someone to look after you properly along the way."

The bitter Melgit stopped shaking his head long enough to stare thoughtfully at the group. Four fools throwing their lives away on a whim. He hooked his thumbs into his belt when he stood. A tender peace hovered in his eyes.

"This is madness to be sure. I do not approve of this plan at all, but I can see a fire in you we sorely need. Perhaps Averon has a future if others of this caliber can come together. My best and fastest steeds are in your service. May they carry you far."

Steleon smiled. "Indeed, all the way to Aingaard and the keep of the Silver Mage should the way prove kind. Draw your supplies, as much as you need. That won't be an issue. I think it best you leave as soon as possible, under the cover of darkness. Your one hope lies in traveling upriver through the Old Forest up to Thuil Lake. From there turn east to Gren. Aingaard will be easy enough to find. I do not envy your task. You have the hardest jobs of us all, if there were any way…"

His voice trailed off and Steleon suddenly found himself looking at each as if they were his own children. The pain in his heart was hard to bear, but he understood the need for sacrifice during war. Even if they failed, Averon would fight on until the last peasant was slain or made slave.

He went to each and laid a loving hand on both boys' shoulders.

"Take your rest these coming days. Gather as much strength as you can for there will be little time for such along the way. Good night my friends."

Already assigned to guard duty on his very first night in the army, Tolis Scarn tried as best he could to keep his growing disappointment to himself. This was not the life he ever wanted to lead. Let the two lands slaughter each other to ruin. He didn't care. He also knew there would be fresh jobs aplenty in the aftermath no matter who was the victor. The thought warmed him against the chill night. Then he heard the distinct rumblings of a Dwarf. Recognition sparked and a whisper of success crept back.

Scarn crept from his post to follow the small group of four. One of them had the stone. He knew it. One of them held the key to his freedom and untold riches. He would like nothing better than to kill them now and escape. Then he'd be rid of the Hooded Man and free to do as he chose. If only it were so easy. One of them had the stone, but which one? As much as he hated to admit it, Scarn needed them alive until the one with the prize revealed himself. He quietly followed them back to their tent, content in the knowledge that he was very close to freedom.

Ten leagues from the encampment and the security of the Thorn River, hidden among the rolling foothills of the Gren Mountains, waited a pair of Averonian scouts. They'd been deployed on rotating watches by Steleon since the first day in the field. For a week and a half scouts ranged the wild lands, searching for likely avenues of approach. They remained hidden in case the enemy also had spies.

There had been no sign of Gren until now. Sparse torches cast a flickering light among the dark rocks, turning shadows into restless demons devouring the night. A great and terrible rustling followed close. Goblins in full body armor. Finished with their plunder and reorganization, their dark master had given the word to invade. His very life seemed bent on it. Now the war machine marched. The scouts listened in horror at the confidence in the Goblin war chants as they marched. The two fled into the night as the marching got closer. War had finally come to Averon.

THIRTY-FOUR
War Councils

The smell of rotting flesh and destruction was thick in the air. Heavy clouds plagued the skies and refused the sun. Jervis Hoole couldn't have asked for a better day to begin the invasion of the lowlands. Tiny flakes of snow were already falling on the mountaintops and the higher reaches of the pass. He knew the wrath of winter was close and it spurred him harder. Not even the Mage's magic was enough to deter the weather long enough for him to bring his army down.

The dragon was gone, much to the relief of his Goblins. They, like most creatures, were in fear of the great wyrm. Hoole didn't care. He wanted out of the mountains. Gren Mot was taking too long to clear. His stringy, black hair flipped about in the restless breeze. Instinct stirred inside, ones he never knew he had. He longed to gaze upon the forests and emerald grasslands of his foe. To see the sparkling blue rivers and field of golden wheat. These had always been denied to him.

His war horse carefully picked its steps while taking them farther down the mountain pass. Soon he would be king of Averon and punish those who called themselves his betters. Soon they would come to understand the pain and suffering of Gren.

Sunrise brought a freezing chill. Frost blanketed the lands and little stirred. It wasn't so cold as to freeze the river just yet. Everyone knew it wasn't long off. Winter was barreling down on them. Steleon stood next to the small fire burning from the pit in the center of his tents, calmly warming his hands. It was already midday and the temperature had barely risen from the morning. Compounding this misery was the disturbing lack of sleep he'd had lately. Fennic's plan lay at the heart of his worries. Tens of thousands of lives were unknowingly depending on an eighteen year old boy to defeat a centuries old wizard with enough power to eternally condemn the world. Steleon wondered if it was going to be enough, magic sword or no.

The tired commander thought of his own family and suddenly found himself thinking of retirement. He was getting too old for battle. But he wasn't foolish enough to believe a world of peace could exist. Man seemed intent on destroying each other. And if that be the way of the world, then he would do his best to preserve what life he could. His thoughts turned back to Hallis and Norgen. Both seemed capable enough in the field and showed a genuine interest in the boys. He wished he could spare more for this venture, but too many would be easily detected and secrecy was their only hope for success.

A runner approached. He was wearing the royal gold and green of the state. Steleon gestured his guards to let the man through and then went back into his tent.

"Greetings from King Maelor," the runner said with a deep bow.

Steleon eyed him, sternly sizing him up. "What news from Paedwyn?"

"The king and a full regiment of the royal guard left this morning under cover of darkness and are heading this way."

"What! Does the king no longer value his life? Tell me boy, why would he wish to come to this tragic place?"

Steleon stood there stunned. This was disturbing news at best. Most of Averon was too young to remember the last time their king had willingly gone in to battle, or even when he had lost his life. Steleon wasn't. He remembered it vividly. He was there when they stood the line against the evil tide. He remembered the fathers of both boys. And he remembered Wiffe and that terrible Star Silver sword. What carnage he reaped that day. The three of them gave up the rich life of Paedwyn and left for some minor village on the border in the hopes that their children would never have to see the things they had. Steleon snorted at the bitter irony of it.

The runner shook his head fervently. "No sir. King Maelor decided that it was his day and was going to stand the line with you and the army as a king should. His own words, sir."

Steleon realized his anger was being directed at the wrong person and smiled back at the runner. "Run back to Maelor and give him my warmest regards. Tell him to ride in at dawn so as to bring hope to our men. It would be an honor to fight alongside him."

"Yes sir," he replied and ducked back outside.

Steleon sighed. The last thing the kingdom needed was the death of their king. Provided they won the war, Averon would need strong nobility to see them through the rebuilding and winter months. His thoughts were disturbed as the first cries of alarm rang throughout the camp. Darkness was falling. He took up his sword and stormed outside. It didn't take long for him to see the problem. Distant torch light announced the arrival of Gren. Soldiers darted through the camp en route to battle positions. Members of the war council gathered. The clamor of steel and armor sang loudly as the army of Averon readied to do battle. Steleon raised his looking glass and spied the enemy. A thin smile cracked his lips. With the light of the dying day he could make out the mass of Goblins heading towards them. It was only the vanguard. The main body was nowhere in sight. Still, the van held thousands of soldiers. Steleon decided to take the war to them.

"Captain Melgit!" he called out, and the cavalryman appeared.

Desire blazed in his eyes. The vengeance in his heart was more than enough to do what needed to be done. He had a broad smile, as if he already knew what he was being asked to do.

"The enemy is foolishly taking their time in deploying. Take your force across the river just upstream from here and show them the importance of speed. Do as much damage as you can and get back here. Don't become so engaged that you can't escape. I have need of you once the main body arrives. We'll provide archers and pike men to cover your retreat."

Melgit nodded approvingly. "Five hundred is a good number. Give the boys a chance to wet their blades properly."

"You're a dangerous man," Steleon laughed. "I think you already had that plan in mind by the time you got here." He laid a reassuring hand on Melgit's shoulder and said, "Bring as many of our boys home as you can. This skirmish is just the beginning. Nothing foolish."

"On my honor," smiled Melgit before he strode off shouting orders.

Steleon almost felt sorry for the unsuspecting Goblins and the fury he just unleashed.

The sounds of battle drifted across the open plain to the western bank of the Thorn River where Steleon waited. Frigid waters surged up to lap at the cold mud. The air was chill and downright freezing when the winds blew. He was mildly surprised it hadn't started snowing yet.

The thunder of hooves, cries and screams of death, and the unforgiving sound of steel piercing flesh echoed into the night. Steleon stood and listened to the carnage for close to an hour before leaving the river bank. His heart started to race the way it always did during a battle. He knew Melgit would return soon and there was more to plan, much more. He retreated behind the line of archers and waited.

Hallis and Norgen were there as well, waiting for the chance to join the fight. The archers drew back and raised their bows to the sky. Ranks of horsemen came flying back across the river. There were hundreds of Goblins on their trail. Steleon tried counting empty saddles as they sped past but the task was too difficult in the dark. Then the arrows loosed. Goblin bodies fell. Some tumbled into the river and were washed away, their dark blood polluting the waters. Archers fired as fast as targets were made available.

Melgit was the last to cross, smiling viciously. The Goblins finally realized the severity of their situation and began a disorderly retreat. The van had been routed. Steleon ordered the cease fire and walked up to Melgit's frothing horse. The army cheered and roared at the victory. Hundreds of bodies lay across the river in a twisted mass of flesh. The enemy had finally been bled.

"You should have seen their eyes!" Melgit exclaimed. "It must have been like the underworld opening up for them. Ha. We made three passes before they managed a defense. I'd say we took down over a fifth of their strength."

One fifth. One thousand enemy soldiers. Steleon wanted to rejoice, if even for a moment, but couldn't. Tens of thousands more were marching on them.

"How many did we lose?" he asked.

"Fifteen," Melgit answered. "Not bad for our first night's work."

That much they agreed on.

"Have your men stand down. They did a fine job and deserve the rest. I'll send a runner for you when I need you," he said and then added, "thank you for not getting killed."

Melgit laughed again. "As if they had a chance."

There were times Steleon thought his own army was going to do him in long before the enemy got the chance.

Sometime during the night, hours after the battle and still more before the dawn, King Maelor and his royal guard entered the camp. Sentries snapped to attention and readied to rouse the general but the king wished them to stand at ease and remain on duty. The soldiers needed their sleep more than he needed an official welcome. His band continued the ride into the camp. Maelor was little surprised upon seeing Steleon warming himself before a small fire, as if he'd been waiting all night.

"Don't you ever sleep?" Maelor asked and pulled his leather gloves off to warm his own hands after dismounting.

Steleon smirked. "Not if I can help it. How was your journey, sire?"

"Uneventful. Though I hear there was a bit of excitement earlier?"

"It seems there are spies everywhere these days," Steleon replied.

He offered his friend, the king, a chair so they could sit and speak of what had already happened and what he was expecting in the coming days. Dawn arrived and found them moved on to the dilemmas of tactics and supply trains. Halfway through the morning sleep finally took them.

THIRTY-FIVE
Shadom Gein

The lightened peaks of the Thed Mountains lacked majesty and impression. They were nowhere near the height of the eastern Gren range and lacked much of the menace. Rich in ore, Dwarves and men had long fought over the mines. Their gentle slopes were inviting right up to the snow laden peaks. The Sibit River laid a dozen leagues away, hidden behind rolling hills and lightly forested plains. Eagles circled the treetops, stretching their wings in the chill afternoon. A brown rabbit pricked up its ears at the sound of approaching hoof beats.

Tarren rode on Ris Kaverling's back as she had every day for the past two weeks. He and his band of Centaurs were friendly enough and twice as deadly when it came to battle. She felt entirely protected from harm. They'd seen no signs of another Goblin war party since that first day and that bolstered her confidence. Ris even cheered up, offering his time to tell her the how and whys of Goblins and the bitter wars fought between them and the fair races of Malweir.

Dark clouds moved in not long past noon, bringing with them the first true whispers of winter. Delicate flakes drifted down and melted the instant they touched the near frozen ground. Tarren pulled her dark blue hood up to protect her against the angry winds.

"Not a good sign," Ris told her. "It'll make for easy tracking if it sticks. We should hurry before more Goblins come."

Tarren wasn't so sure. "Do you really think they're still hunting us? There has been no sign for days. Vinz and the others haven't seen anything. Surely the Goblins must have given up already."

"The enemy is many things, Tarren. Deceitful most of all. They will lull us into thinking we are safe and come upon us unawares. No, Tarren, we must remain vigilant though it pains us at times."

"I was only thinking," she dejectedly said.

Ris nodded. "I know, and I know this is a strange life for you, but this is a dangerous world. I wish it were otherwise. Trust in me as Dakeb has. He believes you have yet to play an important role in the way the future will unfold."

To this she took heart. She thought of her family and how much she missed them. No doubt they felt the same, perhaps even thinking she was dead. The notion chilled her. Most of all, she desperately wanted to see Delin again. He was the sole reason for her leaving home. All she wanted was to find her friends and bring them all home so they could grow old in Fel Darrins and live unadventurous lives. It was a simple dream for a simpler time.

Another hour went by and then the first great rock formation came into view. Heavy shadows fell, prematurely darkening the area. Tarren's heart felt cold, warning her not to enter. The Centaurs reined to a halt.

"Make camp. We enter at dawn," Ris ordered. He turned to Tarren and added, "There are many creatures in this maze that I have no wish to confront in the night. Thuil Lake and Ipn Shal lay but two days hence. There is time still."

"What is this place? Why does it feel so cold?" she asked.

"'Tis an evil place name Shadom Gein, my lady. Many Mages died here. Some were good and some evil. It is said their ghosts still haunt the rocks. I, for one, will not venture inside without the power of the sun," Ris replied.

A deep horn blow cut his thoughts off.

"Goblins!"

Torches could be seen moving through the tree behind them and from the right. The trap was carefully set, pinching the small band of Centaurs between them and the haunted rocks of Shadom Gein.

Ris looked at her with concern. "There are too many to fight. We now have no choice but to enter."

Vinz edged closer, sword in hand. "Let us fight past them. They can't be as organized as we believe."

"No. I'll not risk another life to foolishness."

"Yet you will risk us all in there?" Vinz exclaimed. His fear of Shadom Gein was etched upon his face.

Demon faces formed in the rocks, mocking them to come and find doom. Tarren shuddered. To her, this was the darkest place in the world. Poison tipped arrows began darting past. Some struck the rock faces in a shower of sparks. The Centaurs returned fire and Goblins fell. Blood lust raged in the Goblins eyes.

"Quickly! Into the rocks!" Ris shouted.

Vinz grabbed his forearm. "You'll kill us all."

"Then we're dead either way."

Javelins and arrows started falling around them in thicker clouds. Time was up. Tarren clutched tightly to Ris's back as they dashed into Shadom Gein. They heard the Goblin cheer but kept running. The risk was worth it as far as Ris was concerned.

"Barse, Vinz, slow them down," Ris barked.

Both Centaurs nodded once and stalked back towards the enemy. Each knew what was being asked of them. Vinz held his tongue, uneasy with the decision. He didn't approve of entering the haunted place, but he wasn't exactly ready to die either. The choice was beyond him however, so he silently agreed to face down the Goblins. At least his death would be honorable.

"You're asking them to die," Tarren whispered.

Ris didn't slow. "I'm asking them to keep us alive."

The six remaining Centaurs rode on in silence, the only sound was that of their hooves on the forbidding stone. Moans and wails drifted up from the rocks. Whispers of terrible deaths. There were no warnings, no threats to turn back. It was as if the dark spirits wanted them to continue. A pale glow crept around the corner towards them. They halted and pranced nervously. Snow continued to fall, driven down by forceful winds. The moon's haunting light emerged briefly from behind the clouds. Temperatures dropped sharply until they could see their breath. Tarren shivered and pulled her cloak even tighter. Trapped between Goblins and ghouls, she wished she had planned better by bringing more than just the tiny dagger at her hip.

"Keep your eyes closed and you shouldn't be harmed," Ris told her. "Spirits often lose their focus when they discover no one is paying attention."

He then spoke to his brothers in their own tongue. Convincing them to carry on was a formidable task but they finally relented and entered the eerie glow. The first skeleton they saw was partially decomposed and rotting away. None could guess what it had once been, only that it had been dead for a very long time. More and more skeletons awaited them as they wound through the mist enshrouded maze. Piles of gnawed upon bones lay heaped and broken in the corners. There were so many that Ris felt like he was back on a battlefield again.

Madness was said to haunt this place, ensnaring all who were foolish enough to enter. Tarren began to regret their decision. She could feel the hatred and envy weeping from the very rock. Ris suddenly stopped. Foul tendril of crimson red stabbed their way through the ground and convulsed in a mass of smoke and wonder. Some of the Centaurs turned to flee, but Ris knew it was already too late.

A wraith stood before them. It was a full seven feet tall and menacing from beneath a shimmering cloak of mists. The body had no substance but reeked menace. Ris and Tarren felt their very bones grow cold. The wraith pointed a long, bony finger at them and spoke in a grinding voice.

"You should not have come here. Only the dead may travel freely through Shadom Gein. Go back now else evil befalls you."

Tarren gripped Ris harder until her knuckles bled white.

The Centaur lowered his weapons. He knew he was taking a chance with their lives, but the wraith was warning them. It could easily have killed them all by now.

"Our enemies hunt us from behind and are many. If we were to turn back it would end in our deaths. Forward is the only path we have," he told the wraith.

The wraith stared back menacingly. "Why have you come here?"

More spirits formed, quickly surrounding the tiny band.

"We serve Dakeb the Mage," Ris told them. "We must reach Ipn Shal and this is our only option."

The wraiths seemed to recoil at the name of their ruined home. Once, it was a mighty place of knowledge and friendship. Once, but no more. Whispers danced from the rocks. Dakeb, they exclaimed. How could he still live? Some were angry, others curious. The leader drifted closer to Ris.

"How is it you know Dakeb?"

The Centaur refused to back down. "He has been a friend of my people for years. The Silver Mage has returned and seeks to enslave us all. Dakeb fights him. We are trying to help preserve our world from that evil."

Agonizing wails went up upon hearing Sidian's name. His most loyal supporters raised their hands to sky to smite down these intruders but the souls of the good stopped them. Wraith battled wraith until only one remained. He turned his empty hood back on the small band of Centaurs.

"You may pass, but you must deliver this message. Tell Dakeb that his friends of old are here for him when the need arises. We shall remove your enemy, but you may never again enter this land. To do so is forfeit of your souls."

The wraith disappeared back into the nothing. When Ris looked again he was met with the gruesome sight of the remains of soldiers and guards. All were armed and rotted and ready to do battle. They turned as one in a crisp movement accented by the ringing of steel. One by one the ranks stole away into the maze of Shadom Gein to meet the Goblins head on.

Ris wasted no time. He and the others ran for their lives. The way was surprisingly straight. It was one long stretch until they came into open fields beyond the gloom and haze. They finally came to a halt not far from the last walls of Shadom Gein and rested. All were covered in a slick sheen of sweat and breathing hard.

Back inside the rock maze a chorus of screams bleated into the heavy air. They knew without asking that the Goblins were being slaughtered to the last.

THIRTY-SIX
The Halls of Ipn Shal

The light of a single torch barely lit the darkened halls. Once there was great life here. A grand environment with purpose and intent. The future had been so bright then, back before the greed and corruption moved like a snake through the undercurrent to deceive and destroy. Kings and heads of state often visited, partaking in lavish balls and grand feasts worthy of the gods themselves.

Joy left the world the day evil was allowed to flourish and expand beyond the walls. Malweir forever changed that day. Both good and bad suddenly had direction and the war was begun. They fought for months and years. They fought for control of all around them. They fought until they no longer knew why they were fighting. League upon league was destroyed in this ignorance. In the end only a handful remained. Their kind was all but extinct. Most of the survivors tucked themselves away in quieter lands untouched by the war and were lost to time. But there was one who refused to let the quest die.

He slipped into another land and seduced the leaders. He spent centuries searching for the four shards of the cracked crystal and bled the world for them. Dakeb had fought him before, and barely survived. But Sidian was crafty and found a new land to conquer. The land of Gren. It was an easy target, for the rulers were weak men seeded with jealousy and corruption. Soon the Silver Mage owned Gren and enslaved all within.

Dakeb reflected on those distant moments as he strode through the once splendid halls of his ancient home. Born from the bloodlines of fallen Gaimos, the Order of Mages built a fine tradition for thousands of years. Now Ipn Shal was dusty and filled with cobwebs. A broken ruin of what once was.

Centuries of dust hid the magnificence, but he could still see it if he looked hard enough. The halls and chambers were the same as they had been. Rats and other vermin ran from him, startled as much by his presence as he was by theirs. His heart grew tired from it all. This was the first time he had returned to the fortress city since its destruction all those long years ago. Haunting feelings assailed him endlessly. Dakeb did his best to shake off the demons of his past. He knew time was running out and there was much to do. He needed to hurry.

Sidian was already making his move for Averon. The first units of his army were already marching down onto the plains. Brave as they were, not even King Maelor's men had a chance against so many. The dragon alone saw to that. Dakeb forced a smile. He'd faced one of Sidian's flying beasts long ago and won. But those were different times, with different allies. As it stood now, his new friends were coming to him. The sword and the stone were already moving and the girl was closer than all. Perhaps there was hope after all.

The elder Mage found the winding staircase he'd been searching for and started to go down. Ipn Shal held many basements and sublevels. Most were used for storage and the like, even barracks for the Mage army when the need arose. There were also great libraries unparalleled in any land. Dakeb knew his foe never showed much interest in reading and now planned on using it to his full advantage. Dakeb reached the main library hall and stood in awe. Somewhere in the thousands upon thousands of books was the one he needed. Inspiring considering the order of Mages was born from the blood of the ancient warrior race of Gaimos.

He resignedly shook his head and set to work. His thoughts constantly returned to the girl, Tarren. She was a truly lovely woman and he was sad at the role she must play. Hers was perhaps the most important of all. Thankfully she had a good head on her shoulders and the resolve to see things through. The thought of her brought a smile to his face. There was hope for humanity so long as people like her chose to stand for right.

He was on his third torch by the time he found the book he was searching for: *A Composite History of the Crystal of Tol Shere and its uses in Practical Magic.* Dakeb had two weeks left before Winter's Day and the day Sidian planned his hideous ceremony. Satisfied for the moment, Dakeb sat down to read.

The inhabitants of the Old Forest spoke of invasion and following strife. Whispers and rumors drifted back to Elvanara, the woodland home of the most ancient of the Elven people. King Alsenal warned his folk to stay within the boundaries of the forest where his magic could protect them. He knew firsthand the dangers the Silver Mage possessed and was unwilling to let his people suffer. Celegon, his son, begged and pleaded for the Elves to get involved and help the race of men but the Elf king was adamant. Enough Elven blood had already been spilled in the past.

His sentiment went unheard among the youth. Most of it began with the king's son and trickled down through the community until a strong following to enter the war was raised. Alsenal remained stolid. Celegon defied his father's wishes and readied his friends for the inevitable. War was coming and not even the magic of the Elves was going to be of use if they were too late.

"You can't go against his wishes. He is the king, and your father!" Derlith warned.

Celegon continued to pack for his trip.

"What if you're wrong, eh? What if the Silver Mage doesn't bother to look this way? You'll risk us all if they discover Elves fighting alongside those men."

The Elf prince turned calmly to his friend. "Do you really believe he has forgotten or forgiven the part we played in his last defeat? No. We are all in danger. My father is too old and set in his ways to accept it."

He laid a friendly hand on Derlith's shoulder. "You've seen what Averon is facing. There is no hope for any of us unless we stand together. Come with me. I need as many friends as I can find."

Some of the edge left the Elf warrior's eyes. "Aye. I will follow you, but not for the reasons you think. If war is coming, you'll need someone to keep you out of trouble."

They shared a quiet laugh and slipped unnoticed from the house. Twenty others were waiting on horseback below. They were a guard of honor. A token force to show Averon that the Elves were behind them. He wished the Aeldruin were near, for their support might tips the scales. Celegon climbed aboard his roan and looked upon his home for what might be the last time. A tear in his eyes, he turned and headed south.

THIRTY-SEVEN
Gren Arrives

The unexpected battle with the vanguard of the Gren army pushed back Fennic's departure a few days. Steleon wanted them gone as soon as possible but wasn't willing to risk it with the enemy so close and focused. Two days after that battle the main army came down onto the plain and began arraying itself for campaign. They were an awesome sight to behold. Their armor glimmered in the pale winter sun, and each bore weapons sharp and eager for battle. Steleon was left with no choice but to delay their departure yet again.

A day and half passed while the armies of Gren took the field. The defenders reeled in shock at the size of the formations. Rumors spread. The Goblins were going to kill every last one of them. Fear stretched into the deepest reaches of their souls that day. Hallis stood with the others atop a low rise watching the parade across the river. His muscles tensed as painful memories tormented him.

"I've never seen such a sight," Fennic exhaled. He suddenly felt very small.

Thumbing the blade of his axe, Norgen nodded. "This is just the beginning. What you see is nothing compared to what awaits us. Gren holds many evils, lads."

Delin's stomach dropped. "We don't stand a chance."

Norgen laughed. "Nonsense! War is a fickle bitch. Size doesn't always promise victory. You saw how easily the horsemen ran those others down. They may be many, but Goblins are notoriously poor fighters."

Hallis smiled. "Don't fret. Our intent is to slip into Gren unseen. We won't have a foe that big to face."

"Just the Silver Mage and his dragon," Delin replied.

They said nothing more. Across the river, the massive army continued to emplace.

The first sounds of battle began not long after midnight to the heavy song of catapults firing. Goblin units managed to sneak close enough to the Thorn River in an attempt at establishing a bridgehead. Only the artillery of Averon turned them back, leaving a bloody mess in their wake. Archers formed ranks and began a wholesale slaughter of any Goblin soldiers in range. The units already in the water were decimated entirely.

Steleon burst from his tent with sword in hand. He fumed at the desperation of it. There was no reason why the enemy got so close without his scouts spying them first. He swore to himself that someone was going to pay. He was pleasantly surprised when he reached the front lines. Unit commanders were moving their men into battle ranks and repelling the Goblin assault. The edge left him. Satisfied the situation was still manageable, he began moving up and down the line shouting encouragement.

The Goblins retreated.

Steleon summoned his commanders and issued orders in case the enemy returned and went off to find Hallis.

After warming his hands at the fire, Steleon said, "You must leave tonight. This was just the beginning. We can only expect worse."

Hallis agreed. "We are packed and ready to make the trip upstream."

"The river isn't safe. You need another plan. The best bet is to double back a league or so and move north. The enemy wouldn't see you from there, even if they manage to break through here," Steleon told them.

"None of this makes sense," Norgen commented. "They attack before they are ready and waste lives. Why? As much as I hate to say it, we need to gain the Old Forest and the protection of the Elves before the enemy catches on to us."

Steleon merely nodded. "Indeed. I'm going to send a small detachment with you. Once you reach the forest they'll return to me. If there were more I could do…."

"Forget about us," Norgen told him. "You have more pressing matters that need dealing with. I wish I could stay and split a few skulls."

Steleon snorted. "Indeed. Good luck, my friends. I fear you may need it more than us."

The catapults started firing again. The army commander sagged slightly. He was tired and this was but the first night. The long, lonely call to arms blared on trumpets across the front. Soldiers readied for the charge.

"Leave now, this is your best chance," Steleon said and walked away. "Sergeant at arms!"

Less than an hour later the tiny band of would be heroes stood atop the highest rise surrounding the main encampment watching the second battle rage. Fires raged out of control in scores of places across the far shore, the flames offering brief glimpses of the mass of enemy warriors. Delin couldn't figure how Steleon planned on winning. Not against these odds.

"Come," Hallis said. "Let us go before it's too late."

They turned and began the two day trek to the Old Forest. Ten soldiers rode with them. All were scouts and rangers. None wore uniforms and they were armed to the tooth. They were easily as lethal as a full company of conventional infantry. As such, they possessed the ability to move stealthily through the land and strike without warning. Unrecognizable by all but their own commanders, they did the dirty work the king couldn't admit to. Officially they didn't exist.

When Tolis Scarn learned of their special assignment, his instincts prickled. He'd never owned a uniform and had comparable skills to the men he secretly joined. Most of the rangers didn't know each other so it was no big feat slipping into the end of the column as it left the camp. Scarn thanked his luck. If it weren't for the incoming round that exploded in his tent and killed three men, he never would have found the boys and Dwarf. He used the confusion to his advantage and scurried away. Once in the shadows he overheard their last goodbyes and waited. This was the perfect opportunity. Lady chance was finally smiling on him.

They camped shortly after dawn, drawing up in a tight circle. Five rangers took off in different directions to scout the surrounding countryside. Hallis chanced a small fire and soon had a shank of venison roasting. Norgen stood off by a sapling elm tree smoking his pipe.

"I don't like this," he grumbled. "Fire is dangerous, no matter how many men of the wild are with us."

"At least we'll know if Goblins come close," Hallis replied. "Enjoy the hot meal while you can. There will be none soon enough."

A long plume of bluish smoke drifted up from the bowl of his pipe. "There are worse things than Goblins to fear."

"Phaelor will warn us if another Gnaal comes," Fennic confidently said.

Norgen snorted and stalked away, mumbling under his breath.

A light snow trickled down, briefly coating the land. Still too warm for it to stick, the white powder melted on contact with the ground. Delin warmed his hands and remembered reading stories of old heroes traveling the lands on epic quests. They always faced terrors incomparable than anything imaginable. Nowhere did he ever read about how hard and cruel the travels were. Or how inhospitable nature was to those few who braved doing the right thing. He found his own adventure was miserable at times and frightening at others. Delin wondered how his tale was going to be told in the ages to come.

"The Dwarf is right. Having a fire in the open is hazardous to us all," Scarn warned.

He wrapped his cloak a little tighter and continued watching the tree line. It wouldn't do them any good if Goblins ambushed them now. Scarn had been careful not to talk too much for he wasn't sure exactly what the rangers had been given for orders. He took his turns off in the wild and performed those duties to the best of his abilities. Deciding he'd said enough, he turned and walked away.

"Maybe we should put it out," Delin suggested against his better judgment.

Fennic immediately found it odd that none of the other rangers had commented on the fire. Suspicions formed about that man. Even Phaelor was trying to warn him, but why? He decided to watch him closely until he knew for certain what was foul about him.

Hallis smiled fondly at Delin. "We will put it out as soon as the meat is cooked. Will that help ease your troubled minds?"

"Greatly."

Soon enough they were enjoying the hot meat dripping fats and grease. Delin couldn't recall anything tastier. The rangers declined, much to Scarn's disappointment. They kept to themselves and ate a meager meal of dried meats and nuts. The boys traded tales of their youth once their bellies were full. They stopped short of mentioning finding the sword or the stone because Fennic's mistrust of Scarn was growing. All too soon Hallis ended their merriment by scooping dirt over the flames. Norgen's heavy snoring was prompt enough for the rest to bundle up in their cloaks and try to rest.

It was hours later when the lead ranger, a tall man with a hideous scar running down his face gently kicked them awake. It was time to move on. Hallis and Norgen were up and moving as if they had been the entire night, while the boys grumbled and couldn't stop yawning. Very shortly they were riding towards the Old Forest. Their scouts returned and were instantly replaced by another set. Fennic was greatly relieved to see Scarn ride out with them.

"The Elf King does not permit men to walk under the leaves of the forest," Hallis explained to them. "It has been decades since anyone from Averon was allowed to do so."

Norgen spat. "All the more reason not to trust them."

"Why is that?" Delin asked. The animosity between the races seemed to tense and fester the closer they got.

Norgen surprised them all by laughing. "Who can trust a race that keeps their borders closed and dissuades friendship? Besides, they live in trees! Man is bad enough, but we tolerate them all the same. It seems only the Dwarves are smart enough to live in the great halls of the world. And rightly so I say."

Fennic stifled a giggle. "What makes living underground any better than the open air?"

"Why!" the Dwarf flustered. He scowled at them and said nothing more for a fair stretch.

They'd just halted for dinner when one of the rangers came flying back. His face was beaded with sweat and he came from the direction of the Old Forest. There was a wild look of terror in his eyes. He spoke with Scarface in hushed tones and was sent back out as quickly as he arrived. Obviously terrified, the man obeyed his orders without question.

Scarface solemnly rode up to Hallis. His face was as grim as the cold, cold stone. "We are being hunted."

"By what?" Hallis asked, his hand dancing on the hilt of his sword.

Fennic looked down at Phaelor and recoiled. There was a soft glow coming from the sheath. Danger!

"My man says it is a great beast more terrible than his imagination capable of. It is the color of darkness and reeks of death. It can only be a Gnaal," replied Scarface. His voice betrayed no emotion. "He went back out to try and draw it away from us, back into the wild."

"A wasted effort, my friend," Norgen grimaced, axe in hand.

"Regardless, it is what we must do if we are to succeed in getting you to the Elves alive."

Delin felt his world crumble. They'd only just begun their quest and ruin was upon them. He knew that if there was one hunting them there must be more.

Looking at each man individually, Hallis tightened his grip on the reins. "We must hurry."

THIRTY-EIGHT
Fear and Fight

They pushed hard, struggling to gain the security of the forest. But it was simply too far away and the Gnaal was bound to find them before long. Scarface reluctantly slowed them to a walk. Killing them now would do no good for anyone. Fennic constantly checked Phaelor for changes but the sword remained the same. Danger was close, but far enough away to be of little importance to the sword.

"You make sure to tell us when Phaelor starts acting up, Fennic. I don't want to run into another one of those Gnaals," Delin whispered.

"Don't worry. We know how to fight them now."

"If there's more than one?"

Fennic shrugged. "The more the merrier I suppose."

His voice was uncharacteristically cruel, almost as if he were looking forward to the battle. An unearthly scream shattered the still of the night. It was coming their way. The darkness crept in a little closer, threatening to choke them into submission. A second scream answered. Scarface clenched his jaw and rode on. The moon rose slowly. The light was chill and offered haunting images of the night. Suddenly the world became evil and threatening. Gnaals could pass through the black unseen and strike at any moment. Any of the shadows might be the enemy.

Phaelor hummed. Delin stole a glance at it and shuddered. He was no fan of magic. He'd never met an Elf and certainly had no reason to trust their weapons. Not after what Norgen had said. An owl hooted in the dark. A wolf bayed. Goosebumps prickled down Delin's spine. The fear chilled his soul. He felt everything turning against him. Too soon he doubted if he'd ever sleep again.

Hallis saw the fear about to consume Delin. "Relax, Master Kerny. There are real enough dangers out there. Don't focus on your fears. You'll be fine so long as you keep your wits about you."

Norgen also added his encouragement. "You have an advantage over these rangers."

"What is that?"

"You've been hunted by a Gnaal before and lived to tell of it. That makes the four of us legends already. I think they should fear us instead."

Delin smiled despite himself.

He was almost feeling good again when a riderless horse walked up to them. Scarface grabbed the reins and tried soothing the animal. Dark blood ran from claw-like wounds on its flanks. Fennic recognized the horse. It belonged to the ranger who had come back to warn them. Fennic wanted to cry. The night was hunting them one at a time.

Scarface pushed them on. His emotions remained his alone. He'd known the dead man and had grown up with him. But Scarface wouldn't cry. He couldn't. Crying didn't bring back the dead. Neither did vengeance, but at least that road was accessible.

The column pressed onward.

Nothing more happened that night. Another ranger was sent out to replace the fallen one. He went without pause, knowing what was expected of him. Fennic scowled when he saw Scarn ride back into the main body. Of all the people to live through the night, he cursed. They stopped at dawn to eat a cold meal. Scarface warned against staying too long and much too soon they were moving again. Much too slowly, the distance between them and the forest shrank.

Scarface reined to a halt and wiped his stringy, black hair from his face. His cold eyes searched the area for sign of the Gnaal. They were less than a day from the sanctuary of the Old Forest. He silently hoped they made it. He let his gaze fall upon the ragged bunch he was told to guide. The boys were small and weak in his opinion, dressed in woodland colors and looking near mangy from the escape. Hallis was an old hand and could hold his own. The Dwarf, well, that was another issue. Norgen stood in his rust colored armor scowling again. His dark red hair and beard reminded Scarface of the blood on the freshly fallen snow.

Hallis approached. "What now?"

"This next stretch of land is ripe with places for ambush. There are too many hills and valleys. This is going to be dangerous," he replied.

"Can we go around?"

Scarface shook his head. "No. It will cost us five days at least. We don't have that kind of time. The river keeps our right flank but may prove deadly if we're trapped against it. The nearest ford is leagues away and more than likely patrolled by Goblins. The best chance we have is to ride straight through."

Hallis grimly agreed and they set out at a quickened pace.

A heavy crashing came from the trees to the right once the column entered a twisting valley. Delin's eyes bled white. They'd been discovered at last. His deepest fears were becoming reality. The Gnaals were coming back to finish what they began on the road to Paedwyn. Fennic grinned and drew Phaelor. Dusk was falling, leaving the snow-covered world a haunting shade of its former self. The rangers lit torches and drew in closer for the coming attack.

A large, black shape flew past Delin and off into the darkness. He turned in time to see a torch fall to the ground from a riderless horse. A trail of crimson blood smeared the snow. Arrows flew in the same direction though it was a useless gesture. The Gnaal had struck and one of theirs was dead. Scarface recognized the seriousness of the situation and knew they only had one chance.

"Run!" he yelled.

Panic gripped Delin. He began to sweat and then tremble. A shout brought him out of his delirium. He was just about to drive his heel into his horse to get moving when the great demon of the dark landed in front of him. The horse bucked up on hind legs, throwing Delin before the Gnaal slashed it in half. Blood and ichors splashed both the ground and Delin. Steam rose from the carcass, making him gag. Hot blood coated Delin's face and he started to cry.

The Gnaal stepped closer, sensing death. Delin dared a closer look at his murderer. Massive lesions wept a dark substance coating most of its body. Scaled appendages lashed out at him. A foul odor filled Delin's mouth with bile. He screamed when the decaying flesh curled around his calf. *Tarren, I love you.*

Then the Gnaal dropped him. Darkness fled, leaving the boy and beast in devious golden glow. He looked up into a row of soulless eyes void of color and comprehension. Razor sharp fangs glistened with thick strands of saliva filled the Gnaal's face. Roaring, it turned on a new foe.

Fennic roared back and charged with Phaelor waiving menacingly in front of him. Magic met monster in a blinding flash of light. The shockwave of the blast threw everyone nearby to the ground. The Gnaal screamed again through serrated vocal chords and fell. Sweet pain melted its flesh beyond regeneration. It flapped its ragged wings in a futile attempt at escape. Fennic struggled to his feet and stalked the monster down, leveling the Elven sword as he'd been taught. Using every ounce of strength, he stabbed Phaelor down into the Gnaal's chest. Golden light wepted from every pore until the great demon evaporated into nothing. Fennic dropped unconscious.

"Fennic!" Delin cried and crawled to his best friend.

Norgen and Hallis ran to them. Fennic wasn't moving, though his chest rose and fell softly.

"Fennic, wake up," Delin begged. He looked to the others for help.

Hallis gently picked Fennic's limp body up. "He lives. That is all we can hope for now. The Elves have a healing magic."

Another scream shattered the still. And then another.

Scarface wheeled on them with a menacing look. It was the single most frightening thing Delin had ever seen in a man. "Get them out of here now. You must flee while you still can."

"What about you?" Delin managed.

The ranger smiled. "I'm going to do my job. The dawn is your ally. Ride hard and gain the forest. You'll be safe then."

Scarface looked around and settled his gaze on Scarn, who was the only other ranger close enough. "Keep them safe. All Averon depends on them."

Scarn nodded, slightly stunned from the battle. He thought he'd seen horror before, but never anything so graphic and disturbing. "You have my word," he said.

Hallis herded them onto their horses and led them out of the valley. Horses snickered with fear and anxiety as they broke into a full gallop. The danger of stumbling and breaking an ankle was just as real as the Gnaal, but it was a risk the sergeant was willing to take. They had to gain the Old Forest.

A pair of Gnaals burst from the shadows as the last horse broke away and attacked. Scarface met the charge with despair. Both beasts were twice as large as the first and equally menacing. He looked left and right and sighed. There were six rangers with him. He knew six was not going to be enough to win. Scarface raised his sword and spurred his horse on.

Screams filled the valley in a sea of pain and blood.

THIRTY-NINE
The Old Forest

Dawn nipped hard on their heels. Rays of orange and yellow pierced the clouds, turning the sky a brilliant shade of reddish-pink. There was a heavy chill in the air, and just the slightest hint of wind reflecting off the ice crystals that had formed on everything during the night. When the sun at last crested the horizon, the weary band of heroes had slowed to a walk.

They were exhausted, the adrenaline having left them cold in the middle of the night. Their horses were coated with sweat and breathing hard. All were teetering on the edge of collapse. Sometime during the night Fennic's condition worsened and he now hung near death. An infection was spreading through his body and they were powerless to stop it. The only chance they had was reaching the Elves. His flesh turned a pallid shade, his breathing slowed. Delin, for all his doubts and personal fears, buckled down to stay beside his friend. Fennic needed him now more than ever.

Darkness slowly lost sway and the world returned to normal. Warmth edged back into them. Boulders and trees lost their haunting shadows as the frost melted in the morning glow. And then, just around the last bend, Delin spied a sight he knew would stay with him for the rest of his days. It was the edge of the Old Forest. They had made it.

"Look Fennic, we're there," he excitedly announced.

Delin looked at the majesty of the ancient trees through his tears. They speared hundreds of feet into the sky. It was said some took more than ten men to circle their huge trunks, others were as small as children. Though winter was fast upon them, the Old Forest maintained the splendor of greens it was famous for.

Bright light reflected through the branches, striking the ground in a mottled array of brilliance. Nowhere but in Delin's fanciest dreams could he have envisioned such a place. So full of life. Their problems suddenly seemed insignificant. Here lay peace and a promise of a golden tomorrow. There were no dark Mages, no armies intent on their destruction. Danger was a forgotten mortal punishment. The glories of freedom and life stood in a great expanse before them.

Delin took hope again. Still some distance away, the vision alone was enough to boost his spirits. He could almost feel the warmth reaching out to secure him in a tender embrace. Evil, however, had other plans.

The Gnaal's bellow shook the foundations of the world. All turned to see how close the nightmare was. Fresh terror sprang to life in Scarn's eyes. He'd never been forced to endure such levels of torment. He felt condemned.

"We're dead," he said. "We must use the boy and his magic sword. It's the only way for some of us to escape."

Hallis felt a rage grow. Suspicions about this ranger formed. The old sergeant acted quickly. His hand flashed out and grabbed Scarn by the throat.

"I will not use Fennic just to save your hide. That boy is the reason we are alive now and we owe him better. We ride for the forest. It's not far."

"We'll die before we make it," Scarn choked out. He stopped struggling. Hallis was too strong. A new hatred seethed inside. He knew he was going to kill the man before it was said and done. Dark visions tempted him even before Hallis let go.

"Then we take that chance. Now ride!"

They rode faster than before. The landscape whirled past in streaks of colors. Slowly, the Old Forest loomed closer. They raced forward for another league before Hallis turned. He instantly wished he hadn't. The Gnaal was behind them and closing fast. He watched the monster speed across the frozen ground. It ran like one of the great cats used in the gladiator arenas, fluid and graceful despite its malevolent intention. Heavy muscles rippled from the strain of pursuit. Then Hallis noticed something. There was only one. He wondered if Scarface and the rangers had killed the other. Doubtful as it seemed, Hallis took hope from the thought. One was better than two of the beasts.

They fell under the shadows of the hulking trees and the Gnaal slowed. It was reluctant to come closer. It remembered the pain caused by the Elves so many years ago. Ancient fears resurfaced. The Master would accept no failure. The Gnaal was driven by one binding command. Kill the sword bearer. The Gnaal must kill or be destroyed at the hands of the Silver Mage. With a reckless howl, the great demon of Gren charged.

"We're out of time," Norgen shouted. "The horses are spent and still it comes. Let us take our chances and make a stand, Hallis. At least we can say we made a worthy end."

Hallis finally let his shoulders drop in defeat. To come so close, he thought. He was tired. Tired of running. Tired of fighting for his life. Norgen was right. If they were going to die, they might as well salvage what dignity they could. Fate seemed against them from the beginning, always conspiring to steal hope when it was within their grasp.

"So be it," he said in a grim voice. "Let's end this."

He eased his horse to a stop and slid to the ground. The air sang with the sound of steel being drawn. Hallis tried thinking back to happier times, times when his life was full of promise. He relived his first meeting with his wife when he was a mere ranker, barely old enough to hold a sword. She was the daughter of simple market owners. They'd fallen in love that day and his life was richer for it. His love went beyond the power of mere words.

"Fates be damned," Hallis growled.

Norgen stood beside him with his axe in hand. The blades glimmered menacingly in the morning light. He prayed to his god, Gru, for the strength to meet death bravely. With the Gnaal so close, there seemed little doubt he would be meeting his god soon.

"You're all mad!" Scarn shouted. "Didn't you see what happened to the others? Didn't you? You'll be killed for sure."

He looked at Fennic, who was hardly awake. Delin clutched him, his eyes screwed shut.

Scarn circled his horse towards Hallis. "I was wrong about using the boy, but we can still make it into the forest. It's right there."

His voice was weak and pleading with a hint of shame. Never had he been forced to beg another man, but what was about to happen was worse than his darkest torments. Not even the agony caused by the Hooded Man was so great. The Hooded Man, Scarn cursed him. He vividly recalled the day they met and how much he hated the man. The thunderstorm. The night drenched in rain and wreathed in lightning. He almost wished to be back in that drunken stupor. Perhaps it might help combat the terror barreling towards them.

"No. We stand," Hallis said.

"Smile, ranger. This is what you wanted. A straight fight," Norgen added with a grunt.

The Gnaal was barreling down on them and was meters away when it slowed. It felt the sword. Phaelor's power mocked it. The stench of death choked the air around them. Sharp claws flexed with anticipation. Axe and sword wavered before it. The distance gently closed. The Gnaal reached back to strike and roared in rage.

"Attack!" came a fair voice from the rise behind them.

Only Scarn took time to look back. He was greeted by a sight as terrifying as it was comforting. Twenty slender warriors sprang from the snowbanks, dressed in light leathers of green and brown. Their faces were painted dark with mud, lending them a dangerous appeal. Tolis Scarn was staring at a company of Elves with bows drawn and aimed. The Elves showed no emotion as they loosed the first volley at the Gnaal.

Confused by their sudden appearance, the Gnaal halted and lost the advantage. Another ten Elves appeared from the right and launched long, barbed javelins that struck with bone crunching impacts. Sickly ichor bled from the wounds. The arrows feathered its head and neck, causing the Gnaal to rear back and try to block them. Norgen bellowed and launched a smaller axe made for throwing. The Gnaal groaned and reeled from minor pain. The arrows normally wouldn't have had much effect, but these were Elven weapons and were enchanted. It felt unprecedented pain.

The Elves moved quickly to surround the monster. The Gnaal screeched from the intensity of the assault. Soon it dropped to its knees. A hundred small wounds took their vicious toll. Hallis stayed Norgen from charging in and getting himself killed by a stray bolt. Together they watched with amazement at the precision of the Elves.

They moved in a well-rehearsed orchestra, like a pack of wolves. Their actions were slow and deliberate as if they'd done this a hundred times. The Gnaal sank lower to the ground. It saw death coming and welcomed the embrace. The Gnaal was tired and broken. Long centuries of fear and loathing left it cold. It wanted to die. The Elves drew the noose tighter and made for the killing stroke.

An Elf slightly taller than the rest left his kinsmen and walked directly to Fennic. He laid a tender hand on the boy's forehead and whispered words none of them understood. When he finished, Fennic was awake and moving. His heart warmed at the Elf's touch. The Elf nodded at him appraisingly.

"Now boy, finish this ere it has the chance to recover and come at us anew," he told Fennic. When he spoke, the words were melodious and precise.

Fennic sighed and let the Elf help him to his feet. He drew Phaelor on his own and limped towards the fallen Gnaal. The Elf was beside him every step. Menacing eyes glared up at the pair, and the sword. The Gnaal silently pleaded for a merciful demise. For reasons he'd never know, Fennic felt his contempt and fear ebb. The Gnaal was merely another of the Silver Mage's pawns. It didn't have a choice any more than he or Delin. Fennic plunged Phaelor into the Gnaal's heart with one swift stroke.

A gasp escaped the dying body and the Gnaal was no more. Ashes of the corpse drifted away on the morning winds. One by one the Elves disappeared until only the one remained. He stood beside Fennic like a father.

"Well done," he praised. He then turned to the others, noting with interest the presence of a Dwarf. "I am Celegon, son of King Alsenal. You are safe here now."

Hallis bowed his respect. He was about to reply when Fennic's eyes rolled to the back of his head and he collapsed.

FORTY
Foul Memories

The Cracked Crystal of Tol Shere was a delicate myth for the majority of Malweir's population. For Sidian, the Silver Mage of forgotten Ipn Shal, it represented a lifetime of lust and desire. He'd spent decades searching for the shards. Only when all four were found and the crystal was remade would it unlock the secrets of magic long lost. His very will was bound by that desire. Sidian knew it was the lure of power and the unobtainable. The energy and magic spent to find them left him a haggard shell of the man he once was. Once the crystal was complete, he would be new again. Whole to reign over the world with an iron hand. He shivered at the thought.

It took him one hundred and fifty years to recover the first three, with Dakeb hounding him at every turn. The first was the easiest to find. It was buried and warded by the dead in the Zurn Swamp at the base of the Acrafen Mountains in southern Antheneon. The wards set by his former brothers were simple, hardly problematic though more than enough to keep mortals away. Then again, the Mages never counted on one of their own ranks to betray their trust.

The second he found protected by sea monsters in the Bay of Cuerlon. Again, it was only slightly more difficult than the spirits of Zurn. The third was the trickiest for it was hidden deep in the heart of the land of Chrysrar, home of the dragon men. The sentient saurians kept the shard deep in the Crystal Mountain where their queens hatched and dwelled.

He had the fourth in his grasp once, more than a hundred years ago, but was again stopped by the aging Mage. Sidian bitterly remembered the battle in the Deadlands, far to the north when Dakeb slipped in and stole the fourth and final shard from under him and the last of the great dragons. Perhaps it was because Sidian was in the process of subjugating Gren at the time, or just maybe Dakeb was that good. Either way, Sidian lost the shard and never came close again, until now.

He cursed Dakeb's name and all the man stood for. He once thought the goodness of Ipn Shal and the Order of Mages was destroyed. He knew for certain Dakeb had been killed during that fateful night when dozens of Mages, dark and light, lost their lives. He was wrong. Dakeb returned again and again to foil his desires. How? He didn't have the answer and it plagued his dreams.

Alone in his private tower, Sidian paced tirelessly. Worries creased his brow. There were too many unanswered questions bothering him. A pang of doubt surfaced. Every other person involved with the shards of the crystal were dead and gone. He'd made sure of that, one way or another. Two questions lingered above the others. How did Dakeb manage to survive time and again, and how did he learn of his quest? Neither presented answers.

And now the quest was almost finished. The final shard was almost in his grasp. If it hadn't been for Dakeb stealing it all those years ago, Sidian would never have been forced to hire Tolis Scarn. Sidian hated the man. He found Scarn incompetent and a small time thief and murderer. His value depreciated over time until Sidian was ready to kill the man himself and find someone else. It was only blind luck that Scarn managed to stumble onto the shard and the damned Elven sword. Sidian idly toyed with the thought of turning Scarn into a Gnaal or something worse. Perhaps, he'd just have Hoole slit his throat.

Winter's Day was only ten days away. If the crystal wasn't complete by then he'd be forced to wait another thousand years to open the gateway to the nether world and release the dark gods. Sidian wasn't entirely confident he had a hundred years remaining. His enemies would rally together and invade Gren in a wave of unsuppressed fury. Aingaard would be destroyed and he would die. That much was certain for those same armies made that mistake once before and let him live. He made all of them pay but one, Averon. Their time was now and Sidian was going to make it bloody.

He let his eyes focus on the dark vermillion glow coming from under the door to his right. Sidian carefully stepped towards the chamber where the crystal was. Even now he was wary of the raw power. Not all of its secrets had been discovered. Thousands of years passed since its creation and he knew there was still much to learn. He felt the energy coming from it. It spoke to him. The crystal wanted to be remade. The dark light throbbed in his old heart.

A heavy rapping on the main door disturbed his ecstasy. Sidian crossed the chambers and opened the door with a wicked glare. Before him stood a man flanked by a pair of Goblin guards. He was dressed in the traditional furs of his people and was lean and hard. His features were angular and vile. There was no shortage of weapons on him. Rage flickered in Sidian's eyes.

"You know not to disturb me when I am in here, Spendak," he growled.

The man, Spendak, bowed curtly. "Forgiveness, Master. But word has come from the front."

"Speak."

One of the Goblins twitched nervously. Sidian noticed this and whispered dark words. The Goblin burst apart into mist with a muted scream.

"Lord Hoole is making the initial assault. All units are in battle positions and awaiting further instructions. The war is proceeding as planned."

Sidian wasn't particularly interested in that. It was what Spendak didn't say that he wanted to know. "There is more you are keeping from me," he seethed.

Not wanting to go the way of the Goblin, Spendak cleared his throat and said, "A Gnaal has returned with news of the stone."

Sidian beckoned the man into his sacred chamber and closed the door.

FORTY-ONE
The Eve of Battle

Black smoke billowed from scores of fires on both sides of the river. Sparks and ash clogged the air making it nigh impossible to breathe. The very land had become death for hundreds of meters. The very world was strewn with carnage and hundreds of mangled corpses. Soldiers for both armies ran to put out the flames before they burned the camps to the ground. Heavy clouds completely blocked the light of the moon. It also kept the temperature from dropping below freezing.

Steleon walked up and down the lines offering encouragement and praise. As much as he was doing, he knew there was so much more needed. Fighting the Goblins was one thing, and now he had to contend with the burst of winter hammering them. Steleon knew he would lose more than one man to frostbite. Surgeons and field medics were in place and ready, but they'd be swarmed soon enough. Steleon wondered how many men would die waiting to be seen by one of the surgeons. It was a grim thought.

The roar of catapults firing overhead brought him from his daze. The assault had begun anew. Steleon drew his sword and bellowed threats at the enemy. His men took heart from it and joined in. Rocks and burning pitch exploded throughout the camp. Soldiers took cover as best they could while commanders growled for them to stand fast. It was ungainly to show fear in the face of the enemy. Steleon was proud of them all, but he couldn't let that distract him now. He knew what was coming next.

Battalions of Goblins massed just beyond the range of sight and waited for the horn that would signal their attack. Ten thousand of the gray warriors huddled together in the darkness and readied to advance. There was a latent fear rippling through the ranks. The same fear any army felt on the verge of battle. Soon bodies would be pierced and torn apart in a brutal bombardment of arrows and catapult fire. The survivors would impale themselves on the outer defenses of the enemy bank and then push through to meet pike and sword. They'd seen it before and knew they would see it again.

The horn blew deep and hollow. As one, the Goblin battalions chosen for the initial assault rose and advanced on the river. They struck the icy water at its lowest point and waded through. Dozens of bodies fell in the counterattack. The Goblins didn't stop. Survivors trampled over the fallen, using the bodies for traction. They had rage. The people of Averon had made them suffer too many times and it was time now for revenge. They met the defensive line and roared. Pikes dropped, skewering scores more while arrows continued to rain down into their massed ranks. The attack withered and finally died. Those few hundred that survived turned and fled for their lives.

Steleon finally fell back from the front rank of defenders. His sword arm was sore, and he was exhausted. War was a game for the young. Men clapped him on the back and cheered his name as the grizzled commander left the line. He had much planning to do and needed as many able bodied commanders in the command tent at once. He had a feeling the Goblins would be throwing themselves at them like that all night. The king was waiting for him not far from the line. There was a patch of drying blood on his armor. Steleon knew it wasn't Maelor's.

"It's been a long time since we've had a fight like that," Maelor said, offering a small flagon of red wine to his friend. "Good weather for it. I never liked fighting in the heat. Too much work for limited results. The men tire too easily in summer."

Steleon had to agree, though the king's presence made him nervous for obvious reasons. "Sire, we're outnumbered four to one with more coming down from the mountains every hour. Not to mention the dragon we haven't seen yet. The enemy is focusing on this camp from all reports. It is dangerous for you to be here. I have a feeling the Silver Mage knows you are among us."

Maelor scowled slightly. "We are not having this discussion again. I am king, and my decision is final. Where else would I belong if not with my army at their darkest times? I stay."

Cool winds snuck under the tent flaps, rustling around just enough to chill their legs. Tongues of flames leapt up to lick at the fresh air.

"The winter will be cold this year. I often wonder how my father handled such times. It's a hard life, that of king. If only things were different. Maybe the weight wouldn't be so oppressive."

Flames reflected in the king's deep eyes, though Steleon was sure a tear formed.

"I think you've had the better of it," he said. "You're a lucky man, Steleon. No politics or politicians pulling you away from your intended course. Just a soldier with an army. Just a man." The old king fell silent, suddenly feeling much older than his fifty-four years.

Melgit burst into the tent. His eyes were bloodshot and had dark rings around them from the lack of sleep. "Word has reached me that the enemy is more cunning than we presumed. It appears they are led by a man, not Goblin. Our scouts returned with confirmation of a tall man directing the movements and attacks. His peers whipped the Goblins into ranks and pushed them forward in a foul language none should remember."

A shudder passed through the king's heavy frame. "The language of ancient Gren, before the Mage contaminated it. Once they were no different from us, then generations of servitude corrupted them. They are his prime power, holding the throne for him. They are worse than any Goblin or Troll. These men represent what each of us has buried inside."

"This complicates matter," Steleon said. "I have a feeling that we are in a far more perilous place than we were five minutes ago."

"We've fought men before," Maelor reminded them. "They bleed and die the same as us. All it takes is a longer spear."

Maelor placed a hand on each of their shoulders. "I believe our priorities have changed. Pass the word to our archers. I want them to kill every man they see walking among the enemy first. If we kill their officers, the army might crumble."

Jervis Hoole stepped from his tent and lifted his long, pointed nose to the acrid smoke clinging to the air. Normally, he took comfort in the odor. It helped him soothe when times grew trying. This morning there was a different taint to it. The air wasn't quite so bitter. Something new rode the morning winds. Perhaps it was merely being so far from his ruined homeland that weakened his senses. Or just perhaps it was the Silver Mage at his strongest. He was finally exposing his plans to the world.

Hoole hated the Mage. The throne of Averon was already promised to him, but Hoole wanted more. So long as Sidian breathed, that wasn't going to happen. Thoughts of the Mage dead or in shackles amused him. His hatred ran deep for the man that turned his once proud civilization into a mass of murderous slaves. Hoole wanted Gren. His darkest heart wanted to see the world burn for the damnation of Gren. Burn for the wrongs committed against his people. Jervis Hoole hated life and could think of no better way for it to end than in flame.

He stood on a low rise and watched as the last of his Goblins retreated from the icy water. So few had returned. No matter, he told himself. They were fodder anyways. The fewer Goblins he had to contend with once the war was done the better. His aide, a greasy man with the features of a weasel, narrowed his eyes.

"Shall I order the catapults to provide cover fire until they are safe?" he asked.

Hoole snorted a laugh. "To what point? I wasn't expecting any of them to survive. The few who did now have a greater appreciation for their pathetic lives."

"The Mage won't be pleased," hissed the reply.

Jervis Hoole squared on the smaller man. "Who's going to tell him? This is my army."

"Only when he's not here. He will not be pleased with this."

Moving faster than the aide could react, Hoole drew his dagger and slammed it to the hilt in the man's stomach. A prolonged gasp escaped his as he clutched at the wound and fell to the ground. Dark blood trickled down onto the fresh snow. Hoole smiled, knowing it would take long for the man to die. He watched the whole time. Finally, when the man was dead, Hoole blinked.

"Perhaps your ghost can tell him," he whispered to the corpse.

He summoned a pair of Goblins to haul the body off and tried wiping some of the spattering of blood from his boots. Inside his tent, he found his war captains arguing over the best way to attack the enemy. None of their plans particularly interested him. Nor did the men. They were a bitter lot, of which less than half fully supported his ultimate plans. Hoole let them argue and walked on to the rear of the tent where his private chamber was. He was surprised at the simple pleasure a cot offered.

The night, however, was different. Troubled dreams tormented his sleep, stealing away the pretense of normalcy. Monstrous faces hidden by disease and shadow leered back at him. The more he struggled, the tighter their grip became. He was soon at their mercy. Hoole screamed as their fingers dug into his flesh, sinking deep into muscle and bone. He was lost. The man clung tighter and Hoole knew he was going to die. The glory of tomorrow was a forgotten dream as the light left his eyes.

Jervis Hoole awoke in a cold sweat. His heart threatened to explode. His head throbbed in anguish. He was afraid. The dreams were steadily getting worse and more intense. Still shaking, Hoole decided to see if his captains were still there. A gleam danced in his eyes. Demented as his dreams were, they inspired new heights of torment. He now had a plan.

The battle lines of Gren formed not long past midday. Battalions formed ranks as deep as they were long. Men rode up and down the line with curses and promises of endless misery upon failure. Their whips cracked and lashed out at the diseased flesh. Goblins snarled and pointed their weapons. The hatred was mutual. A bugle trumpeted over the eastern shore and the army stepped forward in rolling mass of contempt. It was an awesome sight to behold. Tens of thousands of the squat Goblins bristling in black mail and arms chanting in their foul language. A cheer roared when they saw the men of Averon blanch. The Goblins took strength from their fear as the river drew closer. None of them wondered why the enemy wasn't opening fire yet, for they were engrossed in the myth of their strength. Another five hundred meters and the first ranks would be at the frigid waters of the Thorn River.

They were his heavy infantry, designed to smash through the defenses and let the lighter, more agile units pass. If they could break a hole in the lines and reach the enemy command area, Hoole knew his odds at winning the war were unbeatable. He watched the battle develop through the looking glass. It was going almost too smoothly. Then he noticed why. The enemy wasn't moving. They were just standing there. The time it took him to realize the problem, and issue orders, was already too late.

"Sound the halt!" he bellowed.

It was already too late. Hoole watched in horror as ranks of Averonian archers appeared on the berms with arrows nocked. The world slowed until he watched it all in slow motion. He saw every splendid detail as arrows plunged into his army. But it wasn't Goblins being killed. They were aimed at the men of Gren. The Goblins continued to press the attack, oblivious to what was happening. All the officers were being struck down. Without them, the advance would crumble. Hoole cursed and watched helplessly.

Then the distinctive whump of a catapult firing sang clear. Then another, and another. The air grew so thick with smoke and bodies he quickly lost sight of the slaughter.

A wave of black and gray desperately tried to turn and flee, but the rear ranks were still pushing forward. Maelor and Steleon watched the chaos develop. Their gamble paid off. Hundreds were already dead and more fell every moment.

"That seems to have worked," Maelor said.

Steleon agreed. "This time. Whoever leads them won't be so careless again. The officers will lead from the rear, out of bowshot."

"You take our success too lightly. Everyone we killed today is one less to lead them. Goblins can't fight without a leader," Maelor scolded.

"Spoken like a politician," Steleon replied. "What comes next? The dragon? All out invasion? We cannot hope to hold them forever. Soon they'll set aside the feints and ploys and drive a stake through us."

"Then we must beat them to it."

"Attack them?" Steleon asked in shock.

Maelor emphatically shook his head. "Goodness no. That's suicide and even I can appreciate that. Our allies will be here soon." He paused. "We've dealt them a heavy blow, Steleon. They'll not be so eager to come at us again. Let as many men stand down as you can afford. This battle is going to end sooner or later, and we'll need all our strength to see it through."

The middle aged king walked away to be with his men. Their love for him was apparent, though Steleon could see the cracks in his rigid foundations. He was afraid the man was going to break and lead them all to ruin. After all, no man was his own father. Baeleon's reputation as king and soldier was harder than most to live up to. The general hoped Maelor was equal to the task, else the kingdom of Averon would perish.

FORTY-TWO
Recovery

Fennic lay at death's foot. His breathing was shallow, and his skin had turned a waxy shade of pale. Delin knelt by his side, softly weeping for his best friend. The others stood around the boys in a loose circle. Elves watched the perimeter for another Gnaal, though none believed another was coming. After leaving the battlefield, they'd ridden until sunset and stopped only when they reached the security of the borders of the Old Forest. At first, a little fresh water and dried fruit seemed to help Fennic, but his condition worsened until he was but the shell of the boy he used to be. They dismounted in a soft clearing and tended their wounds. Most of them were unharmed, though Scarn was exhausted beyond measure. He wished he'd listened to his father those long years ago. If he had, he wouldn't be in this dire predicament.

Celegon frowned, his pointed ears barely visible under his flowing golden hair. He was by no means a healer. The son of a king and next in line to ascend to the throne, Celegon was trained in war and affairs of state. He'd never known love and often contemplated leaving for adventures. Family life never suited his desires. Now he found himself in the middle of war he knew nothing about and the life of a boy slipping from his grasp.

"I cannot heal him. His ailments are of the mind, not body. There are many wicked weapons of Gren and the Mage," Celegon said quietly. "Perhaps my father may help, but there is nothing I can do."

"If he'll see us at all," Derlith spoke.

Hallis sensed the division between them and became irritated. "There must be some way. Why else would he be chosen to carry that damned sword…"

His voice trailed off as Phaelor began to glow. Hallis suddenly had an idea. He rushed over and pulled Delin up. The boy didn't resist. If there was a chance to save his best friend then he would do what he could.

"Draw the sword, Delin," Hallis told him.

Doubt flickered in his blue eyes. "Are you sure? I thought it chose Fennic?"

"No, I'm not sure," Hallis admitted, "but I have an idea. Look at the way Phaelor glows. It is not the aggressive amber of combat. See, look how it turns an almost azure color. I think the sword wants to help."

Delin eased mighty Phaelor from the scabbard, feeling a pleasant tingling move through his body. The sword talked to him. It sang of peace and joy, filling the tiny glade with new hope and inspirations. Even Scarn believed in the magic at that moment. A soft humming reached out to soothe them all.

"Now what, Hallis?"

Celegon slid forward. "Look for a wound. He has to be injured."

The Elf prince knelt and started at Fennic's feet. He rolled up the left pant leg and suddenly rocked back in shock. There was a foot long gash on his calf, dripping puss and a black fluid that smelled poisoned and rotten. Delin threw up.

"Quickly, touch the sword to the wound," Celegon excitedly said.

There was a blinding flash as sword met flesh. A foul hiss tainted the crystalline air. Fennic cried out from unconsciousness and fell back. Pale green fog seeped up from the wound, evaporating as it touched the air of the forest. Phaelor lost its glow.

"Did it work?" Norgen asked. It was the first time he'd spoken since joining the Elves.

Celegon looked down at the Dwarf. His eyes were hard and unforgiving, as if Norgen committed some personal crime at some point in their lives. Old hatreds were hard to let go. "I cannot say. This is a different brand of magic. None but the Silver Mage knows its depth. Ah, look! Already the wound heals."

Flesh knitted back together in an ugly scar. Fennic didn't stir. His memory of the pain keeping him asleep for the time. The Elves went about making camp for the night. There was no way the boy was going to move anytime soon and the others needed the rest. A pair of hunters returned carrying a field dressed boar and a sack filled with wild vegetables and roots. Norgen's stomach growled despite his worries. Dried meats and old cheese only went so far. He watched the Elves prepare the boar, already selecting which shank he planned on eating.

Delin felt a small measure of strength creep back to him. Maybe it was the heat from the roaring fire, or the thought of fresh food. Either way, he was slowly forgetting the horrors of the last battle. He knew, deep down inside, that there was no going back to his old life. He'd seen and done too much for that. He idly fingered the purple stone in his pocket and sat down to eat. Stomach full and his mind at peace, Delin yawned and curled up on a bed of pine needles and went to sleep.

"Those boys have been through a lot," Hallis said.

"We all have," Norgen added. "They're good lads."

Celegon spoke to one of his warriors who nodded and disappeared into the night with three others.

"You have nothing to fear so long as you remain in our lands. Evil has no purchase in the Old Forest," he assured them. "It was not always so. There was a time when Goblins and Ogres used to cross our borders regularly. The Mages helped end that. Master Thellios established a ward around the forest preventing the Dweilfolk from entering. That magic remains as strong today as it did all those hundreds of years ago. You may all rest in peace here."

"That may be well and fine, but we can't stay hidden here forever," Norgen said a little harsher than he intended.

"Your quest is known to us, Master Dwarf. The full armies of my father will not commit to war, for he has long held the belief that we need not worry in mortal affairs. I and a few of my closest supporters can see different. My people are at your disposal."

Scarn struggled to keep the feeling of disgust building in him from showing.

Hallis swallowed a mouthful of red wine and asked, "How many are in your army?"

Celegon was hesitant to respond, for his people were one of secrecy. If too much became known of them it would embolden their enemies. Even among those he'd just saved, he was ill advised to tell. But trust had to begin somewhere. The dilemma was more entertaining than he thought possible. His loyalty to his people was fierce, but he knew they had no hope of standing alone against the powers of the Silver Mage.

"We number in the thousands. They are loyal to the king and will not fight. I have three hundred with me," he finally said.

Norgen snorted his disgust. "Three hundred against all of Gren? Stay in your trees, Elf. The end will come rushing to you."

Scarn entered the conversation. "I don't remember seeing an army of Dwarves coming to the rescue."

Norgen's hand crept to his axe.

"There will be no violence here," Celegon sternly commanded. He turned back to Hallis. "My father does not believe we should involve ourselves in the affairs of men. I think he fails to see what is truly happening. If the Mage wins he will mire the world in darkness. All races will wither and perish. Phaelor coming back to our borders confirms my worst fears. The Elves must play a part in winning this war."

"Can the sword kill him?" Hallis asked.

"Very likely. The smiths who wrought it were a secretive bunch, the last of our druids. My own mother was one. They disappeared not long after the sword was finished and presented as a gift to the King of Averon. None can say what it was designed for, only that it is a dangerous tool of magic."

Scarn listened to the conversation with a guarded interest. He didn't know what was going on and didn't care. None of them had even hinted at the stone yet and that made him suspicious. He guessed one of the boys had it, but they were never left unattended. The Hooded Man was waiting and Scarn was running out of options. Very soon he knew he was going to have to kill them in their sleep and flee. If only the Elves would stop watching for a few moments. Their eyes never left him, nor did the silent knowing twinkle in them. Scarn felt afraid.

The Elf prince suddenly turned his head towards Scarn and whispered, "wi tolo fel sa doma?"

Scarn stared blankly back as if in a daze. Satisfied, Celegon continued. "A small number of us have gone against my father's wishes as best we could without openly rebelling. Goblins and the like may not be able to enter our lands now, but there's no lack of them scouring the perimeter. We hunt and kill them where we find them, but their numbers are strong. Long has it been since we saw so many outside of Gren."

"They have come down from the mountains in force," Hallis told him. "War is openly ravaging Averon now."

"The mountain fortress fell?" Celegon asked. "I bore witness to some of that battle. Your people fought valiantly."

Hallis struggled to contain his emotions. So many of his friends had died there.

"We heard rumors of a dragon, but one of the great wyrms has not been since in ages," Celegon went on, hoping to find some trace of denial in their faces. His heart sagged when they remained silent. "My father must be warned of these developments. The world is in more danger than I thought."

"Makes you thirsty for a mug of frothing ale, doesn't it?" Norgen asked with a smug look. He was content that the Elves were feeling the same pain as the rest.

Celegon eyed the Dwarf appraisingly. "Actually, I think it does."

Thus began a hesitant friendship.

Hallis went on to explain how they'd arrived at the Old Forest and the importance of their quest. Some of the Elves visibly balked at the tale. Only Tolis Scarn sat impassive through it all. He was finally getting the missing pieces he needed. In the middle of hearing about Mages and magic, a thought stuck. Could the Hooded Man and this Sidian be one and the same? It would explain much. New avenues of approach came to him and he started thinking about the future.

"The way to Gren will not be easy," Celegon said once Hallis was done. "Snows already claim the mountain passes. This year threatens to be worse than recent memory. Most, if not all, of the ways into Gren will be guarded or blocked. It is nigh impossible to enter the foul land in winter."

"Impossible or not, we have little choice. Too many lives depend on our success," Hallis replied.

"And they don't even know it," Derlith remarked.

Rubbing his frustrations from his brow, the lean Elf prince exhaled deeply. "That ale is sounding better by the moment, Master Norgen."

Norgen laughed deep and resounding. Truth be told, he found himself starting to like the Elf, despite their differences. Dwarves were known to be jolly, in their own fashion, and enjoyed a good laugh almost as much as a good fight.

Celegon stood. "My three hundred can take you as far as the borders of Gren. After that it falls on you to reach Aingaard. I wish there were more, but you'd need an army to assault the capital. Three of us, me included, will accompany you if you'll have us. The others return to Averon to fight the Goblins. Either way, death will be our boon companion."

"Then it already knows where it stands," Norgen growled with a chuckle. He exhaled a long plume of bluish smoke.

Celegon nodded approvingly. "Rest now. We make for my city in the morning."

FORTY-THREE
Of Elves

Long ago, in the ages before man first set foot on these shores, there came a race of beings as close to the gods as possible. They were tall and elegant, wise beyond reckoning. They spoke in flowing sentences in a golden language soothing to both mind and spirit. They were fair, in both deed and appearance. They lacked the dark hearts commonly found in lesser races. By the hundreds they came and settled in quiet places they knew weren't likely to be discovered very easily. Centuries came and went and their communities thrived.

Then the darkness came. Goblins and Trolls and a host of other foul creatures came up from the depths of the world and ravaged Malweir. They had grown tired of living in the dirt and rock and wanted the world for their own. But the light hurt their eyes and forced them back underground until the sun went down. In the night, they were murderous. They killed everything they could find in their unholy thirst for vengeance. The First Ones assembled an army and met them in their mountain homes. The battles were fast and deliberate. Thousands were slain and there was no end in sight. Slowly, the Dweilfolk spread, pushing the First Ones back.

Men discovered the land not long after, not knowing the dangers they stumbled into. They found the First Ones and named them Elves, for the language was too much for their tongues. An alliance was formed and together they took the war back to the Goblins. But the caverns of the world were deep and there seemed an endless line of enemy warriors. In the end, the alliance won. The Goblins retreated underground to plot and fight with each other.

For a time, men and Elves lived peacefully. But the Elves were never many and soon they found the cities of men encroaching on their lands. The Elves retreated into the forests and forgotten places of the world. Men quickly forgot the past. Elves left Malweir by the hundreds. Those who stay were cursed to live through the time of the Mages. Nothing was ever the same after.

Delin stared at the Elf prince with wonder. He'd never heard such a tragic and grand tale and the world of the Elves suddenly intrigued him. There was nothing comparable in Fel Darrins. He wondered if anyone back home would believe him when he returned and told his own tale. He doubted it, after all, he wouldn't believe it himself.

Celegon led them down a gentle slope and at last the great city of the Elves came into view. Even Norgen gasped. The Old Forest grew thick in the river rich valley. Shades of brilliant green softened their eyes. Birds and butterflies were everywhere. In the center of the vale stood an enormous tree, stretching for a league in any direction. The canopy reached high into the sky and sunlight fell in dazzling sheets. There were flowers of every color and the very air smelled of nectar and honey.

"Behold, Elvanara, my city," Celegon announced with pride. "It is a series of thousands of trees connected at root and branch. Most of the buildings are in the air. So high one cannot see them from afar. You are welcome here for as long as you are my guests. My father will wish to see you soon. Let us take Fennic to our healers. I pray it is not too late."

"I've never seen anything so beautiful," Delin breathed. His skin was warm and felt rejuvenated from the touch of the sun.

Celegon smiled. "Nor will you ever. Our time is ended. Once my people owned the world, only to find out it wasn't what we wanted. Someday Men will come to understand this as well and it will fall upon future generations to right the wrongs of our fathers. But take heart my friends. This is the safest place in all Malweir."

Word had already spread through the Elven city of their arrival. People stopped what they were doing to watch the odd procession go by. Strangers hadn't been seen or welcome here since the Mage Wars. A heavily armed patrol of city watchmen marched out to meet them. They wore hard looks and leather plated armor. Each was armed with sword and bow. The leader stepped forward and held up his hand.

"They cannot be here," he told them.

Celegon refrained from sneering at him. "I must see my father, Nalit. These are my guests."

The Elf guard was not impressed. He'd never took a liking to the prince and this was the perfect opportunity to exercise his authority over him.

"You know the laws, prince," he said. "They must be taken to the cells for judgment."

Celegon slid from the saddle and walked up to the guard. Contempt blazed in his crystalline blue eyes. Nalit balked, his sword arm raising.

Celegon snarled. "Raise your sword and I'll take your head."

Nalit hesitated, seeing something in the prince's eyes that made him wary. "Your father's laws are clear in this matter."

"I am taking them to my father. If you think you can stop me, then try."

The guard's face flushed. He very much wanted to duel this wayward prince and show him who his better was. Just then Norgen coughed. The Elf guard looked up and saw his bearded face leering down on him, axe haft in hand. Nalit knew this was a fight he could not win. Embarrassed and angry, he stepped aside to let them by.

They wound their way through the great Elf city without further problems.

Celegon returned to his joyful self, offering hints and bits of history of his beloved land. They found a reception from the king's chamberlain and a contingent of private guards awaiting them at the base of the palace steps. Word already reached Alsenal and he was expecting them. They were escorted into the king's personal chambers and waited until the lord of the Elves entered.

Father and son embraced, though it was stiff and awkward. Alsenal turned and looked upon the others with mild interest. He was taller than the other Elves they'd seen. His eyes were stern and unyielding, befitting a king. An extraordinary life lent him an air of authority and wisdom beyond reckoning. His features were sharp and angled with just a hint of menace. He was exactly the way Delin thought a king should look.

"I have been told of your trials," he said to them in a calculating, drawn out voice. "It is unfortunate that ones so young must endure so much, but necessary I think. Be that as it may, you are not welcome here. Man rejected our bond of fellowship long ago and I am not willing to sacrifice all that we've built to harbor fugitives."

"Father!" Celegon protested.

Hallis bowed slightly. "Fugitives we are not. The boy carries Phaelor, the sword your people created. I think you are more involved in matters than you care to believe. We go to Gren to end the work of the Silver Mage. This is a task for all races, king."

Alsenal raged inside. His fury grew, but the words rang true. Elves created Phaelor for intended purposes and then they turned their back on the rest of the world. This left the Mages alone before the task was complete. A war soon followed and nearly succeeded in tearing the world apart.

"Those days are gone from us. My people have watched as you continue to destroy the world. Men are creatures of war, and I'll have none of it," he said. "Healers will see to your young friend. May he find peace. The rest of you will be placed in quarters befitting my…. guests. I will decide what to do with you later. Celegon, you will remain with them. Do not let them leave this city."

King Alsenal turned and left, his cape of forest greens shimmering in the reflected light off the leaves. A pair of female healers entered not long after and carried Fennic away to the healing houses. Food and drink was provided in abundance for the others and for a brief time the war was forgotten. They made small conversation and tried their best to relax, but there was still something uneasy about the situation. Only Scarn remained reclusive. He watched them without betraying his inner hatreds. Unfortunate circumstances made them allies and he tried to be hospitable at least. He knew that while he was in the Elven city he needed to mind himself. There was little doubt the Elves would take care of him quickly if he made the wrong move. He saw it in their eyes. They knew he was a bad man.

Most of them were dozing lightly when a house servant came for Celegon. The king was demanding his presence. The young prince held his head high as he walked into the polished halls and to his father. Alsenal sat at the head of a long mahogany table. A half empty wine glass sat before him. The servant closed the door behind Celegon.

Celegon felt his father's wizened eyes rising to meet his own. "What did I do wrong?" Alsenal asked.

"Nothing, Father. This is the way it must be."

The king snorted a laugh. "Your foolishness has put our entire way of life in jeopardy. Even if the Silver Mage wasn't turning his eye on us we are surely a target now. He will be tracking Phaelor and will know it is here."

Celegon clenched his fists behind his back. "I've seen the world, Father. It is cold and dangerous and no one race can stand alone against it. The Mage has loosed his wrath upon Malweir. Averon is just the beginning. Do you think he has forgotten what the Elves did to him all those years ago?"

"Your mother was just like you, proud, tireless and stuck on her convictions," Alsenal said. His tone lost some of its edge. "Do you remember when she disappeared? I tried talking her out of leaving, but she wouldn't listen. Foolishness! The whole lot of them. Why the druids ever listened to that madman is beyond me. And now no one has seen or heard from them in what?"

"Three hundred years."

Alsenal vividly recalled the day the Elf druids left them. They were under the guidance of Vandir Olthan. He was on a proclaimed crusade for the lost relics of a time long past. His madness stole fifty good Elves, including Alsenal's wife. Three hundred years past and the king's sadness deepened daily.

"We can't keep living in the past, Father," Celegon whispered. "Time has come for us to reclaim part of the world. Surely you must understand that we are at least partly responsible for the shape of the future? The Silver Mage is just as much our problem as theirs."

Alsenal closed his eyes and bowed his head. His shoulder's sagged, losing some of their rigidness. "I have grown tired, son. It is time for me to step down as king. It is a burden and treasure. I have tried to lead our people as best I could, but the years have grown long on me. I find I no longer have the taste for it. Will you take my place, Celegon?"

Celegon was dumbstruck. This was the last thing he expected to hear. For a while he stood and stared at the proud man who was his father. Was he serious? Celegon felt a twinge of regret and pain for what he had to say.

"There is a matter I must attend to first, Father," he said, suddenly unsure of himself.

Alsenal covered his eyes with his hand. "You always did have too much of your mother in you, boy. Why do you wish to throw your life away?"

Celegon wanted to reach out and hold his father. He wanted to help him forget the pain and see the joy in life. But now was not the time. He had to be strong, for the both of them.

"Father, we have a chance to end this war now, before it comes to our lands. If my displeasing you is the price I pay to save our people, so be it."

He was dismissed with a bitter wave. "Go then. Do as you will. Leave me now."

Celegon closed the door behind him and fought to keep the tear from breaking free.

"Where do we go from here?" Delin asked.

He felt stronger. The good food of the Elves put meat back on his bones and cheered him greatly. There was a magic about Elvanara he wished was everywhere. His biggest concern was in Fennic recovering. They'd heard no word since the healers took him away, a day ago.

Hallis rubbed the fresh stubble on his chin. "North, past the Thuil Lake and the end of the Gren Mountains. There will be enemies about, but it is less guarded than the passes south."

"That's if the Elf king allows us freedom," Scarn reminded with a scowl.

He was trying his best to fit in, relieve some of the suspicion and maintain the solitary attitude of a ranger of Averon. Perhaps he tried too hard. He knew they watched his every move. It was as if they were waiting for him to reveal his true purpose. Scarn was jumpy in the tree city. One wrong move and his future ended. He suddenly regretted speaking.

"It serves no purpose to keep us," Norgen spat. "We are not the enemy."

Delin turned from the conversation. It was the same they'd been having since they became guests. He looked out the window, down the soft fern covered ground, where children played.

"I have a bad feeling about this, Hallis," he admitted. "I can feel the world constricting on us and there's nothing we can do to stop it."

The old soldier walked over and laid a gentle hand on the boy's shoulder. "Don't speak of such things. There are many leagues ahead of us and none know the future. Hope," he paused to touch his heart, "Hope lies in here. Never forget that, Delin."

The door opened without a sound and Celegon entered. A troubled brow marred his handsome face. There was a new weight on his shoulders.

"Our healers say young Fennic is improving, though by no magic of theirs. He is still ill, but out of danger for the moment. It's quite remarkable. The sword must be staving off the infection," he told them.

"Is he well enough to travel?" Hallis asked. He hated to sound cruel, but time was against him. Winter's Day was fast approaching and he had a feeling that whatever was going to happen was going to be on that day.

"Aye, but not fast or hard," Celegon said. "My father has agreed to let you go as soon as the boy is moveable. As I said before, my men will be with you."

Norgen nodded thoughtfully. "That should make for interesting company."

The Elf prince looked down on him quizzically.

They were ready within the hour. It was all faster than Delin liked. Being here among the Elves helped him remember a happier time. Back before the notion of traipsing around the world really formed. He desperately wanted to see his family again, Tarren most of all. Leaving Fel Darrins, the way they did, was wrong. He knew that now. The madness of it was passed and he felt glum over what his parents must be feeling. He had just finished saddling his horse when he stopped and stared at Fennic.

The boy crept towards them on unsteady feet. Color was returning to his face, but the horrors he'd endured would forever scar him. They helped him on his horse and pretended as if nothing was wrong. He mumbled his thanks to each of them and let Hallis lead his horse. The small band began their trek out of the Elven haven. There were no crowds, no spectators to see the heroes off. Not even the once mighty king looked down on them. The last image they saw was of children playing in the ferns.

Winter's Day was eight days off.

FORTY-FOUR
At Ipn Shal

A pale, shapeless fog covered the land. Tarren held out her hand but still couldn't see it. The heavy cloak she wore did little to stop the chill from seeping in. She shivered atop Ris Kaverling as the Centaurs marched on. He often spoke with her, keeping her company and taking her mind off the winter. The harshness of Shadom Gein lay behind them and was already a dwindling memory. They'd seen things that no one ever should and lost two friends in the process. Tarren almost felt sorry for the Goblins pursuing them. Almost. Their screams would forever haunt her dreams.

The deep chill penetrated to her very bones and it took a concentrated effort not to let her teeth chatter. She focused on why she was here, and why she even left Fel Darrins in the first place. It was all for Delin and Fennic. She'd left home nearly a month ago and didn't feel any closer to finding them than she did when she left. All her adventures amounted to nothing. Despair tried stealing her will and everyday was a struggle to avoid it.

Tarren rode on. She remained grim set and determined to save her friends. Only the Fates knew what was in store. She felt miserable. Her one moment of happiness came from Ris and his friends. She almost cried when he told her how they'd met Delin and Fennic some weeks prior. They didn't know where the boys were headed, but it was enough for Tarren to keep hope.

Ever since she left home Tarren felt pulled in a certain direction. First it was the pony in the forest and then by the conversations with the Centaurs. Fate clearly wanted her to be more than she imagined. Thoughts of returning home didn't even enter her mind anymore. She'd come too far to turn back. Deep down inside she knew Papa would be proud of her. The smooth sound of water lapping at the shore brought her from her thoughts. She shivered even more as the wind howled across the water.

"What is this place?" she asked, fighting to keep her voice from trembling.

"Thuil Lake," Ris replied. "This was once a wondrous place, full of life and cheer. The Mages and their greed ended all that. There are stories of villages along the shore that were wiped out during the war. I have seen some of the ruins. Strangely, no ghosts haunt this land. There is a great void. Nothing grows or lives. There is nothing but emptiness from here to the ruined fortress."

"Ipn Shal," she whispered.

"Yes," he said, "the ancient home of Mage kind."

He said nothing more for a time, for the way was laden with dangers. The Mages had set up protective wards in the surrounding countryside and it would do them ill to run afoul of one. Plenty of folk lost their way in these parts and were never heard from again. He silently prayed the way Dakeb taught him was still clear.

"You'll be leaving once we reach the castle, won't you?" she finally asked him.

"I'm afraid so. There are more Goblins threatening our village. My people will have need of me if we are to survive," he told her with a tinge of sadness. "Take heart, Tarren. You have friends where you least expect it. The one awaiting you is dearer than you could imagine."

She was confused. "Who? I've not even spoken a word to anyone but you since I left home. I haven't met anyone else."

"You'll see," he chuckled. "I have a feeling all will be explained once we reach Ipn Shal." Tarren grew flustered. She knew he wasn't going to say anymore and that bothered her. She felt he knew the answers to her questions and wasn't telling her.

"I wish you didn't speak in riddles," she sighed.

"And I wish I could tell you more, but I have been sworn to secrecy. I can only tell what I am allowed. Trust me, please. That's all I can ask. It may not seem like a smart thing, but it will work out," he tried to reassure her.

"Very well. As long as I have no choice. I promise, no more questions," she submitted.

They rode on. The air grew slightly warmer as they moved away from the great lake, though it was hardly enough to take away the chill. Tarren tried to ignore the situation and enjoy the ride. Then a thought struck her and she decided to ask.

"Do you suppose we'll ever see each other after this?"

Ris smiled, but she didn't see it. "Who can say? I've never been so far south as your village. I can imagine the stares from your folk as we rode into town. Ha! Perhaps I just might find my way south once this war is done. It would feel good to stretch my legs on the southern plains."

Nothing seemed to bother her after that. Calm took her. Delin and Fennic were out there somewhere and she was going to find them. It was that simple. The rest of the world was a minor consequence.

They finally caught sight of the massive ruins just before dusk. Bulky and overrun by nature, the mass of Ipn Shal eased into view. Massive buttresses and towers pierced the sky in challenge to the gods. Marble statues and intricate fountains littered the courtyards. Tall windows of every color let the light in from every angle. There were libraries and studies. This was where the Mages did their work and honed their skills. All before the darkness, before the war.

Fires had gutted the keep, erasing the good committed through the years in the span of a single night. Some said you could still hear the screams if you listened at just the right time of the night. Ruined gargoyles, once the untiring and fearless protectors of the keep, stared down mockingly on the lonely band seeking entrance. The drawbridge was down, but was partially rotted away and spanning a muddied moat whose water had long since dried up. The magic of Ipn Shal was gone. Empty windows watched the world pass without concern, for they were broken and black as the dark of hearts. Tarren shivered. They stepped onto the drawbridge.

A man emerged from the shadows. He was smallish yet imposing at the same time. His shadow was large and hulking. Tarren didn't understand, for the sun was already beyond the horizon. She couldn't see any part of him, but he was familiar somehow. He waited for them to enter the courtyard.

The Centaurs bowed as the man slowly removed his hood. Tarren stared into his deep brown eyes. She found them faded and abused from time. He was neither too thin, nor too fat. He had shoulder length hair that framed a wizened face. Time and the elements dried his skin out, stretching away the fat and marking it with rough looking lines. He stared back at Tarren and smiled.

"Hello again friends," the old man joyously said. His voice was strong, with a slight rasp.

Ris reached out and shook his hand. "It hasn't been so long, though the way was perilous. It is good to be here."

"Come," the old man said. "Let's get inside. The snows will be here before long. Let's take that chill off before you get sick."

Tarren, having dismounted, simply stood and stared at the odd man. He seemed to notice this and smiled even deeper.

"My apologies, Ms. Brickton. Solitude often makes me forget my manners. I have many names in many languages, but you can call me Dakeb."

Smells of roasting meat and stewed vegetables laced the air. A large fire burned in the corner of the chamber. Dakeb whistled as he pulled a loaf of fresh bread from a makeshift oven by the fireplace. He seemed pleasant enough to Tarren and she found herself relaxing. This was the first time she'd been able to do so since leaving Fel Darrins. She listened as he started and forgot conversations as he saw fit.

"I know the past few weeks have been strained and arduous for you, and I would truly love to explain everything," he told her.

She groaned inwardly. "But you can't?"

"Oh no, no, no. I know much more than I wish to. No Tarren, I'm simply expecting more guests tonight and don't want to repeat myself. I know it's not exactly polite of me, but once you've lived as long as I have you find yourself settling into old habits. Don't mind me if I start talking to myself from time to time," he said with a wink. "I do hope they arrive before the storm hits." He stopped rambling long enough for a mouthful of venison.

Late in the middle of the night a small band of riders circled Thuil Lake and presented themselves to Ipn Shal and the lone mage. Tarren and the others were already asleep, despite her strange desire to meet these other people. Dakeb alone greeted his guests. Two of them stared back in disbelief. The world was long and wide, holding many secrets and wonders, yet none so great as the meeting at the drawbridge of a place on memories spoke of.

FORTY-FIVE
The Battle for Averon Begins

Most of the fires had been put out. The rest smoldered and cooked among the scrub brush and saplings. A third of the camp's tents were ruined. Ash and soot coated the ground, polluting the snow with a repugnant odor. Those men not needed on the line were immediately ordered to begin cleaning up. Steleon feared subsequent assaults while the army was distracted with cleaning the mess, but it was a chance he was going to have to take. Dead bodies meant disease. As it were, the field hospitals were already overflowing. Too many wounded had to stay outside in the cold. And too many would be found frozen to death the next morning. Steleon shook his head ruefully. This had to end soon, he thought. A foul mood fell upon the defenders. The army of Averon balanced on the silver edge.

"I'd almost forgotten how disgusting this business is," Maelor said as he walked up to the fire Steleon stood by. "How many years do we lose from this madness?"

"Too many, sire," Steleon replied without looking at him.

They stood in silence for a moment. Neither man wished to think about the next attack. Both worried about the forces they'd secretly begun sending across the river. If things went awry, four thousand men were going to die without help.

Steleon sighed. "I've seen worse. We both have. Men die. The sun sets and rises. It's just war, my king. Our focus needs to be on winning this next fight. We have to time it just right, or else…."

He let his words trail off. There wasn't need to speak them. A runner came up just then, out of breath and sweating. He bowed to the king and saluted Steleon.

"Sir, the last units from Commander Melgit's force have finished the crossing. They are getting into position now," he reported.

Steleon smiled inwardly. "Very good, son. Go and get yourself something to eat. I suspect it's going to be a busy day."

"This is an awful gamble, Steleon," the king said once the youth was out of earshot. "A lot is riding on this."

A strong wind blew in from the south, gathering intensity as it went through. It was snowing again. The day promised to be horrid.

Melgit slowly and quietly moved the bulk of his four thousand riders across the fog enshrouded river. They were more than a league upstream and used the darkness of the middle of the night to their full advantage. Doubts and suspicion plagued him, regardless of the situation. His orders were precise but he still had reason for concern. Too many things could go wrong. Just getting across the river undetected was a miracle. His horse snorted its apprehensions.

"I don't like this either," Melgit said in a soothing voice as he gently pat the horses neck. "Not one bit."

A rider pulled alongside him and saluted. "Sir, the last ranks have crossed. All units are forming up in place."

The old cavalryman nodded. There was a distant look in his eyes. "Thank you, Roffort. Ensure the captains set out pickets. I don't want any surprises tonight."

"Sir," Roffort acknowledged and rode away.

When he was gone, and Melgit was alone again, the world seemed a colder place. He sighed and tried not to think about the dawn.

"I'm afraid this is going to be an interesting day," he told his horse.

The darkness started to break.

The snow came down harder as the day broke, driven down by angry winds. White flakes kissed men and horse alike, briefly gracing them with an almost holy appearance before melting away. Melgit watched his breath form heavy plumes of mist. The morn was sharp and cold. A good day for killing, he decided. Winter never held an attraction for him, though he'd lived through his share of them in the field and on campaign. For now, necessity and revenge kept him warm, as it did with most of the men he'd brought back from Gren Mot. This was what they'd been waiting for. Melgit rubbed his frost laden beard as Roffort returned with news.

"Everyone is in place, Commander."

Melgit nodded his approval. They'd spent hours moving everything where it needed to be for the coming assault. It was arduous and painstaking work, for too much noise would alert the enemy and have an entire army breathing down their necks. Melgit was mildly pleased they were still being unnoticed. He looked up at the cloud filled sky and wondered how much longer before he saw the signal. For now, he had nothing to do but wait, and the waiting was worse than the fighting. Melgit tried counting the falling snowflakes to pass the time.

And then he saw it. A brilliant ball of flame shot from one of the catapult batteries. He grinned savagely. It was time for revenge. Melgit drew his sword and began the advance on the Goblin army.

Thick ropes of blood spiraled through the air to the sounds of steel hacking and ripping flesh. Men, Goblin, and horse fell dead in the fury. The attack was swift and brutal, hundreds dying in the first few seconds as the horsemen thundered through the enemy encampment in total surprise. Four thousand riders tore into their foes without remorse. Sword and axe rose and fell, splitting flesh and breaking bones. The first ranks bore steel tipped lances; the second flaming brands. Soon most the Goblin camp was in flames. Screams rose from the dying and the ones who didn't know they were already dead.

Melgit skewered a man of Gren and cursed. Sweat beaded on his brow, mingling with the drying blood and spots of gore. His muscles were sore and ached from the continual strain of so much cleaving. He reined up in the middle of the carnage and looked around. Most of the Goblins were up and arming themselves and preparing a counterassault. His own men had penetrated the enemy lines by five hundred meters and were reaping a terrible price. Occasionally he watched one of his men fall from the saddle or being dragged down by dozens of grey hands. He knew if he stayed any longer the enemy was going to decimate his forces.

"Roffort!" he bellowed. "Have the bugler signal retreat!"

The surviving horsemen disengaged and fled back the way they'd come. Most didn't bother hacking down at the Goblins. Instead they chose to barrel down on them and keep running. Melgit was the last to leave. He turned and looked back at the Goblins and was pleased to see so many following. The enemy was falling into the trap. Melgit only hoped the trap was in place and ready to go. If not….

Jin yawned again. It seemed that's all he'd been doing lately and he couldn't figure out why. Horses snorted and pranced anxiously all around him. The noise was almost deafening. He couldn't even see most of the riders. Like so many others this morning, he too wondered how much longer it was going to be. Then he heard the sounds of thundering hooves coming at them fast. The answer came swiftly. Averonian cavalry emerged from the mists like things from a nightmare. Horse and rider were covered in blood and ruined flesh. The smell of sweat and blood permeated the air. Jin looked into some of their eyes and knew fear. They were the faces of grim death, and they knew it. Melgit was the last to ride in and he halted when he saw the young soldier. A chunk of Goblin flesh clung to his neck, leaking ichor down his armor.

"They're fast behind. No more than a few hundred meters," he told Jin.

The man to Jin's right, old and with a gray beard, clutched his spear tighter. He looked appraisingly at the younger commander and turned to his adjutant. "Sound the call."

Trumpets rang through the formations spanning the width of the valley.

"I didn't think you were going to be joining us this fine morning," Melgit told the rider in purple and black. He noticed the elk head on the man's shield. The riders of Harlegor had finally come to their aid.

Gray Beard aggressively replied, "For too long the Goblins have been free to do their evil. That all ends today."

Melgit took an instant liking to the man.

Small dark shapes began to appear in the mist. The Goblins were upon them. They came on recklessly, frothing at their mouths and cursing guttural cries in their own foul tongues. They were so intent on murder they never saw the six thousand reinforcements charging at them. The lines clashed in a vicious impact. The contest was fierce and bloody and the riders had the advantage. Foot soldiers were no match against heavy cavalry. The Goblins collapsed and were slaughtered to the last. The riders, with Melgit's men reformed and at their center rear, continued the attack into the enemy camp.

The hasty defense Jervis Hoole had erected was no match for the thousands of cavalry fighting for their lives and lands. Men and Goblin alike turned to flee the onslaught. Resistance lightened and the combined forces swept from one end of the camp to the other and rode on south. Both Melgit and Graybeard didn't think the Goblins were going to make the same mistake of following them again and gradually eased their horses to a trot and then a walk. Man and beast were exhausted and the day was still growing.

"I'd say we stung them hard today," Gray Beard laughed.

Melgit agreed. "It was a good day. Let us get back across the river before they decide to finish it. Commander Steleon will want to speak with you."

Jervis Hoole stood in the middle of his encampment seething with rage. Thousands of his forces were dead, butchered was more like it. Those who lived left their fallen comrades and scoured the battlefield in search of dead enemy. The ones they found were torn apart and mutilated beyond recognition. Hoole ordered companies of Battle Trolls to form and prepare to attack. He was not going to let the Mage send in his dragon and rob him of another victory. Gren Mot should have been his, but Sidian stole it. The plains of Averon were not going to be in question. He stood alone, long black hair sweeping across his face, and stared across the river at his hated enemy.

Steleon slid his looking glass closed and let out a pent-up sigh of relief. The raid had been executed better than he hoped. Enemy casualties were atrocious and their camp was now in worse shape than his army. Hundreds of his forces died in the attack, but the cost, as regrettable as it was, was worth the results. The temperature began to drop and it was barely past midday. Maelor folded his arms across his barrel chest and said nothing. Their thoughts quietly turned to Fennic and Delin and the hope of a nation.

FORTY-SIX
Reunion

Winter erupted with a fury. Snow swirled in thick blankets around the ruins of Ipn Shal, covering the ground in a matter of minutes. Howling winds drove the storm to frenzied heights. The stone buildings rocked under the assault. Trees bowed under the combined weight of snow and ice. The desolate land soon became a winter battlefield. Tarren awoke with a start as something heavy crashed against her window. She was comfortable under the thick furs and warm fire burning brightly near the bed. Once her heart slowed, she yawned and stretched. Until now she hadn't realized how worn out she was. One night in a real bed was almost paradise. Tarren slid into her robe and slippers and eased her way downstairs with a rumble in her stomach. She was hungry.

A row of travel packs lined the base of the stairs. Her heart beat a little faster. The guests Dakeb promised where finally here. Now she could learn the full story, or so she hoped. In her mind, Dakeb seemed a little off. Her apprehensions eased somewhat when she entered the kitchens and saw Dakeb preparing breakfast. He looked up at her and smiled.

"Ah, good morning. I trust you slept well enough?" he asked.

She yawned again. "Quite well, thank you. I could have slept that day away."

"And miss my cooking? For shame," he laughed. "You wouldn't do that to an old man, would you? I so rarely get the chance to show my true talents."

Tarren held her hands up defensively. "I'd never." She hesitated before saying, "I see we have company."

Dakeb handed her a cup of tea. "Indeed. They arrived late in the night." He paused and looked out the big bay window. "Just in time I'd say. That storm is terrible. You'll meet them soon."

Tarren just nodded and ate a meal of quail eggs and fried toast. Dakeb refilled her mug and added a drop of honey to it. She thanked him with a warm smile. For a while they sat and talked about nothing at all. They laughed and joked, expressed private sorrows and past pains. It was midday before they knew it. Dakeb excused himself to add more wood to the fire.

Tarren looked up at the sudden movement in the doorway and felt her mouth drop open slightly. Two tall and lean figures with long, flowing hair and sharp features entered and bowed to Dakeb. The old Mage waved their formalities off and gladly introduced them to Tarren. She was almost too shy to say anything to the prince of the Elves. Norgen stumbled in a while later and headed straight for the food. He tore a leg from the roasting lamb and helped himself to a mug of thick mead. Tarren hardly knew what to think. Elves and Dwarves, Centaurs and Mages. She wondered what came next. According to the number of packs in the hall, there were four more guests. Would they be as strange as the ones already present? A child's excitement gripped her.

A pair of men entered, talking in low tones. Both were dressed in rugged clothes and had the look of soldiers. She thought she recognized one of them but couldn't place him. There was a dark air about him and that worried her slightly. Voices came from the hall and her heart stopped. She froze. Delin and Fennic stepped into the kitchen and she almost feinted. Dakeb smiled behind her. Delin stopped short, his dark brown eyes soaking her in. Weeks of travel and hardship did little in the way of diminishing his love for her. He almost thought she was an illusion and was hesitant to speak lest the spell be broken.

"Tarren?"

She broke out in tears and rushed into his arms. They almost fell if not for Fennic putting a steadying hand in his friend's back. The moment was bittersweet for him. Not for the first time he wished he had something so promising to look forward to at the end of the journey. He wasn't jealous per say. Both were good friends and deserved as much, but he wanted his turn. And deep down inside the hurt blossomed.

Hallis leaned close to Norgen and said, "Lovely girl. I see why he goes on about her."

The Dwarf snorted. She didn't have enough hair for his liking and was too thin.

"Cheer up, Master Dwarf. I've lived a dozen lifetimes and love is the one thing I never came to know. This is a queer world indeed," Dakeb told them.

"Wondrous at times," Hallis added. "I was about the same age when I met my Chella."

Tolis Scarn didn't share their enthusiasm. He watched the girl with repressed fascination, certain he knew her from somewhere. Then it dawned on him. The bar maid from that dumpy village he'd visited south of Relin Werd. So, he smirked, he'd been closer to the stone than either he or the Hooded Man believed the whole time. He stood and quietly thought of their differences.

Pain and suffering gripped his life. He'd left home at a young age and grew up alone and empty. He was forced to provide for himself from the age of ten and learned the rules of a hard life. His first lesson was the cruelty of men. Nothing came easy for him. Not from the day he stumbled home to find his papa standing over the corpse of his mama with a bloody dagger in his drunken hand. Tolis ran for his life and never looked back. He left the youth to their pathetic reunion and plotted how to kill them all.

"I never thought I'd see you again," Delin whispered between kisses. "What are you doing here?"

"Looking for you," she replied.

Her eyes darkened when they caught Scarn lingering in the background. Why was he so familiar? He was unkempt, his hair was uneven and stringy and he wore a gnarled beard. The man she feared and spent so many nights dreading was clean-cut and evil. This couldn't be the same man. Mystery swirled around him and it was that moment she decided to stay away from him entirely. Nothing good would come of talking to him. She lost herself in Delin's embrace.

Delin's heart fluttered. The heat from her body ebbed into his own, breaking the growing darkness in his heart. He almost felt alive again, which made his next words even more painful.

"You shouldn't be here, Tarren," he told her. "You have no idea what you've become involved in."

Her eyes narrowed in an accusing glare. "Delin Kerny! I've risked my life in one fashion or another trying to reach you in time. Didn't you know the danger you were in when that stranger came into town asking questions? I've been looking for you to warn you ever since you left Fel Darrins."

Scarn's head snapped up. His eyes bore a subtle glow. What else does this girl know, he wondered.

Delin was confused. "What danger? What man? The first trouble we found was after meeting Norgen in Alloenis."

"Now just a minute. Don't go blaming me for this. I was minding my own business until you two barged in and got us involved in the middle of a war," Norgen growled back. Never mind the fact he was coming for the purpose of going to war to begin with.

Dakeb finished drying his hands on a kitchen cloth and stepped in the middle of them. "Friends, I agree there is much to discuss and many adventures worth telling, but this is not the way to go about it. Eat first. The fate of all Malweir rests in our hands and I'll not make that decision hastily. Not again. Arguing will not solve the riddles in your minds."

One by one they made their way to the enormous oak table where they helped Dakeb pass out plates and mugs and served themselves a hearty stew of duck and winter vegetables. Brutal winds howled and the snow continued to fall. Finally, once the last plate was pushed back, Dakeb looked each of them in the eye while he carefully measured his next words.

"Centuries ago the order of Mages thought it wise to find a way to store all their knowledge for future generations to build and improve on. We developed the Crystal of Tol Shere. You see, it held all our wisdom of magic and life. We poured our very souls into it in the dream of making Malweir a better place. But there were flaws we didn't see. Somehow the crystal became cracked, and darkness crept in. It was unnoticeable at first, but that darkness soon began to corrupt. Sidian, who was a member of the ruling council became too close to the crystal and fell under the darkness. His mind turned to madness and he quietly began subverting our brothers to his dark cause.

"It was only later we learned his true intentions. He aimed to open the paths to the underworld and release a plague of demons upon us. Our wars were long and bloody, and evenly matched in the beginning. Both orders were eventually destroyed. Only a handful survived the final battles and from them I have heard nothing in all my long years of travel. I fear only Sidian and I remain." Sadness lingered in his eyes.

"The crystal was destroyed, or so we thought. The battle here in Ipn Shal shattered it into four equal shards. In fact, it was broken by Phaelor, Fennic, for that was the purpose the Elves built into it. The sword was made to destroy the evil of the crystal and restore order in the world. But it did not destroy the crystal entirely. The four pieces were next to impossible to erase and I hid them in distant parts of the world. The remainder of my life has been devoted to keeping them from Sidian.

"In this I have failed. For he now holds three of the four shards. I was able to recover the last right before he found it and have been in hiding ever since. Regrettably, his agents got too close to me when I was in the south and I was forced to leave the shard with a pair of boys on their way to Paedwyn."

Delin and Fennic both gasped and looked at each other. Delin slowly reached into his pocket and withdrew the purple stone he'd been carrying for so long.

"You're the crazy old man from Relin Werd," Fennic exclaimed.

Dakeb offered a loving smile. "I regret the ruse, but it was necessary. There was so much I needed to prepare for and I had faith in you when I spied Phaelor. You see, you were already involved, though you didn't know it. The instant Phaelor chose you, Fennic, was the day you became a part of this eternal struggle and the fate of the world. I wish it were otherwise, but the sword chooses who it will."

Tarren looked at her love and felt her heart sadden. Dark Mages and war. She had a terrible feeling she was going to lose him forever. Then a thought struck.

"But what about me?" she asked. "What part do I play in all of this?"

Silence filled the kitchen until even the crackling fire became a whisper.

"That," Dakeb answered in a slow voice, "is a matter I can't figure out. My heart tells me that you have an important part in the coming days."

Scarn saw the object of his quest for the first time and felt his throat go dry. After so many days and months searching it was now within his grasp. He forgot the legend the Mage just told and focused on how to steal it back and end his affair with the Hooded Man.

Dakeb held the shard up. "This tiny piece of crystal, without value as a gem, is the very key to existence in Malweir. But there is hope. Phaelor is once again in our hands and even young Tarren is here." He looked at her. "Perhaps you remember a pony in the woods?"

Tarren smiled. All the doubt and emptiness in her left with the knowledge she'd been watched over since she left Fel Darrins.

"What of the rest of us?" Norgen asked. "Just how much time is left before it becomes too late?"

"Very good questions," Dakeb replied. "The second is the more easily answered. Time runs out on Winter's Day. That is the one time of the year Sidian can complete his dark ritual and bring doom unto the world. The crystal must be whole again exactly at midday. Only then will the gate open. That gives us just seven days to reach Aingaard and destroy the crystal once and for all. Your parts in this are unclear.

"Know this. Sidian fears you boys. He fears what he can't control. His agents are scouring the countryside in search of you. They will kill you and steal both sword and stone if they can. We will not let that happen. This is a dangerous time for us all. The balance is disrupted. Not even the Fates can say who might win or lose."

Dakeb's words drowned out for Scarn. He couldn't take his eyes off Tarren. His nerves were jumpy. His chest constricted under the pressure. Play it cool, he had to remind himself. Goblins and the occasional Gnaal would serve to keep their suspicions off him until he found a way to contact the Hooded Man again. His biggest concern lay in Tarren. He saw the way her eyes silently accused him. She knew. She had to know. Scarn decided he needed to get her alone and find out exactly what she knew.

Dakeb calmly finished his spiced cider and covered a belch. The winds howled a little fiercer, desperately trying to bring down the walls of Ipn Shal.

"I must leave you for the time being. Finish your meals and enjoy this reunion. We head to Gren when the storm breaks."

Hope had once again taken root in the fortress of Mages.

FORTY-SEVEN
Departure

It took another full day before the storm dwindled enough to let them leave Ipn Shal. The mood inside the fortress was changed. Reunions were over and it was time for business. They packed their bags and loaded the horses. Tactics and strategies were discussed with interest, for they knew Gren was not going to be forgiving. With the storm gone, they knew it was only a matter of time before Dakeb led them out.

Hallis found the old Mage standing on a snow swept balcony overlooking the courtyard just before dawn. Only a light sprinkle of flurries drifted lazily by. Dakeb had an oddity about him, as if there were a void of life or death.

"What troubles you?" Hallis asked.

"It would be easier to explain what doesn't bother me. The timing of this doesn't make sense. Why do you suppose he sent his armies forward when he doesn't have possession of the fourth shard?"

Hallis stood and watched the dawn break. "He must be searching for it. He has to think he's close to finding it too if matters have gone as far as you say. That would explain the continuous attacks by Gnaals."

Dakeb turned on him with eyebrows raised. "Would it? I believe there is something more sinister at play. Did you know that the Gnaals were once Mages? He discovered a dark lure and changed their very souls, twisting them into the ruin they are today. When he dies, so will they." He paused for a moment. "These boys will need your protection, Hallis. They look to you for advice and as a role model. We are entering a dangerous part of the journey. The Silver Mage grows stronger the closer we get to Winter's Day. Even I may not be able to stop him in time."

Hallis didn't really want to hear a confession like that from the one man they were trusting to see them through the darkness, but he understood the reasoning. He'd lost track of how many times through the years and different campaigns, sitting alone in his tent or pulling guard in the middle of the night, he'd felt the same. Soldiering was a difficult and often loathsome business that demanded a constant strain of the mind and body. He'd done his share of killing, but never took pleasure from it. Hallis killed only in the name of defense and his country.

Friendships were short in his line of work. Too often they ended abruptly. People came and went too fast to remember. A military career wasn't for everyone, in fact only one in twenty decided to make it a lifestyle. A goodly number of those seldom made it longer than five years. Hallis made the mistake of befriending several men over the course of his career and most of them were dead now.

All in all, he had relatively few regrets in life. He had friends sprinkled here and there. A few he even managed to keep track of when he wasn't deployed or on campaign. It was Chella who kept him healthy and sane. Without her, his loneliness would have finished him off already. She was by far the stronger of the two. She had to be. Hallis made a promise to himself that this was it. One way or the other he was going home to his wife for good when this quest finished. But he had to see to the security of Delin and Fennic first. Without them the dream of Averon was ended.

"My sword is theirs for as long as they need it," he finally told the Mage.

He wanted to ask Dakeb what would happen if they simply held the stone here until after Winter's Day, but the answer was painfully obvious. Sidian would come for them in force and wouldn't stop until they were all destroyed. Going to Aingaard and destroying the crystal first seemed the only way to keep the Silver Mage off guard. Even then it was only a small glimmer of hope.

"Good," Dakeb replied. "Now come. I believe it is time for us to leave. It has been so long since I was last on a grand adventure."

"I pray we live to enjoy the tales of it," Hallis said with a stone voice.

So do I. Dakeb silently agreed.

"We're really going to do this?" Tarren asked after mounting her horse. She'd come so far with one thought in her mind and now that it was accomplished she didn't know what to do. The one thing she did know was that she wasn't letting Delin get away from her ever again. Delin reached over and gently squeezed her hand for strength.

Clearing his throat, Norgen said, "Best we get this over with now."

"Indeed," Dakeb said as both he and Hallis entered the stables. "Time is now as much our foe as the Silver Mage. Make no mistake, friends. There can be no hesitation when the time comes. We must strike the head if we are to win the day."

"Let's go," Hallis said. "We have a long road to travel if we're to arrive in Gren on time." He mounted his horse and led them from the ruins of Ipn Shal.

One by one they filed out of the stables and over the shattered drawbridge. The sun was blindingly bright on the pure snow, a stark contrast to the imposed darkness of the old fortress. It was a pleasant enough change made more so by wisps of fading clouds barely gracing the blue sky. The air was suddenly warm again, not enough to enjoy a day outside, but enough to take the chill off until dusk. Ice and snow covered the landscape. Icicles dripped from the fangs of the stone gargoyles and windowsills. Tarren looked at the world with fresh eyes. For the first time life held a certain beauty she'd never noticed.

"It's almost a shame we're leaving. This place must be gorgeous in the spring," she said to Dakeb.

The old Mage pulled his hood over his head and whispered, "Once upon a time."

Scarn was the last to leave the ruins. He held the trail of the formation like he'd seen the other rangers doing before. But mostly he hung back because he needed to think. He wasn't sure how much longer he was going to be able to use his anonymity. The girl was a problem and it troubled him to great lengths. A voice in the back of his head whispered dark plans for her. So Scarn plotted and waited for his chance to strike.

Dakeb turned one last time from atop his roan stallion to gaze upon his ancient home. Memories rushed by him. Halls and conference rooms filled with Mages and delegates from the kingdoms. Children played and sang from the nearby village. Elves and Dwarves visited for advice and wisdom. People of all races came to see if they had the gift of Mage blood. Those days were gone now. Empty windows stared back down on him, featureless eyes haunting his every movement. Mocking centuries of failure laughed at him. Dakeb and Sidian were the last of their breed, and Dakeb had little doubt Malweir would be better off with both gone. He suddenly longed to be with his old friends again. The burning in his heart for lost loved ones was almost too much at times. Hundreds died for the satisfaction of a fallen brother gone mad. Dakeb cursed the paths that led them to this moment in time.

Winds gripped a partially rotted shutter, forcibly slamming it against the stone wall and an already broken window. Life was gone from Ipn Shal. It had become a hall for vagrant spirits and cobwebs. The knowledge buried inside was dangerous and much more than Malweir was ready to handle. Dakeb wished Thellios were there to offer his counsel on the matter. The problem of the great libraries had to be addressed. Thellios and all the rest were no more than spirits and fading memories in an aging man.

"Everything all right?" Hallis asked.

Dakeb smiled weakly. "Yes."

Hallis nodded once and rode on. He left Dakeb to deal with his own miseries. They had five days to reach the morbid throne of Gren and end Sidian's threat. Between them and success lay a slew of obstacles, the least of which being a series of rolling foothills and a great swamp bordering Gren.

The ten of them filed out into the wild. Dakeb hoped the Silver Mage wouldn't learn of them too soon, for he had agents in every land, from Antheneon to the deserts of Jebel.

Steam rose from the sheets of ice blanketing Thuil Lake. The storm left over a foot of ice on the lake and huge snow drifts everywhere else. Thick pine trees littered the land in their eternal green. Clumps of ice and snow weighed the branches down, adding a depressed feel to the day. Black squirrels with fluffed white tails darted among the boughs, pausing occasionally to peer down on the invaders of their territory.

Tarren looked up at the tiny trickles of snow coming down and smiled. She felt her cheeks burn from the wind and her nose grew numb despite the intermittent sunlight poking through. She watched her breath come out in heavy plumes of steam. Her fingertips, lodged deep within fur lined gloves, were getting colder. It didn't take long for the comforts of Ipn Shal to fade from her memory. The hardships of winter travel didn't bother her so much. She had Delin and he was her pillar of strength. She honestly wouldn't know what to do without him.

The very thought of Delin brought a smile. She watched the way his curly hair framed his round face. His eyes were captivating, holding a love so deep and clear. Tarren had no doubt they were meant for each other. She confided her feelings in her mother not too long ago and her mother hugged her tightly and cried. Its love, her mother said, and no better feeling is there in all the world. Whatever destiny the Fates had in store, she was glad they would meet it together.

He was as much her strength as she was his. Weeks of loneliness on the road served to intensify his feelings towards her. That first night in Ipn Shal was almost a dream. They embraced and never let go. Eventually they fell asleep in each other's arms.

It pained Delin to watch her suffer with the rest of them. She deserved better and he knew he couldn't give it to her, not now. He'd promised Fennic to see this matter through and he aimed to keep his word. He laughed to himself. All they had to do was destroy the most powerful man in all Malweir and escape a land teeming with Goblins and worse. He caught her looking at him and blushed. Tarren did her best to stifle a giggle.

"What's so funny?" he asked, his hopes of his embarrassment going unnoticed quickly faded.

"Did you ever think we'd be weeks from home in the company of so many strange folk marching into the very heart of darkness?" she asked to quickly change the subject rather than explain her amusement.

He confessed. "I've always dreamed of taking off like this to find my own adventures. You know that. The stories of the old times did it, I think. If you only knew how I longed to ride into battle and be the hero. The glory, the fame. There was a time when I found it all intoxicating, but no more. My own adventures are dark and filled with nightmares. I don't wish them on anyone, Tarren. I just want to go home now."

"I never wanted to leave to begin with. Momma always said you boys were going to get me into trouble one day," she said with a sly grin. "You've taken me halfway around the world, Delin, and I'm not going to let you get away again. There's only one way you can fix this mess."

He was almost afraid to ask. "How's that?"

"Take me home and never leave my side again." The finality in her voice left little room for doubt. Delin's heart swelled with joy.

Dakeb called a halt as the sun was dropping over the far horizon. Hallis and the Elves left to scout the surrounding areas while the others made a hasty camp. Dakeb waited until they returned with negative reports before letting them start a small cook fire. They ate in relative silence, intent on the heat of the almost timid flames licking at them. Most of them listened to the forests. Every crack or snap was a potential foe. Caution was their greatest ally now.

"How long will we be stopping each night?" Fennic asked.

"Long enough to eat and relieve yourselves," Dakeb said. "I want to get into the foothills before we stop today at least. Remember Fennic, time is against us."

A wolf bayed in the distance.

"Do not fear them. With as many enemies as we have, the wolves may be counted as friends," Dakeb said when he noticed Delin shiver from the sound.

Soon enough they were saddled up and weaving through the land. The smallest sliver of moon shone down in the chill night. Level ground began to give way to rolling slopes and ravines. Scrub brush and boulders were looming shadows in the half light. They'd finally reached the foothills, and the boundary with Gren.

FORTY-EIGHT
Hunted

The moon crept higher into the night sky, almost gaining its zenith before Dakeb called a halt for the night. Dakeb reasoned that this close to Gren meant Sidian had wards in place to warn him of invaders. They set camp atop a snow-covered knoll just high enough to make it difficult for attackers to reach them while showing not much of a silhouette. The high ground wouldn't be a deterrent for the frenzied Goblins, but it would at least delay them enough for the small group to flee. The horses were tethered to a stand of white birch trees. Hallis set the guard schedule and one by one they bedded down and went to sleep.

There was no fire that night. Smoke and open flames traveled far in the chill, winter air, and would be an open invitation to the monsters in this part of the land. It was Dakeb's hope that they'd reach Aingaard undetected. That's when their troubles would begin. Cheap disguises and petty tricks wouldn't prevent Sidian from finding and capturing them. Any use of magic was a dead giveaway. Not for the first time did Dakeb find his powers to be more damnation than gift. The dilemma kept the old Mage awake for the rest of the night. He had to find a way to breech Sidian's defenses before it was too late.

The Elves were the last to return from their scouting expedition before discussing what they'd seen with Hallis and Dakeb.

"We found nothing to the south," Derlith told the Mage.

"Nor to the east," Llem, the third Elf said.

Dakeb found his report surprising considering east was the direction they were heading.

"That doesn't make sense. We'll enter Gren tomorrow," Hallis said. "I doubt the Silver Mage will leave an open avenue into his lands."

"Unless they're expecting us," Celegon said. "I saw signs about a half league back. We're being tracked."

Hallis nodded grimly. "I saw the same to the north. The enemy knows we are moving again."

"Then they will attack soon," Derlith added. His almond eyes pierced the surrounding darkness for signs of the enemy.

"Perhaps not," Hallis offered.

"Why wouldn't they? Sidian must know by now the threat we pose. He may not know where the fourth shard is, but he will have learned of the Star Silver sword by now. He must have spies and legions out searching for us by now," Celegon said.

Dakeb finally spoke up. "That would imply trust in his subordinates. Sidian has none of that. He knows he stole Gren and there are many who would seek to supplant him as the dictator. His rule of fear and terror has seen to that. We are being followed, yes, and watched closely. Perhaps he even has a spy within our own ranks."

"I've felt the same since finding those Gnaals hunting you south of the Old Forest. Someone had to be leading them," Celegon told them. "The noose is tightening."

"The ranger doesn't feel right to me, Dakeb," he went on. "I've met some of the rangers of Averon. This man is not who he pretends to be."

"We've kept a steady watch on him since that first night, but he's shown no signs of treachery yet," Derlith said. "Say the word and it will be my pleasure to make him talk now."

He ran a long finger down the rune etched blade of his dagger.

"No," Dakeb ordered. "Make no move against him. If he is working for Sidian we don't want to tip our hand just yet. Keep watching him and when the time comes we shall be in place to deal with him. Keep a close watch on the Goblins tracking us as well. Part of me thinks they're driving us in the direction they want us to go. We are fortunate not to have a Gnaal too close right now."

"The Gnaal is far behind," Celegon announced. "I saw a dark taint in the ground where his tracks were. How many there are I do not know. They clearly are in fear of the boy and his sword. We need to use that to our advantage."

"Do we circle back and try to kill it?" Llem asked nervously.

He was afraid of the beasts, and for good reason. No one should ever witness the horrors of what he saw during the battle at the Old Forest. There'd been times in the days since he felt sure death was stalking him. Fear nagged at the back of his mind, haunting his actions. It whispered to him to give up while the choice remained his.

"We avoid the Gnaal as best as possible," Celegon told his friend. "There's no sense in risking everything until we get closer to Aingaard. Those boys are our biggest asset and it would be ill to use them uselessly against a foe with night unlimited resources."

"Agreed," Hallis said. "I say we march on as planned. We can't stop and fight every detachment of Goblins along the way."

"Get some rest now, friends," Dakeb told them. "I will stand the watch, for there is much I need to think on tonight. We break camp before the dawn."

His gaze lingered to where the three villagers from obscure Fel Darrins slept. That's when he noticed Tarren and Scarn were both missing.

Tarren shivered as she pulled her trousers back up and laced them. The night was much colder than she remembered. Then again, she'd never been so far north in the winter. Either way, the chilled burrowed into her bones. Tightening her cloak, Tarren headed back to Delin and her sleeping bag. The moon turned the world around her to a shimmering dream of a pale enchantment. She remembered being a little girl and sneaking out of the house on nights the moon was full. She'd count the stars until sleep took her. Her parents knew she did because she always woke up tucked into her bed the next morning. She wished she were home again. As far away from the war as possible.

The shadows suddenly came to life and fell on her.

"I... I didn't mean to startle you," Scarn said after stepping back to let her see him. "I am merely on my way to do the same thing you just did."

She waited for her heart to settle, but the beat remained fast and strong. If it were anyone but him, she thought. "I thought I was the only one still up. Good night."

Tarren hurriedly brushed past him, not wanting to be caught alone with the man so far from immediate help.

"Wait," he called.

Her legs betrayed her. Tarren stopped and turned. They stood and stared at each other.

"I disturb you, don't I?" Scarn asked her and took a step forward. "I'd really like to know. This is a dangerous time and we need to be able to trust one another if the Mage's plan is going to work. Please don't fear me."

"I'm not afraid," she replied, her voice barely a whisper.

Scarn eased closer, his boots crunching through the thin layer of ice covering the snow. His eyes burned into hers, almost seducing her to keep looking. "Aren't you? I wonder. I can smell fear on you, girl. It's in your eyes. The way you watch me. The way your body tenses when I'm near. Tell me what you're afraid of. You can trust me."

He moved closer still, until he was directly in front of her.

"You want to hurt us," she said with an almost trance-like voice. "Why else would you follow us so far from Fel Darrins?"

He smiled, toothy and demanding.

"I know nothing of those boys and didn't see them for the first time until the battle at the Thorn River. They're not my concern, nor was your little village. I was hired by a nobleman from the east to find his wayward grandfather," he lied. "The trail merely went through your village. Sadly, I found him dead in Relin Werd."

Tarren merely stared with suspicion.

"You don't believe me?" he innocently asked.

Scarn took his index finger and traced a line from her soft lips down past her jaw. He lightly touched her flesh down her neck and stopped at the top of her blouse. Her mouth trembled. The cloak slipped from her shoulders, leaving her exposed to his lingering gaze. Fear coursed through her but there was something else. Something primal deep inside. Could it be arousal? She wasn't sure but her mouth involuntarily opened when he brought a finger back to her lips.

"Tell me you believe me, Tarren," he whispered in her ear.

She answered without hesitation, "Yes. I believe you."

"Good girl," he cooed. "Now I want you to go back and sleep. Forget this conversation even happened." *Or things might not go so well the next time.*

Tarren snatched up her cloak and ran off. The moment was already fading from memory. She curled up next to Delin and drifted off to sleep. Her dagger was clutched to her breast the entire night.

Tolis Scarn collapsed once she was out of sight. Blood trickled from his nose onto the pure white snow, making it look violent. He looked around and wondered why he was so far from camp and the fire. It didn't make sense. The last thing he remembered was wanting to confront Tarren and find out what she knew about him. And now he was lying in snow covered bushes far from the others. Reluctantly, he picked himself up and went back to his bedroll. Sleep didn't come to him for the rest of the night. He was too busy plotting.

Dakeb roused them much too soon and they ate a meager meal of apples, old bread, and cheese in the predawn cold. They were sore from sleeping on the unforgiving ground. Hallis and Celegon rode the perimeter again and came back with grim faces. The enemy moved within visual range during the night and were pulled back just far enough to melt into the fading night. They agreed to keep the information to themselves for the while, at least until the old man managed to sneak them into Gren successfully.

"Good morning, Tarren," Norgen grumbled to her.

She flashed a brief smile back. She didn't know it was out of character for the Dwarf to be so cordial. Delin noticed it immediately and decided to watch her closer.

"Everything all right?" he asked once he thought they were alone.

Scarn's head rose at the sound of his voice, just enough to get her attention without arousing questions.

"Fine. I'm just sore from sleeping on the ground," she replied. A nagging feeling in her brain told her there was more, but what she had no clue.

Scarn finished buckling the strap around his horse's belly and walked away. His confusion over the events of the night prior was disturbing. He vaguely remembered being there and speaking to her. The voice and body were his but the words weren't. Had he been possessed? Scarn didn't know the answer and that frightened him.

Dark, thick clouds hung low over the towers of Aingaard, choking the air in a pall of oppression. Lightning scored the ground around the palace but never once inside the decaying walls. The same magic responsible for the coming darkness protected the city from all out destruction. Fires spit from the fissure surrounding the city. The very ground was turned to ash and charcoal. Sidian's will alone kept this brand of Hell from taking control.

Spendak stood outside the Silver Mage's door, fingers lightly rapping the hilt of his sword. He didn't know why he'd been summoned but knew better to question. Sidian was steadily becoming unstable. Executions were increasing. Rows of heads impaled on pikes ringed the parapet. Screams from those being flayed alive lasted the night. Matters were getting out of control. On top of that was word from Hoole and the battle in Averon. A second army was hastily being formed to follow the invasion force. The iron door groaned open and the Silver Mage appeared. His hair was frazzled and his face dark and drawn. Even his robes, normally spotless and impressive, were wrinkled in disarray.

"How long have you been standing here?" he asked accusingly.

"A few moments, my lord."

Sidian glared at the man, searching for hints of betrayal or sedition. "Come with me. There is much to be done."

Spendak obediently followed him down a marble stairwell.

"What more can we do? Our borders are protected. Lord Hoole and the army are engaged in Averon and we know the location of the fourth shard," he reported.

"Do we? The crystal left Ipn Shal yesterday. They are bringing it here."

Spendak couldn't believe it. "What? That makes no sense. Why would they risk it?"

Sidian laughed. It was a wicked sound.

"They're coming to kill me and they bring an old friend. The one man capable of doing just that. This will prove interesting." The thought amused him.

He'd never liked Dakeb. The youth had been the first to recognize the threat of Sidian's scheme. He organized the resistance and became the main reason for the division and the war among the Mages. Sidian admitted their wholesale destruction was the ultimate goal, but he wasn't ready to implement his plan when Dakeb struck back. Too many died before he was ready and the crystal of Tol Shere was ruined. Centuries were lost because of Dakeb. Sidian was going to take extreme pleasure from ripping his old friend's body apart. Just the thought of dark rivers of blood made him giddy with excitement. Five more days and it would all be over. Finally.

"Are you sure? Your agent must be returning it," Spendak offered. The potential disaster of the former left him cold inside. Armies he could fight, but he'd never had to battle a Mage before.

"No," Sidian answered. "The fool still doesn't know my true identity. I suspect he may have a better idea though after last night."

While alone in his inner sanctum, Sidian used his powers to seek out the crystal and his enemies. He was only slightly surprised to find them on the border of his lands. He'd been tracking Scarn through a minor spell from the moment he hired the petty thug. It was then Sidian decided to possess the man's mind and learn what he could. By doing so he set the future in motion. Already his forces were herding the small group of would be heroes in the direction he wanted. All was going according to plan. Yet his worries depended with each passing moment.

Spendak pressed further. "Let me take a battalion out and finish them before they gain the Nveden Plains."

They both knew Dakeb had a chance to disappear on the vast plains.

"My lord, please. We can't afford to take the chance."

Sidian raised an eyebrow in question. "And if you fail? Will they slip back into Averon? Or perhaps the Old Forest and those retched Elves? Your head would be the next on a pike, Spendak. Do not fail me. My generosity has expired. I want them hunted and harried all the way to Aingaard. Only then will I release my true fury."

The man of Gren turned to leave. He was angered and confused with his orders. Sidian was taking unnecessary risks with the future of the kingdom. Spendak entertained the thought that the Silver Mage may need to be dealt with before too long.

"Oh and Spendak, make sure you remain in the city and oversee the defenses. Just in case Dakeb finds a way through your forces."

Spendak marched off in a brooding silence, leaving the Silver Mage to wallow in the maddening dreams of the future.

FORTY-NINE
Treachery

The wind swirled the loose snow into a gentle funnel that ranged through the valley. Around them the foothills rose in gradual slopes reminding them of a long forgotten peace. Hallis came upon numerous tracks but not the kind he feared. So far it had been reduced to just animals and birds. He knew better than to relax though. Dakeb and the Elves said the enemy was still there tracking them, and the closer they got to Aingaard the more dangerous it was getting.

The scouts ranged back and forth, easily covering twice the distance the main body went. Hallis was relatively sure they weren't fooling anyone and that they were being watched every step of the way. He made sure to keep Scarn in his line of sight as much as possible. They consulted on several occasions and Scarn always gave limited opinions and answers, and each lie confirmed their suspicions of the thief.

They called the halt just shy of midday and let their horses graze on the shoots not completely buried under the snow. A crow cawed from the upper branches of a lone pine, mocking them with a haunting call. Pitch black eyes watched them with interest.

"Bah, vile things," Norgen scowled.

Fennic looked up. "I think that's the first crow I've seen since leaving home."

"Our elders say they bring curses," the Dwarf said. "'Tis a bad omen too see one so close to Gren. Nothing good will come from this."

Dakeb let out a heavy sigh. "Nonsense, Master Dwarf. A crow is more than a bird. I knew many Mages who kept them as pets. Superstitions won't do you any good now. Rely on your cunning and strength if you wish to see Breilnor again."

Norgen's face burned crimson. "Ha! Easy for a Mage to say. I should be so brave with the aid magic. Common folk don't have the luxuries of some."

"There is no luxury in my life," Dakeb snapped back, losing his temper for the first time. "I've seen more hardship and heartache than you can imagine. Would you be so strong to watch everything you ever knew destroyed in a single night? Friends, family, loves, and interests? Do not speak to me of luxury. Time and again I've wanted to end this pain of mine. The choice to march into Gren or sail back across the waters looms in my mind every day. But I stay. I'm the only one left who can stop Sidian."

"What about the sword?" Tarren asked. She was uncomfortable with the argument and wanted to change the subject.

"Phaelor is a tool, an instrument if you will. Young Fennic can wield the sword and carry out its destiny, but he alone cannot kill Sidian."

"I don't understand then," Fennic chimed in. "I thought Phaelor was designed to choose its handler until the day it was finally needed?"

"It was, but magic is complex, more so than you think. The Elves knew this, at least to an extent. They watched our war grow and became disgusted by it. Their druids forged the sword in the depths of the Old Forest thinking it would protect them against the fury of our magic. Their thinking was admirable, but off the mark. Phaelor destroys products of magic, but not the creator of such. Gnaals and other terrible creatures can be cut down without much effort once the blade touches them."

"So even if I stabbed him it wouldn't do any good?" Fennic asked.

"Oh, he can be wounded. After all he is a man. But do not make the mistake of trying to kill him. His magic will destroy you, Fennic."

The conversation slowly faded. Each of them ate a silent meal and readied for the next leg of the journey. Dakeb's last words opened a new realization none of them wanted to think of. The threat of death was a constant companion until the end of their adventures. The air suddenly grew colder. Tarren wanted to bury herself in Delin's arms and forget this entire affair. The old Mage realized his mistake at mentioning potential doom and tried to make amends.

"I remember the last time I was in Fel Darrins," he gaily said. "Oh, it was long before any of you were born. Must have been when your grandparents were as young as you are now. It's a quaint village. The townsfolk treated me like royalty, and I was dressed a mere pauper. I've never met more polite people."

Tarren smiled. She tried imagining what her parents were like as children. She desperately wanted to go home, but it was too late. Now she had to find the warmth of home and her childhood in the depths of her heart. For now though, Dakeb gave it all back to her in his gentle words.

"What brought you there?" Delin asked, suddenly curious. In his short time with the man he'd come to understand Dakeb never did anything without a motive.

"I was in the employ of King Baeleon, Maelor's sire. He'd just taken the throne when the Silver Mage rose to attack Averon the first time. It was a bitter war, not quite so threatening as the events unfolding around us. We beat him back in a resounding defeat and then stopped. I sometimes think that was

Baeleon's weakness. We could have gone into Gren and ended it once and for all, but he halted and had Gren Mot reoccupied to defend his people.

"I traveled with your grandfathers back to Fel Darrins. They were tired of the big city life and the toils of warfare. They both agreed to raise their families in peace in a quiet part of the world few knew. They wanted to be as far away from kings and politics and corruption as possible. I often visited them until they passed." Dakeb felt his heart swell at the thought of dear friends.

"You knew Old Man Wiffe too," Fennic surmised.

Dakeb didn't wish to respond. "Yes. And I knew Phaelor and its potential to shape the future."

Fennic's heart skipped. "Did you know I was going to be chosen?"

"No."

Fennic stared blankly at him.

"Prophecy is a dangerous tool. It's one I will not attempt. There's something wrong about meddling with the future. Nothing good comes from manipulating lives. Not even the Elven druids understood the full potential of what they'd done."

"Does that make the sword alive?" Tarren asked.

"In a manner of speaking. Phaelor knows who the next bearer will be long before the current one is done with his task. None of us ever truly figured out how, and the Elves who created it disappeared long ago. In all that time we never came to understand how the sword worked."

"That isn't reassuring," Fennic said.

"Fear not. So long as it is in my power, no harm shall come to you," Dakeb told him. "Nor to any of you. Besides, I'd very much like to see Fel Darrins again. I can still recall bouncing your father's off my knee. They will be very proud of you."

Delin tried to put the pieces together. He'd been given a huge puzzle and aimed to solve it before they reached Aingaard. He didn't remember a single time when either of their parents mentioned knowing a Mage. Then again, he assumed Mages weren't overly popular after the terrible wars they fought. His parents never mentioned Old Man Wiffe either, at least not until after he was found dead. The call to break camp came too soon for him to come to any conclusions.

Dakeb led them on for the rest of day and they stopped again much sooner than the day prior. They looked around to see the foothills all but gone. It was like stepping into another world. The snow and ice was behind them as well, replaced with thick vegetation and an ungodly stench. Vines as thick as a human leg curled around the molding trees. The air grew heavy with sudden humidity, making it harder for them to breathe.

"What place is this?" Norgen asked. He resisted the urge to vomit.

"This," Dakeb announced, "is the border of Gren. The Sanken Swamp. It's a lifeless place. If we entered without the Elves, chances are we'd never find Celegon or the others again."

Fennic looked around at the vast expanse of rotted greens. "Should we go find them?"

The Mage emphatically shook his head. "Where would we begin? I can't find them even with my magic. Certainly not this close to Sidian. We wait here."

"But how will they know to come?" Delin asked.

Dakeb flashed a private smile.

Hallis drank sparingly from his canteen and put the stop back in. The air was cold. His breath froze the moment it left him. Beads of perspiration dotted his face, matting his hair down. He knew he'd pay for it later when he stopped moving. The sweat would turn to ice. The wind chilled him even more. Fortunately, he didn't have to wait long for the return of the Elves.

"Did you find anything?" he asked as Celegon emerged from a copse of pine.

"Nothing. Not even a track," the Elf prince replied. His voice thinly disguised his disappointment. With the swamp not far off, the enemy should be teeming the last few foothills.

Hallis gestured to Llem and Derlith. "Ride ahead to the border of the swamp and let Dakeb know our findings. I don't like what's happening here."

"What are you thinking?" Celegon asked. His hand dropped to his sword.

"I think the Goblins circled around beyond our range so they can attack while we're separated like this. It's the only thing that makes sense. This is their chance to pick us off one by one," Hallis said.

Celegon agreed. "Perhaps our ranger friend has been feeding them information when we're not looking?"

Hallis forced a laugh. He'd been suspecting much the same. The wind flipped his long hair about wildly. Hallis stretched as best he could and tried to loosen up. Then Scarn came back. His horse came flying around the bend, kicking mud and snow up. His eyes betrayed fear as he whipped his horse to go faster. Squat bodies in chain mail and waving barbed spears came running close behind. Goblins!

"Run!" he yelled.

Celegon aimed his bow and fired in one swift motion as Hallis climbed back on his horse. A second Goblin was dead before the first hit the ground. Both riders turned to flee when a hideous scream shredded the air. It was the roar of a Mountain Troll. They had to flee now, before it was too late. Even with Scarn, they'd be hard pressed to defeat one of the lumbering giants. With a compliment of Goblins following it, Celegon knew it was a losing battle.

The ground trembled under the weight of the approaching footsteps. Snow fell from the branches and pine needles. Thunder frightened the land. Barbed laughter rose from the Goblin ranks as their foe fled. A dark shadow suddenly towered over them, blocking the sun. The thunder stopped and the only sound was the whistle of a soft wind careening off the snow laden slopes. The Troll came into view. It was an ugly beast over three meters tall and close to a thousand pounds of muscle and hatred. The Troll was a sickly color, pale and wreaking in death.

A massive forehead made his eyes hollow and smaller than they were. Clumps of bluish hair dotted his head, some as long as three feet. Scars riddled his body. Wounds new and old served as a reminder to the pain and hardships of perpetual struggle. The Troll leapt towards the Elf and Man. He hit the ground with a roar and swung his heavy cudgel at the nearest rider. The heavy weapon barely missed, instead striking and shattering a slender tree into slivers and dust.

The Troll recovered quickly and attacked with frightening speed. Goblins roared in approval. Celegon and Hallis disappeared into the trees. Enraged by not having fresh blood in its hands, the Troll turned on the smaller Goblins and crushed one with his fist. Only then did it stop. It was breathing hard, and steam rose from its back in waves.

Scarn slowed not long after passing his companions. He knew the Goblins would make short work of them and give up the hunt. Two horsemen against a Mountain Troll was hardly a contest. Scarn already had his story ready for when he returned to the Mage. He'd speak of their bravery and give an oath of revenge, even if meant killing the Silver Mage himself. To be honest, the Goblins ambushed him perfectly. His clothes were ripped, and his body bruised. He wasn't sure, but he thought a rib was broken as well.

He wiggled his lower jaw, thinking that punch was harder than he believed. The voice in his head told him not to worry, and to let the Goblins do their job once they had him in their grasp. Only now did he realize the voice was coming from the Hooded Man, or should he say the Silver Mage. Either way, he did what the darkness commanded. There was no other way.

Doubts and questions plagued his every thought. The Silver Mage invaded his mind more than Scarn wanted. Time was almost up and they'd never been so close to the fourth stone as now. Day by day Scarn felt himself slipping deeper in the Mage's grip.

It all started simple enough. One man hiring him for a quiet job no one would even be concerned with. The Hooded Man quickly lost patience and the quest dragged on. Then came the promises of violence and damnation. He'd even come under physical assault. Scarn wanted nothing more than to forget this entire mess and lose himself in a good bottle of ale. Hopefully his reward would be enough to entice a few women to his bed. That would go a long way in easing the anguish suffered. He was smiling when Hallis and Celegon came riding up to him. They eyed him suspiciously, almost bordering on open hatred. His smile faded as they flanked him.

"Glad to see you made it," Hallis said through grated teeth.

Celegon fingered his dagger and added, "Yes. We would have felt terrible if you'd have risked yourself trying to help us."

"So I could die too?" Scarn spat back. "My orders are to ensure the safety of those boys. An Elf and a soldier should be able to defend themselves. What more do you want of me? I warned you. You had enough time to run."

Hallis leaned menacingly close. "I think you led them right to us."

"Why would I do that?" There was a sliver of apprehension in his voice.

"You tell us," Celegon said.

Scarn tried to laugh. "What is it about me that arouses your suspicions? Am I that imposing a figure? Am I? I think you overestimate my importance."

"Tell us who you really work for," Hallis demanded. "We know it's not the king."

Part of Scarn wanted to tell it all and have it done with. In relation to the part of him who knew what true suffering was, that part was very small. Living was more important than these fools having their concerns vindicated.

He vehemently pointed at his bruised face. "Does this look like I work for anyone?"

Celegon was about to reply when the chorus of howls began again. The enemy was back on the hunt.

"We'll finish this later," Hallis promised.

He and the Elf prince vaulted towards the end of the foothills and the border of the Sanken Swamp where Dakeb was waiting. Scarn followed closely behind. They rode as fast as they dared, unwilling to risk their mounts by stepping in a covered hole or stumbling over rocks and other hazards buried in the snow. Goblins were no match for horses on the open field, but here the odds were greatly evened. Soon enough the sounds of pursuit faded, and all that remained were the three riders. Hallis slowed them to a walk. The swamp was near.

They reached the bottom of the valley just as the sun was disappearing behind the mountains. Norgen was the first to see them. He was already standing with his legs apart and his axe on the ground and hands on the hilt as if contemplating cursing them for taking so long. The rest of the group were off behind him. Celegon noticed they were all ready for battle.

"What kept you?" the Dwarf growled.

"Unexpected business," Celegon replied with a sideways glance at Scarn.

Dakeb took each of them in. He kept his opinions to himself for the moment. There were more important issues at hand.

"We must hurry. The swamp is a dangerous place, especially at night. Creatures dwell within that even I refuse to deal with."

FIFTY
Battle for Tarren's Soul

The Sanken Swamp was a place revered through much of Malweir as evil. A darkness so foul all life suddenly ended without cause was said to dwell within. Monsters and other hideous creatures, afraid to enter the light, stalked the deepest regions of the swamp. Horrible noises wailed throughout the nights, always threatening yet distant. The moon was setting by the time Dakeb led them through the far side of the swamp and onto the fringes of the nightmarish expanse of the Nveden Plains.

The plains ran the length of Gren and were a barren wasteland, uninhabitable by all but the most desperate tribes of men and Goblins. Fugitives and outlaws mostly populated the major villages along the path to Aingaard. The lowlands were a miserable place of greed and avarice. People were raised to be judgmental and cruel. The wickedness of the Silver Mage was complete.

Once Gren was a beautiful land filled with life and green. That was before Sidian and his visions of madness. Now it was the epitome of disaster. Massive cave and tunnel complexes underlined the plains from the mountains to the peaks of Aingaard. With no protection from the searing heat and light of the sun, the Goblins dug deep into the earth. Often they dug too deep, breeching lava veins of the few volcanoes dotting the land.

Dakeb remembered the world the way it used to be. He remembered the birds of every color gracing the skies and trees. Children played in the huge ponds at the base of waterfalls while their parents talked and ate along the shore. There wasn't any war back then, and the Goblins seldom left their mountain caves. Those days were long faded, and the world was less of a place. Dakeb struggled to keep a tear from falling. Black clouds hid the moon, locking the plains in a cruel form of darkness. Fires sprang up here and there for as far as the eye could see, and a noxious odor tainted the air. Gren was truly a nightmare.

"This is what we have to look forward to?" Norgen scowled. Even used to dwelling deep in the earth he found the land repulsive.

Dakeb nodded. "All the way to Aingaard and beyond I'm afraid."

Hallis found himself attacked by bad memories. The battle of Gren Mot was fresh in his mind despite the trials since then. The smell on the wind was overpowering and he felt his stomach tighten spasmodically. He very much wanted to leave this place.

"What lies beyond the city?" Fennic asked.

There was a wild look in his eyes. Phaelor's power was reaching up through the sword to take control again.

"No one knows," the Mage replied. "All who once did are gone."

Delin looked up. "How can everyone forget? I'd think kings and lords would want to know as much about Malweir as possible."

The gleam in Dakeb's eye faded. "There are some things best left forgotten. Even I have no desire to remember all I've learned through the ages. I have grown weary of this life. Perhaps I can rest once this is ended."

"Aren't Mages immortal?" Tarren asked.

"Sadly, no. We die when our task is complete or whenever the Fates decide. We can be killed as easily as normal men."

"Can't you use your magic to keep you alive?" Delin pressed. There was something in Dakeb's voice he found disturbing.

"Yes and no. Magic isn't so simple as you think. Some spells I can perform but once, and others a thousand times without effect. A Mage draws his power from the earth, even the dark ones did. All this," he gestured towards the distance, "is a result of Sidian's overuse of his skills. He's turned a beautiful land into barren misery."

He paused to think. "Magic is about limitations, both physical and mental. When those limitations are breeched, an anomaly occurs. Dangerous things happen. The making of the sword was one. The druids weren't clear with what they were dealing. Truth be told, by creating Phaelor they helped disrupt the balance. Once that act was done it was a small matter for Sidian to rise so quickly."

Fennic scratched the stubble on his chin. "If the balance has been disrupted what can we do to stop him?"

"Sidian has one flaw that may prove fatal. His quest for the crystal consumes him. It drives the rest of the world from his mind. He's distracted now, solely focused on opening the paths of doom."

"Phaelor," Fennic uttered.

"Yes, Phaelor. Sidian never paid attention to the little things in life. The Star Silver sword is not only the cause of the imbalance, but the cure as well. While you cannot kill Sidian himself, you can restore the world to rights. All you need to do is stand near enough to the crystal when he inserts the last shard."

"What!" Tarren exclaimed. "I thought we wanted to keep him from putting the crystal back together."

"This is more complicated than you know. Phaelor can only succeed if it's used at precisely the moment Sidian places the fourth shard with the rest. Strike the crystal and it all ends," Dakeb explained. "The key is timing.

If we strike too soon we run the risk of letting his evil cover the world. Just a fraction of a moment off and the nightmares begin."

"How will I know when it is the right time?" Fennic asked.

The Mage gave him a kindly smile. "You'll know."

Scarn listened closely, wondering how he was going to use this knowledge to his advantage. The prospect of unholy armies rampaging across Malweir left little room for men the likes of him. There was also no way he could get out of delivering the stone now. He'd already been possessed twice. Escape was impossible. Too many ifs lingered in the corners of his mind. He was trapped and knew it. Scarn didn't like it one bit.

They continued riding until the dawn. The small column inched ever closer to their goal and the battle at the end of the world. The landscape never changed. Much of it was scored from lightning strikes and rampant fires. Thistle and burdock bushes sparingly covered this part of the plains. Every so often they came across a dry creek bed. Rotted carcasses littered the area. The smell was putrid. By the time dawn bleakly broke, they were beyond exhaustion.

"There is a group of large boulders to the south. They should be sufficient to conceal us," Celegon spied.

Hallis asked, "How far are they?"

"Less than a league."

"Dakeb, we should pick up the pace before that Mountain Troll following us figures out where we are and comes calling," Hallis said.

"Why can't we just walk into battle like civilized folk?" Norgen asked before kicking his mount into a full gallop.

The last rider slipped into the circle of boulders less than a half hour later. Llem turned to ensure no one was following. Satisfied, he followed the others by dismounting and seeing to his horse. Tarren let out a prolonged yawn that expressed the fatigue they were all feeling.

"Bed down," Hallis ordered. "We set back out in four hours."

Celegon nodded to his brethren. "We shall stand the watch."

"I'll help."

The Elf prince shook his head. "There's no need. Rest and recover your strength. Conflict is racing to find us. You will have need of it soon."

Hallis didn't argue. He felt it in his bones. He was exhausted. He quickly laid out his riding blanket and was snoring in minutes. Thunder rumbled across the distant horizon. The air suddenly had an acidic tang to it. Dark clouds rushed in. Celegon sighed. He didn't relish the prospect of crossing Gren in a maelstrom. For the first time since witnessing the battle at Gren Mot he wondered what he'd gotten himself into. Dakeb assured him they all had a part to play. They'd known each other for centuries and he chose to trust the old Mage.

The Elf prince watched his sleeping companions. Men seemed to share a bond none of the other races had. They made as many friends as enemies, and strife was a constant threat due to the sheer size of their populations. His own people, first to colonize here, were never so great. They built things of wonder and mystery, but never had the large numbers Man created. If only, he thought. Dwarves were another matter. Ill-mannered and direct, the Dwarves kept to themselves and were the least known about.

Celegon laughed at having one for a companion now. There were others of course. Sprites and Nymphs were a rarity that few living could remember. Of all the races he'd come across, Man offered unity. He looked down at the two boys huddled beneath their blankets and smiled. A strong gust of wind brought a chill to his bones and carried the sounds he hoped not to hear. Celegon melted into the shadows.

The column was a hundred strong and marching in files of twenty-five. A trio of blonde men lashed them on with forked whips. Their very actions suggested pure hatred for the Goblin soldiers in their command. Celegon watched the men of vanquished Gren and snarled. There was but one reason a unit this big was in the far north country. The Silver Mage was on their trail.

The Goblins groaned and cursed under the whip. Disgruntled and seething in violence, they marched on. Celegon drew his bow and set and arrow to string. He knew Derlith and Llem had done the same. Their situation was precarious. The protection of the rocks could easily be turned against them, ensuring a violent demise. He braced for battle. But the Goblins shuffled past without so much as a sidelong glance. Celegon exhaled a slow breath and released the tension on his bow. They were safe for now.

Thick mists swirled around Tarren's ankles as she ran for her life. They tried to grab her and steal her away from reality. Footsteps echoed behind her, heavy and menacing. Tarren feared for her life. She knew if they caught her she was dead. She ran even harder. Trees sprang up to block her way. Rubber branches laced with thorns cut her as she ran past. Tiny trickles of blood leaked from a score of wounds. She didn't slow down though. She knew she couldn't. The footsteps got closer. Another heartbeat and....

She was seized by a powerful grip. Tarren screamed. A deep, booming laugh echoed across the nightmarish world. Her attacker wasted no time pinning her arms behind her back with a thick cord. Any hope of escape quickly left her.

"Just be still, pretty. This isn't going to be as bad as you think," a familiar voice crooned.

His breath was hot on her neck. His hair, greasy to the touch, fell across her blood spotted cheek.

"What…what do you want from me?" she stuttered.

The more she struggled to break free, the deeper into bondage she fell. If she could just reach her dagger.

"That, is a surprise," he replied.

Tarren's eyes widened with shock. She suddenly knew her abductor. There was no way she could mistake Scarn's voice. She knew then that she was doomed. A strong shove in her back kept her moving but towards what she didn't know. The trees gradually thinned. Tarren saw glimpses of terrible, misshapen creatures crawling towards her. And out of nowhere there stood before her a man dressed in a concealing black robe. Emptiness beckoned from beneath the hood. A voice in her head whispered for her to approach.

Her feet betrayed her, shuffling her closer to the Hooded Man. He raised a hand and her bonds fell away. Tarren felt warmth through her body and her eyes glazed over. Rich laughter came from the depths of the hood.

"Kneel," the Hooded Man commanded.

Tarren obeyed.

The Hooded Man bent down, revealing his eyes to her. They were tiny and a crimson red. They stared deep into the core of her soul. She felt him reach into her flesh and grip her weary heart in the palm of his hand. Terror coursed through her veins. All her secrets were revealed to him and he laughed mightily. Darkness settled around her, forcing her to bow subserviently to his will. When it seemed she was lost, a brilliant light surrounded her and drove the darkness away.

Tarren remembered nothing.

The golden light faded from Dakeb's fingertips and the Mage pulled his hands from Tarren's forehead. The danger was past. Both sweated profusely and he was trembling. He relaxed from the strain of using so much magic. It wasn't long after they went to sleep he found Tarren thrashing wildly in her sleep. He wasn't really surprised, though it troubled him to great lengths. Both he and Celegon had been watching her closely since that night she and Scarn disappeared in the woods at the same time. Only now did he realize that Sidian wanted her mind. He'd barely been in time to save her, this time. The last spell Dakeb left on her would make her forget this nightmare. Or so he hoped. Either way, he didn't leave her side for the rest of the night. Tarren woke to find the kindly Mage sitting nearby with a smile on his face.

"Good morning, young lady," he said.

A sharp pain lanced through her forehead. "What happened?" she asked, almost in a daze. "I feel so bad."

"Oh, I imagine it's just the combination of the lack of sleep and riding so hard. It's hard to stay hydrated and eat right on these kinds of adventures," Dakeb lied. "You'll be fine once you get a little food in your belly."

He didn't have the heart to tell her the truth. But there was more. He was deeply concerned with the way Sidian had been attacking her and he didn't know why. *What games are you playing at my old friend?* Soon enough they were on their way across the horrors of the Nveden Plains again.

FIFTY-ONE
The Dragon Comes

The morning sun evaporated the mist rising off the frigid waters of the Thorn River. Dawn was just beginning to break, spreading tendrils of light through the veil of night. The battling armies rose late this day, as if the commanders knew what was going to happen. A light wind danced over the battlefield, taking some of the gruesome stench of death and decay away. Mounds of bodies were piled in the rear of the assembly area. There were too many to count. Not that it mattered. Continuous reinforcements were pouring down into the lowlands from Gren daily.

Thus far, each attack had met failure. The riders from Harlegor nearly broke their backs, despite the numbers of Goblins. Jervis Hoole was losing his patience. Enemy catapults rained down mercilessly on his positions. Buzzards and crows flew overhead by the thousands. Hoole looked out at his disheartened army with disgust. The memories of the victory at Gren Mot were already gone. Some of his forces were already bordering on mutiny. Apart from the outright slaughter of anyone seditious, Hoole had one plan in mind to raise their spirits and renew the battle. He smirked at the thought of the look of surprise on his foes' faces when he sent in his battalions of Trolls. They'd arrived under the cover of darkness and were anxious for a brawl. Once his front line forces pulled back to retire for the day, Hoole was going to send the Trolls crushing into the heart of the enemy.

The throne of Averon was close now. One step away and all the lowlands would be his to rule. He briefly imagined how it would feel to be free of the Silver Mage and let it pass. Too much was at stake. Only one other knew of his seditious intentions and Hoole had been forced to promise the governorship of Gren to the man before he agreed not to run to the Silver Mage. In the end the idea was grand. One king with two lands.

Hoole smiled as he returned to his tent.

"I don't like this."

Steleon clenched his jaw and stared off at the enemy camps. He was against the wall and he knew it. The battle was going his way for all intents and purposes, but the balance was fragile. All it would take is one concentrated push and his army would fold. The only way he'd been able to stay alive this long was through tricks and guerrilla tactics. It kept the armies of Gren off guard and hesitant to take the offensive. Steleon knew that wasn't going to last long. He needed a way to change that.

Melgit didn't answer for a moment. He thoughtfully stroked his black beard. Young Graeme was standing at his side, as he had since the battle began.

"What's to like?" he finally said. "This is war."

"No," Steleon replied. "This goes beyond just war."

"It's what we must weather and endure if Averon is to have a future," Maelor said as he walked up the gentle slope to them.

Both snapped to the position of attention. "Sire."

Maelor waved off the formality. "I don't imagine this lull is going to last much longer."

"No," agreed Steleon. "They're preparing their final assault. My scouts are reporting a massive build up. It won't be long at all."

"Are you sure?" Maelor asked.

"Yes. See how they're forming up? They're going to strike us with three prongs and try to drive us back far enough to gain the banks. Once they've established a crossing they can pour their full weight down on us."

"How prepared is the defense?"

Steleon shook his head slightly. "I've ordered the front trench abandoned. We flooded sections of it and emplaced iron tipped stakes at the bottom. That should slow them down enough for the pikemen to get in place. The catapult batteries will start firing the instant their front ranks begin the advance. Archers and javelins will add fire to the far shore. The cavalry and infantry are in reserve until the time comes.

Maelor nodded approval. He'd always liked his field commander and knew why his father had spoken so highly of the man. "We stop them on the banks. Why the despair then? I can feel it in the way you hold yourself."

"Have you ever known a battle to go as planned?"

Maelor didn't respond.

"There's still the rumors of the dragon," Melgit brought up.

Graeme repressed a shudder.

"Which no one has seen since the fall of Gren Mot," Melgit added.

"That doesn't mean it's not out there. More than likely perched on some distant mountaintop awaiting instructions from the Mage," Steleon snapped back. "I prefer to concentrate on what I see before me."

"When the dragon comes?"

"We die."

The sun continued to sink over the horizon. A lone, baleful horn blew from across the shore. It was time.

Goblin arrows sailed across the river. The defenders ducked behind an interlocking wall of shields. Occasionally one fell with an arrow in him. The rate of fire gradually slackened as the first battalions began the lunged towards the river. War drums pounded on the night air. The moon hadn't risen yet and eastern Averon sat in darkness.

Steleon's catapults opened fire, throwing death and vengeance into the enemy ranks. The drums beat harder. The Goblins inched closer. The defenders nervously waited in position. Sweat ran down their faces. Their hearts roared. Each of them knew what awaited. The actions on this night meant the future for their kingdom and quite possibly the rest of Malweir. Each of them made peace with their personal deity and readied for the worst. The differences between veteran and recruit were gone. They were all the same now.

The Goblin army marched closer. Their dark shapes slowly came into sight. A brutal realization dawned on Steleon. The shapes were much larger than Goblins.

"No," he whispered.

His fears were realized a moment later when the front ranks came into plain sight. Trolls, and a lot of them. Steleon knew he had nothing capable of beating back such an assault. He snatched Graeme by the shoulder and tried to prevent a total disaster.

"Run to the catapults. Tell them to shift their fire to the river. It's the only chance we have at slowing them," he shouted.

The boy ran for his life, and the lives of every man, woman, and child in Averon. Trolls splashed into the river. Steleon joined the ranks of pikemen waiting in the second trench.

"Stand the line!" he yelled above the approaching clamor. He raised his sword in challenge to the enemy. "Even Trolls have weakness. Fight for your lives!"

Pikes lowered. Steleon wanted to believe in his words, but he'd be damned if he knew where a Troll was weakest. They were going to need a miracle if they were going to survive this. Arrows would be wasted on their armor like hides, so he reserved them for the small Goblins. At speeds greater than a horse could run, the arrows would make short work of the foot soldiers. Steleon resolved himself not to retreat. It was here or nowhere. The front lines were going to bear the full weight of the storm.

"For Averon and King Maelor!" he roared.

His army echoed the cry.

Icy waters poured from the Trolls massive bodies as they climbed from the frozen river and onto the western shore. Balls of flaming pitch sizzled overhead, dripping down on the defenders. Fire exploded on the nearest Troll's chest and he staggered. The Troll dropped his weapon in the river and fell to his knees. Another round hit, and then another. The Trolls were massed so closely it was impossible to miss. Unfortunately, the pitch wasn't stopping them. The Trolls kept coming. Cudgels and mighty tulwars hammered down on the defender ranks, crushing and battering them aside. Pikes thrust back with little or no results. Occasionally a Troll did fall from wounds, but the defenders paid a heavy toll. Little by little the line was driven backwards. Steleon saw the doom of Averon approaching. Hope was fading.

It took the Trolls practically no time to break through the lines and strike at the heart of the infantry. The soldiers fought bravely and hard, but they were no match for the battle hardened Mountain Trolls. Steleon took his infantry into the heart of the battle. A horribly scarred Troll swung for his head, flakes of burned skin peeling off his ruined flesh. Steleon tried to step back but tripped over a body and fell. The cudgel came crashing down.

Steleon saw death coming and was surprisingly calm. Then he noticed a small figure dart in and slash the Troll across the back of the hand. The beast roared back and slapped the soldier hard. Bones crunched and organs burst from the blow. The soldier landed a few meters away and didn't move.

"Strad cu grashk!"

The battle cry was echoed by thousands of gravely voices. Steleon and the Troll looked up at the same time in bewilderment. Trolls up and down the line did the same. They knew the cry and felt fear for the first time since entering the battle. They began a disorderly retreat across the river. Many of them slipped and fell into the trench and were impaled. The enemy line broke. Trolls turned and fled as thick, wooden missiles whistled into their ranks and struck them down. The smaller Goblins were crushed and trampled to death without a chance.

Steleon rolled to his feet and readied for a trick. None came. The Trolls were terrified of this new threat and had lost the will to fight. More of the wooden missiles struck home. Steleon's heart filled with hope. He didn't know what was happening but wasn't about to complain. He watched the enemy retreat and finally breathed in relief. A great clamor arose from the center of the burning camp. The sound of steel and boots marching closer echoed across the plain. All around his men cheered. Then the first of the Dwarven army came into view, axes hungry and restless. The Dwarves marched past the broken lines of defenders and met the enemy. Blood and mayhem raged. The Dwarves fearlessly drove into the Trolls. Axes hewed flesh and cudgels smashed down. The battle was swift and vicious. Trapped against the river, the Trolls fought hard for their lives. Dozens fell from both sides. The Dwarves quickly advanced to the bank.

Steleon regained his senses and immediately ordered his cavalry back across the river. Infantry and reserve units were ordered behind the Dwarves. This was his one chance to end the siege and relieve the pressure on Averon. He looked about for council. Now was not the time to get carried away like his opponent. The battle was far from being decided. Catapults fired as fast as they could be loaded, and archers shot arrow after arrow.

A half-moon was rising over the peaks of the Gren Mountains, giving many their first views of the developing slaughter. Rank upon rank of the Dwarven army marched past the battered men of Averon. Melgit's cavalry, strengthened by the riders from Harlegor, wheeled around the battlefield and made ready to drive through the retreating masses. The army of Gren had no defensive positions prepared and they were exposed to the combined fury of man and Dwarf. Hundreds died in the first moments. Steleon watched the battle develop with interest until he noticed the body of the man who'd saved his life.

Part of him was reluctant to see who it was. He felt a shadow in his soul whispering names and possibilities. Dead bodies weren't new to him. He'd had a long and storied career in the military. Dying was just another aspect of the job. Steleon knelt and slowly turned the body over. Sorrow gripped his heart as he looked into the twisted face of his savior. It was Graeme. Steleon wanted to cry. The boy had survived a dragon attack, capture by the Goblins, and endured the mental anguish of watching all his friends die around him, and here he lay. Steleon stopped the two closest soldiers and ordered the body taken back to the command area. There'd be a hero's burial when this night was done.

Then he noticed a stout Dwarf with sharp eyes approaching.

"You be the one in command?" the Dwarf asked with a rough tone.

"For what it's worth, I am," Steleon answered. "High Commander Steleon, at your service."

The Dwarf bowed slightly. "I am Ordein, brother of Norgen and commander of the Bairn army."

"You came at the right time. I fear we were about to break," Steleon replied.

Ordein had a knowing look in his black eyes. "Timing is critical in war against Trolls. If we came sooner they wouldn't have committed to the fight. A Troll can be formidable, but we've had long wars with them and they know us as well. I think they were more surprised than your own folk."

"How did you come so quickly? The last time I saw your brother he doubted if word even reached your halls."

The Dwarf lord laughed deep and rich. He explained how his brother sent a carrier pigeon from Alloenis explaining everything. The warning gave the Dwarf army ample time to form and march on Paedwyn. They'd been harried along the way but avoided any serious engagements. No one was fool enough to attack a force of over two thousand battle thirsty Dwarves, not even a Gnaal. The two commanders quickly conferred, telling each what they knew of the situation. By the time they finished, Steleon figured they'd be able to drive the enemy back into the mountains.

Steleon sent runners to every major command with instructions to get on line and push forward. Surgeons, cooks, and the rest of the support personnel busied with policing up the battlefield and trying to save as many lives as possible. The stacks of corpses continued to grow. The battle edged further and further from the river. Ordein's Dwarves were pushing the Goblin army back towards Gren.

"By Gru! This is a glorious night," Ordein howled with delight. Triumph laced his words. "I was beginning to think we'd never cross your lands."

"Let's hope the Silver Mage doesn't have any tricks left to pull while the three armies are strung out like this," Steleon added. His voice lacked the fire or fervor of his stout counterpart.

"What more can he possibly have? Nothing worse than Trolls."

Steleon barely whispered, "A dragon."

Ordein faltered. "Hasn't been a dragon in the world for a very long time."

They left it at that and continued the battle. Steleon called for his horse while Ordein followed his army on foot. Both were eager to see the night done.

Blood boiled and temperatures ran hot, but the rout was finally brought to a halt just before the dawn. Dwarves and men shouted curses and taunts at the fleeing Goblins hordes. Hardly an inch of ground was left uncovered with either blood or body parts for nearly half a league back to the Thorn River. Weeks would pass before anyone got an accurate casualty count. For now it was enough. Averon held the field. Picket lines were established and the men formed ranks to await fresh orders. Most of them could barely stand.

The physical toll was almost as great as the emotional one. They all knew what was coming next. The enemy was beaten here, but far from broken. The invasion of Gren was the only logical next step. Steleon and Maelor trooped the line, speaking to as many of the men as possible. Cook fires soon ranged the field and a crude gruel was prepared to warm them some on the cold winter dawn. Steleon almost ordered kegs of mead brought up, but it was too soon for that. They needed rest first.

"This was a good fight," Ordein announced when they rejoined him. His axe blade was buried deep in the chest of a dead Goblin. "It's been a long time since my folk were able to whet our appetites like this."

"This was a costly battle," Steleon quietly drew out. "We cannot thank you enough. Those ballistae saved the day."

Maelor readily agreed. "Indeed. We are in your debt Master Ordein. I hope this war ends quickly so that we may begin a new era of trade and peace between our two peoples."

"Sire, there's still the small matter of an enemy army on Averonian soil. This war is far from being over," Melgit said. His left arm was slung in a bloody bandage.

Maelor was about to respond when a loud boom raced across the sky. Everyone looked up, shielding their eyes against the rising sun. A great, dark shape came speeding towards them from the mountains. Steleon felt the color drain from his face. The Silver Mage had finally released his wyrm. Flames spouted from the dragon's nostrils and mouth and even from a distance the defenders knew it was over.

Ordein tugged on his beard in disbelief and began barking orders. "All right you bloody bastards! Back in ranks and ready to fire!"

Adrenalin coursed through Jervis Hoole. This was the day he was supposed to become king. He'd spied Maelor's colors on the field and knew it was over. All it was going to take was his Trolls crushing into the enemy and the battle was his. Hoole howled with glee as his army attacked. Then his world crashed. Had he been closer to the front they might have averted the disaster, but he wasn't. The army of Gren was quickly turned on its heels. He struggled to see what was happening and why his forces were turning to run. He saw massive Trolls on fire and trampling the smaller Goblins in their fright. The moonlight finally allowed him to notice the small figures charging recklessly into his ranks. Dwarves! Hoole spat the name. Where did they come from? An aide rushed to his side.

"We must flee now," he yelled. "Back to Gren Mot where we might have a chance! We cannot hold here anymore, Lord Hoole."

Jervis Hoole slid the tip of his dagger at his aide's throat in the blink of an eye.

"Run if you wish. Sound the retreat, though I doubt they'll listen. See how the enemy cavalry already race to block our exit? We are all of us doomed this night. Go and run. We'll see how far you get before death comes to claim you. Be gone from my sight before I kill you myself."

The aide carefully stepped back. A foul look scored his face. "Wait until the Mage learns of this. You'll pay for leading his army to ruin."

Hoole crossed the distance between them and ran the dagger deep into the aide's chest. Snarling, Hoole drew his sword and struck the head from the shoulders. Blood fountained as the body fell.

"You had your chance," he told the corpse.

Hoole wiped the blood from his sword and went off in search for a horse. He had to flee if there was to be a chance for the future. His future. Jervis Hoole fled for his life.

FIFTY-TWO
Shifting Tides

The retreating Goblins stopped upon seeing the great dragon overhead. Little by little they turned back towards the plain to watch the beast blow his kiss of death. The devastation of Gren Mot was still strong in their memories, and out here was a much easier killing ground. A great cheer rose from their haggard ranks. The enemy had nowhere to escape the dragon's fury. Odors of sulfur and brimstone contaminated the battlefield. Men and Dwarf doubled over and wretched from the smell. Arrows raced up to meet the wyrm and bounced harmlessly away from the heavy scales. Rocks and burning pitch followed and met with the same results. Some swore they heard the dragon laugh. Heavy ballista missiles came next and the dragon barely had to swerve to miss them. Then the beast tucked its wings in and dropped low over the field, sweeping hundred from their feet. Flames spit out and turned man and beast to ash.

Steleon picked himself up and watched as the dragon circled around for another pass. Soldiers ran in fear while others tried to extinguish the flames murdering their friends. Still others tried to form some semblance of defense. Steleon knew it was futile. The dragon wouldn't even need to try to thoroughly destroy them. He noticed something strange when the dragon turned. The sun caught the flying beast at the right moment and a glint of something shiny sparkled. He didn't know what the significance might be, but it kept his attention. Steleon grabbed for Ordein.

"Did you see that?"

The Dwarf had a certain wildness in his eyes, as if he knew he was about to die. "Aye, tis a terrible way to die."

"No. Look at the throat. There's something different about it," he insisted.

The dragon swooped in for another pass. This time they both saw the object clearly before jets of flame washed over more of their forces. It was a jade amulet wreathed in silver and clasped on an iron chain.

"It's the amulet! We need to break the amulet around his neck!"

Ordein scowled, "Why?"

"That has to be the source of the Mage's power. You said it yourself, no dragons have been seen in hundreds of years. Break it and we break the spell," Steleon said.

Ordein looked at him skeptically. He was afraid the man had lost it. Black smoke curled up from the tips of the flames spreading throughout the army. The dragon attacked again and more died. Steleon didn't wait for Ordein to make up his mind. He got up and ran to the archers that were left.

"Aim for that jade around his neck!" he shouted to them.

One by one they raised their bows and took aim.

"It's coming back again!" Ordein shouted before diving to the ground.

The great serpent barrel rolled, spitting flames a hundred feet through the air. Noxious fumes made them swoon. Some dropped unconscious while others were roasted alive. Arrows raced back, striking the wyrm in a hundred places with no effect. Steleon saw the gleam of recognition in the wyrm's eyes as it rolled over and came straight for them. Steleon looked back into those cold eyes and saw rage and confusion. The dragon landed in front of them and reared back. The wingspan was well over a hundred meters. His body was covered in rust colored scales. Wicked fangs dripped acid and the very air was one of twisted malevolence. The single horn sloping from the top of his head shook with fury. Slowly, the dragon drew a deep breath and readied to strike.

A single arrow whistled past Steleon's head, brushing his hair and kissing his cheek as it went. He watched the tip strike the jade jewel perfectly in the center. The explosion of brilliant green light pulsed from the dragon's heart and knocked them all to the ground. Steleon slowly tried to pick himself up and looked in time to see the dragon shake off whatever spell once held it. He'd been right. The Mage was controlling the dragon through sorcery. Freed from the curse, the dragon stared down his opponents one last time and took to the skies. It was heading back to Gren. Steleon whistled under his breath. Ancient legends whispered that dragons were among the smartest of all races. If that were the case, woe be to the slave masters in Gren.

"I'll be damned," Ordein exclaimed. His axe rested over one shoulder. "A single shot."

"No one could have done that in one shot," Steleon said. "Whoever it was deserves our highest praise and award."

King Maelor walked up to them, an ash bow in his left hand. "Save the decorations for those soldiers out there."

He dropped his bow and walked to where the remains of the amulet had fallen. He had a grimace of disgust when he picked up the cursed jewelry. An uneasy feeling coursed through him at the slightest touch. He felt as if the Silver Mage was staring into his very soul, stealing the warmth. Maelor handed it off to the nearest soldier.

"Take this to the smithy and have it smelted and poured into the river. It is an evil thing and I'll not have it stain my lands again," he ordered.

"I wouldn't believe it if I hadn't seen it," Ordein told him as Maelor rejoined them.

Maelor offered a weak smile. He was as worn down as the others but knew he couldn't let it show. "Years of hunting excursions and a hard task master when I was growing up are to thank for that. I've spent more time on the archery range than I care to recall. I think this just might be cause for celebration."

Ordein said, "I like how you think, king. Let us discuss the future over a pint of beer."

Steleon shook his head in defeat. Recollections of drinking with Norgen disturbed him and he had no desire to repeat the performance with his brother. Besides, there were more pressing issues at hand. Melgit and the cavalry were still running down the enemy and if they got too far from the main body there was the potential for disaster, especially among the boulders and crags of the foothills.

The whoosh of fresh flames hit before the actual fires burned into the retreating Goblins. The dragon was taking revenge and in a cruel way. Thankfully, Melgit had ordered a halt and even now formations of riders were doubling back away from the combat zone. No one had the desire to see even their enemies flamed alive.

"Sire, I believe we've won the field. Do we now follow the remnants of their army back into Gren and end the threat for good or do we trust that a small band of heroes can actually defeat the Mage?" Steleon asked.

Maelor placed his hands on his hips and surveyed the carnage around them. A great sadness welled inside. So much death and chaos and for what? One man's greed. He wanted nothing more than to plunge his father's sword into the Silver Mage's cold, dead heart.

"See to the dead and wounded. Give the men rest for a day. They earned it. Break out the ale and mead. But no one is to get drunk or I'll have them flogged for it. We are still at war, my friends. Set the picket lines and bring the camps forward. I want all field commanders in the tent in two hours."

"My Dwarves will take the front lines," Ordein volunteered. "We're the most rested and ready for what might come in the night."

Maelor nodded. "Thank you."

The group broke up, each going their different ways. The sun was dropping by the time the commanders assembled for Maelor. A little at a time, the soldiers from Averon, Harlegor, and the Bairn Hills settled down and relaxed. The tension and anxiety remained, as it would for days to come.

Many fell asleep the moment they sat down, too tired to even enjoy the king's ale. Up in the mountains, the orange glow of the dragon's hell continued.

Alone at last, Steleon dropped onto his cot and stared at the tender flames in the fire pit. He placed his head in his hands and cried for all those lost today. He suddenly felt very old. The weight of his days bore down heavily on his tired shoulders. Graeme reentered his thoughts and haunted him with his bravery. He'd been only a boy and should have been home with friends and family. Not out here. He wasn't the only one, Steleon lamented. Somewhere out in the wilds were Delin and Fennic. Images of the boys being tortured and killed tormented his mind. For the thousandth time he wished he hadn't let them go so easily. A guard entered with a bowl of stew. Steleon wordlessly took the bowl. He knew then what needed to be done. Finished eating, he gathered himself and went to the king's meeting.

"Ah Steleon," Maelor said. "It's been a long day, hasn't it?"

He agreed after a moment of silence. "Yes, sire. It has indeed."

"I've seen worse," Ordein offered in casual dismissal. "Though that wyrm was nearly the end of us. You have a fine army. It just took my axes to get you moving again. Ha! I name you Dwarf friend, Steleon. You'll forever be welcome in the halls of my people."

Steleon smiled back. "I'd be more than happy to take you up on that offer once this business is finished, but we have much to do before the end."

Melgit and a dark-haired man of middle age entered the tent just then and all eyes turned to them.

"Sire, this is Lord Flonish, captain of the Harlegor cavalry," he told those assembled.

Ordein eyed the newcomer with a natural mistrust for horsemen. Steleon clasped Melgit's hand with a genuine relief.

"Glad to see you made it through," he told them both. "What are our losses?"

Melgit shrugged. "They're manageable. We lost a few hundred altogether but are still in good shape. A lot of horses went down and broke their legs when the dragon attacked. That'll give you more infantry at least."

Flonish agreed. "This little war of yours is proving costly. There is a decided lack of interest across the kingdoms. Antheneon refuses to get involved and my kingdom is already stretched thin. We've heard rumors of smaller kingdoms joining forces with Gren and have been forced to double the watch on the southern borders. But my men are here to see it through. What is the next step?"

The truth in his first statement was painfully clear. Only three nations rallied to fight the Silver Mage. Three out of more than a dozen. Steleon doubted it would be enough.

"I don't think anyone understands the seriousness of the threat this time. We cannot afford to fight a war on two fronts. This battle here nearly finished us," he said. "We have to find a way to end the war now, before they regroup and strike again."

"What do you have in mind?" asked Maelor as he warmed his hands on the fire.

"Is there any choice? This is our best chance at invading Gren, while their armies are in full retreat. Strike now while we have the advantage," he replied with a cold voice.

"Go into Gren?" Melgit exclaimed. "I don't think you understand what you say. We would be effectively blind and at a disadvantage. This puts the army at grave risk."

"We are in grave risk to begin with," Steleon bit back. "Remember that we are not the only ones going to Gren."

Only Flonish looked confused.

"As much as I'm inclined to agree with you, we need to assess the situation more carefully. The weather is already changing. I believe a storm is coming in from the east. Mountain crossings are dangerous enough in good weather. But to do so in a winter storm is suicidal. Even if we do make it through before the storm hits, we'll be cut off without follow on reinforcements or supplies," he told them.

Many heads nodded agreement.

Steleon said, "Sire, we need to do something to help Hallis and his group. They are the only ones capable of winning this war for us. Let us take the armies and create a diversion so they can reach Aingaard and put an end to the Mage once and for all."

The idea was less than appealing, but they knew how important that tiny group of insurgents was to winning the war. Maelor knew he had to give them every chance for success. It was the only way.

"Sound the call to march," he said in a measured voice. "We go to Gren. This is a momentous occasion for all our peoples. Not in a hundred years has a combined army marched against the Silver Mage. I leave the details to you. Gentlemen."

They rose and bowed as he left them to their war games.

Steleon turned to Melgit. "I want scouts out immediately. Have them sweep the plain all the way to the edge of the pass. Take nothing for granted. The enemy may be regrouping as we speak. No one rides alone either."

"I'll handle it," Melgit replied. "We've already got roving patrols out. Redirecting them won't be an issue."

Flonish folded his thick arms across his chest. "Let me know how many men you need. We will cover down."

"I suppose there's no place for my Dwarves in all of this?" Ordein growled in outrage at being excluded.

"On the contrary," Steleon said. "We have need of every able bodied soldier. I just as soon keep your forces consolidated and near the front just in case the Goblins return."

Beaming with pride, the Dwarf lord exclaimed, "I'll lead the march all the way to Aingaard myself."

"Let's not be too hasty," Steleon cautioned. "We have five days until Winter's Day. Can we make it in time to stop the Mage?"

"Depends on the weather," Melgit replied. "It'll take four days to gain the Nveden Plains if the way is clear and we'd be ready to fight by that afternoon. I don't think we'll be able to move any quicker."

"That doesn't leave us much time."

"It's the best we can hope for," Melgit answered.

Locked in the security of his inner sanctum, Sidian paced. Unanswered questions tormented him. The strain of maintaining the war and his spells was wearing him thin. And now the defeat in Averon added to his misery. Sharp pain racked his bony frame, forcing him to his knees as he screamed in horror. Not even his command of magic was enough to stop the pain. He lay writhing on the floor for over an hour before it stopped. He knew then that his plans for Averon had failed. The dragon was free from his spell and wreaking terrible havoc on the Goblin army.

Sidian cursed Jervis Hoole and his incompetence. The army was broken and his greatest asset was lost. The path into Gren lay exposed. He didn't doubt Maelor would wait long before coming. It was inevitable. As depressing as that seemed, Sidian had a greater concern. The final shard was in Gren and coming to him. Plots and counterplots at work in his mind; Sidian finally pulled himself from the floor and opened the door for Spendak.

The warrior eased uncertainly into the sanctum.

"I have a task for you," Sidian croaked out. "You will personally lead a company to Greeth and awaited our enemies. The enemy has passed the swamps and made it past your soldiers. You will be awaiting them when they arrive. Once you have them in your possession, take their weapons and bring them back to me alive and unspoiled. Go now and do not fail me."

Spendak bowed curtly and was gone. The danger was increasing and he worried about the stability of Sidian's mind. More than once he considered running a sword through him and being done with the whole affair. Perhaps King Maelor would accept terms for surrender. Either way, the hourglass was draining on this whole, horrible affair. The end was coming quickly.

FIFTY-THREE
Tough Choices

Heavy winds slashed across the barren Nveden Plains. Dust and ash hammered into the tiny band, forcing them to huddle together. Darkness had settled in, though in comparison daylight wasn't much different. The smell of death permeated the air. An occasional rotten corpse lay in a ditch or crevice. Such was the land of Gren, and they wanted nothing more than to turn around and go home. Dakeb, of them all, frowned in sorrow at what was once a beautiful land.

Dawn broke. The village of Greeth lay less than an hour away. Smaller than either Feist or Alloenis, Greeth was Gren's second largest city. The disorganized rows of buildings were primitive at best, most with broken doors and cracked walls. Few buildings had windows and the ones that did were fragile and shattered. The villagers were mostly men. They were the last remnants of the ancient Grelnor. Goblins and other foul creatures preferred the dark caverns running underground and in the mountains. Tales of cannibalism revolved around the broken village.

"We're going there why?" Norgen asked once Dakeb finished speaking.

Dakeb sighed. "Circumstances have changed. Time is running out. If we continue to slink across the plains we'll never reach Aingaard in time."

"What are you saying?" Hallis asked. A familiar prickling itched his skin. The last time he felt such was back in the Gren pass before he was ambushed.

Celegon added, "We never discussed this course of action."

"Because there is no time for a debate on the matter. The longer we spend arguing over the finer points of how to go about what needs to be done, the further from the goal we are. I have my reasons for keeping my own council. You, Lord Celegon, of all people should understand the burdens of leadership," Dakeb shot back. His voice was uncharacteristically heated.

"So now you're our leader in this merry little adventure?" Scarn scoffed.

Tarren passed him a sideways glance laden with disgust. Her fears and misgivings towards the man grew each day. She knew he was going to try something foul soon but couldn't prove it.

"Mind your tongue, ranger," Norgen spat, finally fed up with human bickering. "I haven't seen you do much of anything since joining us, not even when your brothers fell that first night."

Scarn drew his sword. The Dwarf crouched low and readied to attack.

"Enough of this!" Dakeb snarled. "Do not for one instant allow yourselves to be fooled. We must all unite for the darkest hour, lest the enemy steal his victory. This is the most dangerous time. Think of those men fighting on the Thorn River. Their blood is buying us precious time."

"You're planning on letting us get captured, aren't you," Hallis quietly asked.

"It's the only way. I wish there were some other way to get there, but even I cannot make miracles happen," he replied apologetically.

"What's to keep them from just taking the crystal, and killing us on the spot?"

Dakeb answered, "It's too risky for him. Sidian won't feel secure unless he sees us in defeat and destroyed by his own hand. Either choice is a grave risk for us. The potential for failure is great, but there is no other option. It's the only way we're going to get into his fortress of Aingaard in time to stop the ceremony."

An uneasy silence settled over them. Each was forced to struggle with their personal demons and darkest thoughts. Only Scarn found no trouble with the plan. In fact, he couldn't have asked for things to turn out better. He was finally going to be free from the Hooded Man, and his visions of bitter promise. Scarn didn't even care if he got paid or not anymore. He just wanted to be done with the deal so he could put it behind him and never look back. After all these long months, hope took purchase.

Norgen wore his usual scowl. Hunted and harassed from the moment he left his mountain halls, the Dwarf managed to stay one step ahead of the enemy until now. Others died so he might stand here in Gren today. All their blood and sacrifice would mean nothing if he failed. For a moment, he thought of his brother Ordein and what he would do. When he came to a conclusion he spoke in careful prose.

"Three Elves and a Dwarf are not welcome sights in this accursed land, Dakeb. If this goes wrong our lives are forfeit." He sighed, "but that is a risk I swore to take when I signed on. I will follow your lead."

"Thank you," Dakeb replied. He took a small measure of hope in the stout Dwarf's words. Now if only the others would go along, they might still have a chance at stealing the day from the Silver Mage.

The Dwarf folded his burly arms across his chest and went to stand behind Delin and Fennic. He wasn't going to leave the boys unless death took him first. One by one the others joined him until all but Dakeb stood together. The old Mage sighed in relief. He'd known since leaving Ipn Shal that this was going to be his hardest test. He looked into each of their eyes, silently noting how Scarn looked away. There were hints of latent fear in Tarren's eyes and he knew why. The issue between the girl and the false ranger was becoming grave. Nothing good would come of it if Dakeb didn't step in first. Unfortunately, that was going to have to wait.

"We march throughout the day and enter Greeth at dusk," he told them. "After all, we don't want to make it look like we want to be captured. The journey has not been easy and we are in need of rest. Much strength will be needed if we are to defeat Sidian in the heart of his power."

"I'm scared, Delin," Tarren whispered between bites of dried deer meat.

Delin fought the urge to cradle her in his arms and steal them back to Fel Darrins.

"We're all afraid. I don't think any of us would have ever left home if we knew what was going to happen. This is beyond me, beyond all of us. We'll be fine as long as we have faith in each other, Tarren," he told her in a soothing voice.

She emphatically shook her head. "That's not what's troubling me."

Delin coughed. "What is it then?"

"Scarn," she replied.

He was confused. "The ranger?"

"Come on, Delin. He's no ranger. I know little enough about both, but a blind woman can see through his ruse. He's dangerous. Always watching me from the corner of his eye as if he's waiting for me to reveal his secrets. I can't sleep at night. The dreams are constant and horrible. The sad part is I find myself enjoying them a little more each time. I don't know what's happening to me. I'm so scared."

They'd all been troubled with nightmares of late, though none seemed so disturbing as hers. He didn't know what to say. What could he do to comfort her from the pain of sleep? Delin simply held her close and whispered it was going to be all right. Her weeping face buried in his chest as he struggled to believe his own words.

Tolis Scarn took his gaze off the cuddling couple, content that his secrets were still safe, and resumed brushing down his horse. The game between the girl and himself was growing increasingly dangerous. He wasn't sure how much longer he could keep her intimidated from talking. Even if the Mage's plan were successful, all it would take was a word from her and he'd never live to see Aingaard or his freedom. His choices were becoming severely limited.

Still, he found a certain arousal towards the girl. She was a comely thing, and part of him wanted to feel the softness of her flesh, see the curve of her hip. He didn't remember the last time he'd been with a woman, but it was long enough that the dream was nearly a forgotten pleasure. It was a shame she needed to die. He could use a pet to relieve his frustrations for a night. Maybe the Hooded Man would give her to him as a reward. Scarn curled up in his bedroll and went to sleep with thoughts of her. His dagger lay clenched in his right fist.

For all intents and purposes, Dakeb was fast asleep. Cross legged, eyes closed and snoring, the Mage was anything but. His breathing was slow and deliberate. It was an old trick dating back to the awakenings of the first Mages to roam Malweir. With his energies consolidated, Dakeb was able to see into the deepest regions of the mind and soul. He reached out and entered Tarren's mind. She was in the most danger of them all. He worried that she wasn't going to be able to endure the test of the final days. Scarn and something else was driving her deeper into dementia.

Fevered images clouded her thoughts, inching deeper into her conscience. They were trying to control her. Darkness threatened to seduce her with its wicked ways and torrid tasks. The purity of her soul had dimmed considerably since leaving Ipn Shal. Each time they stopped, Dakeb found himself drifting back to her to try and salvage what he could. It was a task that demanded much of his energy, and he knew he'd need everything to confront Sidian. Focusing his powers into a thin beam of energy, Dakeb sent it coursing through Tarren's sleeping body. Alone, it lacked sufficient power to fend off Sidian's curse, but he may just save her long enough to see the battle ended. Another day closer to what he hoped was his final task. Sweat beaded on his weathered brow. His muscles ached from the latent strain of the magic. His body hurt from days and decades of struggle. Finished for now, Dakeb released his hold on the magic and sank into unconsciousness.

Dusk ushered in a near perfect darkness, tainted only by the menacing glow of apocalyptic fires burning across the Nveden Plains. Horrors unbound, lay as far as they imagination lay. Greeth stretched out before the band of weary travelers at the base of a low rise. Sporadic lights gave off little of the city. Dozens of shapes scurried off into the shadows. A pall of terror and sickness seemed to hang over the city, permeating the very air with a special brand of sickness. Dakeb led them down.

"I can't believe we're actually doing this," Delin whispered to Fennic.

Fennic shrugged. He could already feel Phaelor trying to take control again. Power and temptations trickled into his veins. It was enough to make him swoon. The sword wanted to fight. It needed to fight. It was the only way. Destiny lay but a heartbeat away.

"Much is unbelievable these days," Dakeb cautioned. He caught the troubled look in Fennic's eyes. Yet another potential for disaster lay in wait. If the Star Silver Sword took control of the boy there would be a nightmare to pay. He decided to let it rest for the moment and tried to calm Delin. "Often the hardest part in belief is taking the first step. Your heart will lead you where you need to go. I've found life is peculiar that way."

"Hmmph," Norgen said, "nice to see one of us can see a brighter shade of things."

"Practicality, Norgen. It's all practicality," the Mage replied with annoyance.

Norgen wasn't as convinced.

Small bands of Goblins and corrupted men could now be seen. They roamed about in search of a meal or trouble. Greeth loomed ever closer. The column slowly wound into town. There was no confusion or pause on their part. Dakeb led them true. No one even bothered to look their way as they finally entered the fringes of town.

"Keep your mouths shut and your hoods up," Dakeb warned them. "These are crude creatures, but generally keep to themselves. Do the same and they will leave us alone."

Celegon leaned in and asked, "This is all well and fine, but I was under the impression we were trying to get captured? Why all the secrecy?"

Dakeb quickly answered. "Because we're looking for the right person."

They each eyed the old Mage but kept quiet. He'd been right so far, and they knew when not to ask questions. They didn't need to wait long for the riddle to solve itself. Beady eyes watched them from the shadows. Spies and hopeful thieves looked to gain a quick profit should the opportunity arise. The smarter ones slipped away unseen, but one eased off to report to his masters. The enemy knew Dakeb had come.

"Now what?" Hallis hissed once they entered a large open square in the heart of the city.

They were the only ones on the streets. Windows and doors were closed and locked. The tiny group crowded closer together in anticipation of a fight. The heavy sounds of footsteps running at them echoed off the walls. Goblins poured from the alleys until the roads became impassable. Spears and halberds lowered menacingly as the circle tightened. Trolls and a few gangly men moved to the front of the crowd. Snarls and curses filled the night. They were threats of unbridled hatred.

A tall, thin man with greasy hair and sparkling black armor, gilded in patterns of dragons and studded with gems, edged his way through until he came to stop in front of the Mage. The cruel look on his face was one of complete and total victory. The sword in his hand emphasized the point.

FIFTY-FOUR
Captured

"In the name of Lord Sidian, the Silver Mage and ruler of mighty Aingaard, I place you under arrest. Drop your weapons and climb down from the horses," Spendak growled to them.

A Troll stepped menacingly closer, the heavy tulwar anxious in his huge hands. One of the horses reared up in fright. One by one they dropped to the ground and began unbuckling their swords and weapons. Winds lashed around them, kicking up dust and a foul stench from the alleys. Spendak's hair blew wildly, lending him a demonic look.

"Now, off with the hoods. I want to see your faces," he ordered and raised his sword level with Dakeb's chest.

Goblins ducked in and took the reins and led the horses off. Others began picking up the pile of assorted weapons. They stopped when they got close to Fennic. Phaelor was glowing hotly, as if tempting them to touch it to know what true hell was. A lone, dark hand with gnarled fingers reached out to grasp the sword. The Goblin nervously touched the cold hilt and screamed in pain. Lancing pain shot through his veins. Smoke poured from his flesh. Flames erupted from his nose, mouth, and ears. Dead before he knew what killed him, the Goblin's charred corpse dropped heavily. The others cringed back. Even Spendak betrayed a hint of fear.

"The Star Silver Sword," he whispered, coming out of his shock. "Sidian was right. You are as dangerous as he warned."

Fennic too was shocked, but he quickly snapped out of it. "Touch it if you will," he warned with a snarl. "Death wants a companion."

Spendak leaned forward, "Sharp tongue for a boy. Perhaps I should kill you now and have done with it."

A collective gasp escaped the Goblins and took attention away from the two men. Celegon and the others chose that moment to remove their hoods. Elves! The enemy of a thousand years had returned. The very sight of the long, pointed ears sticking out of the flowing hair was enough to inspire new fear in the Goblins, and even the more stalwart Trolls.

"Come on then," Norgen growled. "Let's finish this."

The Dwarf stood with his legs slightly apart, in challenge of his hated foe. His copper beard was tied in a tight tail and garnished by several gold rings. Hatred flared in his dark eyes.

Spendak was impressed, if only slightly. He alone knew who it was that intended to kill Sidian. "My, my. What a curious group you've assembled, old man. I wonder how you expected to complete your task. Elves, a Dwarf, an old man, and children. What did you hope to accomplish? Surely you don't think you can actually kill Sidian?"

Hallis took a step forward. A dozen archers raised their bows and took aim.

"I wouldn't," Spendak cautioned. "The boy can keep his toothpick, but one wrong move and you all die. My Goblins have been aching for target practice lately." He turned to his forces, "Bring the chains and bind them. I want to be back on the road to Aingaard in an hour."

Several Goblins moved forward with the heavy manacles. They were quickly bound and pushed along the road to where a rickety wagon awaited. Hallis was surprised none of them had been beaten yet. Not in a hurry to be pummeled by a Troll, Hallis decided to cooperate and held his hands out. The iron was cold and tight on his flesh. A pair of Trolls easily picked them up and dropped them in the back of the prison wagon. Both had pleased looks on their tusked faces. The wagon was locked and chained. It offered no protection from the elements, as it was a simple cage of iron bars and reinforced flooring. Hallis hoped the trek to Aingaard wasn't going to be too long.

Spendak stopped gloating over his prize. He'd been expecting them to put up a fight and was somewhat disappointed he didn't have the opportunity to kill one or two. His hatred for the Elves ran almost as deep as for the disgusting Goblins Sidian insisted on using. *Elves*, he cursed. If their kind had stayed and fought the Silver Mage when he first came to Gren none of this would be happening. But like so many before them, the Elves chose to flee and leave the people of Gren to their doom. Not even the once vaunted combat skills of the Grelnor were enough to stop the evil from consuming them.

"We are ready, my lord," the wagon master snarled.

Spendak nodded. "Bring their horses. We can always use them in Aingaard."

The capital city lay to the south, less than a day's ride. The Nveden Plains were unusually harsh but wouldn't pose too much of a problem. Sidian didn't need the stone for another two nights. Spendak had plenty of time to deliver his prize. With a slight motion of his head, he urged the wagon master to proceed. The column started the long, slow crawl to Aingaard and the fate of the world.

Fennic watched the empty desolation of the plains roll by in a collage of shadows and menacing shapes. His initial impression of the land of Gren hadn't changed much, and then it was for the worse. He didn't understand how anything could stand to live like this. He hated the land, hated it with all his heart. The smell was enough to inspire nightmares and the people were a ruined waste of culture, and it only got worse the deeper they traveled.

It was only Dakeb's silent warning that kept him from using Phaelor to strike down their foes when they were captured. He knew Phaelor would have made quick work of them, regardless of their numbers. After all, wasn't he the Gnaal killer? Now bound like his friends, Fennic seethed in silent rage.

"Relax, Fennic," Dakeb told him. "We didn't come here to fight. Not now."

Fennic thought otherwise. "We still should have tried."

"To what end? You'd be dead, and Sidian would still have the rest of us. Remember, Phaelor chose you for a reason. Your time is yet to come."

"Just give me one swing and I'll end his terror forever," Fennic announced.

Dakeb watched the boy with growing concern. Phaelor was consuming him, and he didn't know how to stop or even slow it. "I've already told you what will happen if you strike Sidian. Has this rage consumed you beyond reason?"

"Listen to him, boy," Norgen growled.

He liked being caged least of all, but he also knew how foolish resisting was. Besides, the Mage had a plan. Norgen recalled his father's words: Fight with your head, not your emotions. Don't ever give the enemy the upper hand. They were sound words and he wished he could drive them home with Fennic.

"This is the chance we've been waiting for. Think about it," Norgen continued.

"The sword is still in our possession and we're being taken to the heart of the enemy."

Delin watched his best friend with fright. This was the first time Phaelor had taken so strong a hold on him. He was afraid for Fennic's soul. The sword was dangerous, and everyone could see it but Fennic. He clutched Tarren's hand for support and was comforted when she returned the gesture. Times were bad enough without fits of insanity or delusions of grandeur. He hoped and prayed the end wouldn't come down to him having to choose who to save, because he truly didn't know anymore.

The wagon rolled deeper into the night.

"Dakeb, now that we've been given this opportunity, how do you intend on using it to our advantage? There's not much we can do with these chains on," Celegon asked.

There was a twinkle in the old Mage's eyes. "I do happen to be a Mage, you know. How good would I be if I gave away all my secrets?

Predictability is a crutch. Do the unexpected when they're looking the other way, I say."

"So we can assume you're not going to tell us what to expect," Hallis added.

Dakeb chuckled.

"You have to admit, despite the situation, this is easier than riding the way ourselves. Maybe we should have taken a wagon from the beginning," Dakeb brought up after a few hours had passed. "We certainly could have loaded more to eat. I'm starving. I'll have to remember that for the next time."

"The next time?" Scarn asked skeptically.

"There's always a next time."

Scarn fell silent and kept to himself, every so often stealing glances at Tarren. She was convinced she knew who he was, and that troubled him. He desperately needed to do something about her before the others found out and turned on him. But what? He didn't know. Hopefully time would play out in his favor. That was providing his guess was accurate and the Silver Mage and the Hooded Man were one and the same.

Tarren burrowed her head into Delin's shoulder and tried to sleep. Thoughts of home strayed into her dreams. A month ago she'd been a simple girl from a small town most of the world never heard of. She didn't know what she wanted out of life nor where to find it when she figured it out. She hadn't even known her love for Delin until he and Fennic left on their quest. Tarren's heart nearly broke that day.

Since then she'd found herself growing in every sense of the word. Her mind and spirit evolved the further into this dark journey she traveled. She'd gone from a naïve village girl to a young woman wary of the world. Her body was changing as well. She was developing into a full grown woman. Maybe that was why Scarn kept eyeing her and making her uncomfortable. Maybe, but she knew better.

Tarren regretted it all. She hated the reasons she was forced to grow up, and the split-second decisions that brought her to this foul land. All she wanted was the chance to go home and never leave again. Delin just being there gave her strength and hope, but the taint of evil here was so strong. She felt things inside her changing. She was more callous than she used to be. Her body often flashed hot for no reason at all. Dakeb remained ever secretive and she was sure he was hiding something from her. Tarren wanted to know what.

The moment passed, and Tarren let it go with a sigh. There was too much she didn't have control over. She finally pulled her head away from Delin's shoulder and wasn't surprised to see Scarn's cold eyes staring back at her.

The Elves sat huddled together in the back of the wagon talking in their own language. They all knew the risks involved with joining Dakeb. Many of their kind had fallen during the Mage Wars and their quests over the centuries. Never before had the task been so dire.

"This isn't looking good," Llem said. "We've been in tight places before, but none this bad. Too much can go wrong."

Celegon dismissed his concerns with a wave of his hand. "The Mage knows what he's doing. Besides, a thousand things could have already gone wrong. Events are developing according to the Mage's plan. Soon enough we'll be inside Sidian's keep. Then we can finally end his reign."

"And these manacles?" Derlith asked, raising his bound hands. "I too have doubts. It's one Mage against another. Shouldn't their magic cancel each other? This battle could well destroy the foundations of the world. Can we so confidently trust him with our lives so recklessly?"

"Dakeb has been a friend for centuries. Our lives have been in his hands since we arrived at Ipn Shal. Two more days can't hurt," Celegon said.

A pair of Goblins snarled at them.

Llem eyed them casually and asked, "What about weapons? Providing we can make it to the throne room without losing our heads, we're going to need a way to defend ourselves."

The Elf prince shrugged.

"You're not very inspiring," Derlith scowled. "And then there's that one. The so called ranger. He's becoming a liability. We should finish him before we reach Aingaard."

Scarn shifted in his sleep and started to snore.

"Dangerous," Celegon agreed, "but the Mage claims we all have a part to play. Killing him now may upset that balance. I'll not take the chance. Not yet."

Night gradually turned into day. Distorted sunlight reflected off the snowcapped peaks of the Gren Mountains, turning the snow a soft pink. A flock of geese in a V formation honked in passing. Tarren watched until the clouds swallowed them. One of the guards tossed a stale loaf of bread into the wagon. Depression settled back in. A few more hours and they'd be in Aingaard. The pace quickened.

Spendak glanced back at the wagon from time to time. Only the Mage disturbed him. He should have at least put up a fight, but the old man calmly accepted his fate. What game was he playing at? Sidian didn't bother explaining who the other prisoners were, only to be wary of the Mage. He could easily tear the Goblins apart with the flick of his wrist. Spendak contemplated the future as they rode on.

Norgen came awake with a loud snore and shielded his eyes from the dim glare of the sun. He was sore and angry, much as he'd been for the last few weeks.

"Good morning," Dakeb cheerfully told him. The smile on his face was bright considering the situation.

"At least one of us is in a good mood," Norgen replied in a sour tone. "I'd give anything to get my hands on my axe and cleave a few Goblins necks."

"How much longer until we get there?" Hallis asked. There were too many eager ears nearby to let Norgen keep talking like that.

"Sometime around dusk I should think. It's been a long time since I was last here," Dakeb answered.

Hallis wanted to ask the obvious question but held his tongue. Some secrets weren't meant to be shared. Instead, he said, "That's cutting it pretty close to Winter's Day."

"So it is," Dakeb agreed. "But the ritual must be performed at precisely the right minute on Winter's Day. Otherwise Sidian must wait another thousand years. It's a complicated issue, but I'll do my best to explain."

By the time he finished, they all wished Hallis had never approached the subject. He told them of the origins of the Mage Order from the blood of the Gaimosian Knights and how the dark gods strove to return from their banishment to conquer the world they claimed their own. It was a sordid tale. The sun was going down and not one of them had a clue about what Dakeb had said. Another loaf of moldy bread was tossed in, and the wagon stopped long enough for them to relieve themselves. Then the wagon rolled on through the night to a chorus of metallic groans and creaks.

The violent sound of thunder and lightning awakened those that had drifted off. The night sky continued to darken. Fires raged in tune with the madness in the skies, and a sleeting rain attacked them. The Goblins marched on under the whip. Fissures and crevices opened around them, inviting them with certain doom. Rock formations broke the ground like jagged teeth waiting to impale angels should they descend. Gren had suddenly transformed into a vicious place.

And there, silhouetted against the pale orange glow of the horizon, sat the ruined city of Aingaard. Dawn was still some hours off, making it look like the end had come to Malweir. Blue tinged lightning struck not far away, sending a shower of sparks into the wagon. Hairs stood on end. Electricity tainted the air. Their flesh became goose pimpled. A metallic taste stuck in their mouths. Heavy winds rushed in, buffeting the fragile wagon to the point of destruction. Even the assurances of reaching the enemy citadel was stolen now. Hope diminished.

The storms became increasingly violent the closer to the city they got. All around was a world gone mad. The Silver Mage had managed to destroy the balance of nature. The world was collapsing in on itself as it played closer to oblivion. The city of Aingaard was somehow untouched. Dakeb attributed this to magic, a serious misuse of magic. When the Silver Mage perished, so to would this nightmare.

The wagon clattered across the cobblestone bridge spanning a fire laden chasm ringing the city. The gates were open, for no enemy had attacked in centuries. Dozens of Goblins and Trolls lined the way, all were dressed in sparkling dark armor. They had malicious glares and polished weapons. A trumpet sang to all, announcing the enemies of Gren had come. There was cheering in the streets from the massed crowds. Threats and promises of death rose from the myriad voices. In twelve hours the gateway to the under-world would be open and Gren's ascension to the domination of Malweir would begin.

FIFTY-FIVE
The Army Goes to Gren

The combined armies of Averon and Harlegor marched towards Gren in a long, winding column singing cadence and traditional battle hymns. Advance units had already made contact with the enemy in the ruins of Gren Mot and were in the process of cleaning out the fortress. On the lower plains, the last scatterings of Goblins were being hunted down and destroyed. Few of the dark host remained in Averon. Still, Steleon and Maelor were cautious in their approach. The victory on the Thorn River was a gift and it wouldn't do to squander this one chance in a fool's charge.

Bodies lined the walls of the mountain pass. Steleon sent squads of pikemen forward to ensure the dead were just that. Goblins often used deceit to gain the upper hand and with quarters so tight in the pass, the potential for disaster was high. The northern winds blew strongly for most of the morning and early afternoon. Snow powder drifted down from the ragged peaks. Golden sunlight reflected off the slopes, though little of the warmth made it to the bottom of the pass. Halfway through their march, Steleon spied an omen. A lone eagle, large and inspiring, followed their progress as it soared through the eastern skies. The men took heart and marched faster.

But not even the coming of an omen was enough to stay their nervousness long. Shadows and cold draped over the column. Soldiers quickly complained from the bone numbing chill and a prolonged lack of sleep. The campaign had been tiring and demanding. Hundreds of their comrades and friends were already dead, and hundreds more would soon be joining them. The promise of vengeance pushed the survivors.

Steleon felt their pain, for he was suffering too. He wasn't as young as he used to be, and the long years of battle and campaign were wearing him down. Still, he knew they had to move quickly if they had a chance at defeating the Silver Mage. Speed was the key. The sheer boldness of their plan hadn't been done in military history for centuries, not since the last time the Elves went to war against the northern Goblin nations. They simply had to reach the Nveden Plains and be arrayed in battle formation in time, or else the entire gamble was a failure. Either way, one of the great nations in Malweir was going to fall. He just wasn't sure which one.

It was close to dusk when he first spied what remained of Gren Mot. The smell was sickening and many soldiers heaved their stomachs up. Long dried blood stains added to the morbidity of the place. Bodies lay in ruined heaps, some having been chewed and eaten. Worst of all was the huge pile of heads in the center courtyard. Hundreds more were impaled on long poles along the parapets. Steleon fought to contain his emotions. He pushed the men harder, ordering them to clear the fortress and press on into the plains of Gren. He silently hoped they would use what they saw here and bring that fury down on the enemy.

"Keep them moving," he barked to Melgit. "Push them down onto the plains before this place has the chance to affect them."

Melgit only nodded. He couldn't speak. The horrors of seeing the butchered remains of so many men he served with and knew personally ate at his soul. He knew that his head should be in that pile along with better men. It took a concentrated effort to bring him from his daze.

"Move out!" he finally yelled to his men as they trudged past. "We march down to the plains and await our enemy! Move out!"

Steleon sighed with relief. He'd been afraid of how Melgit would react upon returning to this dead place. The danger was passed for the moment. Now he needed to worry about getting his full army down through the mountains.

Drinking deeply from his canteen, Steleon stopped long enough to wipe away some of the sweat and grime from the long day's march. He, Maelor and the rest of the key leaders were assembled in a small cut off the main path beyond the fortress. Banners of dozens of units went by. Soldiers cheered their king and commander. The spirit of the army was still strong, despite the nightmares witnessed in Gren Mot. The tired commander hoped it would last long enough.

"Impressive," Ordein commented. "I've been a warrior all my life. I've seen many wars and battles, armies marching off to join steel with the foe. This is the first time I've seen an army so grand and proud. The Silver Mage ought to tremble in his dark tower at the thought of this mighty war machine. By Gru! How can we fail?"

Maelor weighed the question carefully for a moment. Although he wholeheartedly agreed with the stout Dwarf, he had doubts over Sidian's preparedness for their invasion. "This war is far from over. We've won the last battle, true, but the enemy is vast and full of deceit and surprise. We should not take the Mage too lightly."

"That's defeatist talk. My folk came here to fight," Ordein snarled in response.

Steleon saw the argument brewing and moved to cut it off. It wouldn't do them any good to fight amongst themselves with the enemy so close. "There'll be plenty of fighting ahead, I can promise you that. Let us use caution a while longer. At least until we see what surprises the Silver Mage has in store for us."

"Bah! We have them on the run now. It's been two days since we last saw sign of the foe. Let me take my Dwarves and finish this. The very road to Aingaard may lie open and you speak of caution. I say we press the attack."

Steleon shook his head. It appeared a Dwarf's blood contained as much steel as his axe. "I'm afraid it's not so simple. The enemy still has his magic. Not even the tenacity of your folk is enough to best such."

"What of Fennic and the sword?" Melgit asked. His newly appointed general's rank glittered in the fading sun.

Lord Flonish of Harlegor added, "I think we need fear the worst. If they've been gone this long and we've heard no word, disaster may have befallen them."

"Whether they've fallen or not, I know not. Should they fail we'll be all that stands between Malweir and the horrors of Gren. The very conquest of the world is at our door. It's a fine line we walk," Steleon said.

"Dead or not, we keep moving. Winter's Day is three days away and I have a strong desire to see this through. The Silver Mage will have the same notion. It's a matter of time now," Maelor said.

He looked around and focused on the passing men. "Leave a battalion of engineers at Gren Mot. I want them to take care of our dead and begin rebuilding the defenses. I'm sure word of our coming has already reached Aingaard. Make sure the cavalry and siege machines are in the flatlands before this army stops moving for the night. Set up the picket lines and post my colors in the center of the field. I think it's time for Sidian to know who comes calling."

"Sire, this is a haunted place. Many a good man won't risk his life to Gren and the ghosts both," Melgit cautioned.

"Then we exorcise those ghosts with steel," Maelor replied and rode off.

Ordein grinned.

Melgit rode back to the ruins in middle of the night to confront his nightmares. He stood in the remnants of the command tower and surveyed what remained. The view to the east stretched a good half league, with the occasional glimpse down onto the Nveden Plains. This was the place he had watched the beginnings of the war unfold.

He could still imagine his friends: Fynten steaming over the map table. Wiln and Surnish arguing over tactics. The sour look constantly marring Prelin's scarred face. Even quiet Crespith and that damned fool dagger he always carried. Melgit fought back the tears as long as he could before succumbing finally. He hadn't realized how much he lost that day. He had a feeling he'd soon be joining his friends. Kicking at the piles of soot, he sat on a window bench and cried away the pain.

"My bones tell me snow is coming," Flonish said. Total darkness surrounded them. Heavy clouds swept in, low to the ground and hateful. The promise of storm rode with them. It sat ill on his fears.

Ordein nodded hasty agreement. "Winter in Gren is not a healthy thought. Defeating the Mage will be difficult at best. It will take our combined force to drive his armies off."

Steleon listened to the useless conversation. They all knew the Silver Mage wasn't going to postpone his war until spring. Each of them understood the seriousness of the situation yet persisted in arguing over non-factors. They had less than three days before the dark Mage was going to do what he intended. That was it. The redundancy of their arguments was numbing. Steleon wondered how they could be expected to fight as one and win this war. Matters were much simpler when he was the sole voice of the army. He closed his eyes and prayed that Delin and Fennic were close to finishing their quest.

"We continue the march," he finally said in a stern, controlled voice. "I'll not sit idle and let this fine army lose all momentum at the threat of snow. Should we become trapped in Gren we ride south past the mountains and into Antheneon. Remember gentlemen, if we can't ride the pass neither can they. If it comes to retreat, we make the Silver Mage pay with every foot of ground."

"I'm not so sure the Antheni will appreciate our advance through their lands," Melgit said. "Rumors have it they deal with the Silver Mage."

Maelor smashed his fist into the small table. The candle flickered softly. "Damn them all. They should be fighting alongside us. Their policy of non-commitment will be the ruin of the east. If needs be, we'll slam through them as well. I will see this war finished. By the gods I will."

Ordein nudged Flonish and beamed, "He'd make a good Dwarf."

The Dwarf lord rose slowly, his four foot frame somehow impressive in the confines of the small tent. "It's clear to me that we have lost focus with that one victory on the river. The Silver Mage seeks to open the paths to the underworld, just as he has in the past. Either we stand and fight, or we run and die. There are no other choices. My folk will gladly lend a hand in rebuilding your fortress once this war is done. Gru knows the world needs more beauty created by the Dwarves. We push on and fight. Here, now."

He sat down with a smug look. Their argument was effectively finished.

Steleon smiled for the first time in a week.

"Ordein has the right of it," he told them. "Stopping the Mage is a task appointed to others. Ours is to destroy his armies. Have all units form battle lines and prepare for the attack. We march like that until we meet resistance. The enemy will be caught off guard. Let them die that way. General Melgit, how long before the army is ready to advance?"

"The majority have been on the plains for about two hours now," he said after a moment. "Say another two before they're rested enough to do the job."

"Will that give enough time?" Flonish asked. "My cavalry need little enough to deploy, but I think the infantry and artillery will need longer. Nine thousand riders make a handsome opponent but won't stand long if the enemy attacks too soon."

Steleon said, "You'll have the men of the vanguard with you should it come to it, and the might of the Dwarven Hammer. Though I doubt the enemy will attack."

"Why not?" Maelor asked skeptically.

The old warrior explained, "Their army was shattered at the Thorn River. What units did survive most likely turned south to skirt around the mountains rather than stay in our path. The Silver Mage will know this. He'll be more cautious about sending his forces in. Most of their leadership can be presumed destroyed. Goblins don't fight well without a leader. Any that did survive more than likely took to ground rather than risk the wrath of the Mage. That makes the rest of the army potentially blind to our moves. I believe we can be arrayed in battle ranks and ready to fight before the enemy has the chance to react."

Melgit added, "Sir, I'm taking a small staff forward with the van. That'll give me better control of the situation. I don't want to be caught with my pants down again."

The Dwarf lord quit tugging on his beard long enough to say, "What happens if we're wrong? The army needs good leaders. Soldiers will do as their told, and sergeants will hold units together under the darkest conditions. Officers are hit and miss, but true combat leaders are special. Those we need more than anything. To put yourself at risk like that is brash, boyo."

"There is danger in any move we make. I wouldn't mind getting a glimpse of what's in store for us myself," Maelor said suddenly.

"Absolutely not, sire," Steleon bit out. "You are Averon. If you fall we shall too. A general can be replaced. The king cannot. General Melgit, though I disapprove of the mission, I see the necessity in it. Request granted but keep your staff small. You may leave at your discretion."

Melgit gave a sharp nod and exited the tent.

"I think I'll head down there as well. Wouldn't mind stepping in front of the lads for a while," Ordein said. "Might even get to wet my axe in the process."

Two hours later the army groaned to their feet again. They complained and griped the way good soldiers are supposed to and struck the camp. Quickly they were packed up and moving again. They could feel the end drawing near. The final battle of this terrible war was upon them. Anticipation buzzed through the ranks. There was no cadence or cheer this march, for the once defenders had become invaders and required stealth.

Light snow was falling, coating the outcroppings of rock and dead trees lining the road. Moonlight painted the clouds a ghastly color. The brunt of the storm was still hours away and already the Nveden Plains were changing for the worse. Banners fluttered in the wind. The mixed colors of three nations united to end an ages old evil. The soldier's faces were grim, determined to see this through so that they may return to their families and loved ones. Soon, very soon, the army would meet the enemy in battle, and the fate of Malweir would at last be decided.

FIFTY-SIX
The Battle of Nveden Plains

Melgit's first true glimpse of Gren abhorred him. He'd heard all the stories and tales old grandmothers told at night to keep the children in line. Until now he'd never put much stock in them. These visions of ruination would forever scar his memory. A small part of him now understood why the Grelnor hated the men of the lowlands. It wasn't hate. It was envy. This was the very birthplace of death and decay. How many generations were forced to grow up and only dream of color and warmth? To wish for the one thing they couldn't obtain, a world free from the yoke of tyranny. It was a forgotten dream.

He closed his looking glass and shook his head in disgust. Beside him, Commander Slephen yawned. He was undaunted by the sights. He'd been a soldier all his life and had seen his share of blood and horror. Gren presented a new challenge, to be sure, but they were all the same when it came down to winning and surviving.

"Lovely place to wage war," he casually remarked through another yawn. "At least we don't need to worry about snow."

Melgit forced a laugh and eyed his adjutant oddly. He didn't understand how the man was so calm. "Nice to see one of my commanders still has a sense of humor."

Slephen shrugged. "It helps. Besides, with magic and dragons, we need something to keep us going. This war is nasty business."

"I wonder if your king will appreciate such candor when the blood flows," Ordein asked.

For the hundredth time Melgit wondered if he was trapped amongst madmen. "Have your scouts found anything significant yet?"

"We captured a few Goblins," Slephen replied. "I think we're about to catch them off guard and take the day, General."

"Don't be too hasty. This land is riddled with underground caverns connected by a massive tunnel complex. There's plenty enough room to conceal an army until the time is right," he paused. "Commander, deploy your forces along that crevasse to the right about six hundred meters out. That should give you enough maneuverability in case they launch their own assault. The rest of the army will form on your flank."

"Would you like my personal or professional opinion, sir?" he asked.

A raised eyebrow was his response.

"It's not my choice of ground, but it's a damned sight easier than most we've had to fight on. I'll have the boys moving and in place within the hour," Slephen told him.

The man saluted and rode off. Melgit watched him go. Slephen was whistling.

King Maelor and the lead elements of the main body slowly moved into battle position. Guides came forward and began issuing orders for emplacement and the order of battle being passed down from Melgit.

"So far so good," he said as the army marched by. "I think we've taken them by surprise after all."

Loath as he was to admit it, Steleon found himself agreeing. Aside from limited Goblin scouts, it appeared Gren was caught off guard. "It appears so, sire. I recommend caution nonetheless. We've been tricked before."

"We've also beaten back everything thrown at us," Maelor reminded him.

Steleon remained quiet. Too many dark thoughts were going through his head. He stood and watched the occupation of Gren proceed.

Fierce winds howled across the barren plains, battering the single story stone buildings. A pair of Goblin sentries stood by the door of the largest, braving the hazardous weather. Inside sat the three Generals of the armies of the Silver Mage. They quietly discussed their next move. Arms folded across his chest, General Eorgis took in his peers with a foul look. A spider web of scars ran down the side of his face, ending where his left eye once was. A proven veteran, he'd been given command of the defense of Gren upon hearing the news from the Averon. With Jervis Hoole missing, and the dragon no longer under the Mage's control, Eorgis and his forces were all that stood between the enemy and Aingaard.

"Enter," he bellowed at the sound a heavy knock.

A young soldier walked in. He was covered with sweat and out of breath. Eorgis eyed him disgustedly. Hoole's lack of training had ruined too many good young men and he was being forced to pick up the scraps.

"Do you plan on reporting or am I to guess what you have to say?" he ground out in metered hatred.

"Sir, the enemy is down from the mountains. They are taking up positions along the plains and preparing for battle."

So, it was finally time. "How many do they bring?"

"It looks like his entire army, sir. Tens of thousands at least."

Eorgis dismissed the boy with a wave and went back to his generals. He had a battle to plan.

The mighty war machine of Gren groaned to life. Battalions of Goblins and Trolls streamed up from their caves and laagers with fire in their blood. They sang as they marched, for the prospect of havoc was too strong to be denied. It had been long since they fought the hated Elves and Dwarves. Trolls and Goblins howled with excitement. Doom marched on the winds as the gap between armies closed.

"Damn this country," Slephen cursed, wiping the sweat from his brow for the third time in as many minutes. His earlier indifference was gone.

Ordein chuckled. "Aye. It's the perfect place to wage a war."

"Why would you say that?" Slephen asked him.

"No one will care if this place is destroyed. Not like fighting back in the streets of Paedwyn or in the halls of Breilnor," the Dwarf replied.

He'd never thought of it that way. Just being in Gren was more than enough for him. Slephen was from a small village near Relin Werd and Fel Darrins. This was his first taste of such vast emptiness, and it disgusted him.

"Well, if they don't make a move soon, we'll be at Aingaard before long," he said. "Won't be much of a fight."

The winds continued to pick up. Riders started coming in, driven on by the strength of the approaching storm. All wore grim looks. Ordein gripped his axe haft a little tighter. He was sure something terrible rode on the winds. The moment he'd been waiting for was fast upon them. He knew it.

"The enemy is approaching!" one of the scouts reported with a grimace.

Slephen failed to see the excitement in it. "From where and how many?"

"They're coming from due east and it looks like they're bringing everything they have. We're outnumbered, sir."

Slephen frowned. With the riders of Harlegor and the Dwarves they numbered around thirty thousand. If they were outnumbered, the Mage must be throwing his entire reserves at them. It was a time of desperation for both armies.

"Take word back to the main body with my compliments," he ordered.

Ordein asked, "What are we going to do?"

Slephen still wasn't sure. He eyed the Dwarf with a deadpan look and said, "We're going to try and slow them down until Steleon is ready."

Melgit and Steleon listened to the scouting reports with growing interest and distaste. They'd been expecting opposition, but nothing on the scale being reported. This was developing into a losing situation and neither liked it.

Maelor brushed a hand through his coal black hair. "It seems we're not going to gain Aingaard before Winter's Day. The fight is here."

"We could draw back into the canyon. Deploy the lines and bring up the artillery," Melgit offered. "Give the enemy a smaller front to engage us on."

"That won't work," Steleon immediately said. "Seventy percent of our combat strength would be bottled up in the pass and we don't know how many tunnels they have leading up behind us. They could come in from the west and cut us in two before we knew what was happening. Reinforce the lines and put your cavalry in reserve on the left flank. I want those catapults emplaced to be able to range the entire front. Seal the gaps. No one gets behind us or we're ruined."

General Melgit strode confidently off and began barking orders. Maelor and Steleon looked at one another with doubt.

Pikes lowered and arrows nocked at the first signs of advancing Goblins. Four thousand men howled once and made a mad dash towards the Averonian lines. The catapults were loaded and awaited the order to unleash their specific brand of hell upon the foe. Melgit watched the developments through his looking glass. He held the order to fire. The small, dark shapes grew larger. But at such a distance he couldn't make out friend or foe. Then he noticed the first of the shapes in plain view. The short bodies brandished battle axes and bore fierce looks. They were breathing hard and covered in blood and gore. It was the vanguard! He'd had no word from Slephen in some time and was beginning to fear the worst. From the looks of it, they'd already been engaged. If he guessed correctly, a host of enemy would be hot on their heels.

"Open the lines and prepare to attack!" he shouted.

They listened without comment as Ordein and Slephen recounted the first battle in Gren. Greatly outnumbered, they stood their ground and attacked. The enemy army hadn't been expecting such and complete surprise was in Slephen's favor. The vanguard split into two wedges and drove into the heart of the attackers while they were still unorganized. The attack was a rousing success.

"We didn't abandon the assault until they brought their full weight to bear on us," Slephen explained. "Any longer and we would have been cut off and destroyed."

Maelor listened with growing interest. Even one friendly casualty was too many. "How many did we lose?"

"Close to a thousand all told, sire. Most were killed but some were taken prisoner," he replied with a heavy heart.

"They are dead either way," Jin replied. The newly appointed commander of the cavalry still felt uneasy in the king's council.

No one disputed his comment.

"The enemy?" Maelor pressed. He already knew they were outnumbered by at least three to one and hoped the vanguard managed to whittle that number down some. As it stood, the potential for slaughter was all too real.

"Three, maybe four thousand," Ordein answered with a scowl. He'd been hoping for more.

"Sire, we must also take into account that we did catch them off guard. I doubt we'll find success so easily the next time. They know we're here now," Slephen added.

Steleon rubbed his bloodshot eyes. "Thank you, Commander. I'm placing you in reserve. Take your troops and try to get some rest while you can."

Slephen saluted and left them.

"What do you think?" Steleon asked Maelor once the two of them were alone.

Cracking his knuckles in anxiety, Maelor calmly replied, "This is your war, Steleon. I trust your decisions completely."

Steleon barely managed to conceal his surprise.

Winter's Day dawned with unusual ceremony. Lightning wreathed the purple sky with malicious intent. Heavy shades of red and orange marked the rising sun, adding seriousness to the affair. Storm clouds rolled across the Nveden Plains. Dormant volcanoes rumbled awake from far away. Fire and smoke spit into the sky. Then came the drums. The sound was incredible. Hordes of Trolls and Goblins howled and cheered as they advanced. The very ground trembled at their approach. Already angered at having been blooded so deep in their own lands, their army surged forward with vicious thoughts. They wanted the blood of every man standing before them. Once that was done, they intended to slaughter every man, woman, and child in Malweir.

The combined armies of Averon, Harlegor, and the dwarves of Breilnor rallied under their flags. The sheer size of the enemy horde was intimidating. Steleon watched the armies of Gren march closer. They were more than a league away and moving slowly. This was done on purpose, of course, to inspire fear and doubts in the waiting ranks. Steleon sent runners up and down the lines with orders. The wait was going to prove as hard as the assault. He hoped that Delin and Fennic finished what they set out to do. The alternative made him shudder. The commander of Averon turned to his generals. It was time to finish the war.

FIFTY-SEVEN
Betrayal

Jervis Hoole was forced to stop much sooner than he wanted to. His horse was lathered in a thick sheen of sweat and was breathing too heavily. If he didn't slow now, he'd be moving on foot through enemy held territory. Hoole dismounted and led the poor beast to a nearby stream. A full day and night had passed since the disaster at the river. So far there hadn't been any signs of pursuit. He refused to be fooled though. His list of enemies was long and no doubt included a fair amount of his own soldiers. That made every gulley or depression the perfect place for ambush.

For the first time in his life he had no direction. He couldn't return to Gren or his life was forfeit. All the dreams and visions of the future were smashed in a single ill-fated battle. Never again could he go home, and that pained him. He had a sinking feeling that all his friends and family were being systematically rounded up and executed on Sidian's orders. The Silver Mage didn't tolerate failure.

Careful not to let the horse drink too much, Hoole led them to a stand of ash trees. He dropped a handful of oats and let the horse feed while he took care of his own needs. The caw of a crow shook him. He hadn't realized until now how quiet it was. Almost deathly quiet. Hoole immediately recognized the danger and began saddling his horse again. There was no time. Any illusions were gone. His life was in jeopardy.

The southern tip of the Gren Mountains was almost in sight now, gradually petering out into sloping foothills more manageable for both the weary horse and rider. Open plains gave way to lightly forested areas. All he had to do was make it to the forest, another day's ride away, and Hoole was confident he could disappear successfully.

The arrow biting into the tree next to his head changed all that. He didn't see where it came from, but there was no mistaking the origin. Hoole sneered at the short Goblin arrow. A pair of feathers, dislodged from the fleeing crow, drifted down among the loose snow knocked off the branches. Another arrow sped by; this one inches from his face. Hoole swore he caught the sounds of a foul laugh.

Easing into the trees a little deeper, he carefully plotted his next move. Running too soon risked certain ambush and death. Goblins and Trolls weren't noted for their tactical prowess, but there was no end to their tenacity and thirst for revenge. In addition, he had no idea how many Men of Grelnor were hunting him. Two more arrows whistled past before he decided to flee. Kicking his horse hard in the sides, Hoole launched from the stand of trees and rode for his life. Arrows struck all around, and he wondered if an entire legion of archers was after him. Then a spray of blood, hot and steaming, erupted from his horse's throat. The beast screamed and fell dead.

Hoole managed to roll clear before the massive animal crushed him. He rose to a knee and tried to spy his enemy. Not that it mattered, he mused. He was caught and knew it. Mud and snow dirtied his face and hands. He was tired and worn down by weeks of war. At last Jervis Hoole understood. It was time. He slowly rose to his full height and drew his sword. A pool of crimson spread violently from the horse's body.

"Come out and face me, cowards!" he bellowed in challenge.

A lonely wind howled across the fields.

Hoole struggled with the emotions threatening to consume him. Anger, hatred, and humiliation ate at the edges of his soul. He knew he was surrounded. A single man emerged from the nothing before him and halted a goodly distance away. They stood still and eyed one another for a time. Neither seemed in a great hurry. A light snow began to fall.

Hoole broke the silence. "I should have killed you when I had the chance, Nintel. You are a disgrace to our people."

Nintel laughed, his voice ragged and piercing. The former, and latest, adjutant eyed Hoole with open malice. "I disgrace our people? Take a cold, hard look at yourself before making those accusations, Hoole. How many good men lay dead because of your ambitions? These are your last few moments, I suggest you make better use of them than throwing empty threats. You betrayed us, and for that you shall pay."

Hoole spit. "Everything I did was for Gren! I have no shame in that. But you, worm, you have sold it all to be a puppet for the Mage. Gladly will I trade my life for that."

An Ogre inched into view to his left, as did a pair of Goblin archers behind Nintel.

"You shall die content then. I aim to tear your heart out and send it back to Sidian. Don't run, it will spoil the thrill of this," Nintel said dryly.

He drew his sword and stalked forward to meet his foe. The knowledge of immediate death made the battle easier for Hoole, and he fought with ruthless abandon. His thrusts pushed Nintel back far enough for the archers had a clear shot. They took it. Two arrows thumped into Hoole's chest. He dropped his sword as pain shot through his body. The once proud leader of the Grelnor dropped to his knees and gasped for breath. Blood poured from the wounds to mingle with the already drying pools from his horse.

Nintel walked up and kicked away the now useless sword. He was fully aware of the level of treachery in Hoole's heart and wasn't willing to take chances. Jervis Hoole leaned forward, placing one hand on the ground. Blood trickled down the shafts in his chest. His chest was tight. He couldn't feel his limbs anymore. He tried to speak but the words wouldn't form. Nintel laughed again.

"Oh how the foolish have fallen, eh old friend?" he asked, leaning as close as he dared. Hoole now lay prone on his back. Empty eyes stared back at Nintel.

"You always thought you were so much smarter than the rest of us. Too bad you couldn't see past your own ignorance."

Nintel collected his band of assassins and left the body for the vultures. The reign of Jervis Hoole was ended.

FIFTY-EIGHT
Tarren Falls

The smell was worse than anything Delin ever experienced. It reminded him of the day he and his father stumbled upon a family of rabbits drowned in a well. He'd vomited three times and never forgot how awful it was when his father pulled the waterlogged carcasses from the water. The skin peeled away, making the task twice as difficult as it normally would have been. The memory remained unpleasant, especially since they'd been cast into Aingaard's foulest dungeons.

He looked around, but the lighting was minimal and offered only vague glimpses of those around him. He was chained by leg and wrist to the slime covered walls. Delin found it distressing that Sidian's henchmen stole the last shard of the crystal when they searched the prisoners. Despite all Dakeb's reassurances, it was beginning to look like the end after all. If they didn't find a way out of this miserable dungeon soon Malweir had no hope. Right now he was wondering how long the Silver Mage intended on torturing them.

He saw a large rat scurry through the muck along the wall. Even rats had to eat, he supposed. Empty manacles caked in dried blood hung between him and who he guessed to be Tolis Scarn. They offered a worrying glimpse of things to come. Sadness claimed him, though none of it was for himself. He regretted what he'd done to Tarren, and his poor mother back home. She'd spend the rest of her life never knowing what happened to her little boy.

"A fine mess you've landed us in, Mage," Scarn spat from the shadows.

As much as it grated his nerves to listen to Scarn speak, Delin was grateful to be taken from his private lament.

To his surprise, Dakeb laughed. "I do apologize, but I can't recall hearing a better way to gain access to Aingaard along the way."

"We're a bit past that," Hallis said. "I'd like to know why the Mage didn't recognize you. He should have been able to pick you out from the beginning."

"I'm a minor concern to him now. He won't come to see me for himself until he feels he has all the pieces in place. Then he'll want to come and gloat. That means bringing us to his chambers to watch the end of the world. Sidian never could resist showing off, even when he was a young man. This should prove interesting."

Norgen rattled against his chains from the far side of the room. "Interesting? I say we break out now and take his head. Finish this task the right way. The boy still has his sword. No one is going to even try and take it. That's our advantage."

Delin tried to find his best friend in the gloom. He could barely make out Phaelor's soft glow from his hip. That sinking feeling of despair crept back in with the knowledge that Fennic was just as helpless as he.

"Why are we arguing?" Tarren asked finally. "We should be focusing on finding a way out of here before he gets to the end of the world."

"Such a smart girl," Dakeb smiled warmly. "I admit I tend to drift off the subject from time to time. It's quite easy to forget things once you've lived a few hundred years. Why one time I...."

"The stone," Celegon reminded.

"Ah yes, the stone. The fourth and final shard of the cracked crystal of Tol Shere. Sounds a might ominous, doesn't it? Imagine the thousands of people who haven't the slightest their world may soon be over. Sidian has yet to complete the crystal. I imagine he's sitting in his tower toying with it now. He knows nothing can stop him. All his enemies are either dead or captured. So much power has got to be disillusioning him, intoxicating his senses beyond reality. This is all to our advantage."

"How so?" Hallis asked. He didn't understand how being a prisoner was in his favor.

A shimmer passed through the Mage. "Consider this stone like a drug. He's drunk with power and thinks he has all the loose ends sown up. The Tol Shere crystal may well be the ultimate power source in all Malweir. Would you fear a bedraggled band of prisoners safely tucked away in a secure dungeon with only hours left before the culmination of five hundred years' worth of hardship? I wouldn't. There is no way he thinks he can lose. We have him right where we need him," Dakeb explained.

Scarn laughed again, mocking them all with his disdain. "You've led us into ruin, old man. I've heard stories of these dungeons and now we're living this nightmare. Lucky for you we're chained."

"Or what? You'd stab him in the back and run?" Fennic shot back. "You're nothing but a lying coward."

"Mind your tongue, boy, I hold you accountable as well," Scarn snarled.

Norgen's deep, booming laugh echoed throughout the fetid cell. "Feisty, isn't he?"

Any response was cut off by the sound of approaching footsteps. Half a dozen heavily armed Goblins entered the chamber, followed closely by a nasty looking man. It was the same man who'd captured them in Greeth. The Goblins split into two ranks, each aiming their crossbows at the helpless prisoners along the walls. With a nod from Spendak, one of the guards produced a set of keys and advanced on Scarn.

"It appears our master has taken an interest in you, thief," Spendak told him. "He wishes to thank you for your services, personally."

Tolis Scarn smiled. This was almost too good to be true. He didn't care about hiding his identity anymore. He just wanted out. Collect his payment and leave the rotten land of Gren forever. Scarn rubbed at his chaffed wrists and headed for the stairwell. He was finally free. He stopped when his foot was about to touch the first step and turned around. Hatred blazed in his eyes as he walked up to Hallis.

"You don't know how much I've wanted to do this," he whispered. His fist was balled so tight the color drained away.

Scarn punched as hard as he could. The blow to the stomach was sweet, but he wished he had one of his long knives with him. Then he could show the soldier what true power was. He drew back to strike again but was stopped by Spendak. The man of Gren had little patience and even less liking for the thief. Scarn was hurried up the stairs. That done, Spendak turned on the others and smiled at Tarren. His teeth were dark and wicked. A pair of Goblins moved forward and unchained her.

"What are you doing to her?" Delin shouted. His voice was almost lost amidst her cries and struggles.

Spendak turned on the boy. "Oh don't worry about her. The Master has plans for your young girlfriend."

Tarren twisted and jerked and very nearly broke free. Spendak was amused but had seen enough. He grabbed her by the shoulder and slapped her hard across the face with the back of his gloved hand. She fell unconscious in a heap at his feet. Laughing, Spendak had his Goblins pick Tarren up and take her from the dungeon. Delin screamed out her name.

Tarren woke with a groan. Her head was pounding. She didn't know how long she'd been unconscious, or where she was. There was a bump on her forehead and her jaw was sore. Panic seized her momentarily. Then she noticed she was in a plush bed with down pillows and soft sheets. Her tattered dress was gone and a strange jeweled necklace hung around her throat. Looking around she noticed a luxurious black dress that offered little to the imagination hanging at the foot of the bed. There was a tray of fruits and cheese next to the bed. Otherwise the room was empty.

It took her a while, but hunger finally won. She reached out and took one of the dark red apples and ravenously devoured it. She quickly lost herself to the virtual feast before her, knowing deep in her mind that her friends were starving and in torment. A gentle creak announced she had a visitor. Tarren ducked back into the bed and pulled the blanket high so nothing was exposed. Fear radiated from her. Shadows flowed into the room, followed closely by a frail looking man in dark gray robes.

He had a sort of calmness about him, a serenity she'd never seen. His manner was seductive, though he didn't utter a word. His eyes seemed to mesmerize her. Soft humming escorted him to the foot of the bed. It caressed her in a soothing way. Tarren's eyes drifted close. Her hands released the blanket, dropping both shamelessly to her sides. The Silver Mage held up his hand, palm facing her. The necklace began to glow with a strange warmth spreading through her body. Tarren gasped softly and swung her legs out of bed. Without knowing what she was doing, she headed for the gown and began to get dressed.

Tolis Scarn paced back and forth in the tiny room he'd been confined in. Spendak had assured him that it was only temporary until the Mage finished with his other guest. That had been some hours ago and Scarn had yet to see another living soul. He felt he was being suckered again. The Hooded Man had played him for the fool for almost a year, and Scarn wanted his due. The wait prompted doubts. No one in their right mind would invite a killer and thief into the heart of their empire and let him leave in one piece.

The Hooded Man. Scarn laughed at the thought. How could he have been so blind as not to see the Mage's true identity? He'd been outright fooled from the beginning, plain and simple. Swords and stones; Elves and Dwarves. All of that was behind him now. He had to think of way out of this death trap before it was too late. Hands clasped behind his back, Scarn continued to pace. A knock on the door brought him back to reality.

He knew who it was before he even made for the door. Sidian gracefully walked in, his heavy robes flowing around him. Behind came a gorgeous young woman in a low cut black gown. Scarn forced himself to look twice. It couldn't be. He recognized Tarren and wondered what had happened while he'd been locked away. She was the last one he expected to be converted. A familiar lust began to boil in him. The Mage smiled, wicked and inviting.

"I've been looking forward to meeting you, thief. My associates aren't exactly pleased about it, but I'll think they'll soon get over it. You might even say I've had a vision," Sidian chuckled. He slowly removed his hood, perhaps as much for the dramatic effect as for letting Scarn finally see the face behind the shadows.

The face staring back at Scarn was like any other old man. Old beyond years, with hollow cheeks and frail, blue lips. Sidian's gray hair drifted down past his shoulders, making him appear older than he was. Liver spots peppered his skin and his eyes seemed empty despite the heavy crow's feet eating the edges.

"You seem disappointed," Sidian said. "Perhaps I'm not the imposing figure they've made me out to be, eh?" he leaned menacingly close. "I assure you, I am everything horrible they ever said."

"Why should I think that you're actually going to pay me and let me go then?" Scarn asked. "I think there's a dagger up your sleeve waiting for my back."

He hoped the fear in his voice wasn't overly displayed. This was the critical moment for him and he needed to play it just right.

Sidian laughed. "You have my word, master thief. Tarren, be a dear and bring our friend his payment."

Hips swaying in a provocative manner she never had before, Tarren smiled and walked up to Scarn with a large bag of coins in her hands. He watched as her breasts swayed back and forth in tune with her body. The fabric of the gown was almost transparent. What he couldn't see his imagination provided. Scarn made out the hardness of her nipples and forced himself to take the purse. Her eyes burned holes into him, as if begging him to give in to those rising urges. Sidian looked on with limited interest.

"I trust you'll find enough coin to keep you occupied for a good while. You may leave once the ceremony is completed. That is my word," Sidian went on to explain. "Until then, I shall have food and drink brought to you. If you desire anything else, my staff is at your disposal. Good day, Master Scarn."

Tarren at his heels, Sidian left. Scarn remained where he was until long after the door clicked shut. He felt like a school boy being given his first kiss. Better. He dumped the purse on his bed, laughed at the sound of so many coins clinking against each other. Gold reflected in his eyes. He was rich! There was enough here to buy his own small kingdom. On his knees, scooping his future up and letting it slip slowly between his fingers, Tolis Scarn was in bliss. That's when a soft knock came. His heart raced. The trap was sprung. Sidian had lied to him again. He'd seen too much and knew too much that could damage the Mage if it fell into the wrong hands. Scarn scrambled for his weapons and moved next to the door.

"Come in," he said.

The door opened but a crack, as if the person on the other side knew what he planned. There was little hope of escape, as the room had no window.

Scarn was determined not to die alone. He drew back to strike. The slender, feminine hand on the doorknob stopped him. Tarren Brickton slid into the room like a ghost. Seeing the opportunity, Scarn quickly checked the hallway to see if she was alone before closing the door. The dagger wavered cautiously before him.

Her eyes rested on the well-used steel. Her full lips curled into a seductive smile. "I know that isn't for me," she coyly said.

He didn't know how, or when, but Tarren had become a woman. Her long hair lay draped over her shoulders, concealing most of her breasts in a pleasing way. He slowly took in every inch of her. She wore flat sandals with crisscrossing straps halfway up her calves. Her gown was slit to the waist on each side, offering him glimpses of her smooth legs and just a hint of buttocks. Designed to show off her lithe body, it also displayed her womanly curves. She turned to prove she was weaponless.

"Why are you here?" he demanded. "Did he send you?"

She extended her arms and slowly turned to face him. "Do you remember that night in the woods beyond Ipn Shal? The night you touched me? Did you enjoy it?"

His mind reeled. "Yes," he found himself answering.

A low purr escaped her lips. "Here I am. All alone, just the two of us. Wouldn't it feel good to touch me like that again?"

"Yes," he said, his voice even weaker.

"I promise not to tell," she teased.

Scarn reached for her, but she was too fast. Her gown twirled from the motion as she ducked out of reach. She had a deliciously wicked smile. One that he knew all too well.

"Do you like what you see?" she asked in a throaty voice.

He stood speechless as she danced in front of the soft glow of the fire. Scarn drank in her beauty. All thoughts of leaving slowly faded as he grew enchanted with her. She wiggled her hips, as if inviting him to come and indulge in his darkest desires. The roundness of her breasts enticed him greatly. The curve of her legs beckoned his touch. Scarn slowly stripped his shirt and went for her again.

Tarren welcomed him with open arms. His kisses were hard and urgent. His tongue pushed past her teeth and swirled in her mouth as his hands groped and caressed her oiled body. She slowly curled a long leg around his waist. Pressure was building between them. An unquenchable lust added to their passion. Tarren moaned from his touch.

"I've dreamed of this moment," she whispered through clenched teeth.

Her necklace glowed as they fell onto the bed. Tarren smiled as she reached for the dagger he carelessly dropped. Not that Scarn was paying any attention to her. His kisses moved to her neck and the tops of her breasts. Tarren traced a line down his spine with a painted fingernail. He moaned once before the dagger came slamming into him. She drove the dagger into him again and again, holding him tightly with the leg still around his waist. Dark blood rolled across his back and he screamed just once. The final blow pierced his heart and Scarn fell dead atop her. Tarren savagely ripped the dagger free and kicked his corpse to the floor. Smiling, Tarren arose and rearranged her gown. Her task complete, she returned to her master. Scarn's empty eyes stared up at the ceiling in eternal shock.

FIFTY-NINE
Winter's Day

The sudden torchlight flickering down the slime covered stairs was slightly blinding to the prisoners in the dungeon. The foul speech of Goblins accompanied the light. Dakeb slumped in his iron manacles, contemplating defeat. Unless Sidian made a rather large mistake, the dark powers were going to win. Now, in this darkest hour of need, Dakeb's foresight abandoned him. His heart ached upon sensing the corrupted presence coming down with the Goblins.

He'd done everything he could to prevent Sidian from taking control, but in the end he was no match for the Silver Mage. Heightened by the powers of the joining at hand, Sidian quickly unraveled Dakeb's hard worked plans. His heart cried as he caught the first faint whisper of perfume heading towards them. He cried for Delin and Tarren, for he'd grown especially fond of them over the last few weeks. They'd been forced to endure more than anyone should in a lifetime, and he couldn't have gotten half as far without them. But now, Dakeb felt all was lost. Tarren descended the stairs like a dark angel. Vengeance burned in her once gentle eyes. She saw her once friends chained and dejected along the walls and laughed. It was a cruel and wicked sound. Hatred radiated from her pores.

"Quickly, chain and gag them. The Master is awaiting," she ordered the Goblin guards.

Delin froze, his heart stopping. Confusion gripped him. It couldn't be Tarren, it just couldn't.

"Yes, Mistress," the Goblins snarled in reply and went about their task.

"Tarren?" Delin asked in pain. "What happened to you? What are you doing?"

"Silence slave!" she hissed. Hands on her lush hips, the newly created mistress of the dark stalked into the cell. Her eyes were hard, spitting fire through the slits. A cold hand stretched forth to caress Delin's cheek. "Poor Delin. You didn't think you could actually contend with the Master's will, did you?"

Looking down at her scantily clad body Delin was both aroused and disgusted. She wasn't even a shell of the girl he'd fallen in love with. His stomach felt uneasy being so close to her.

She laughed at his dejected look. "I feel more alive than I've ever been. The Master has opened up my true self." Her gaze lingered thoughtfully on Dakeb. "He especially looks forward to your reunion, old man."

One by one they were led up through the winding passage and decaying corridors. The Silver Mage wanted them to witness his crowning achievement of nearly seven hundred years of toil and hardship. At first, they struggled against their captors, but Dakeb's silent urging ended it. It was no use, and if his hunch was correct, the Goblins were taking them directly to Sidian and the end of things.

Delin walked behind Tarren and fought back the tears. She was evil now. He had no doubts. He cursed the day this adventure first came into his head, and the day he and Fennic found that sword. It was the source of their ruin and had led Tarren down a dark and unforgivable road. Oblivious to his torment, Tarren led the captives up the winding stairs of Aingaard's tallest tower. The specially prepared ritual chamber awaited.

A pair of Goblin warriors guarded the warped door at the edge of the landing. Their axes were crossed and the looks on their faces was pure malevolence. Spendak emerged from the shadows of a recess. His eyes lingered on Tarren with mistrust. She was still one of them as far as he was concerned. It didn't matter what the Silver Mage had done. Her being here was a beacon for potential disaster.

"Open the door," Spendak commanded. "They are expected."

He waited until they shuffled by before reaching out to grab Tarren by the upper arm. "Remember your place, girl. I know who you really are. Don't presume for a moment that you have replaced me in his graces."

She had the dagger strapped to her thigh, the same dagger she'd used to kill Scarn, out and at his throat before he could blink. "I think you'll find a great many things are about to change. With me at his side, the Master no longer has need of your filth."

Glaring, Spendak stood and let her pass. He quickly followed her in and noted the positions of the prisoners. The Elves and Norgen made up the back row. Cruel looking spears pushed them close together. Hallis and the others lined the front, all except for Delin. He had been taken to a massive slab of granite next to the marble pedestal holding the cracked crystal. Tarren herself was the one who tied him down. He didn't even struggle. There was no point in it.

With a barely perceivable nod, she bade the Goblins to begin. They released a stone lever and the granite slab slowly began to stand on its end. Delin found himself hanging down, looking at the crystal. He recognized the irony but found no humor in it. Directly below, lay the fourth and final shard of the crystal he'd been carrying for months. A dark flavor emanated from the three shards already together. The pull of magic urged the fourth to rejoin them.

"Relax, lover," Tarren cooed in an unforgiving tone. "This will all be over soon." Even as the words left her lips a sliver of resentment trickled through her. Doubt began to take purchase in the forgotten corners of her soul.

Dakeb took it all in with great interest. He too had waited lifetimes for this single event. Tonight was as much about his destiny as it was Sidian's. There was a wall sized mirror hanging opposite of Delin, gripped on both sides by massive hands carved from bone. His eyes were drawn to the fallen majesty of the crystal. What had once been hailed as a triumph for Malweir and the future of all life was now a shallow terror. He felt the evil pulsing through the crystal and knew sadness and regret.

A stout Goblin entered the chamber and slammed the mighty staff he was carrying into the marble floor three times. All eyes slowly turned to the doorway and the ancient figure moving through. The Silver Mage, sovereign of Gren and usurper of life, strode into the ritual chamber dressed in a splendid white robe gilded with gold. Tarren and the others dropped to their knees and bowed so low their heads touched the ground. Hands clasped in front of him, Sidian took in his guests with a mischievous gleam. A cruel smile formed when his finally laid eyes on Dakeb.

"My old friend," he said in a measured breath. "I knew you'd come to me in the end. You never could mind your own business. You should have never tried to stop me."

He motioned for the guards to remove Dakeb's gag.

Dakeb smiled curtly in reply. "We do as we must, old friend. This scheme of yours isn't going to work. I promise you that. You've been stopped before and will be stopped now."

Sidian raised his eyebrows in a curious arch and leaned closer. "How do you expect to stop me? Your hands and feet are chained. I finally possess the final shard of the crystal and you've never let me get this far before. I've won Dakeb. You and all the others could not stop me before. The crystal showed me the true way of the world, where the absolute power lies. Here, at this nexus you will witness the return of the dark gods. Look around you. My new pet is ready to sacrifice the boy on my command and the hour is upon us. Shortly you will bear witness to the true power of the dark gods. Your precious Tarren has already been elevated. See how willingly she gives herself?"

"Ensorcelled is more like it. She's nothing but a harmless child who knows nothing of this war. Let her go, Sidian," Dakeb warned.

"I think not. Her role is too important. See the dagger she bears? Tarren, please rise and tell these people what you did to earn it."

Tarren slowly drew to her full height and stared back at the captives. Wickedness blazed in the fiber of her being. "This dagger I plunged into Scarn's back until he was dead. I stood and watched his blood seep out and coat the floor in a beautiful red. And when the hour draws nigh, I will stab this very same dagger into Delin's heart. His blood will drop onto the completed crystal and open the gates to the netherworlds. Then the dark gods shall be freed at last."

Sidian Laughed. "You see? Already she has traveled deeper into darkness than many before her. She gives her soul so willingly. She'll make a fine bride once my task has been completed, don't you think?"

Delin's eyes flew wide in terror. This was all his fault. If only he'd never left home, none of this would ever have happened to them. His heart broke then, chained and gagged on the foul altar. Dakeb, however, seemed enthralled by all he'd learned. The final mysteries of his long lifetime had been revealed. He knew as much as he needed to know. He was ready to act and take his battle to the Silver Mage.

"Pure blood," he said, almost in a whisper.

Sidian nodded. "Yes. Innocent blood spilled at the hand of the one who loves him the most. You have done all the work for me, Dakeb. After all these years, your insecurities have given me the strength I need to finish my task. Soon legions of unholy warriors will pour through the gateway and consume Malweir in a plague of blood and hatred. Thellios never understood the crystal's true powers. None of you did. And for that blindness you shall suffer. You've failed, Dakeb."

Dakeb stayed silent. Nothing more needed saying. Time marched on. Any moment now Sidian would begin the ceremony and embark upon a reign of terror unparalleled throughout history. The sand in the hourglass trickled down to the last grains. The horn sounded again and Sidian moved to the base of the granite altar. Whispered chants grew louder around him as he began the ancient spells. A strong gust of wind blew out the torches. Tarren's hair and gown blew wildly in the wind. Dust and debris were kicked up, pelting the exposed skin without mercy. A deep green glow started filling the chamber.

Outside, Gren was thrown into turmoil. Fires sputtered into infernos sweeping across the plains and into the mountains. Volcanoes spit doom up to the heavens, threatening to burn them down. The earth quaked, threatened to rip itself apart.

Nightmares sprang to life. Sidian's chants continued. Kneeling at the base of the altar, Tarren raised the dagger overhead with both hands, swaying to the rhythm beating in her veins. Her eyes glossed over. The jeweled necklace radiated a sick light. Pieces of the ceiling broke off and crashed down around them. The mirror suddenly went black.

Sidian reached and grasped the fourth shard of the crystal and stared wildly at it. A pair of glowing eyes opened in the darkness of the mirror. The first of the dark gods. Soon they would be free and their legions unleashed. The Goblins cringed. One cast down his spear and made to flee. Spendak took his head in one clean blow of his sword. It took all his might and will not to reach out and do the same to Sidian and his pet whore. He knew his lands would be saved if he did, but the power of the crystal commanded obedience. So, the Grelnor stood his station and watched.

Violent light pulsed from the crystal as Sidian lovingly placed the final shard with the others. Remade whole, the crystal of Tol Shere fed electricity in the air. Centuries had come and gone, bringing the world full circle. Darkness crept back into the land. The hour of doom had at last arrived. Clicking into place, the four shards melted into one. The dark gods smiled from their exile.

Tarren took her dagger, handling it like a childhood friend, and cut a line across the palm of her hand. Bright red blood escaped her flesh and she laughed when she dripped it down onto the crystal. Green turned to crimson. Aingaard trembled. The Silver Mage stepped forward, prepared to meet his master. Delin swore he heard the crystal growl hungrily as the dagger inched close to his heart. She ripped his shirt open, exposing flesh and muscle, then paused for the Mage. Sidian clapped.

The hourglass was almost empty. Tension filled the room. Spendak suddenly realized how foolish his plots and plans were. The Goblins forgot the threat of being killed and edged closer to the door. The power of the netherworld was too great. Spendak himself was already waiting by the door just in case.

Sidian turned to Dakeb and said, "See how hopeless your situation is? Evil has matured, Dakeb. I will finally take what is mine. Tarren, spill his blood and open the way. Quickly."

Delin jerked at the touch of the cold steel, wincing as pain lanced through him when the point broke through the first layers of flesh. The last grain of sand trickled out of the hourglass. A single drop of blood splashed down, kissing the crystal. The mirror trembled. The gates to the netherworld began to grow and pulse with energy. Tarren slowly pushed the dagger deeper until a steady flow of blood escaped. Her eyes were ablaze with violence.

Dakeb went into action. This was the moment he'd awaited and feared for so long.

SIXTY

A Moment of Pain

Dakeb mumbled a spell and their gags softly fell away. Their bonds disappeared into thin air, all except for Delin. Hallis was the first to act. He ducked right to avoid being skewered by a wildly thrust spear. Grabbing the shaft with both hands, he kicked the Goblin in the throat. The spear was in his hands and aimed at the next before anyone else could move. Norgen and the Elves erupted into action, quickly disarming and killing the nearest guards. All but one. The Goblin ran screaming from the chamber and the alarm was raised throughout all Aingaard. Hallis knew they'd be trapped and destroyed if the house guard reacted in time. There was little time.

"Celegon! Take the stairs," Hallis yelled as he dropped to a knee and thrust the spear at Spendak.

The Elf prince ripped a spear from a nearby corpse and rushed out the door with his fellow Elves. If the three of them could keep the way open long enough they might have a chance. Norgen moved to follow but was tripped by a fallen guard. The Elves ran off without him. Lithe and fleet of foot, the trio made it to the bottom of the stairwell and quickly established a defensive position. The house guards would soon be coming. Armed with two spears and a short sword, they didn't wait long.

The familiar clamor of armor and booted feet rushed towards them. Celegon watched the mass of Goblins approach warily. He could tell by the looks in their eyes they were bloodthirsty and ready for revenge. Sensing the danger, Celegon resisted the urge to strike first. He knew that in doing so they'd be exposed and torn apart. Llem wasn't as patient. He brandished the stolen spear and charged.

The first Goblin was taken by surprise and skewered through the heart. Llem struck a second across the face with the haft of the spear before the others reacted. Daggers and swords flashed. The Elf held his own for a brief time, but the Goblins were too many and he was cut off from help. Blood leaked from a dozen wounds, driving him to his knees. Celegon and Derlith attacked from the rear, hoping to rescue their friend before it was too late. The Elf prince met the enemy blade to blade as Derlith dragged Llem away. Two Goblins fell immediately to the Elf's skill. Their bodies blocked the hall enough for the trio to retreat to the stairwell where it was more easily defended. A strangled sound came from behind him and Celegon dropped his head. Llem was dead.

Norgen gasped as one of his ribs snapped from the force of the Goblin kick. The sturdy Dwarf stumbled back, losing the grip on his weapon in the process. The Goblin pressed his advantage. Spittle and blood drooled from his hungry mouth in anticipation of killing the Dwarf. Norgen lashed out and kicked his attacker in the side of the knee. The Goblin fell with a cry but was still able to bring his sword down. The blade pierced Norgen's side. Snarling, the Dwarf reached out and wrenched the sword from the Goblin and struck off his head in one hard swing. Losing blood fast, Norgen slumped down unconscious as the battle raged around him. His last sights before passing out were of the Grelnor man advancing on Hallis.

Grinning from ear to ear, Spendak raised his sword. He welcomed the chance to fight a real man again, not the disgusting Goblins or any of the other folk. The temptation had been gnawing at him since Greeth and it took greater control to hold himself as the time of the ceremony neared. Now he could unbridle his blood lust and let his sword do the work. He was going to enjoy this.

"That's it, come to me," he goaded.

Hallis said nothing. Unlike the Gren, he was a professional soldier. Trained and disciplined over a lifetime of trials, Hallis allowed his reflexes to take over. He made a light feint, testing Spendak's defenses. Spendak parried right, bringing both weapons together in a shower of sparks. The Grelnor laughed.

"You can't possibly think you'll defeat me. I've killed many that were better than you," Spendak boasted as he circled his foe.

Hallis stabbed again. He sensed weakness in the man and used it to his advantage. His spear tip came down on Spendak's forearm, drawing a thin red line through the sleeve. Cursing, Spendak lunged. It was a reckless move in which he traded balance and poise for anger. Anger and carelessness led many a man to his untimely demise, and that was exactly where Hallis hoped to take him. Swinging the spear like a club, Hallis continued his attack. The last thing he wanted was for Spendak to recover. As it was, the Grelnor was knocked off balance, narrowly avoiding a slash across his throat.

Spendak reacted aggressively, rising and bringing his sword to bear with his full weight. The force of the blow halved the spear and sent Hallis reeling back. Spendak smiled moved in for the kill. The sword struck but Hallis moved just in time. Steel scraped against the stone wall. Hallis used those few seconds to his advantage by dropping to a knee and slamming the broken haft into Spendak's stomach with all his might. Sparks fell around the two. Hot blood splashed the marble floor. Spendak stared in disbelief as the life slowly faded from his eyes. The sword dropped away.

"How?" he asked with his last breath.

Delin's blood dripped unchecked onto the crystal. Each drop widened the gateway to the netherworld. Sidian, despite the triumph of the moment, saw the battle rage around him and felt his world slipping away. Centuries of scheming and endless wait were crashing down around him. He had to act now or all was lost forever.

"Kill him now!" he shrieked. Sweat cascaded down his brow. "Release the dark gods!"

Tarren pushed the blade deeper. Delin looked into her eyes and recognized death. He was helpless to stop her. The hope Dakeb once offered was already dim. Pain burned his chest and lungs.

"Tarren, don't," he pleaded. Tears stained his dirty face. "Don't let him take you from me. Come back, please come back. I...I love you."

She hesitated. Doubt flickered briefly behind the façade of evil. Delin's voice was weak, trembling from a hundred hurtful emotions. The pressure behind the dagger eased. Delin looked down at his love, amazed at what he saw. He took reassurance in her doubt but didn't think it was going to be enough. Time slowed around them, until it was just the two of them.

"I love you, Tarren," he repeated with more fervor.

Tarren didn't know why, but she removed the knife from his flesh. The spell binding her faltered, and she caught a glimpse of freedom beyond. Love swelled into her heart and did battle with the cancer of her soul. Feeling his control slipping, Sidian raged. The amulet around her neck flared hotly and she screamed in pain. Her eyes rolled back into her head and she collapsed in a ragged mess of flesh. Her body shook and trembled under the torture of the Mage. Delin knew that once he finished with her, he was going to turn his evil back onto him, and that would be the end.

Blue lightning shot from his fingertip and struck Delin in the chest and arms. Smoke lifted off his charred body. The smell of roasting meat filled the chamber. The Silver Mage glided forward. Despite the intensity of his deeds, he looked frail and weak.

"Your pathetic attempt to save your precious Tarren has failed, boy. Now you will know the true horrors of what my gods offer," he seethed. Rage consumed him.

"Mage!" bellowed a voice from behind.

Everyone turned, eyes widening in shock. Fennic charged with Phaelor. The sword glowed golden and violent. Sidian stumbled backwards, caught off guard. The pedestal blocked his way. He reached out with a withered hand and touched the crystal, channeling its power into his being.

Fennic charged ahead. Phaelor drove him on, ignoring Dakeb's previous warnings.

"Fennic, no!" Dakeb shouted.

But it was already too late. Phaelor swung through the air, hissing as it lashed out to stab Sidian in the side. Buried deep in his belly, Sidian gasped in pain as the golden light flooded his body. He felt the first hints of death creep into his veins, inviting him into oblivion. Fennic shouted in a short-lived triumph. He drove the sword deeper, confident that he had fulfilled Phaelor's destiny and ended the reign of the Silver Mage. A bitter sensation edged through him. Too late, Fennic realized his mistake. By touching the crystal, Sidian was able to channel their combined energy through Phaelor and into Fennic. Fennic screamed once before the explosion drove them apart.

Dakeb rushed to his side, but it was too late. Fennic Attleford lay dead at his feet. Smoke and steam rose from his eyes and mouth. A single tear formed in the corner of Dakeb's eye. With sorrow, he looked up to see the broken corpse of Sidian laying twisted along the wall. The Silver Mage was dead. Hundreds of years after the war had begun, the last of the dark Mages was destroyed and their evil faded. Behind them, the dark gods roared against their eternal bonds. Dakeb shot a wall of white fire at the gateway, temporarily holding the evil at bay. His strength was waning and knew it wouldn't be long before the power of the crystal drove him back. He knew there was but one way for them to end this once and for all.

"Hallis, cut Delin free. Time is almost gone. He and Tarren must use their love to end this or we are doomed," he strained to say.

Sweat streamed down his face now. The sheer heat of the energy being used burned his hands and face. The last Mage grimaced under the strain.

"How?" Delin asked as he dropped to the floor and scooped Tarren up.

Dakeb buckled under the power of the dark god's assault. "Trust your hearts. That is all I can tell you."

Tarren awoke. Her eyes were soft and filled with love again. Delin looked down in sadness and pain. So many had died for them. The world was dying and the evil of the Silver Mage still threatened to steal them all away. They realized at that moment that if nothing else came from the nightmare surrounding them, they loved each other with all their hearts. Delin bent down and kissed her.

SIXTY-ONE
The Silver Mage Falls

Their lips touched, sparking unabashed romance between them. The feeling went far beyond physical constraints, drawing deeply from a sense of spirituality. Love thrived between Tarren and Delin and filled the ritual chamber. All from the breath of a single kiss. Evil washed away under the power. Delin's face flushed and Tarren felt giddy and weak in the knees. Their hearts fluttered. They stood there and held each other's hands, waiting for the end. But it was an end neither expected.

The power of the crystal dimmed. The violent light was drowned under the weight of love, rapidly losing ground as the influence of the Silver Mage ebbed. The darkness from beyond the gateway collapsed on itself. The volume of power began to suck the very air from the room. Dakeb collapsed. The others struggled for their next breath. Slowly the gate drew shut. The dark gods railed against the light but were helpless to prevent it. They knew that this time was come and gone and another way into the world of the living was needed. They had failed.

Tarren, on impulse, reached out to clutch the crystal of Tol Shere. The dying flicker called to her, tempting its way back into her mind. She fought with mind and soul, her grip tightening on the crystal. It burned her hand but she didn't cry out. She took pain in penance for the crimes she'd committed earlier in the night. With a heavy toss, she threw the crystal into the closing gateway before it disappeared. The crystal was finally gone.

"What have you done?" Dakeb whispered in shock.

Lightning struck the tower, collapsing a good portion of the roof around them. Norgen bellowed in pain as a large chunk of rock smashed into his leg. The world went mad outside. With Sidian dead, the spells holding Gren together faded. Time and nature returned with a bitter vengeance.

"Someone get this damned rock off of me!" Norgen growled weakly. His blood surrounded him in vast, dark pools. He knew he would die if they didn't escape soon.

Dakeb struggled back to his feet, dust and debris falling around him. He reached out to touch the surface of the mirror, now plain and unimaginative. The glass shattered at the faintest touch, leaving empty claws grasping the air.

"The crystal," he muttered to himself.

Tarren looked up through her pain and told him, "I made sure no one would ever try what Sidian did. I saved Malweir from suffering, Dakeb."

"Yes and no. You have rid Malweir of a blight on her past, but in doing so gave the enemy the very object needed to return. If they figure out how to use it we will truly be doomed," Dakeb replied gravely.

Delin left Tarren then to kneel by the body of his best friend. Tears streamed down his face in shame and regret. "Fennic. I'm sorry. It should have been me, not you. I'll never forget and won't let anyone else forget either. I promise."

Aingaard rocked beneath them. The destruction was savage and mounting at an alarming pace. Dakeb gathered his wits and motioned for Hallis to help carry Norgen. Using what magic he could muster, Dakeb sealed Norgen's wounds and tried to ease his pain. The Dwarf, stalwart as he was, passed out. The damage was severe. An ordinary man would have already died. Celegon burst through the door then. He was out of breath and bleeding from several places.

"The house guard is fleeing. We need to get out of here before the castle collapses around us," the Elf prince managed.

Hallis nodded, finally breathing deeply. "Help Dakeb with the Dwarf. I'll grab Fennic. Everyone else down the stairs."

Celegon noticed Fennic's ruined body for the first time and felt a great pain lance his heart. He watched as Delin collected Phaelor, and together with Tarren, moved down the stairs. He realized then that his father was wrong. Men weren't weak or corrupt. There was strength in the hearts of men and for that all Averon should be grateful. Celegon staggered over to help pick Norgen up.

Dust choked the halls, turning night a rusted shade. They found Derlith at the base of the stairs, the body of his friend beside him. Slabs of granite slid from the wall to shatter on the once pure marble floor. The ground shook.

"This way," Derlith waved at them.

The tower collapsed in on itself as they fled. Cement and stone buried Llem's body just as Derlith was reaching to pick him up. Choking on the dust and debris, the Elf sadly gave up his friend and ran for his own life. Celegon guided them out the palace doors and into a courtyard. Thunder and lightning devastated the city. Whole sections had already fallen off the cliff edge. Flames licked up from the ground, melting walls, and igniting thatch. Aingaard was dying. Soon there'd be nothing left but painful memories and whispers of ancient grandeur.

Hallis was able to find the stable quickly in part to the screams of the panicking horses. They managed to subdue enough for their escape and then let the rest free. Hallis and Celegon strapped Fennic's body down and headed out the stable door. They wasted as little time as possible. Waiting until everyone was safely aboard, Hallis spurred his horse forward.

The column wound through the crumbling streets. Lightning strikes blasted around them, destroying more with each bolt. A building exploded, showering that part of the city in debris and flame. Tarren clutched her reins tighter and closed her eyes. She didn't want to die in this maze of endless streets and gutters. At last they came to the decaying marble bridge spanning the chasm. A wall of flame rose on each side of the bridge, pushing the tiny group harder. Hallis led them to a full gallop and the buildings soon gave way to a ravaged landscape caught in the grip of the underworld. They had returned to the Nveden Plains.

Tremors rocked Gren. Lighting attacked friend as well as foe. The battling armies stopped then. Dead and dying littered the plains. With the death of Sidian, the armies of Gren broke and fled to their underground lairs. Men and Dwarf cheered briefly until they realized the gravity of the situation. Gren was destroying itself around them. Steleon lowered his sword and watched as gaping wounds opened in the ground. Molten fire spit from the holes and the land bled. Nature raged out of control and threatened to claim them all unless they escaped. Violent rains began to whip down on them and the call for retreat was raised. Steleon only prayed it was in time to save what was left of the armies.

Hallis kept the pace until dawn. Their course was due south and most of the damage was lost behind them. The world was less turbulent here. Soon they would reach the mountain border with Antheneon and hopefully freedom beyond. With all of the chaos and confusion, there seemed little chance of being caught by the enemy so he begrudgingly slowed them. Night gracefully turned to day. Feelings of dread evaporated. They stopped to tend to their wounds and try to eat, but none of them could stomach the food. The pain of last night was too sickening.

Eventually they left Gren, entering Antheneon's supple farmlands. The air was easier to breathe. Once again the sky was blue and laced with clouds. The oppression of Gren was behind them. Even though snow blanketed the lands, their spirits were rising. The western lands offered hope and promise. But despair still lurked. The farther they traveled the more their grief grew. Llem and Fennic were dead. Norgen was on death's door, and all of them had wounds needing care. Dakeb could do only so much.

One night, not far from the border of Averon, they sat around a small fire and tried to forget the misery of Gren. There was little conversation in the flickering light, though all had much weighing on their minds. Delin snuck off to be by himself. He sat alone on an ice-covered boulder and cried his pain away. Tarren heard his sobs but left him to his lament.

"Another few days and we should be at the border," Dakeb announced after finishing the last shreds of meat on the rabbit leg he'd been gnawing on.

"We shall take our leave soon," Celegon told them, firelight reflecting in his jeweled eyes. "My father will wish to know of these events."

Dakeb nodded thoughtfully, looking up to see Tarren stalk off in solitude. He found her not far away with her head in her hands. She looked up at the twinkling stars and remembered. Dakeb held back, sensing her desire to be alone, but he knew that doing so wouldn't be good for her. Of all them, she'd been through the worst. He came to stand behind her and watched the stars in silence for a time.

"When I was a boy the world seemed so bright," he told her in a soft voice. "Nowhere I looked could I find darkness. That is the gift of youth, my dear. It is a dream all of us should strive to maintain. Let me show you something wonderful."

She turned. Dakeb slipped a hand into one of his deep pockets and withdrew a butterfly of beautiful light. The colors of the rainbow danced on its wings. Tarren giggled as it flew to her and landed on her shoulder. She sighed as it dissolved into her skin. Dakeb immediately felt the tenseness leave her. A warmth returned, beating back the cold of what she'd done under Sidian's spell.

"You should go and rest now," he told her.

She smiled and left him alone. Dakeb suddenly felt old.

"No one should suffer at such an age," he whispered to her retreating shadow.

The night wore on.

The Elves left them at the border. Celegon promised to send their healers to Averon for Norgen and the other victims of the war. An excitement surged into the group. They were close to home and the end of the road. Almost fifty days ago they'd set out from Paedwyn and gone to war. Fifty days of struggle and misery that would never be forgotten. Now they were almost home. The days trickled by slowly until they found themselves son the last ridge overlooking the white towers of mighty Paedwyn. At last, the adventure was over.

SIXTY-TWO
The Return Home

Time went on much as it always did. Days turned into weeks and then seasons. Scars healed. Spring replaced winter, and then summer came. People came to forget the war. Painful memories were slowly laid to rest. The world returned to what it once was. True to his word, the Elvish healers Celegon promised came to Paedwyn. Skilled as they were, they found Norgen's wounds particularly hard to heal. They spent the better part of a year tending the dying Dwarf. He eventually recovered and once he was well he was back to his ornery self. Word of his recovery was sent to Breilnor and his brother, Ordein. A five hundred Dwarf procession was sent to Paedwyn under the banner of friendship. The majority were engineers who boasted they would have Gren Mot rebuilt and better than before. Plans called for additional defenses that would deter even a Dwarf.

Norgen became his people's ambassador to King Maelor. Averon had become a land of tolerance and acceptance. They'd even gone so far as to send representatives to the Goblin nation, though no response was returned or even expected. Despite this amplified schedule, Norgen held true to his promise and traveled to Fel Darrins. He and his entourage arrived under much fanfare and celebration. Never had Dwarves been seen there. He met old friends and Fennic's family. After a night of hard drinking and discussion, Fennic's father relented to letting the Dwarves bury his son in the halls of their great kings under the Twin Spires of Ragnash. The original adventurers joined them and for the first time another race was privileged to the splendor of the hall of heroes and kings.

Celegon became an ambassador for his people as well. He and King Alsenal settled their differences and traveled to reclaim Phaelor. They believed with the Silver Mage gone and the threat of the crystal ended, Phaelor had no more calling in Malweir. Celegon and Norgen became fast friends over the years, strengthening their bonds until their dying days. Once a year they paid homage to Fennic at the base of the mountains. Slowly the division between their races closed and a new age of trade and prosperity dawned on central Malweir.

The Elves welcomed this change with open arms. Many were tired of the imposed seclusion and eager to see part of what used to their world again. Trade bloomed. Military improvements were made. Before Maelor died he created a joint army command that responded to threats when they arose. But wars were few and far between. Hundreds of years passed before rumors of a new, dark evil surfaced. A war unlike any in the history of Malweir was fought in the ruins of Arlevon Gale far to the northwest of Paedwyn.

But that is another story.

Hallis ended his life in the army without fanfare or thanks and disappeared from Paedwyn. He'd seen enough of war and was ready for a quiet life. Fennic's death proved the catalyst that changed his mind. He'd missed too many precious moments by being out on campaign or suffering in the dead of winter in a foreign land. His beloved Chella deserved better. Years of loneliness had taken their toll on both, making them older than their years. One day, during her solitude there came a knock on the door. Chella made her way to the door and gently opened it. Her eyes filled with tears as she looked upon the bedraggled face of her husband. Hallis smiled weakly and embraced her with all his love. He was finally home. For twenty-three years he never left her side. And then, late one winter night, they went to bed and never woke up. Happy at last, the lovers died in each other's arms, entering the afterlife hand in hand.

Three years after the battle at Aingaard, the adventurers gathered together in the tiny town of Fel Darrins. Dakeb had never been happier. He and Delin stood overlooking the small creek that flowed through the town.

"This is a fine day, my boy," Dakeb told him through a mouthful of roast pheasant.

Delin agreed. He and Tarren had just been married. The sounds of celebration echoed through the streets and homes. Folk from all over Averon were in attendance, including a surprise visit from King Maelor himself. The people of Fel Darrins were overawed by the amount of such high and noble people in their quaint town. Elves, Dwarves, and men from all over had come to pay respects.

"I wish Fennic were here," Delin replied. "He would have liked to have seen this."

"Some things are often beyond our control. Fennic saved us all with his courage. Never take that from his memory. I think even now he is watching down on us," Dakeb said thoughtfully.

"I won't."

They were quiet for a time. Then Delin looked over and asked, "What do you think the future will bring, Dakeb?"

Much of the pain from the war was gone. Tarren had been relieved of her dark memories thanks to the Mage. It took a great deal of effort, but he was rewarded not long before the wedding.

The old man clapped his hands on his knees. "Oh, I don't know. Very hard to predict. The Fates may have a grand design, but they've never been inclined to tell me of it. All we can do is live day to day, mind our own affairs, and ask for a long, healthy life. All that I think you are about to discover. There are a great many things I know nothing of, but I do know this. Your adventures across Malweir are over. Enjoy this life, Delin Kerny. You've earned it."

Delin and Tarren went on to have three children. Aptly, they named their first son Fennic. He was the pride of their lives. All told they spent nearly eighty years together.

Fel Darrins was never the same again. Pilgrims came from all over to see the birthplace of two of Averon's greatest heroes. Taverns and inns sprang up. Monuments were erected. Roads were improved all the way to Alloenis. The population grew, rising dramatically in the span of a decade. Generations were born and passed and soon the world forgot about the events of King Maelor's day. The tales of Phaelor and the cracked crystal of Tol Shere faded into legend.

And of Dakeb? Well, no one rightly knows. He simply stopped coming. They never saw him again. Rumor said that he adopted a young boy and groomed him to carry on the legacy of Mages. Many times through the years people came upon a wild looking old man in one place or another who disappeared as fast as he came. No one ever learned his name or found out where he went

EPILOGUE

A lone man dressed in riding leathers and a light cloak urged his horse to a stop. He'd entered the forest a day ago and still hadn't found what he was looking for. Exhausted and filthy, he practically cried when he saw his reflection in the silver stream, babbling nearby. He'd been on the trail for almost a month, all because of a silly dream. He had no money left and was starting to feel dejected. He was also feeling foolish for following the whim of a dream.

The rider dunked his head in the cool water and instantly felt refreshed. He ran his hands through his wet hair, relishing the simple relief from the summer heat. His horse snorted, making the young man look up in alarm. Three archers stood before him, bows drawn, ready to fire. He looked up in the hardened eyes of the Elven hunter and wondered if he was going to die.

"Why have you come into our lands? This is a secret way by which none shall pass. Who are you and why have you come?" the Elf asked harshly.

"My name is Braeden Kirth. I'm here because a dream told me to come and seek out a sword made of the finest silver," he stammered, shocked and awed at the slender Elves that appeared out of thin air.

Easing the tension on his bow string, Celegon passed a wary glance to Derlith. Six hundred years after the destruction of Gren, it was happening again.

The End

ONE

Kavan

Kavan knelt beside the body and felt for a pulse. The trail of crimson on the pure white snow suggested the answer, but he still had to check. His perceptive eyes were immediately drawn to the growing blood stain in the middle of the boy's back. His muscles tensed under his loose-fitting jerkin. Kavan felt rage. Sickness swelled within him. A closer inspection of the corpse showed him what he both knew and dreaded: teeth and claw marks.

It had been the same for the previous four victims. Kavan instinctively glanced about. The gesture was futile; if the beast was still here, Kavan held little doubt it would already have attacked. Still, Kavan let a hand drop to the hilt of his short sword. Even a Gaimosian Knight could be caught unaware and killed. Kavan had no desire to fall into that category.

A cold wind blew across the open field. The tree line was a hundred meters in any direction. The beast had no fear; that much was obvious from the spot of the kill. Loose snow danced across the field, tickling Kavan's neck and face. Kavan removed a glove and gingerly placed his fingertips in the wound. The blood hadn't begun to dry yet. He smiled, cruel and wicked. The beast was close.

"I've got you," he whispered to the gathering dusk.

The Gaimosian looked around again, this time for a trail. Snow had been falling for the past few hours, but it was still loose enough for him to just make out a set of prints moving east. Kavan looked up towards the forest edge. He could barely distinguish a thin plume of blue smoke rising into the grey skies. With night falling, he knew his task had just gotten more treacherous. The beast was dangerous enough in daylight. Night made it particularly lethal. Kavan drew his sword and left the body behind. The hunt was on.

He moved swiftly and with purpose. Everything he owned was on his back. He was a man without home or family. Revenge drove him, keeping him warm at night when the harsh reality of the world threatened to claim him. He was a man lost, damned for the crimes of a kingdom that no longer existed. Hatred tainted his heart. He, and those few others remaining, roamed the lands eternally in the quest for vengeance. These were the Gaimosian Knights, travelling under the shroud of steel and mysticism. The world knew them as Vengeance Knights: the fallen sons and daughters of once proud Gaimos.

Now Kavan worked for money and the thrill of the hunt. A belief system instilled from birth bade him act in the sake of honor and righteousness. As such, he'd been hunting this beast for nearly a month. Every time he drew close, some form of devilry allowed the beast to escape. Kavan was determined not to let that happen again. He picked up the pace. What was left of the sun now dazzled a demonic red across the horizon.

Kavan viewed it as a good omen. Killing was always easier at night. The blood red sky felt right for the moment. He continued watching for signs of the beast as he got closer to the trees. His boots crunched softly on the under-layer of hardened snow. Stealth had never been his strong suit. He'd ever been one in favor of kicking in the front door and seeing how matters played out. Others of his kind had taken to the shadows and the lives of assassins since the fall of Gaimos. Kavan was better than that.

A howl rose from the mountains. Local wolf packs were on the hunt. Kavan smiled and entered the forest. It was a good night to kill. He paused beside an ancient oak tree and let his eyes adjust to the gloom. The heavy branches stretched far and covered large areas with darkness. He smelled the smoke now and knew he was close to the house, close to the beast and the end of the hunt. The twenty gold pieces promised by the villagers wasn't exactly a king's ransom, but they would more than satisfy his meager needs until something better came along. Anyway, after chasing this beast for close to a month, Kavan was ready to kill it for free.

The sounds of the forest echoed hauntingly. Winds rustled rotted branches and dead leaves not yet covered by the quickly accumulating snow. Kavan wanted the beast to know he was coming. He wanted it to know death approached. After so long, Kavan needed a fight. Low branches reached out to lash at his exposed face and arms as he stalked towards the house.

The smells of roasting meat and burning wood grew stronger. He was close. Kavan felt the shadows creep in around him the deeper he went into the woods. He tilted back his head and sniffed the wind. Death had already beaten him here. The thatch-roofed home came into view. Kavan spied the broken-in front door and lamented for the family. What remained of the door left a gaping wound marred by the invitation of a subtle fire in the hearth. A blood-streaked hand curled up in the doorway. The fingers were broken and gripped a thick tuft of fur.

Kavan instantly decided against going through the front. The beast knew he was coming and would be lying in wait for him to make the fatal error of charging in blindly. A woodpile lay just off to the left of the house.

Snow powder covered the top rows. A crude bronze-edged axe rested deep in a large piece of oak nearby. Fresh snow partly covered dozens of tracks. Some were human; most weren't. Dog tracks intermingled with the rest.

It didn't take Kavan long to discover the fate of the rest of the family. A pair of corpses was stacked by the back door, both bodies savagely torn apart and callously dropped beside the carcasses of the dogs. They'd had their spines broken and throats torn out. Kavan swore under his breath. The dogs would have provided warning to the family, but it hadn't been enough. Only death and evil remained inside the meager cottage. Kavan crept to the back door and stopped to listen.

He knew from experience what was going to happen next. Kavan ducked under the windowsill and crept right. Using the shadows for cover, the Vengeance Knight rose slowly and peered inside. Only his right eye broke the silhouette of the stained window. He scanned the home for signs of his prey. The fire had burned low, offering just enough light for him to make out two more bodies. What he assumed was the father lay in the door while a child of five or six had been butchered beneath the table.

Enraged, Kavan resisted the urge to charge inside. He still didn't know where the beast was. The murder scene was one he'd witnessed a hundred times. Their ordeal was ended. Nothing could be done to assuage their suffering now. Kavan needed patience. He thoroughly searched the rest of the ruined home before his eyes settled on a partially hidden corner by the front door. A shadow stretched just enough past the edge of the light and moved with the gentle rhythm of slow breathing. Kavan narrowed his eyes.

"At last," he whispered.

Kavan was about to slip back to the rear door when a pair of frost blue eyes suddenly opened and fixed him with a baleful glare. Swearing, Kavan ducked as the beast launched at him. Only a lifetime of training saved his life. He dove left, narrowly avoiding the sudden explosion of glass and wood. He felt the rush of a large body pass overhead. The beast reeked, gagging him as he rolled and brought up his sword.

The beast crashed into a small tree. Snow fell from the impact. Kavan rose to one knee and got his first true look at his prey. Stark realization flooded his senses. This was no ordinary creature. He faced a werebeast! Kavan watched in shock as the beast shook off the effects of the collision and recoiled to strike again. Werebeasts hadn't been seen in this half of Malweir in decades. Battling one now didn't make sense. It shouldn't be alive. His chances of surviving were suddenly diminished.

The werebeast lowered its massive head and centered on Kavan. Sheer hatred blazed in those eyes. It was then Kavan noticed something startling. Many of the beast's features were those of a man. What foul arts had twisted this genetic nightmare, he'd never know. Kavan was certain of one fact: some dark evil had created this creature.

Heavily muscled, the beast had a mane of pure black running down its wide spine. Silver hair covered the rest. Hot spittle dripped from menacing fangs lining the mouth. Razor sharp claws dug into the ground. Easily five hundred pounds, the beast went on four legs and had a stubbed tail. Whatever magic was responsible for its creation, Kavan knew the beast was made for the sole purpose of killing. Only one of them would be walking away from this battle. He hoped it would be him. Questions needed answering.

The werebeast flexed, giving Kavan a split second to react before it attacked. Kavan knew he had but one chance to survive. He had to strike fast and sever the beast's head. The theory was untested, but Kavan was certain decapitation killed just about everything. He rolled to his right as the beast crashed into the ground where he'd just stood. Letting out a fierce roar, the Vengeance Knight swung with all his might at the exposed underbelly.

Sharpened steel ripped into the thick hide, tearing a great gash over the sternum and down the rib cage. Blood and fur splattered down. The beast let out a twisted scream as it crashed into the house. Glass burst as the werebeast tumbled through the cottage. Kavan rose in a fluid motion and ran at the dazed and wounded beast. He burst through the ruined front door and aimed his blade. Fast as he was, the werebeast recovered faster. It lashed backward with a hind leg, catching him in the stomach. The force of the blow sent Kavan flying across the family room.

Kavan slid across the already bloodstained floor. Glass and wood shards ripped into his back and neck until he crashed into the fireplace. Stunned, he struggled to rise. The back door exploded in a shower of splinters. The werebeast stalked inside, hungry for the kill. It knew it had the advantage and meant to toy with Kavan before killing him.

Kavan crawled up on his hands and knees. Pain lanced through his entire body. He guessed at least three of his ribs were broken, and he was cut in a dozen places. His vision swirled darkly. He cursed himself for underestimating his enemy. Kavan looked up through his pain and noticed the beast had a heavy limp. A trail of blood and gore followed it into the house.

The werebeast stopped a goodly distance from the stunned knight. As much fun as it had in inflicting suffering, the beast knew it was wounded and grew leery of tasting the bitter steel again. The clouds leaving his vision, Kavan grinned fiercely at the reluctant approach of the beast.

"Hurts, does it?" he asked and raised his sword in challenge.

The beast bellowed in response and attacked. A battle rage came over the Vengeance Knight, and he met the attack head on. They collided in a sickening crunch of bone and flesh. Kavan was driven to the floor. The beast fell on him with malice. Elongated claws snarled around Kavan's torso and squeezed. He felt the breath crushed out of him. He fought back the urge to cry out as the pressure on his ribs intensified.

He started hammering the pommel of his sword into the beast's side, striking just beneath the ear. The beast screamed, and Kavan could have sworn it was the sound of a man in pain. He hit harder despite his own growing agony. The pressure eased suddenly, if just a bit. Kavan turned his sword sideways and drove the wrist guard into the beast's ear canal.

The werebeast let him go and recoiled from intense pain. Kavan struggled to his feet. Brain matter dripped down the sword onto his hand and wrist. He looked down on his wounded enemy and felt…nothing. There was no hatred. No remorse. Pity was absent as well. At this one moment in time, Kavan wanted only to kill the beast and be done. He took an unsteady step forward and raised his sword one last time. The werebeast looked up at him with pleading eyes. Kavan understood it all then. The beast wanted to die.

He stood over his elusive quarry and hefted his mighty broadsword, making ready to strike. Another man might have paused to study the beast or learn from it. Kavan already knew what he wanted. The werebeast had run free and killed for far too long. It was only fitting to repay it in kind. He gathered what little remained of his full strength and brought the sword down with a mighty swing. The werebeast never took its eyes off its killer.

After a sickening crunch followed by brief resistance, the beast was dead. The body fell in a great heap of lifeless flesh as the head rolled to a stop at the foot of the slaughtered farmer's child. Kavan took neither satisfaction nor disgust from the task. He'd been paid to rid the land of a murdering creature and had done just that. He quickly searched the house for a towel and medical supplies before sitting down to clean his sword and dress the more major of his wounds.

Kavan then collected the severed head and wrapped it in a burlap sack. Once finished, he gathered the bodies of the family and set them in the center of the main room. He lacked the time or energy to give them a proper burial, instead choosing to enact an old Gaimosian tradition of burning the bodies. He left the beast where it had died. Some things didn't deserve the honor. Kavan spent a goodly portion of the next hour collecting fuel for the pyre. Setting the pyre to flame, he snatched the severed head and strode out the front door.

It is a troubled time, for the old gods are returning and they want the universe back…

Under the rigid guidance of the Conclave, the seven hundred known worlds carve out a new empire with the compassion and wisdom the gods once offered. But a terrible secret, known only to the most powerful, threatens to undo three millennia of progress. The gods are not dead at all. They merely sleep. And they are being hunted.

Senior Inquisitor Tolde Breed is sent to the planet Crimeat to investigate the escape of one of the deadliest beings in the history of the universe: Amongeratix, one of the fabled THREE, sons of the god-king. Tolde arrives on a world where heresy breeds insurrection and war is only a matter of time. Aided by Sister Abigail of the Order of Blood Witches, and a company of Prekhauten Guards, Tolde hurries to find Amongeratix and return him to Conclave custody before he can restart his reign of terror.

What he doesn't know is that the Three are already operating on Crimeat.

the Dragon Hunters

CHRISTIAN WARREN FREED

The Mage Wars are a fading memory. The kingdoms of Malweir focus on rebuilding what was lost and moving beyond the vast amounts of death and devastation. For some it is easy, others far worse. Some men are made in battle. Grelic of Thrae is one. A seasoned veteran of numerous campaigns and raids, Grelic is a warrior without a war. He languishes under mugs of ale and poor choices that eventually find him locked in the dungeons of King Rentor. His only chance at redemption is an offer tantamount to suicide: travel north with a misfit band of adventurers and learn the truth of what happened in the village of Gend.

Grelic, suddenly tired of his life, reluctantly agrees and meets the only survivor of the horrible massacre: Fitch Iane. Broken, mentally and physically, Fitch babbles about demons stalking through the mists and a terrible monster prowling the skies, breathing fire and death.

What begins as a simple reconnaissance mission quickly turns into a quest to stop Sidian, the Silver Mage from accomplishing his goals in the Deadlands. The last of the dark mages seeks to recover the four shards of the crystal of Tol Shere and open the gateway to release the dark gods from their eternal prison.

Grelic and his team are sorely outnumbered and ill prepared to deal with the combined threats of a dark mage and one of the great dragons from the west. Not even the might of the Aeldruin, high elf mercenaries, and Dakeb, the last of the mages, promises to be enough to stop evil and restore peace to Thrae.

THE
LAZARUS MEN
A LAZARUS MEN AGENDA

CHRISTIAN
WARREN FREED

It is the 23rd century. Humankind has reached the stars, building a tentative empire across a score of worlds. Earth's central government rules weakly as several worlds continue their efforts toward independence. Shadow organizations hide in the midst of the political infighting. Their manifestations of power and influence are beholden only to the highest bidder. The most powerful/insidious/secret of these, The Lazarus Men, has existed for decades, always working outside of morality's constraints. Led by the enigmatic Mr. Shine, their agents are hand selected from the worst humanity has to offer and available for the right price.

Gerald LaPlant lives an ordinary life on Old Earth. That life is thrown into turmoil on the night he stumbles upon the murder of what appears to be a street thief. Fleeing into the night, Gerald finds himself hunted by agents of Roland McMasters, an extremely powerful man dissatisfied with the current regime and with designs on ruling his own empire. In order to do so, McMasters needs the fabled Eye of Karakzaheim, a map leading to immeasurable wealth. Unknown to either man, Mr. Shine has deployed agents in search of the same artifact and will stop at nothing to obtain it.

Running for his life, Gerald quickly becomes embroiled in a conspiracy reaching deep into levels of government that he never imagined existed. His every move is hounded by McMasters' agents and the Lazarus Men. His adventures take him away from the relative safety of Old Earth across the stars and into the heart of McMasters' fledgling empire. The future of the Earth Alliance at stake. If Gerald has any hope of surviving and helping save the alliance he must rely on his wits and awakened instincts while foregoing the one thing that could get him killed more quickly than the rest: trust.

BIO

Christian W. Freed was born in Buffalo, N.Y. more years ago than he would like to remember. After spending more than 20 years in the active duty US Army he has turned his talents to writing. Since retiring, he has gone on to publish more than 20 science fiction and fantasy novels as well as his combat memoirs from his time in Iraq and Afghanistan. His first book, Hammers in the Wind, has been the #1 free book on Kindle 4 times and he holds a fancy certificate from the L Ron Hubbard Writers of the Future Contest.

Passionate about history, he combines his knowledge of the past with modern military tactics to create an engaging, quasi-realistic world for the readers. He graduated from Campbell University with a degree in history and a Masters of Arts degree in Digital Communications from the University of North Carolina at Chapel Hill. He currently lives outside of Raleigh, N.C. and devotes his time to writing, his family, and their two Bernese Mountain Dogs. If you drive by you might just find him on the porch with a cigar in one hand and a pen in the other.

www.ingramcontent.com/pod-product-compliance
Lightning Source LLC
Chambersburg PA
CBHW031613100726
47898CB00006B/1781